ADVANCE PRAISE FOR *RINGS OF FIRE*

"Gregory Shepherd's *Rings of Fire* is a powerhouse of a thriller and a stunning look behind the border walls of North Korea. For fans of Tom Clancy, Brad Thor, and Vince Flynn, *Rings of Fire* is a novel not to be missed."

—Mark Greaney, #1 *New York Times*
bestselling author of *One Minute Out*

"Fast-paced and exciting, Gregory Shepherd's expertise on the Far East shines through on every page. Everything a thriller should be!"

—Ward Larsen, *USA Today*
bestselling author of *Assassin's Run*

"In *Rings of Fire*, Gregory Shepherd has created an enigmatic, engaging, and thrilling portrait of the Far East—a tsunami of a thriller. No one writes thrillers set in Japan better."

—Alex Shaw, bestselling author of *Cold Blood*

"Once again Gregory Shepherd pens a gripping and action-packed counter-terrorism tale set against the backdrop of the Olympics in Japan. You can taste the grit and hear the rifle's crack as JSOC sniper Patrick Featherstone uncovers a twisted plot to kill. The clock ticks down to another unforgettable adventure in *Rings of Fire,* the *must read* of the year."

—Lt. Col. Hunter Ripley ("Rip") Rawlings,
New York Times bestselling author

"Unstoppable. *Rings of Fire* is a geopolitical thriller that gathers speed like an avalanche."

—Timothy Hallinan, author of the Poke Rafferty
series and the Junior Bender series

"Freshly fierce! A uniquely crafted thriller chock-full of rich Asian cultural nuances and hard hitting JSOC mission execution."

—J.T. Patten, Author, Task Force Orange series

Also by Gregory Shepherd

Sea of Fire: A Thriller

a thriller

RINGS OF FIRE

GREGORY SHEPHERD

PERMUTED
PRESS

A PERMUTED PRESS BOOK

ISBN: 978-1-68261-943-8
ISBN (eBook): 978-1-68261-944-5

Rings of Fire:
A Thriller
© 2021 by Gregory Shepherd
All Rights Reserved

PERMUTED
PRESS

Permuted Press, LLC
New York • Nashville
permutedpress.com

Published in the United States of America
1 2 3 4 5 6 7 8 9 10

"In war, truth is the first casualty."
—Aeschylus

PROLOGUE

KAESONG, NORTH KOREA
May 1, 2017
The day of the Glorious Triumvirate Celebration

Comrade Ahn Mun-yin couldn't get enough of the echoing silence of the cave system he explored for his job several days a week far from the crowds and noise of the "surface world," as he called it. And the crowds and noise would be worse than ever today, the day of the Glorious Triumvirate Celebration, a national festival marking the radiant brilliance of the dynasty of Kim Il-sung, Kim Jong-il, and Kim Jong-un. His wife was content to spend a few hours relaxing topside on this beautiful spring day quietly reading to their child as she waited for her husband to emerge from the depths. An hour after his expected exit time, though, she began to worry, as did the man himself when he suddenly heard the sound of rushing water and realized the danger he was in. He hurriedly made for the cave entrance a quarter mile above, with the rumble of the flood pulse growing in intensity like an oncoming freight train. It took him a full hour to reach the surface, the entire cave shaking the whole time as if by an earthquake. He was only fifteen yards from the cave entrance when an enormous torrent of white water suddenly broke forth from the ceiling, spewing tons of falling rock and debris that almost completely blocked the cave entrance. He could just barely see daylight, but there was no way he could get out any time soon without help, so he checked for a signal on his cellphone. He was picking up one bar, but it flickered in and out of reception.

He repeatedly tried calling his wife, but there was no answer, so he yelled at the top of his lungs toward the cave entrance over and over but again heard nothing. Sensing that something had happened to her husband, the wife had hurried back in the direction of Kaesong forty minutes earlier to try to get help. Her husband got as close to the cave entrance as possible and made a call to Pyongyang. Then he turned on his headlamp and began digging. When he emerged from the cave the next morning, he ran all the way home, but his house was deserted.

C H A P T E R 1

TOKYO
Four years later
July 10, 2021

I'm dead! Adrenaline ignited the shooter's viscera, and his grip stiffened against the trigger. He relaxed slightly when he looked up into the rafters of the Olympic stadium and saw it was only a *tombi*, a type of hawk, carrying a midsized carp from the lake in nearby Akasaka Palace in her beak. The tiny squeaks of her hungry chicks in their raftered nest pinged off the canopy as their mother landed and began shredding the fish with razor-like claws. The man swore silently. Although he had breached the highest levels of security and made his way to his hide undetected in the middle of the night, he had just come close to a panic-pull of the trigger. Swearing again, he took several deep breaths, feeling his pulse gradually decrease.

It was just after 3 a.m., exactly two weeks before the Games of the XXXII Olympiad were set to begin, that the squat, powerful-looking figure clothed entirely in black began his ascent of the south wall of the stadium. The raucous frenzy of nightlife in the area had evaporated after the last subway pulled out at midnight. Now the only sounds were the occasional shout of a drunk in the distance. Or the roar of a passing taxi. Or the stifled grunts of the solitary figure as he shimmied himself up the pylons, pausing every once in a while to rechalk his hands and look down on the main concourse. He had timed his ascent to the clockwork punctuality of the eight security guards who were posted below. None of them ever looked up. They had been told that the 5G AI security system was fully operational, even this far out from the start of the Games, and that it was nigh impossible for anyone to fool sensors that could distinguish between those taxis in the distance, or that cat skulking in the shadows, or that human attempting to scale the south wall. But the solitary figure in black who was indeed scaling the south wall had trained at Keumsung Military College, where from morning until night he had hit things, broken things, had things broken on his head, driven nails through boards with his forehead, rolled around in broken glass, pulled trucks filled with soldiers, and hit tiny bull's-eyes one hundred yards away. So breaching a stadium with state-of-the-art security? Child's play, although even he had to admit that architect Kengo Kuma's design, with its tiered gardens protruding twenty feet out on the way up, challenged his climbing skills like few structures had at Keumsung Military College. But now he was settled in his perch high up in the stadium and waiting for his targets to appear. His trigger finger was on hot standby as he beheld the stadium that surrounded him, lit only by starlight.

Situated in what had been designated as the "Heritage Zone," the area where the 1964 Tokyo Olympics were held, Kengo Kuma's sixty-eight-thousand-seat stadium recalled Frank Lloyd Wright's philosophy of creating structures in harmony with their environment. Kuma expressed a desire to go beyond the era of concrete and restore the link that Tokyo lost with nature during the reconstruction of the city after the Great Kanto Earthquake of 1923. His stated goal with his design was what he figuratively called "defeated architecture," by which he meant a stadium that would transcend its design. But if the man in the rafters had his way, defeated architecture would come to mean something quite a bit more literal in the weeks ahead.

Having breached all manner of security on his way up the south wall, the man had found a recessed gap between the nosebleed seats at the top of the stadium and the rafters of the oculus that opened up onto the sky. The gap would be used for TV cameras during the Games, but for now it would serve very nicely as his sniper's hide. He crawled inside and waited, enjoying the hum of quiet as the faint stars in the black sky began to fade into the spreading shades of purple and pearl of astronomical dawn. An hour later, he watched through his rifle scope as a hundred or so men in blue jumpsuits and peaked caps marched in smart files to the middle of the field. He noticed that his finger had unconsciously tightened around the trigger. He relaxed it. *Not yet*, he thought. *Not yet.*

Up until a week earlier, security for the Olympics had been the responsibility of a joint venture made up of fourteen private companies, but Prime Minister Adegawa had decided that the measures that the joint venture had in place were inadequate for ensuring maximum safety, and thus had replaced it with the Japan Intelligence Agency (JIA), which reported directly to him. The JIA men on the field fanned out around the field and began, along with much of the country at the same time, what is known as *rajio taiso,* or "radio calisthenics." The man in the sniper's hide shook his head and smiled in amusement. It was exactly how they did it back home, right down to the little piano ditty that played over the loudspeaker system. He peered intently through his rifle scope, looking for a specific person, a foreigner with Mediterranean features who had grown up in Japan. The shooter had made the man's acquaintance in North Korea four years earlier. Finally he found him. *He's dead!* he thought. Adrenaline again coursed through his viscera. But then he relaxed his finger on the trigger. *Not yet. Not yet…*

The foreigner with Mediterranean features had skipped the morning's calisthenics, since he had gotten up at 3:30 a.m. to do his mixed martial arts kata back home in Kamakura, about forty miles away. He had been a star long-distance runner at Kamakura High School, and his eyes still had the inner intensity that came from churning out mile after mile around the seaside town with nothing in his head except the classical music he loved, especially that of Bach. "Loner music," his father had called it, and he meant it as a compliment. As his eyes took in the stadium, the foreigner thought four weeks ahead to the day of the Closing Ceremony, when the marathoners would be sprinting into the stadium after their twenty-six-mile traversal of Tokyo in stifling heat and humidity. For the briefest of moments he wondered if he might have had a shot at the Olympics had circumstances been different, but he cut himself off in mid-thought. *Coulda woulda shoulda. Total waste of time, especially at my age.*

He had eaten a quick breakfast and ridden his motorcycle up on the all-but-deserted Shuto Expressway, arriving at the stadium ready to begin his first full day with the men who would be serving under him, a foreigner. How Japan had changed in the years since his youth, he marveled, before remembering the many more things about Japan that would never change in a thousand years. He had been hired as chief security consultant for the 2021 Olympics, but many of the old hands in the JIA, Japan's CIA, resented taking orders from a foreigner, xenophobia that had also raised its ugly head when the stadium's first architect, the British-Iraqi Zaha Hadid, a woman no less, was summarily fired in order to bring in Kengo Kuma.

The foreigner had been hired by the new director of the JIA because of allegations of corruption and possible treason within his own agency. Its former director was suspected of being in league with the Chongryon, a Tokyo-based organization with close ties to North Korea, a suspicion that was only strengthened when he bought that group's headquarters on prime Tokyo real estate for a shockingly low price. The new director, Kazuo Hayashida, had been brought in to restore the Agency's reputation, and to that end, he had retained the services of a total outsider, the foreigner on the field, making him instantly unpopular with people in the Agency who had been cozy with the ex-director. The foreigner had jumped at the opportunity since he was, frankly, bored. His newfound domestic tranquility was deeply satisfying on one level, but on a level that he kept to himself, he missed his old life: a hunter of men. He had no idea that at that moment, he was the hunted one....

The sniper set the barrel of his rifle on the small bag of chalk that had given his hands traction on his climb up the south wall. He used the barrel to smooth the chalk powder down into a groove and peered through the sight. His eyes focused on the field below, where the men in blue jumpsuits were now standing in neat rows. He held out his hand in front of him. Steady and firm. His grip tightened around the rifle again, but only to the degree that he might hold one of the baby hawks in the rafters without injuring it. He peered through the optical sight and waited for precisely the right moment, cursing the heat that was causing sweat to pour into his eyes.

The men on the field were cursing it as well. The late summer humid swelter of Tokyo, known locally as *mushiatsui*, or "steam heat," rivals that of the jungles of Borneo to those unaccustomed to it. Adding to the discomfort is the cacophonous booty call of cicadas, whose 120-decibel chirp makes them the loudest insects on earth. As the temperature rises, the cicadas begin their search for a mate even earlier. Even now, at 7 a.m., with the temperature rising above 82°F and the humidity already topping 90 percent, the brain-penetrating whine of the cicadas blared out of the hundreds of oak, cypress, willow, ash, and maple trees surrounding Kengo Kuma's stadium.

Down on the field, Seiji Naya, one of several assistant chiefs of security with JIA, felt himself getting hotter by the minute, and not because of the oppressive heat and humidity. As he read through the day's security update, he swore silently and began storming toward the low riser from which the daily briefings were announced.

The foreigner with Mediterranean features stood at the bottom of the riser, penciling notes onto a page and preparing to deliver the briefing. As the cacophony of the cicadas became more and more irritating, he considered that in a few short weeks they would just be dried out exoskeletons littering the ground, and the larches, oaks, and maples would be brown in another cycle of birth and death. An old haiku came to his mind: *Nothing in the cry / of cicadas suggests they / are about to die.*

The shooter in the rafters followed the action on field through his scope as Naya got closer to the foreigner. Deputy Assistant Watari saw that Naya was, once again, in one of his rages, no doubt with his usual complaint of having to take orders from a *gaijin,* a foreigner. Watari, of a more cosmopolitan world view, moved to intervene, but Naya pushed him roughly aside and situated himself face-to-face with the foreigner. As soon as he looked up from his clipboard and saw that, once again, he would be confronted by Naya, the foreigner set his jaw and raised his chin aggressively.

"This is unacceptable, Mister Featherstone!" Naya began, a vein bulging in his forehead. "We're talking about the security of seventy thousand athletes and spectators at any given time! How can you possibly argue that snipers should be the main tool to counter security threats? The threat can come from anywhere, even outside this stadium! Our Japanese companies have developed a state-of-the-art 5G facial recognition system that can tell identical twins apart. Besides, we in the JIA have been charged with providing security without interfering with the Games. Snipers will only frighten people! Your directive is, frankly, naïve. It's completely beyond me how you managed to persuade Director Hayashida to adopt it!"

He spoke in fluent but heavily accented English, knowing full well that Patrick Featherstone, who had been born in Kamakura forty-one years earlier, was stone-fluent in Japanese. Patrick intentionally used less than honorific verb forms in his Japanese-language response to Naya.

"No one is saying that snipers should be our *only* tool, Naya-san, only one of our most reliable ones. The 5G AI facial recognition will be fully operational, but as you say, the threat could come from anywhere, and if you don't realize the necessity of having properly positioned snipers as backup for technology that can be hacked, then maybe you shouldn't be involved in guarding those seventy thousand people."

As Patrick said this, his mind went back to Pyongyang a few years earlier, when he and a hastily assembled team had helped to engineer the Rising Tide revolution that brought down the regime of Kim Jong-un, during which Patrick called upon his own sniper skills to take out a hostile shooter a half mile across the Taedong River from Kim Il Sung Square.

The shooter up in the rafters stifled a laugh, watching through his scope as Naya exploded in anger at the foreigner they both hated so much but for different reasons. Patrick Featherstone.

"Shouldn't be involved?" Naya shouted. "How dare you talk to me that way! You're not even Japanese, how could you possibly understand the way things are done in this country? It's completely beyond me why Director Hayashida insisted on having you play even a small role in security, let alone be the main adviser!"

Patrick smiled as Naya raged, which made Naya even angrier, but the little despot had been a thorn in Patrick's side for weeks, and Patrick enjoyed being his superior in the chain of command. Naya was about to continue his tirade when an authoritative voice from behind made them both turn. It was Kazuo Hayashida, the new director of the JIA.

"Gentlemen, it's time we begin the day's planned drills. The Opening Ceremony begins in exactly two weeks. Mister Featherstone, you may begin your presentation." Now it was Hayashida's turn to feel Naya's wrath.

"Mister Director, having a foreign chief security consultant would never have happened under your predecessor who understood the Japanese way!" Naya turned and glared at Patrick as he stalked away. Hayashida sighed in exasperation. Naya was a lifer and couldn't be fired.

As this was going on, a young woman in a navy blue suit came up to Hayashida's side. The contrast between the suit and her light-colored hair was striking. Her facial features were somehow both particular and archetypal. Hayashida said something to her in English. She smiled sympathetically and nodded in response.

Patrick allowed himself a parting smirk at Naya, then glanced briefly at the young woman as he ascended the riser and turned to face the men in blue jumpsuits. The shooter up in his hide squinted through his scope in deep concentration on the scene unfolding on the field below. It was almost time…

"First of all," Patrick Featherstone began, "I want to thank all of you for being part of the most highly trained Olympic security force ever assembled. I'd now like to begin with a review of the potential hostile actors we could be facing. And starting today, two weeks out from the Opening Ceremony, we are on heightened alert." He proceeded to go through a checklist of the groups and individuals he considered the main threats. Deputy Assistant Watari, who also despised Seiji Naya, had taken his place by Patrick's side in a show of international solidarity.

High up in the canopy of the stadium, the shooter keyed a text into the single-use phone he had brought. Patrick felt his phone vibrate but decided to leave it until later. The start of the briefing was already late as it was. He began to run through the usual suspects of terror groups and detailing each of their strengths and weaknesses when JIA Director Kazuo Hayashida was called out of the stadium. As soon as Naya saw him exit, he walked quickly back to the riser where Patrick was making his presentation. He had not finished with this *gaijin*.

Patrick was turning a page on his clipboard when two shots rang out in quick succession, their combined sound waves caroming around the oval structure and out the huge oculus above the track. Naya and Watari lay flat on their backs, gaping holes where their hearts had been. Everyone in the security detail froze in shock. And then chaos broke out, doubling down on Sun Tzu's adage: "Kill one, terrify a thousand."

High up in the rafters of the stadium, the mother *tombi* was alone again with her hatchlings.

CHAPTER 2

Later that day

The incongruity of meal, presentation, and setting was intentionally designed to throw the diners off their bearings and remind them who held the power in this room on the third floor of Toyama Storage, a business in the dockland section of Yokohama. And what a room it was. The real purpose of Toyama Storage was revealed when a black-suited, middle-aged man ceremoniously raised a red velvet curtain and unveiled a coffin which the man's two sons wheeled into the middle of the viewing room. For this was a corpse hotel, one of Japan's most recent and bizarrely ingenious methods of reconciling its mounting elderly death rate with the scarcity of crematoria in a country eternally beset by the NIMBY mentality.

The host of the day's festivities was a man known to all simply as Mr. Lee. He had been a close confidante and successor of the occupant of the coffin, Comrade Moon, one of the most notorious criminals North Korea ever produced and the patron martyr of the people assembled in the viewing room. The expression on his face in the photo atop the coffin was a repellent-to-the-point-of-fascinating mix of charm and wickedness that went far in explaining how he had risen close to the pinnacle of power in the DPRK...

A shy but friendly boy, on his eleventh birthday Comrade Moon witnessed his mother being obliterated by an American bomb during the Korean War. Not a trace of her remained. From that day forward a new person was born, one who would never allow himself to trust another human being, one who would sell his soul for power, if he had one to sell. But it had been obliterated along with his mother by the American bomb.

Attending the prestigious Mangyongdae Revolutionary School in Pyongyang, he was two years younger than the Dear Leader Kim Jong-il, a priggish know-it-all who enjoyed lording it over other students and even faculty and administrators, or as much as someone of Kim's runty stature was able to lord it over anyone. Moon, however, knowing a meal ticket when he saw one, cultivated a friendship with the son of Great Leader Kim Il-sung. Unlike Kim Jong-il, Moon was tall and athletic, which caused no end of jealousy for Kim *fils*, who in later years would describe his appearance as that of a "rat turd." Moon persisted, however, since he could tell even at that age that Jong-il, through his incessant toadying up to his father, was destined for the highest reaches of the regime. And so, in order to curry favor with Jong-il, Moon immersed himself in *kimilsungsa*, or Kim Il-sung Thought, and came to Kim the younger with request after request for elucidation on some arcane point in the many volumes that had allegedly flowed from the Great Leader's pen.

Years later, Moon's encyclopedic mastery of Kim Il-sung Thought led to an audience with the Great Leader himself that Kim Jong-il arranged. But the meeting backfired on Kim Jong-il, as the father saw in Moon the role of regent for his son, a role that Jong-il deeply resented, especially since Moon was younger than he. Thus, after the Great Leader died, Kim Jong-il purged Moon from his lofty position, cognizant of his potential as an adversary.Eventually Moon wheedled his way back into Jong-il's good graces by pledging his undying fealty and guaranteeing it with his life—and that of his family. Kim Jong-il, never one to take the high-sounding words of underlings at face value, demanded literal proof. At one of Kim's legendary drinking parties not long thereafter, Comrade Moon signaled for everyone's attention and once again pledged his loyalty in effusive terms. At the end of his bathos-sodden speech, he drew a pistol from his jacket and shot his wife in the head. A shocked silence fell over the other members of the party, who then hurried away. Kim embraced Moon, pledged his own loyalty in return, and the two of them proceeded to drink their way through three days of mourning for Moon's wife. A dozen concubines from Kim's personal stable were brought in to help comfort the grief-stricken widower, and at the end of the three days, Kim awarded Moon the post of deputy director of the People's Office of Services.

Moon's next rung in the ladder of power was to marry Kim's sister. She died of acute alcoholism within a year, but he was now part of The Family. Overnight, he was admitted into the Dear Leader's inner circle and made head of State Security, the secret police.

He took to dressing flamboyantly, flaunting his access to the Dear Leader with the extravagances that such proximity entailed. His closeness to Kim also enabled him to act with impunity toward underlings, with more than a few of them meeting untimely deaths by his own hand. Thus, in his hand-crafted shoes of the finest Italian leather, he stood splendidly astride a sinful nexus of elegance and criminality.

Moon's next act was to create Bureau 39, a massively tentacled conglomerate of wickedness shrouded in mystery and bringing in billions a year for the senior Pyongyang leadership through drug smuggling, slave labor in the North Korean gulag system, and the counterfeiting of American one-hundred-dollar bills, known as Super Ks. But now Comrade Moon lay in a coffin at Toyama Storage, slain four years earlier during the overthrow of the Kim Jong-un regime by a Japan-born foreigner who went by the name of Patrick Featherstone.

Comrade Moon's successor, Mr. Lee, offered no information about himself, not even a first name or background, although some said he was of North Korean ancestry but had been raised in the Chinese city of Dandong, right across the Yalu River from North Korea. He spoke the languages of both countries with native fluency, along with English and Japanese. Mr. Lee's coyness about all aspects of his identity stemmed not from any sense of modesty or shame, but rather from the tangled web that was his personal history. In fact, "Mr. Lee" was a pseudonym that he and Comrade Moon had decided on to conceal his double identity, one of them legitimate, the other viciously corrupt.

After the red velvet curtain was raised and the corpse hotel's manager's two sons had wheeled Comrade Moon's coffin into the middle of the viewing room, the main door of the room was then opened for the dozen young men who waited outside. All twelve were impeccably groomed and dressed to the nines in ultra-lightweight woolen suits by Armani and Brioni. They were members of the *Bonghwajo*, or Torch Club, children of the DPRK power structure who had been unceremoniously booted out of their luxurious homes in what was known as the "Pyonghattan" section of the North Korean capital after the Rising Tide revolution that toppled the Kim regime. The revolution had taken place four years earlier on the day of the Glorious Triumvirate Celebration, a festival marking the radiant brilliance of the dynasty of Kim Il-sung, Kim Jong-il, and Kim Jong-un. After the fall of that dynasty, which their *nomenklatura* parents had helped prop up for so many years, these pampered one-percenters were down to their last few billion North Korean *won* and searching for a way to regain their former lifestyle. Mr. Lee offered salvation in the form of the insurgency he created in the DPRK known as Chosun Restoration, with *Chosun* being the former name of Korea before Japan colonized it in 1910. Its stated goal was the restoration to power of Kim Jong-un. The twelve youths assembled today were the insurgency's best and brightest.

In accordance with an initiation rite derived from that of the Mafia, Mr. Lee's twelve young apostles of mammon would be served sake from ceremonial flat *sakazuki* cups of solid gold, which they would first hold up in offering to Comrade Moon's coffin. After drinking the sake, they each would present a finger to Mr. Lee, who would prick it with a pin and squeeze so that their blood dripped onto a wad of cotton they each held in their other hand. Mr. Lee would then take a taper, light it from one of the candles surrounding Comrade Moon's coffin, and set the cotton on fire in their hands. They had been instructed to hold it for three seconds before dropping it into a bowl of water that had been placed on the table for the purpose.

"We remember Comrade Moon today and include him in our ritual and feast." As he said the name, Lee's eyes went to the coffin in the middle of the room. "And we ask him in spirit to give his blessing to Chosun Restoration, our army of liberation." Mr. Lee then nodded to the twelve young North Korean men who proceeded to hold the cotton balls in their hands as he pricked their fingers, dripped the blood onto the cotton, and set the balls on fire. After all of them had dropped the cotton into the bowl of water, Mr. Lee led the closing of the ritual, the final words of which were repeated by the inductees: "We dedicate ourselves to Chosun Restoration, and we bind our fates to that of our fellow members."

Mr. Lee then raised his wineglass to the coffin, and the young men followed suit. "We salute Comrade Moon!" they toasted three times in unison. As the ceremony drew to an end, the unearthly aroma of flesh and fat roasting in butter, punctuated with after-notes of vaporized Armagnac brandy, drifted enticingly into the room from the floor below. To Mr. Lee, it seemed only fitting that a meeting to discuss violence and mayhem should be held in this place of death and have ortolan as the featured item of the menu.

After the final toast ended the initiation ceremony, a long table was set in front of Comrade Moon's coffin and the appetizers were brought in. One of the young men likened the lobster bisque and spider crab in sweet-savory foam to inhaling sea spray. Then it was time for the main, highly illegal course. No larger than a baby's fist and weighing less than an ounce, the delicate ortolan songbird is a French delicacy of yore. The birds are encouraged to gorge themselves, and when they are two to three times their normal size, (that is to say, the size of a typical

American, Mr. Lee jokingly told his new acolytes) they are drowned in Armagnac, plucked, and roasted.

As the roasted birds, speckled with an autumn-leaf-fall of truffle shavings, were being carried into the room, their aroma becoming more and more maddeningly tantalizing, everyone murmured in fevered expectation as their individual cocottes were set in front of them. They all then placed oversized linen dinner napkins over their heads as French tradition dictated, hiding their faces from God at the impending sin of eating such a rare and delicate creature.

After the meal, largely silent except for the crunching of bird bones and primal grunts of gustatory passion, Mr. Lee addressed the group.

"Gentlemen. The twelve of you have been chosen carefully from the most elite members of the Bonghwajo Torch Club as Chosun Restoration's advance guard. I have purposely limited your numbers to avoid arousing suspicion until our reinforcements arrive for the latter part of our mission. But you make up for your small numbers by the fact that you are all highly adept at martial arts, gunmanship, and the use of high explosives. We meet today in common cause. As you are all well aware, the interests of Bureau 39 were admirably advanced for many years by Comrade Moon. Now our dear Comrade is no longer with us, and the DPRK is in the midst of great turmoil, following the Rising Tide revolution of four years ago. We are now at a crossroads."

Mr. Lee was a master orator and paused to let the tension build before continuing in a lower-pitched voice.

"When Rising Tide deposed our Brilliant Commander Kim Jong-un on the very day of the Glorious Triumvirate Celebration, it also robbed you of your rightful claim to aristocracy, and greatly diminished Bureau 39's traditional sources of income. However, Rising Tide and its puppet leader Nahm Myung-dae have made the lives of the people far worse, with widespread hunger and the breakdown of order.

"Now, with the upcoming Olympic Games, we have an unprecedented opportunity to take revenge, and for you to regain your former status. Gentlemen, we seek nothing less than the return of the Kim family to the seat of power in the DPRK, with the twelve of you as military regents paving the way for his return. The one hundred or so reinforcements who will arrive later will be our second wave. Let me begin with the details of the first wave for which you will be responsible. My overall plan has five phases, each of which represents one of our enemy's centers of gravity, which we will systematically destroy. In so doing we will bring the enemies of our nation to their knees. Would you now please gather around this map of Tokyo. Mister Pung, who was Comrade Moon's right-hand man, will help me explain."

A thickset, middle-aged Korean man with gunshot residue on his fingers stood. He explained that each of them had a particular mission of destruction meant to sow chaos and terror during the upcoming Olympic Games to demonstrate to the world that Chosun Restoration would avenge the overthrow of Kim Jong-un four years earlier, and would now stop at nothing to restore the Brilliant Commander to power. Pung had begun Phase One of the plan that very morning with the double assassination at the Olympic stadium.

After Pung had finished, Mr. Lee rose from the table and departed. He promised to come back from time to time to check on their progress.

CHAPTER 3

TOKYO
The American embassy
July 10, 11:47 a.m.

A Marine guard placed the rifle that had been recovered from the stadium on the round mahogany table in the middle of CIA Station Chief Norm Hooper's office at the American embassy. Three Agency men immediately took seats around the table, peering intently at the rifle as if expecting it to start moving of its own accord. Hooper's former jock physique had gone flabby in the middle, and he began tapping a soft, slow paradiddle on his belly while lost in thought. His senior CIA case officer, fifty-four-year-old Harmon Phibbs, ran a hand through his thick shock of fiber-optic white hair. Jack Fitzroy, CIA Asia head of clandestine activities, sat next to Hooper with his ever-present cup of coffee. All three were officially cultural attachés, part of the diplomatic minuet danced in every embassy in the world.

"Hot damn, an AK-47," Phibbs muttered under his breath as he leaned forward for a closer look.

As Phibbs made his comment, the three CIA men were joined by Patrick Featherstone, the man who had been conducting the briefing at the Olympic stadium when the two men were shot. Hooper turned to him with his head at an angle and scratched his ear as he spoke. "So, Featherstone, two guys get sniped right after one of them questioned why you were hired."

Patrick's eyes narrowed as he took a seat. "And? What are you implying, I was somehow involved?"

"No, of course not," Hooper said, straightening his head. "I'm just saying…well, shit, I'm going to come out and say it. I think the guy had a point about you being head of security for the Olympics after what happened in Pyongyang." Patrick's posture stiffened, but he said nothing.

Hooper's face tightened into a grimace as he continued. "I just saw a report this morning on what might happen if things go totally to shit in North Korea. It would be catastrophic for the entire region, do you know that?"

"I understand, but what bearing does that have on the Olympics?" Patrick said. "This is four years later, and we have the situation at hand to deal with. You're conflating two totally different things."

Harmon Phibbs took it upon himself to speak for Hooper. "What Norm's saying is that what happened this morning doesn't give you permission to grab your sniper rifle and go off the rez like you did in North Korea," said Phibbs. "That was some spooky kabuki, World War III kind of shit. And now the whole potential refugee crisis in North Korea…"

Hooper held up his hand to his senior case officer. "I can speak for myself, Harmon."

"Sorry, Norm."

While they were having this exchange, two Japanese men were escorted into the room by a Marine guard. Kazuo Hayashida, director of the Japan Intelligence Agency, silently took a seat at the table with a bemused look on his face. The younger man who had accompanied him sat deferentially on a chair away from the table. The way Americans argued without concern for group harmony both fascinated and disgusted Hayashida, especially since two of his main assistants had just been murdered in cold blood. *Americans with their little power games,* he thought sourly. *If everyone spoke their mind like that in Japan, we'd be back to the Warring States period.*

"In any case, gentlemen," Hayashida said, joining the conversation, "we obviously have a grave situation on our hands, and I'd like to thank you, Mister Hooper, as well as President Dillard, for generously allowing the use of the American embassy as the combined security command base for the Olympics. And, of course, thank you as well, Mister Featherstone." He thanked Patrick separately because Patrick had been brought in as a private contractor, not as a representative of the United States.

"By the way," Hayashida continued, indicating the young man with his hand, "this is Minoru Kaga, one of our most promising recruits. He transferred over from the Cabinet Intelligence and Research Office where he found things a bit…well, let's just say he was looking for a bit more of a challenge. I chose him for his fluency in English as well as other abilities."

The young man stood and bowed. "I hope to be of service in any way I can."

Just then, there was a knock on the door, and in walked the young Caucasian woman in the navy pantsuit from the stadium. Her short, dark blonde hair was stylishly gelled, and she had the fresh look of someone who religiously kept in shape, although the creases at the sides of her mouth seemed to indicate someone who had already settled in for the long, hard winter of life.

"Sorry I'm late," she said testily. "Apparently, my security creds didn't make it to the front gate."

"That's our fault, Kirsten," Hooper said, looking sharply at Phibbs whose job it had been. Phibbs picked up his coffee cup and blew upon the cold liquid, saying nothing.

"Patrick, have you met Kirsten Beck?" Hooper said. "She's a liaison from the FBI's Honolulu office and has been working for several weeks with the JIA. Kirsten, Patrick Featherstone is a freelancer who sometimes takes that designation completely literally."

Patrick gave a lopsided smile at Hooper's description of him and rose to shake hands with Kirsten Beck as she took a seat at the table. They regarded each other with professional interest, but not without quick glances at respective ring fingers.

"Oh, you're the man who was doing the briefing at the stadium," she said with sudden recognition. She smiled and said, "I've heard about your fine work in North Korea."

"*Fine work?*" Hooper laughed in sardonic disbelief. To his mind, Patrick's actions leading to the fall of Kim Jong-un had been recklessly dangerous, and he began to let loose with classified information despite Hayashida and Kaga's presence. "Do either of you have any idea how many refugees there could be if the civil war they're projecting in North Korea actually comes to pass? The report I got this morning said twenty million! And do you know how much it would cost the surrounding countries to absorb them when they start streaming across the borders? Trillions, Featherstone, trillions! Thanks so much for your *fine work.*"

A pall of silence fell over the room. Hooper finally broke it with an apology.

"I'm sorry for that, everyone. Kirsten, I didn't mean to jump all over you. It's just that the situation in North Korea is even more unstable now than it was under Kim Jong-un. We all better pray it doesn't turn into another Iraq after Saddam was toppled. Let's get back to this Olympic thing. Again, my apologies."

Kirsten Beck began. "Totally understandable, Norm. Well, as far as this morning's incident goes, I guess my main question is the obvious one: Does anybody have any idea who the shooter was?"

Patrick said, "I have a few ideas along those lines, but I don't think Naya and Watari were the main targets."

"You can't be serious," said Phibbs, putting a hand on the rifle on the table. "They practically got eviscerated with this AK-47."

"What I mean is, whoever the shooter was, he was trying to send a message, rather than take out those two. In fact, I wouldn't doubt if I myself was supposed to be the main recipient of the message."

"What makes you say that?" Phibbs said skeptically. "It was plain as day that Naya and Watari were…"

"Naya and Watari were on either side of me, Phibbs," Patrick said sharply. "The shots came one after the other. Why not take me out, too, since I was right in the middle? Plus, the rifle is a North Korean Type 58, not an AK-47, although I'm sure they look alike to the inexperienced eye." Phibbs's nostrils flared at Patrick's intentional dig.

"I'm also sure it was left on purpose," Patrick continued. "I didn't make many friends in North Korea when I was there, but the people I was up against could have taken me out any time over the past four years… or a few hours ago. I think the shooting was a calling card. Letting me… us…know how easy it is for them to get to us anyplace, anytime, in any way. And also that North Korea is still an active player at some level."

"And just in time for the Olympics when the whole world is watching," said Kirsten Beck, more to herself than to the others. Patrick nodded.

"Jesus, it just occurred to me. North Korea blew up a jetliner to try and sabotage the '88 Olympics in Seoul," said Fitzroy in his authoritative basso. "If there's a Nork connection to all this, we're in for some deep kimchee."

"Agreed," said Patrick. "Also, I found this at the stadium. It was jammed into the ventilation slots of my locker." He took out a small piece of paper from his pocket.

"What's it say?" asked Hooper.

"You must look down upon the enemy, and go to higher ground."

"Sounds like a fortune cookie to me," muttered Phibbs dismissively. "Maybe they couldn't find a waste basket after they sent out for Hu Flung Dung."

Hooper lowered his head into a facepalm of bowel-shriveling embarrassment. Patrick glared at Phibbs and held up the piece of paper he had found in his locker. "I got a text with the same message right before the shootings. You'll notice in the note here that the five Olympic rings are on fire in the background. I think this is a taunt," Patrick said.

"A taunt? Of you personally?" asked Hooper.

Patrick nodded. "The words are a quote from a seventeenth-century samurai named Miyamoto Musashi. He was a master swordsman and artist. And he wrote a treatise called *The Book of Five Rings*. I wrote my art college senior thesis on it and posted it online years ago. My guess is that someone found it and sent me a message."

"So what do you suggest we do, break out the swords?" Phibbs asked.

Patrick replied to everyone while looking directly at Phibbs. "I'll need to bring in some people I trust."

Hooper spat air in disgust.

Patrick continued, "That's not a dig against the whole Agency, Hooper. But there are people I know who have a high level of expertise that comes from personally dealing with North Korea. And to my mind, what happened this morning has North Korea written all over it. I also have a strong feeling that this morning was just the beginning."

CHAPTER 4

After the meeting, Hooper asked Patrick and Japan Intelligence Agency Director Hayashida to stay behind to discuss a matter he didn't want to go beyond the three of them. Hayashida sent Minoru Kaga, his new recruit, back to JIA headquarters. Once the three of them were settled around the table, Hooper began. "Gentlemen, I think an important question that has to be settled soon is, how much information on this morning's incident gets released to the public. I'm talking, of course, about the North Korea connection."

Patrick exhaled and looked up at the ceiling with his mouth set in concern. Hayashida had his eyes closed while Hooper spoke, not in disrespect, but to show that he was taking in every important word. Neither he nor Patrick seemed inclined to be the first to offer an opinion, but seeing Hayashida's closed eyes, Patrick decided to start.

"Well, I'm really just the hired help in terms of security, so I don't know if it's my place to be offering my two yen on a policy issue, but the big question to me is, who were the actors in this morning's assassinations, and do they have anything else planned? If they do, then I think it's our duty to alert the public. And if it really is North Korea behind it, then I think we can be sure it's not a one-off. Also, this morning was a clear indication that whoever it was, North Korean or otherwise, was able to circumvent all sorts of traditional and AI security."

Hayashida began to nod, still with his eyes closed, while Patrick was speaking. When Patrick finished, he opened his eyes and continued to nod.

"I agree with what you say, Mister Featherstone: we just don't know who it was and what else may or may not happen."

Patrick's eyes narrowed and his head went back. Hayashida had just cherry-picked a minor detail of Patrick's argument and ignored his larger point that the public should indeed be alerted. Hayashida turned to Hooper.

"Mister Hooper, I actually asked Prime Minister Adegawa the same question as you did before I arrived," said Hayashida. He cleared his throat and shifted in his seat, which Patrick took as an indication that he was about to impart information that might not fall on welcoming ears.

Hayashida continued. "The Prime Minister and I both agree that these Olympics are hugely important not only for the prestige of Japan, but for lifting the spirits of the Japanese people who, as you know, have suffered greatly in recent years beginning with the 2011 Great Eastern Earthquake. Over twenty thousand of our people perished. And since that time, we've also had earthquakes in Kumamoto and Hokkaido, and the typhoon and massive floods of 2018."

He cleared his throat again. "The Prime Minister feels, and I agree, that whether this morning was an isolated instance or the beginning of a larger plan of attack, we can't allow terrorism to bring the Olympics to a halt. The Prime Minister cited the example of the Munich Olympics where terrorists ran wild, and yet the Games went on."

"Excuse me, Director Hayashida," Hooper interjected before the JIA director could continue, "but the target in those Games was the Israeli team. We can't be certain that whoever committed these murders this morning doesn't have a much larger target. What if they want to bring the Olympics to its knees? Or Japan to its knees?"

Hayashida began nodding again. "Exactly, Mister Hooper. As you say, we can't be certain. Therefore, it is the Prime Minister's decision that the public not be alerted."

Patrick was barely able to stifle a sardonic laugh mixed with grudging respect at Hayashida's adroit closing down of the topic with basically a nonanswer and making it seem as though a consensus had been reached. Death by agreement. He recalled the Japanese proverb, "If the pot stinks, put a lid on it." Since he had grown up in Japan, he knew all too well the futility of trying to counter Hayashida and the Prime Minister's brand of logic with anything actually rooted in the weighing of facts. They were going ahead with the Olympics, case closed. Butt out, *gaijin*.

Instead of wasting his time on a counter-argument, Patrick rose from his seat and said, "If that's the Prime Minister's decision, Mister Hayashida, which I very much disagree with, then I suppose I have work to do." He turned and left the room.

CHAPTER 5

KAMAKURA
That afternoon

After leaving Tokyo for home, Patrick had one more work-related task to attend to before he could unwind. Less than an hour later he arrived in his hometown of Kamakura forty miles south of Tokyo and maneuvered his motorcycle up the steep mountain where he lived. He parked the bike and proceeded on foot to a trail that led deep into the forest. Once on the trailhead he stopped and listened for a full minute. Nothing except the wind and birdsong. Satisfied that he was alone, he lowered himself down a steep declivity off the trail and walked two hundred yards deeper into the forest until he came to a spreading Japanese emperor oak tree with a large branch growing out at an angle. The shovel he had hidden under leaves was still directly under the tree, and he dug down into a foot of soft earth until the shovelhead clanged. Reaching into the hole, he extracted a heavy metal box which he opened almost reverently and took into his hand a well-cared-for Colt .45 1911A semi-automatic pistol that had belonged to his father. The oversized walnut grip was his father's own design. It held a hidden extra round accessible by breaking off the inside grip panel.

Owning a gun, owning a bullet, and pulling a trigger are three separate and very serious criminal offenses in Japan. For years, Patrick had managed to keep his illegal activities out of the eyes of the authorities by virtue of the remoteness of his shooting range and the meticulous care he took in masking any sign of his armaments. Not even his role as chief security consultant for the Olympics gave him leave to own a personal arsenal such as the one he had here. He began the day's target practice by attaching a sound suppressor onto the barrel of the gun and loading a full mag of .45 caliber rimless cartridges. After setting up a paper target on his "range," backstopped by the mountain thirty yards away, he walked back to the oak tree, took aim, and shot from a variety of positions: sitting, prone, legs folded tailor-style, even left-handed. When he retrieved the target, he swore under his breath. In the old days, every shot of the four mags would have hit at least the second ring from the bull's eye. Today only seven rounds had even hit the target. His pistol skills had always lagged behind his rifle skills, but this was inexcusable, especially considering his appointment as chief security consultant for the Olympics. He swore again at his lack of foresight and discipline in setting time aside for the target practice that he obviously sorely needed. But he forgave himself somewhat when he considered the domestic demands on his time, demands he'd never had back when he was a young gunslinger in the Joint Special Operations Command of the U.S. Army.

He checked the time and proceeded to clean the barrel with a bore brush, restoring a glint of silver to the ancient rifling. As he worked the brush into the deepest recesses of the barrel, he smiled as his thoughts turned to an early evening at home, a rarity in the months since his appointment. He carefully placed three pistols into a backpack and set off for home.

Later that afternoon he awoke with a gasp. He had lain down on the tatami floor of his house for a nap but had quickly fallen into a dream in which his longtime lover, Yumi Takara, had her right hand outstretched to him pleadingly with a look of panic on her face. In her left arm she held a child with a gaping hole in his body. In the background of the dream a huge crowd was chanting the words "Rising Tide! Rising Tide!" over and over.

He took several breaths to dismiss the horrific image of the child, then turned to Yumi who was at the other end of the room.

"Same dream?" she asked as she rose to fill his teacup from a pump thermos on the kitchen counter. Patrick nodded and reached up to turn on the air conditioner. The humidity had become unbearable due to an impending storm. He sipped the tea and looked across the room.

"How's he doing?" he said, indicating a little boy who lay on a futon.

"Up and down," Yumi replied. She went over to the boy and began stroking his forehead. He lay sleeping on his back with his head angled up to one side and his mouth open. The happy-faced puppies on his soft cotton pajamas brought a smile to her face, especially since Patrick had picked them out.

"Are the supplements helping?" Patrick asked.

"The doctors seem to think so. But he still has that vacant look from the malnutrition. It's only when he sees you that he seems to focus on anything."

Patrick noticed that Yumi had placed a traditional Korean protective amulet of a three-headed hawk on the boy's pillow despite her avowed disbelief in anything smacking of superstition. He had given it to her after rescuing her from Senghori Prison near the DMZ just before the overthrow of the Kim Jong-un regime. The reason for Yumi's incarceration was the actions of her father. He had run afoul of Comrade Moon, founder of North Korea's Bureau 39, and gone into hiding. In order to force his hand, Moon ordered that Yumi be kidnapped until such time as her father surfaced. He didn't, and she was abducted to Senghori, where Patrick tracked her down and rescued her.

After the overthrow, rather than returning immediately to Japan, she insisted on volunteering at a children's shelter not far from Senghori Prison. Patrick had stayed with her. The North Korean boy who lay on the futon of their home was named Dae-ho. He had been found in the forest near the children's shelter near Kaesong. He was one of seventy or so orphans (the number changed daily due to the mortality rate) in the children's shelter, and Patrick and Yumi had begun adoption proceedings after nursing him back to a semblance of health.

Patrick set down his tea on the low calligraphy table in the middle of the room and went over to where the boy lay. As soon as Patrick approached him, the boy's eyes opened, and he reached out his hand and said, "*Appa*?" (Daddy?). When Yumi tended to him, he would say "*Omma*?" in the same questioning tone. It was all he ever said. Patrick chalked up his muteness to his ongoing recovery from malnutrition, although one of the doctors had mentioned possible autism. It was too early to tell.

Patrick extended two fingers, as was their little ritual. The boy held them tight, closed his eyes, and fell back asleep. Patrick signaled Yumi for his tea as he lowered himself down onto the futon. Even in the early stages of sleep the boy held firm. It wasn't until a half hour later that his breathing got deeper and he relinquished his hold on Patrick's fingers. Patrick rose from the futon.

"He's definitely a fighter," he said, kissing Yumi on the head.

"Just like his new adoptive father."

"Well, not officially yet."

Although Patrick didn't let on to Yumi, he was terrified at the prospect of fatherhood, by adoption or otherwise. His self-doubt increased as he considered the great sacrifices his own parents had gone to in raising him. Kiana Miyamoto, of a well-off family from the island of Kauai in Hawaii, was fourteen years younger than Daniel Featherstone, who wooed the pretty young Eurasian college student when she was attending a seminar on Shakespeare at the University of Tokyo. She was on a full scholarship from the University of Chicago, but abandoned her academic career to stay with the mysterious older man who invited her for coffee and proceeded to win her heart.

Daniel Featherstone had arrived in Japan years earlier as part of Douglas MacArthur's occupation force and found the country fascinating enough to remain in beyond his two-year tour. His easy fluency in

Japanese caught the attention of the head of the CIA's front organization, the Joint Advisory Commission, and he went on to serve in an elite commando unit known as the Special Mission Group (SMG) which engaged in a yearlong campaign of destruction of North Korean coastal railroad tracks and bridges, as well as the planting of landmines and booby traps and the caching of weapons in the cave systems near the city of Kaesong. After the Korean War he taught English at the University of Tokyo where he met Kiana Miyamoto. Both of Patrick's parents came from predominantly Irish families, although one of Kiana's grandfathers was ethnic Japanese. They had hoped to have a large family like the ones they came from, but by the time they got around to having Patrick, her womb was all but depleted. Instead of having their own large family, they both dropped their academic careers and became codirectors of Kamakura's Yukinoshita Orphanage.

Yumi and Patrick had been engaged to marry several years before her abduction. But then Patrick turned to Zen Buddhism as a means of quieting his mind of the endless loop of mistakenly shooting a five-year-old Serbian boy on a Joint Special Operations Command (JSOC) sniper mission. His mind took an impression like wax and it instantly turned to marble, which was a blessing for an artist but a curse for someone with depressive tendencies, as he was. The only way he could clear his mind of the image of the child he had shot was through deep meditation. Before long he broke off his engagement to Yumi to pursue the life of an ordained monk.

After rescuing Yumi from Senghori, Patrick realized that she was the love of his life after all, but Yumi was still bitter over being tossed aside for Patrick's prospective life as a monk, a vocation he later decided against. His love for her went unrequited, but she eventually relented, and they moved back to Patrick's hometown of Kamakura. With the help of sympathetic contacts in the Japanese government, they were allowed to bring with them little Dae-ho, one of the most fragile of the North Korean orphans who had been found wandering in the forest half dead from starvation after the Rising Tide revolution that had toppled the Kim regime.

With the boy fast asleep, Patrick sat down at the low calligraphy table where Yumi had set out their supper. She had prepared his favorite dish of *tonkatsu*, deep fried pork cutlets topped with her signature homemade sauce made from vegetables from her garden along with soy sauce, vinegar, and sugar. Patrick picked up a large bottle of Sapporo draft and poured them each a glass which they clinked together before starting the meal. Patrick ate in silence, staring off into space and preoccupied with what had happened that morning at the stadium. She nudged his knee with hers under the table. "Anybody home?"

Patrick lowered his eyes and smiled. "Sorry. I was just thinking about the next three weeks."

"Any chance you could include me in your thoughts?" she teased. "You're my only contact with the real world until Dae-ho gets better."

"The Olympics aren't the real world. It's a fantasy that happens every four years where everyone pretends to like each other while they march in the Parade of Nations. Have you ever heard the story about the British and German soldiers during World War I who played soccer with each other on the battlefield on Christmas Eve? Then the next morning they went back to shooting each other."

Yumi shook her head and winced. "So cynical. The Parade of Nations is my favorite part. It's so nice to see everyone smiling, unlike you."

Patrick rocked his head noncommittally as he slurped sauce off a strip of tonkatsu. "I suppose."

"Do you think Japan will show its best face as the host country?"

"I can't think of a better host in terms of hospitality, and Japan *always* shows its best face. *Face* is what this country is all about. It's what lies beneath the face that's sometimes a bit problematic."

"You could say the same about any country. It's not like I'm some kind of cheerleader for Japan, but it's got its good points."

"Oh, I agree totally," Patrick said, taking a sip of beer. "I'm sorry if it seems like I'm dragging the country down, but I think as a foreigner who was born here and still can't get citizenship, I see things that other people don't."

"You know the solution to that," Yumi said while demurely dipping a strip of deep-fried pork into the sauce. Patrick nodded.

"Sure. Us getting married. But you'd think that my being born here would count for something at least."

"Tell me again why you felt you had to accept this job. I'm not getting on your case here, I just don't understand why you take things on that you later regret."

"I don't regret it, I just recognize the responsibility it entails, that's all." He left out a major factor: although he felt more content than he ever had in his life, he missed the excitement that the consultant's job promised.

Yumi took a sip of beer and pulled a strand of hair over her upper lip, mustache-like. "I wonder if I would have made a good spy."

"It's not too late, you're not even forty. Hey, maybe you could sign up to be a honey trap." Crow's feet at the corners of his eyes creased into a smile.

She let go of her "mustache" and her eyes widened. "What's that? It sounds dishonorable."

"A honey trap lures enemy spies into her net with the promise of sexual favors. You get to carry a gun in your bra in case there's any trouble."

"No way! I'm a respectable Japanese girl." She fluttered her eyelids, and they both laughed.

They ate in silence for a few minutes. "Any word from over there?" she asked after a while. *Over there* was their code for North Korea.

"Actually, I'm pretty sure I heard from someone personally today."

"Really? Who?" She sat up straighter and her head went forward.

Patrick proceeded to tell her of the assassination of the two security officials at the Olympic stadium and his strong suspicion that the shooter had been North Korean. When he had accepted the job as chief security consultant for the Olympics, Patrick had stipulated that his role would be advisory only. Then today happened, hence his target practice earlier in the afternoon.

"That's terrible!" Yumi said.

Patrick saucered his eyes and nodded vigorously. "Yup."

"Do you think anyone in the pachinko parlors is involved?" she asked. Her own father had been a proprietor of one such parlor in Tokyo, which had been the source of his problems with Comrade Moon. He had used the parlor as a transshipment point for pharmaceutical-grade methamphetamine coming in from Pyongyang.

"That's a good point, I hadn't thought of that angle," Patrick said, crunching on a mouthful of *tsukemono* pickled vegetables. "If drugs are involved, I'm sure the parlors are somehow connected. But something tells me this is different. More political somehow."

Yumi lowered her eyes and began to pick at her own vegetables. "When will you be leaving?" she asked in a quiet voice.

Patrick looked closely at her, investigating her eyes and body language. "Tomorrow, remember? I have to stay in Tokyo during most of the Games as part of my contract." He sipped his miso soup and set the bowl down again. "I'm just a consultant, though. No rough stuff this time, don't worry."

But part of him, a big part, missed being an active participant in the "rough stuff." The urge to hunt. The thirst for revenge slaked only by the blood of the guilty. And despite the vow of nonviolence he had taken when he contemplated becoming a Zen monk, he had to confess that he'd never felt anything quite so instantly gratifying as peering through a sniper's scope and sending 1.5 ounces of hot lead hurtling at the speed of sound at someone who had forfeited the right to continue among civilized humanity. The only problem was, a case could be made that he himself had done something in North Korea which quite possibly forfeited his own right. Yumi said nothing when he promised no rough stuff, but stared at him with skeptical eyes. And Patrick knew why. When they were working at the shelter near the DMZ, he had gone looking for the commandant of Senghori Prison. What happened next was something that Patrick had unsuccessfully tried to rationalize to himself as a manifestation of PTSD. He forced the memory from his mind.

Later in the evening, after Dae-ho had awoken and been fed, Patrick and Yumi settled into their comfortable routine of quiet conversation during their calligraphy practice while the boy doodled silently with his little brush on scrap paper. The narcotically meditative scent of the camphor-based black ink filled the room like incense. Patrick looked over at Yumi who was sitting on the floor absorbed in her practice and smiled to himself. When she sat this way she was the model of fluid grace, but when she sat in a chair, she would cross her legs and arms and suddenly turn into human origami. A sense of peace and fulfillment came over him until the assassinations at the stadium once again intruded into his consciousness. He found his brush almost guided to the character for "crisis." He dipped his brush into the *suzuri* inkwell and compulsively drew the character over and over for a full fifteen minutes. At seven o'clock, he glanced at the clock on the wall and stood.

"I told Yasuhara Roshi [*roshi* is an honorific title reserved for a thoroughly accomplished Zen master] that I'd drop by. Do you want to bring Dae-ho and come with me?"

"That's okay, you go ahead," she said. "There's something I need to look for, and it's easier to find things when you're not in the way." He smiled at her and brought his head down. She looked up and they kissed...chastely for now, for Dae-ho was watching them. Maybe later when the boy was sound asleep.

"I'll leave you to your search, then," he said as he went out the door, smiling at her as he left. "I love you," he added quietly.

"Me too," Yumi said. He smiled at her but crimped his lips in dismay over the fact that she didn't also use the words "I love you" and hadn't since before he had broken off their engagement several years earlier.

CHAPTER 6

TOYAMA STORAGE
Yokohama

As Patrick was getting ready to pay a visit to his Zen teacher, the privileged North Korean Bonghwajo youths from Pyonghattan were hurriedly summoned from their upstairs rooms at the incognito corpse hotel in Yokohama.

"Everyone assemble in the viewing room!" Mr. Pung shouted from the bottom of the stairs. His voice had taken on an added layer of resonance after his shooting of the two security officials at the Olympic stadium.

Immediately after the last of the Bonghwajo had taken their places in front of Comrade Moon's coffin, the front door of Toyama Storage opened and Mr. Lee barreled in as quickly as a man with a limp could be said to barrel. A few of the North Korean youths discreetly looked down at his feet, not having realized that the leader of Chosun Restoration had a disability. At their initiation ritual a few days earlier he had already been seated at his place. Now, with the youths assembled around him, Lee's penetrating gaze took in each boy in turn. Then he abruptly turned his back to them.

"What does the year 1923 mean to you?" he demanded. The youths looked at each other in puzzlement. Lee wheeled around and glared at them. "What? Nothing?"

After an excruciating minute of silence, one of the boys timidly raised his hand. Lee lifted his chin.

"The Great Kanto Earthquake, sir?"

Lee nodded vigorously. "Exactly! And what happened then?"

Several of the other Bonghwajo began to breathe normally. They were now on familiar ground, for they had been told this story since they were young children. A different boy raised his hand, this time with full confidence. Lee recognized him with another upward jut of his chin.

"The Japanese murdered six thousand Korean people, sir."

"Correct!" Lee shouted. "And why did they murder our people?"

The boys were now in open competition to be recognized. Lee pointed at the one at the far end of the assemblage.

"They claimed that our people had poisoned their wells, sir."

"Correct! And who was behind these murders?"

"The Japanese army, sir," several boys shouted in unison.

"Correct! And where are the ashes of these murderers interred?"

All twelve boys were now vying to outdo each other as they answered Mr. Lee's rapid-fire questions.

"And who are the military descendants of these murderers?"

The sinister Socratic dialogue went on for several more minutes, at the end of which Lee announced that a reinforcement cohort of ninety-four members would be arriving in two days from the DPRK. But the advance guard of a dozen Bonghwajo assembled on this night would have the honor of drawing first blood. Tomorrow.

Later that evening Mr. Pung chose six of the twelve and told them to prepare for their missions. The following day they would have the opportunity to prove themselves on the field of battle. All of the youths held Pung in the highest esteem, both for the double assassination he had carried out at the Olympic stadium and for his impeccably sinister background, which they had learned about when they were recruited into Chosun Restoration....

An only child, Pung was actually born in Osaka in 1970 of North Korean parents. His father died of alcoholism when he was still a young boy, and his widowed mother raised him as best she could with her mea-ger earnings as a seamstress. He was a dutiful son whose devotion to his mother was commented on favorably by the neighbors, but his peers at school thought him a mama's boy and ostracized him. Growing up friendless is traumatic for any young child, but especially so in Japan where one's position in a group determines the better part of one's iden-tity: no group, no self. Especially for an ethnic Korean.

When he was thirteen he began associating with a gang of fellow young Koreans who rejected the Japanese society that had rejected them first and embraced Kim Il-sung of North Korea as their heroic surrogate father figure. At the age of sixteen he broke his mother's heart by drop-ping out of school and moving out of the house. He found lodging with a few of the older Koreans who had a cramped apartment in the seedy Juso section of Osaka. They didn't charge Pung any rent at first, but he earned his keep by joining the others on their all-night excursions in the back alleys of Osaka where they would transport small quantities of methamphetamine to different parts of the city. They would sleep all day at the apartment and then smoke the *bingu* for the night's work ahead.

Seeing potential in the young recruit, the head of a local yakuza family with ties to North Korea challenged him to make his bones and join the family by taking out a *wakagashira*, or first lieutenant, in a rival family. He gave Pung a pistol for the job, but Pung, showing an early flair for the dramatic, opted instead for a switchblade which he purposely left at the scene so that his fingerprints could be recovered and his reputation assured. Since he was only sixteen at the time, he was given a four-year sentence followed by probation. But by the end of his hard time, he had attracted the attention of the talent scouts of Bureau 39 and had been persuaded to come live in the land of his ancestors. Before not too many years he became Comrade Moon's right-hand man and main enforcer in the drug trade.

For the first mission of Chosun Restoration involving the Bonghwajo youths, Pung divided the six selected Bonghwajo into two teams of three each to escalate the Phase One attacks that he had begun with the double assassination at the Olympic stadium. The remaining six members would keep a low profile at the corpse hotel, planning the next attacks. The Phase One attacks were specifically aimed at military personnel, and to that end, he would take his six young charges to an area outside of Tokyo where they would hone their shooting skills in preparation for two simultaneous attacks later in the week. All of the young men had had training in firearms as members of the Sarochong, or Party Youth, in North Korea, so the shooting drills they would engage in in the forest would just be a tune-up. Theoretically.

CHAPTER 7

As Patrick got ready to leave for his visit to his Zen teacher, his mind wandered back to when Yumi had last said the words "I love you" to him…

After the debacle in Serbia, when Patrick had accidentally shot the Serbian boy, he returned to Kamakura and embarked on a long alcoholic binge in a vain attempt to expunge the memory that kept percolating to the surface of his consciousness like a weighted corpse rising from the depths of a swamp. The memories subsided only when he took up Zen meditation at a temple near the center of the coastal town. One day a young artist in her early thirties came to the temple to practice zazen as well. She was a practitioner of traditional Japanese calligraphy and sumi-e ink-brush painting which had been Patrick's major at the university. As she entered the kitchen where Patrick sat chatting with the abbot of the temple, she stopped and stared. Patrick stared back at her with his lips parted. The rest of the world fell away. The very air around her took on an incandescent glow. Her thick, lustrous hair was full of lights that burned holes in his heart. In no time they had fallen in love, despite widely divergent sensibilities.

They weren't the type of couple whose temperaments chimed perfectly at all hours of the day and night, but when things were just right between them, they were a seamless meshing of body, mind, and spirit, a mysterious fusion, like Einstein's space-time. Lying in listless bliss after making love for the first time, he spoke to her softly just to make sure she was real, and she answered for the same reason. But it was as if they were one being, with no "I" or "you." Just oneness calling and answering itself: *I love you/I love you too.*

"Let's stay here forever," Patrick whispered in her ear.

"We can't just make the rest of the world go away," Yumi chided him gently.

"We can try."

But things were not always right between them, and their personalities often jabbed against each other like sharp rocks in a burlap sack. Their life together was a never-ending back-and-forth between the two extremes. Usually it was his long silences that would precipitate the oscillation from bliss to rancor. At first she read his unwillingness to talk as disinterest or even disaffection with her. But along with his black Irish penchant for depression and brooding, he had been cursed with a technicolor visual memory, and the image of the boy he had shot in Serbia was never far from his mind. In time the memories receded in inverse proportion to his love for her. Now, all these years later, Yumi had accomplished the impossible: she had guided his solitary and turbulent soul into a stable love. He couldn't be more content on one hand, but part of him still yearned for the thrill of the hunt. The thrill of the kill.

Once outside his house he mulled over whether to take his Harley Road King or the old Toyota Stout light truck he had restored, and opted for the Stout. He didn't want the throaty engine of the 1500cc hog to explode into life right next to the house and frighten Dae-ho at this time of the evening which had gotten even more oppressively humid. Patrick wiped the sweat from his eyes with the back of his hand before putting the Stout into gear.

Along his route to Yasuhara Roshi's temple he picked out the parts of Kamakura that had meant so much to him growing up, including the famous Great Buddha dating back to the thirteenth century. He had been fascinated as a young boy when his father told him that the oxidization they saw blackening its interior was the preserved exhalations of pilgrims who had been dead for more than seven hundred years. A smaller, less famous temple two blocks away known as the Hase Kannon, however, had always impressed him even more deeply. Something about the heavy-lidded eyes of one of the statues as it reclined in royal ease in the half-lit sanctuary room affected him with a sense of unfathomable mystery, as if he were being afforded a glimpse into the very heart of the universe. The sense of ancientness was such that he half expected to see twelfth-century monks rounding a corner on their way to the meditation hall. It was the deep peace he felt there that first led him to Zen.

It took him fifteen minutes to reach Eiwa-ji (Temple of Eternal Peace). When he got out of the truck, he paused on the short access road to the temple and just stood there, letting the susurration of the bamboo in the evening breeze wash over him. Something between a heavy mist and a light drizzle softened the air. A few minutes later he walked to the front door and opened it a crack. "*Gomen kudasai,*" he called out softly, apologizing in advance for any disturbance.

"*Hai,*" an old voice called out from a back room. His teacher was over ninety, but despite cheeks clawed by age and a scholar's hump from all the reading he had done over the years, he was as energetic as a fifty-year-old, fully recovered from a serious illness several years back. Even as he moved briskly along the polished hardwood floor, he had about him an inner stillness that Patrick hoped to find in his own heart someday.

"You're back," Yasuhara Roshi said with a wide smile, and invited Patrick into his small private apartment where he insisted on preparing large bowls of *matcha*, the brew used in a traditional tea ceremony. Patrick usually stayed away from the thick, bitter tea at night because of its high caffeine content, but he welcomed the roshi's idea with manufactured enthusiasm and an inner sigh. He would be up late tonight. As he picked up his tea bowl, he admired how the *craquerie* of its lacquer picked up light that a more perfect bowl would have merely reflected. The bowl must have been at least a hundred years old.

The roshi saw him admiring it and said, "*Wabi* and *sabi.*"

Patrick nodded. *Wabi* and *sabi* were Japanese concepts that elevated imperfection into an aesthetic ideal. The world and all its objects were perfect in their imperfections, not despite them. In order to remain sane in this world and appreciate the beauty it has to offer, one has to be an imperfectionist.

"The older I get, the more I appreciate those two words," Patrick said wistfully. Yasuhara Roshi laughed. "You're still a young man. Me, on the other hand…" He left the thought unfinished. As they sipped the matcha, they chatted amiably, and the teacher asked after Dae-ho.

"He's doing okay," Patrick replied, looking into his tea.

"Just okay. That doesn't sound promising. I'll be sure to include him in our morning *sutra* service tomorrow morning, although only a few of the old timers come around anymore."

"Thank you, Roshi, I would appreciate that."

The old teacher took another sip of his tea. "I've come to believe that Buddhism in Japan is more and more like a dead cicada. It *looks* no different than a live cicada, but there's just the body left, no life." He sighed. "I don't know how much more time I have either. But I'm no different from anyone else. 'Life and death is the Great Matter,'" he said, quoting one of the main tenets of his faith. "'All things pass quickly away.'"

"I'm sure you'll be around a while longer, Roshi," Patrick said in a teasing tone. "Didn't Bodhidharma live to be one hundred and fifty?"

"Oh, spare me that. Can you imagine what kind of life that was for him? And that was fifteen hundred years ago before they invented air conditioning. I have a hard enough time at ninety-two. Still, I'm surprised at how quickly it happened."

"How quickly what happened?"

"Getting old. It didn't sneak up on me at all. One day I was sixty, then all of a sudden, I'm ninety-two. I don't know where all that time went."

"Have you heard of John Lennon?"

"Of course."

"He said that life is what happens when you're making other plans."

Yasuhara Roshi laughed. "That's good. And true. You're still young, but it will happen to you, too, you know. Make sure you have things in your life that are deeply important to you, not just work."

Patrick thought of Yumi and Dae-ho. Then he thought of the two men who were shot on either side of him at the Olympic stadium that morning.

"Do you fear death, Roshi?"

The old teacher set down his bowl. "When you reach my age, you think about getting old and dying every day. There's a haiku by Basho. 'This autumn why am I growing old? Bird disappearing among clouds.'"

Patrick looked intently at his teacher. Yasuhara Roshi continued.

"I think I have a serenity now that wouldn't have been possible to me even ten years ago, let alone when I was your age. Plus, my mind is very quiet now. I think it's from letting go. It's as if all the years behind me are now preparing me for the end. Believe it or not, old age has its own blessings that aren't available to the young." He stared into his tea.

"I watch the children in the neighborhood play, and I see them growing from week to week. And when I compare myself to how strong I was when I was your age? I even feel a sense of quiet satisfaction about that. 'Was I really that strong?' I think to myself. And then I laugh to see how much weaker I am now. But now, unlike before, I have a long lifetime of memories to enjoy at odd times. Young people can't do this. For one thing, they don't have all that many memories. For another, they don't give themselves the time to appreciate the moments they have now. They go looking for things outside themselves. But if they had all the money in the world, a beautiful house and famous friends, deep down they'd still be thinking, 'Is this it?'"

Patrick loved when his teacher talked like this. His mind ran along the same lines, and this was the only opportunity he had to share similar thoughts with someone who wouldn't dismiss him as morbid. The roshi continued.

"This life is just so beautiful and just so meaningless. And the strange thing is, the meaninglessness makes it even more beautiful. It's untethered to any need to mean anything. It just floats, changes, and is gone, like a cloud that you imagine is a flower, and then a mountain, and on and on." He turned to a bookshelf behind him, took down a thin volume, and began paging through it with white, corded hands. When he found what he was looking for, he looked up at Patrick.

"I read something not long ago by this man. Do you know him? The Russian author Solzhenitsyn." He held up the cover for Patrick to see.

"Solzhenitsyn said, 'Growing old serenely is not a downhill path, but an ascent.' I like that. An *ascent*. So to answer your question, no, I don't fear death." He paused and looked at Patrick. "How about you?"

Patrick looked into his tea bowl. "I think I've had enough near-death experiences that I don't really fear it the same way I did when death was an abstraction. I guess what I fear most is being separated from the people I love. And I fear that they would be sad if I weren't around. I don't want to cause that kind of sadness."

Yasuhara Roshi laughed softly. "Always so serious. You've been this way your whole life, I think. You should live more lightly. But I know why you're talking like this. I heard about your new job. And these days terrorism seems to be all around us. Be careful, alright?"

Patrick smiled. "Maybe I'll lighten up after the Olympics," he said. Then his tone became more serious. "I think I've taken on too much with this job."

"I'm sure you're perfect for it. Just remember to relax your fingers." Patrick smiled again. Yasuhara Roshi was a calligraphy master, and he had always admonished Patrick to relax his fingers when he was gripping the ink brush too tightly. The advice was transferable to gripping a gun or a rifle. They chatted in a lighter vein for a while longer until Patrick saw his teacher stifle a yawn. How the old man was able to put back gallons of matcha throughout the day and have no trouble sleeping was beyond him. He rose from his *zabuton* cushion.

"I'll be back before too long. And one of these days I'll come to early morning meditation, if only to keep you company. But it has to be on a morning after I haven't had so much matcha the night before." They both laughed and then bowed to each other.

"Stay well, Patrick."

"And you too, Roshi."

CHAPTER 8

After his visit to the temple, Patrick took the long way home in hopes of burning off some of the caffeine in his system. He drove along the road fronting the Kamakura shoreline and thought back to his youth, when he would crank his old but well-maintained Indian motorcycle to life in the middle of the night and speed down this same road at speeds of up to 120 miles per hour, reveling in the utter ecstasy of no barriers. Sometimes he would go further inland, even as far as the Mount Fuji area seventy miles away, and engage the local motorcycle punks in bloodcurdling contests of nerves along hairpin mountain passes. As he smiled at his youthful foolishness, a motorcyclist roared past him, waving to Patrick as he did. Patrick recognized the man's bike and gave chase. The pursuit was all in fun, though, because the young man was a friend whom Patrick had helped turn away from a gang of *bosozoku,* motorcycle thugs who deal in drugs and prostitution and act as enforcers for yakuza families.

On his rambling motorcycle rides through the surrounding countryside years earlier, Patrick had an encounter with the boy's gang as they were busy turning donuts on Kamakura's shore road at night, intentionally bringing the traffic to a halt and generally making nuisances of themselves. As Patrick attempted to go around them on the side of the road, one of the gang members, a scrawny-looking punk in an outsized leather jacket, tried to cut him off. Since the traffic was stopped in both directions, Patrick was able to reach out and grab the kid with a powerful hand by his jacket and pull him off his bike, which then crashed to the ground. The other gang members hooted at their mate's bad luck in being confronted by someone who actually had the courage to fight back. They roared off still laughing, abandoning their hapless buddy to this vaguely Italian-looking *gaijin*.

The kid was terrified, and he began apologizing profusely, saying that the other gang members had ordered him to do it, since he was still just a pledge. Patrick could easily see that he was a typical confused delinquent whose antisocial behavior masked a frightened heart and a desperate desire to belong. He brushed the kid's jacket off and told him his punishment was to follow him to the rest stop across the highway. The kid regarded him suspiciously, not sure what Patrick's intentions were, but he dutifully followed. Patrick bought them each a soda and proceeded to read him the riot act. At the end of their little chat, he got the boy to promise to stop associating with morons who wouldn't even back him up against the guy who stood up to them.

"You're right, they're all *baka* (idiots)," the boy said hanging his head.

As it turned out, the kid lived not that far from Patrick, and they would wave to each other while out on their bike runs. Eventually, they started meeting up for more of Patrick's little sermons on the proper way to live, especially since Patrick always paid for lunch. Soon they were friends, albeit separated in age by a good fifteen years.

Back in his gang days, the young man had kept his hair long and styled into a ridiculous pompadour, but these days it was lopped down to a buzz cut. He was an ethnic Korean named Yi Beom-su, but he now self-mockingly dubbed himself *Bozu*, the Japanese term for a shaved-headed monk. Patrick thought it a bit too close to Bozo as a nickname, but he didn't mention it to the boy. One of Bozu's motivations in taking a nickname was so as not to call attention to his Korean-ness in homogeneous Japan.

Though his life as a gang member was behind him, one thing Bozu would never give up was his beloved 1200cc Suzuki Bandit, and on this night of too much caffeine after his visit with Yasuhara Roshi, Patrick invited Bozu to meet him at a late-night bar called Seedless along

Kamakura's shore road. As Bozu got off his bike and Patrick out of his truck a short ride later, they came over to each other and embraced. When Patrick was growing up in Kamakura, it was almost unheard of for young men to hug each other, but years of Western movies and internet images had made displays of affection more prevalent in the more urban areas.

Once inside the bar's tower-like upper level, Bozu ordered coffee and Patrick ordered *Calpis*, a cloyingly sweetened fermented milk drink that one either loves or loathes at first taste. Neither dared to order anything alcoholic since Japan's drunk driving laws are some of the strictest in the world. Their common language was Japanese, although Patrick's Korean was quite fluent, even more fluent than Bozu's, who had turned his back on his native heritage to better blend into Japan's often cruelly homogeneous society. He had learned the hard way the Japanese adage, "The nail that sticks out will be hammered down." There had always been a lot of people with hammers in Bozu's life.

As they sipped their drinks and looked out upon the ocean, they chatted about their recent lives while thunder rolled in the distance. The long white curtains inside their section of the restaurant billowed and snapped like mainsails in the rising wind. Patrick told Bozu of his travels to North Korea, leaving out his role in helping to instigate the uprising that had toppled the Kim regime.

"North Korea?" Bozu asked with raised eyebrows. "Why the hell would anyone want to go there? I've met some North Koreans. They made my old friends in the gang look like school kids." He then went uncharacteristically silent except to light a cigarette. Patrick waited several minutes for him to open up with what appeared to be bothering him.

"Patrick, do you believe in patriotism?"

This was not what Patrick was expecting. "Patriotism? You mean like those idiots who want to restore the Emperor as a god?"

"No, not like that. I mean like owing something to your country."

"I suppose I do, if it doesn't involve anything too crazy."

"And if you knew that someone was trying to harm your country, would you kill them?"

"Hang on, Bozu, are you talking about Korea?"

"No, I'm talking about Japan. Even though I was born in Korea, I was raised here."

"So you're talking about patriotism toward Japan. Let me guess, someone's been giving you shit because you're Korean."

Bozu waved his hand dismissively. "That always happens. Japanese can be really racist, but if it hadn't been for this country, my family would probably be digging cabbages back where we came from. I'm just wondering what you think about owing a debt to the country where you were raised."

"I definitely feel a debt to Japan, even though I've been on the receiving end of a lot of racism too. It's still an amazing culture, and most of the people aren't like that. Where are you going with all this, anyway?"

Bozu shrugged. "I guess I'm just getting philosophical as I get older," he said, stubbing out his cigarette.

Patrick laughed, and Bozu smiled at his own self-seriousness. He was all of twenty-six years old.

"One of these days when you're feeling extra philosophical, I'll take you to the temple where I do my meditation," Patrick said. "You'll find that a lot of the questions in life answer themselves when you just sit quietly. Plus, with that haircut of yours, you'll fit right in. You might even be motivated to quit those things," he said, pointing to the ashtray.

After Bozu went on his way, Patrick sat in the Toyota Stout in the parking lot and let his mind wander. When he was young, Patrick and his father often went surfing together in this same area of the Kamakura seaside known as Shonan, whose dark, volcanic sands extend about thirty miles along the shoreline. Daniel Featherstone, codirector with his wife of the Yukinoshita Orphanage in the heart of Kamakura, would drive the orphanage's old-but-dependable Stout along National Route 134, with Patrick and a few of his friends rumbling along in the back, checking out the various beaches for the day's best and steadiest swells. Irony of ironies, years later Patrick and Yumi had both worked in a North Korean shelter and were now looking to adopt a North Korean boy.

Patrick's father would ferry the group from Yukinoshita Orphanage to the beaches in the Shonan area. Rarely do the waves there exceed a few feet in height, except during the late summer typhoon season, but Patrick had an indelible memory of catching his first four-footer at the age of eight on an exceptionally brilliant August morning the night after a raging thunderstorm had blown away the heat and humidity, with Mount Fuji, clear as a bell, witnessing his accomplishment from seventy miles away.

When he and Yumi returned from North Korea after the overthrow of the Kim regime, he decided to take up the sport again, hoping to recapture the ineffable sensation of freedom and oneness with the ocean he remembered fondly from his youth. The salt air, the gentle rocking of the waves, the indescribable walking-on-water experience when the board dropped into the pocket—all of these called to him from across the echoing years. He also wanted to reestablish a spiritual connection with his father, who had been lost at sea when his fishing boat went down in a gale off the Shonan coast when Patrick was fifteen. During his attempt to rescue Yumi from Senghori Prison near the DMZ a few years earlier, Patrick had two visions of Daniel Featherstone while in the throes of near-death experiences, but he had never mentioned these visions to Yumi or anyone else. His father, plain as day, had spoken to him, encouraging him to live for Yumi whose life depended on Patrick's survival.

Before he was invited to be the chief security consultant for the Olympics, and while Yumi was doing most of the work of tending to Dae-ho, Patrick was at loose ends for a project of some kind, especially after the heady danger of their time in North Korea. So he decided to restore Yukinoshita Orphanage's ancient Stout into a surf truck, rebuilding its engine and transmission, installing new seats, and painting it the brilliant canary yellow his father had painted it all those years ago so that the orphans could always spot it when they went out on their daytrips. As Patrick was tearing out the old seats, the dank, organic closeness of the rotting upholstery gave way to its old, evocative 1950s car smell and conjured obscure memories, the detail and sheer number of which took his breath away.

There was his best friend from age nine, Taiki Inamura, exaggerating the truck's bounce by launching himself off his butt as high into the air as possible, making Patrick and the others erupt into the unchecked hysterics of youth. And there was little round-faced Masako Fujino, with her short rice-bowl haircut, timidly holding onto her twin sister, Yoko, who would assure her that everything was okay when the truck hit a dip in the pockmarked road. During every stage of the vehicle's restoration, Patrick would sit on the ground from time to time, enveloped in the cloistral hush of deep reminiscence, gazing at the truck and allowing his senses to be flooded with the subtle ecstasy of nostalgia.

But some of the memories that percolated into his consciousness weren't so pleasant. The reason Masako Fujino was so timid could be seen in the cigarette burn marks on her arms. Her sister Yoko, who also had scars on her body, actually fought back against her father and called the cops. None of the relatives wanted the responsibility of raising the girls, so they were sent by the court to Yukinoshita Orphanage. Other kids at the home were similarly abused, some sexually, and Patrick traced his fury bordering on madness toward child abusers to knowing these kids as a child and feeling a sense of guilt that he had been so lucky to have two parents who loved him.

Once work on the truck was finished, it was time to set aside painful memories and put the truck back to the use he remembered best: as a surf jalopy. Turning heads as he drove it along Route 134, the truck elicited two-handed waves, hoots of approval, and shaka signs. Patrick would head to a semisecret cove along the Shonan coast that his father had discovered years ago. Only he and a few select friends even knew that the cove existed, let alone that it was accessible if one didn't mind hiking through dense sticker bushes. One day he turned off the main road, parked fifty yards from the narrow access trail, and began lugging the eight-footer he had bought used from a friend who owned the nearby Blue Peter Surf Club. As he crested the ridge, he saw no one in the breeze-wrinkled sea, no doubt a result of the sixty-five-degree water temperature, but he had changed into a wetsuit in the jalopy. After waxing the board and attaching a leash to a plug on its underside, he carried the board to the edge of the water, where four-footers were breaking with surging energy. It was a perfect day to reignite an old passion, and rising up from the Kanto Plain, Mount Fuji seemed to be acknowledging his return.

The bracing water turned his hands bluish white at first, but once he began paddling out beyond the impact zone, adrenaline and high spirits restored circulation to his exposed extremities. A long groundswell set was coming in from the southeast in a steady period, generated by a storm hundreds of miles away. Its outermost wave was the one he would claim from the sea. An offshore wind was keeping the waves tailored and well groomed, with hardly even a drop of spray blown off their crests. As his wave got closer with each rolling swell, exhilaration filled his belly, and when he finally launched his feet up onto the deck, an idiot grin plastered on his face, he felt for the first time in years the ecstasy of oneness with the ocean's primal might.

Now, as he gazed upon the ocean months later from the upstairs veranda at Seedless, he wistfully recalled that wild sense of perfect self-sufficiency. He then thought of Yumi and Dae-ho at home and wondered once again if he was really cut out for the settled life. Sighing away this conflict that he kept hidden in a secret room of his heart, he finally broke off his reverie and started home. The evening air had gotten even denser with humidity, and tiny droplets of rain began to fall steadily, as if the sky itself were sweating. Capillaries of lightning pulsed inside huge nimbus clouds, and just as he was getting into his truck, the heavens opened up. When he reached his house on the top of the mountain, the rain was marching in sheets across the fields, and he ran inside the house stripping off his wet clothes and heading straight for the shower. He passed Dae-ho, who was sleeping again in his little tatami room. The double whammy of pellagra and beriberi from coming close to starving to death in the woods was still taking its toll on his fragile little body. After emerging from the shower and putting on dry clothes, Patrick lowered himself to the boy's futon and kissed him on the forehead, but the boy didn't stir from his dreams.

"Find what you were looking for?" he asked Yumi as he came out of Dae-ho's room, toweling off his hair.

With a look of triumph on her face, Yumi took out an ancient-looking book she had been holding behind her back.

"Remember this?"

Patrick bent down to look at the title. She held in her hands an early edition of *The Book of Five Rings* by Miyamoto Musashi, the seventeenth-century artist/samurai. The same samurai whose quote was texted to Patrick by parties unknown after the double assassination at the Olympic stadium. One of Patrick's main motivations for entering the JSOC years earlier was Miyamoto's insistence on the interdependence of martial skill and artistic accomplishment.

"Of course I remember it. I wrote my senior thesis on that book. My mother gave me that copy for my graduation. I'm surprised you were able to find it. I was just talking about it today. How did you know about it?"

"I remembered seeing it in here somewhere. It's a treasure. You should take better care of it."

"I didn't even know I had it anymore. Why did you go looking for it?"

"Miyamoto Musashi was one of the foremost samurai in history and a great artist to boot. I thought of him in connection with your new job. And didn't your mother say that the Japanese side of your family was descended from him?"

Patrick shrugged. "Her maiden name was Miyamoto, but she was a staunch Catholic, and Musashi was a Buddhist. My mother didn't have much use for the whole Buddhist thing, so if she said we're related to Miyamoto, then I'm inclined to believe it, even if there's no direct proof other than family hand-me-down history."

"Maybe you can learn something from him for your Olympic job. Plus, if they interview you on TV, you can tell them about the connection."

"I'm not looking to be interviewed on TV," he said with a testiness he hadn't intended. "I want to stay in the background."

"Okay, okay."

"Sorry. Those killings in the stadium today have me on edge." He hesitated before bringing up the next bit of information and tried to sound casual when he did.

"By the way, I'm bringing in our old friends Tyler Kang and Inspector Choy to help with security."

Yumi was silent for a moment. Then, "Those two are coming, and you'll just stay in the background," she said, suddenly darkening. "And no 'rough stuff,' I suppose."

Both of the men Patrick mentioned had helped save their lives in Pyongyang, but Yumi quite rightly associated them with the opposite of the domestic tranquility she and Patrick were enjoying in their new life in Kamakura. Seeing her worried look, Patrick put the towel he was using to dry his hair around his neck and went over to her. He began massaging her shoulders. She sighed and said, "I just don't want any more trouble, that's all. I want us to be happy. Is that too much to ask?"

Patrick whispered in her ear, "Shhh. That's what we both want." The rain was coming down harder and his words were almost inaudible, but he could feel her begin to relax. After a few minutes, he turned her shoulders so that they were face-to-face. He guided her face to his with his fingertips. They kissed. She shuddered. Their breathing became faster and deeper as the rain came down harder. Patrick moved the low calligraphy table out of their way and lowered her to the tatami.

Suddenly, they both stopped and looked in the direction of Dae-ho's room. Nothing. They looked at each other and stifled giggles like high schoolers. Then they picked up where they had left off.

The following morning broke clear and bright with an agate sky softly marbled with milkweed clouds. It would last at most an hour before the humidity drifted in from the ocean. They both dreaded this moment, because starting today, Patrick was contracted to be in Tokyo almost continuously for the next three weeks. After a mostly silent breakfast, they rose from the table and embraced.

"I have to go now."

She nodded into his shoulder.

"You'll be alright?" he asked.

"Go."

"You okay?"

"Go."

"I love you."

"Me too."

CHAPTER 9

July 18

Pung drove the six Bonghwajo he had chosen to a wooded area called Otaki in Chiba Prefecture, and after ensuring they were alone, they got out of the car and followed Pung deep into the forest. They carried their Type 58 rifles in long canvas baseball bat bags with Waseda University Baseball Club emblazoned on the sides. Two hours later, Pung was perplexed. While all six youths were highly skilled in the mechanics of riflery, they showed an appalling lack of discipline when it came to coordinating their efforts in even the simplest drills. Spoiled brats unused to working well with others, they seemed more interested in outdoing each other in target practice than being part of a team that would imminently be engaging the enemy in a dual attack. Pung called Mr. Lee to see if the mission could be pushed back, but Lee refused, saying they were already behind on their schedule of terror. Pung had them gather up their equipment for the ride back to Tokyo. But first he sent a text on another burner phone.

On the ride up to Tokyo Patrick felt his phone vibrate. Thinking it might be Yumi, he pulled off to the side of the highway. The text read, *"The true warrior should dress like a commoner. Wearing a uniform is like painting a target on your back."* This was an obscure quote that Patrick discovered in the course of his thesis research on Miyamoto Musashi. It was confirmation that whoever was sending the texts was indeed taunting him. But like the text at the stadium, it was too general to be of preemptive value.

Unlike many of Japan's temples and shrines which date back centuries, Tokyo's Yasukuni Shrine was built relatively recently in 1869 to commemorate the nation's war dead. After World War II, however, the shrine began accepting the remains of Class-A war criminals including wartime Prime Minister Hideki Tojo and several of Emperor Hirohito's top generals. Moreover, the shrine's museum exhibit descriptions and website began criticizing the United States for "convincing" the Empire of Japan to launch the attack on Pearl Harbor in order to justify its own war effort. Paying respects at the shrine is *de rigeur* for current members of Japan's Self-Defense Forces (SDF).

The Self-Defense Forces were created in 1954 following the abolishment of the Imperial Army. While not a standing army per se, the SDF is charged with maintaining domestic order in times of crisis, although its role has expanded in recent years with China's threatening moves against the Senkaku Islands off the coast of Okinawa. Just how much of a defense the SDF could mount to an outside threat is open to question and even ridicule, and the top brass of the organization bristle when their military effectiveness is called into question, particularly when a BBC report called the Force a "toothless tiger" with its chances of effectively countering a military threat as likely as Godzilla reemerging from the Sea of Japan.

After the double assassination at the stadium, though, Patrick had requested that the SDF be placed on standby at all Olympic venues, including the Nippon Budokan, an arena in which the judo competitions would be held the day after the Opening Ceremony. Judo teams from around the world were being allowed in to practice in the weeks leading up to the official opening of the Games. SDF reinforcements were sent in from various bases in the Tokyo area, and thus, when a group of three young men in brand new full battle rattle showed up at the North Gate of the Budokan and flashed expertly forged IDs of soldiers from Camp Asaka in northwest Tokyo, the civilian security guard waved them through unchallenged.

Once inside the main gate, the three quickly and silently ascended the steep staircase leading to the arena and proceeded to the SDF rallying point on the opposite side of the sprawling compound near the rear gate. They set their bags down on the ground, unzipped them, and took out three of the same Type 58 North Korean AK-47 knockoffs that Pung had used to such great effect in the stadium. But a sharp-eyed lieutenant, his suspicions aroused by the spotless and creased newness of their battle uniforms, had been discreetly following them from the main gate. When he saw that their rifles bore little resemblance to the standard-issue Howa battle rifle, he drew his 9mm sidearm.

"Halt where you are," he called out in Japanese, aiming the pistol at them. The three young men, who were unaware they had been followed, quickly turned their rifles on the lieutenant and fired. The lieutenant managed to get off four quick shots, one of which found its mark, before dropping to the ground with grievous wounds to his midsection, but the commotion had alerted soldiers in the improvised mess hall, and a dozen of them came charging out with weapons drawn. The three young Bonghwajo, one of them wounded in the shoulder, began firing in all directions, something they had been planning to do anyway but not with the kind of resistance they were encountering. The SDF men had just come off of a live-fire exercise at a camp near Mount Fuji, where their superior officers, in an effort at motivating them, read article after article effectively denigrating their manhood by lambasting the Force as "an army of clowns" as one reporter put it. Thus, their reflexes were honed, and their honor was on the line, and here was an opportunity to set the record straight. A volley of 9mm bullets from a dozen Minebea handguns cut down the three young men in a matter of seconds and continued long after they were ever going to get up again. But not before the young men had inflicted major casualties on the enemy.

Less than a quarter mile away and a few minutes later, the three other Bonghwajo mounted a near-simultaneous attack on Yasukuni Shrine, storming the small *Chinreisha*, or Spirit Pacifying Subshrine that honors Japanese war criminals, among others. But when reports came into the shrine of the attack a few minutes earlier on the Budokan, the SDF members of the Olympic judo team who were paying their respects at Yasukuni were on high alert as the young men charged through the main gate. All three Bonghwajo were killed with not a single Japanese casualty.

CHAPTER 10

When he first recruited his team of North Korean young men of privilege, Mr. Lee was concerned that they might not have grasped the fact that they were now in a very real sense soldiers in the fight to restore the Kim family to power and to reclaim their rightful place at the apex of North Korean society. But he could tell from the grim looks on the faces of the remaining members at the corpse hotel that they now fully realized the danger their mission entailed. All they had to do was look at the six empty chairs at the table.

"No battle has ever been won without casualties," Mr. Lee began. Every eye in the room was riveted on him. "Losses are to be expected. But I would never have recruited a single one of you into the advance guard if I didn't feel to the core of my being that our cause was just. Similarly, I would never have chosen a single one of you if I didn't feel that you were all exceptionally qualified for the mission we have undertaken to restore justice to the DPRK." At his mention of the word "mission," he noticed that one or two of the young men fidgeted ever so slightly, an indication that they themselves had doubts about their abilities. The eyes of the others, though, burned with zeal and determination. Lee would choose his next group of warriors accordingly.

"Phase One of our mission is complete. We have engaged the uniformed forces of the enemy, and we have wounded the bull, so to speak, first with Mister Pung's exceptional marksmanship at the Olympic stadium, and now with the heroic actions of our fallen comrades who inflicted great losses upon the enemy, killing eleven of them." The eyes of some of the remaining six went wide. They hadn't realized that their confreres had been so successful before being cut down. Lee continued.

"As a prelude to the arrival of our reinforcement contingent, we will now move on to Phase Two of our mission: the civilian population. We will wound the bull even further and soften the resolve of the enemy." He looked around the room, and as he had suspected, several of them looked troubled. One of them raised his hand. "Will these civilian targets be ones who have been responsible for what happened to our homeland?"

Lee was ready for the question. "Were the ones who overthrew the government of our Brilliant Commander concerned about the civilian casualties they inflicted? And was it not the civilians of Japan who shouted 'Banzai!' to the emperor who sent his army to enslave us?" He looked around the room.

"How many of you have heard of the Battle of Pochonbo?" he asked. Every hand in the room shot up. "Of course you have. You have been taught from a very early age of the heroic actions of the Great Leader Kim Il-sung who at the age of twenty-four led a rebellion against the unheard-of fascist tyranny of the Japanese against the Korean people. Twenty-four years old. Only a few years older than all of you here. The Great Leader fired a shot in the sky, and the battle commenced. Following his sterling example, Mister Pung and our fallen comrades also fired shots, beginning our own battle for national liberation.

"And the Great Leader showed at the Battle of Pochonbo that the Japanese imperialists could be smashed and burned up like rubbish. The flames over the night sky of Pochonbo in the fatherland heralded the dawn of liberation in Korea. It was a historic battle which gave the Korean people the confidence that they could achieve national independence and liberation. Have I answered your question?" The young man who had asked it nodded his head up and down vigorously. Lee continued.

"Our cause is just, and our aim is true. In Phase Two, following the example of the Great Leader, we will show no mercy until our mission is complete and successful. No mercy at all. Our objective is terror, pure and simple." He then chose three of the remaining six Bonghwajo for the first mission of Phase Two and turned to Mr. Pung, who brought forth their weapons. To prevent a repeat of the debacle at Yasukuni Shrine, where the attackers were wiped out without any loss of life on the Japanese side, Pung brought them back to the training ground in nearby Chiba Prefecture for a two-hour seminar on tactics that included a blistering lecture on firing discipline and the drawbacks of the ready-fire-aim strategy that had gotten their friends killed at the shrine.

After Pung departed the corpse hotel with the three attackers, the remaining three met upstairs. They had known each other all through their school years and trusted each other implicitly. As Bonghwajo, they took the English nickname "Bong Boys" for their three-member clique, and they met to discuss how not to become like their fallen comrades. It was not as if the three friends harbored a scintilla of doubt about what Mr. Lee had just told them; it was just that there must be a way to insulate themselves from the danger that had led to the loss of half of their original number. The three of them talked well into the night about how to not only advance Mr. Lee's objectives, but also to survive the upcoming battles so that they would not become suicide missions. Someone needed to be alive at the end of this all to reclaim their rightful place at the forefront of North Korean society.

CHAPTER 11

LAS VEGAS
One week earlier

"His mouth wrote a check that his ass couldn't cash," explained an Asian man in an Air Force uniform to a duo of Las Vegas cops as a man in a red do-rag lay on the sidewalk in front of them, out cold. The cops happened to be passing by when they saw the much larger man, dripping with bling, shouting racist slurs and shoving the Asian who now identified himself as Captain Tyler Kang, USAF. Apparently, Kang had accidentally brushed into the man, and when the guy called him a Chink and reached his hand out aggressively, Kang slapped the hand aside, sweep-kicked his legs out from under him, and thrust the palm of his right hand into the man's left temple. He would live, but would probably choose his future adversaries a bit more judiciously.

"Watch out," one of the cops said. "This guy's a known gangbanger and his friends will probably come looking for you."

"Too bad for them," Kang replied. The cops had seen clearly that it was self-defense, so they had to let him go.

His taekwondo teacher had once described Kang as a giant fast-twitch muscle, so quick were his reflexes even now in his early forties. The precision of his kicks and punches had propelled him to the top of the men's taekwondo competition in preparation for the Olympic trials, the oldest military man ever to make it that far.

Tyler Kang's military career began in the Joint Special Operations Command where he trained as a sniper alongside Patrick Featherstone.

Located at Pope Air Force Base and Fort Bragg in North Carolina, JSOC is technically prohibited from conducting covert action operations, but it gets around this inconvenience by working closely with the CIA's Special Activities Division. In the early years of its existence, the most promising prospects from JSOC's Tier One Unit were trained in the latest paramilitary operational techniques by the CIA's own elite. This super-secret commando unit was known as Team Red. Tyler Kang and Patrick Featherstone quickly became legends in the unit.

After an initial basic training period, Tyler and Patrick were stationed at Fort Bragg for advanced instruction that included learning ballistic tables for every rifle imaginable, from the M1 carbine to the German Mauser to the M16. Every day they were tasked with breaking down and reassembling in a dark room whatever rifle they happened to be working with, thus becoming intimately familiar with every spring, rod, lever, and screw. They also practiced shooting with either hand, firing controlled three-shot bursts rather than emptying entire magazines, and varying patterns in their assault drills, never doing the same thing the same way twice. If they made it through advanced training, each would then move on to sniper training and be assigned a partner.

After being partnered together, Tyler and Patrick alternated between the duties of "first" and "second," the former being the trigger-puller and the latter the spotter who pinpoints targets, ascertains distance, and calculates windage for the dope book, a pocket-sized tablet used to record all the factors that go into a setting up a shot. Their success rate with distant dummy targets was unparalleled. Both young men bridled against authority, however, and they earned a deserved reputation as mavericks, especially Tyler, who was forever questioning the judgment of their instructors. But their superiors decided to keep them together after graduation for the simple reason that they were so damn good, especially as a team. From then on, their targets would be flesh and blood.

Their first mission took them to Sarajevo, where they were assigned to take out the Serbs of "Sniper Alley," a boulevard where over one hundred innocent people, including dozens of children, had already been shot for the crime of attempting to cross from one part of the city to the other. Tyler and Patrick painstakingly set up their hide in one of the high-rises that lined the boulevard. There they spent over an hour zeroing their Barrett M82 rifle, calculating possible thermals from buildings, the funneling of the wind, and the elevation to probable target areas. Their preparation was exhaustive and rigorous. Only when both were satisfied that they would be able to liquidate anyone in the target area without fail would one of them train the 20X Unertl spotting scope on the surrounding hills and give the other the okay to fire. In their first week of rotating first and second, they had fourteen confirmed kills.

Their commanding officer, Major Ken Cestari, sent for them one afternoon after they had been in Serbia for almost two weeks. He had a special mission for them for the following day. They had been chosen over three other sniper teams. They arrived at dawn for the briefing.

"This one's not nearly as easy as Sniper Alley, but it's ten times more important," Cestari began. "And it's also black. Off the books, never-happened kind of thing. There's a man here who will give you the details." He turned and opened the back door of his office. In strode a stockily-built man in his mid-thirties. Neatly brushed short hair, not a strand out of place. Uniform devoid of rank or insignia. Spy.

"This is Norm Hooper. He'll give you the specifics of the mission."

Hooper introduced himself with only a bit more detail. He was from the Special Operations Group of the CIA's Special Activities Division. *Wet boy*, thought Tyler and Patrick simultaneously. Years later, Norm Hooper became the CIA station chief at the American embassy in Tokyo.

"We have a very thin timeline, gentlemen, so let's get to it." Hooper nodded to Cestari, who unfurled a topo map of the area. "This is the town of Pale, about ten klicks from here. Right in between here and Pale there's this castle." Hooper used a long pointer with a black rubber tip to indicate a king's crown on the map.

"There's a guy living here known as 'the Hun.' He's not really German, but he's an admirer of Hitler, so…" Hooper flipped several color photos onto the map table. They had obviously been taken at a distance but were clear enough. The man's ice-blue eyes were windows into a heart of pure wickedness.

"A local warlord, probably behind a lot of the sniping you guys've been up against in the Alley. Real name: Ranko Djanic. Up to his ears in corruption. Brings in heroin from the Beqaa Valley in Lebanon, sells it, and uses it to buy arms. That's the part that got our attention. He's looking to profit from destabilizing the whole Balkan area. Sells to both sides, profits from both." He paused and looked at Patrick and Tyler. "He has to go. You guys get to punch his ticket."

Tyler and Patrick pored over the map. Hooper appraised their demeanor and facial expressions with unblinking, red-threaded eyes. The two partners in assassination had a pact, expressed only between themselves, that they would refuse targets that were, to their minds, not up to a certain standard of wrongdoing. Ranko Djanic clearly exceeded that standard.

"Just one question," Tyler said, looking up from the map. "Why is it black? Why not go with regular ROE [rules of engagement]?"

Hooper replied without hesitation. "Because we want to send a clear message to anyone else who might be entertaining the same idea: we can operate outside the law like they do. And they just might be next on our honey-do list."

"And who gave the order?" asked Patrick.

Hooper shrugged. He just pointed up and said, "On high."

But Tyler and Patrick's partnership and friendship came to an abrupt end with the mission. At the exact moment that Tyler called for the shot, Ranko Djanic's five-year-old son ran out from behind a tree where he had been hiding in a game with his friends and raced obliviously in his father's direction, laughing giddily as his friends tried to catch him. Patrick's and Tyler's focuses were through telescopic lenses that narrowed their fields of vision to Djanic's upper body and head. Patrick squeezed the trigger through its final ounce of pressure, and a tremendous echo resounded through the mountain pass. But instead of hitting Djanic, the young child who had run into the sight picture was practically blown in two. His body lifted briefly into the air and then fell inertly to the ground.

"Jesus!" Patrick yelled in disbelief, a starburst of adrenaline exploding through his nervous system. "Why didn't you tell me the kid was there?"

"I swear to God I didn't see him!" Tyler screamed back.

"And now he's dead, you fucking idiot!"

"I told you, I didn't see him, dammit!"

A mandatory after-action review ensued, and Patrick, being the shooter, was court-martialed. Tyler, on the advice of his JAG lawyer, testified that the shooter has final responsibility for making sure the target area is clear of civilians, and that Patrick had taken the shot anyway. Patrick testified that the high-tech scope he had been issued for the mission had failed, but Tyler testified that he wasn't aware of any malfunction.

"I told you that right before the limousine pulled in!" Patrick shouted out in court.

"Your exact words were, 'This thing is fucked,'" Tyler retorted. "I thought you meant the mission, not the scope." Patrick was court-martialed, found culpable but not guilty of criminality, and discharged. His life was ruined, as was their friendship. But the two were reunited in North Korea where they helped bring down the regime of Kim Jong-un, with Tyler saving Patrick's life in the process. Their friendship was inevitably rekindled.

After the fall of Kim, Tyler went on to earn a master's degree in aerospace engineering and reenlisted in the military, this time as a member of the "Chair Force" of drone operators at Creech Air Force Base outside Las Vegas. He would sit for eight hours a day in a darkened, air-conditioned room seven thousand, five hundred miles from Afghanistan dressed in a flight suit and remotely controlling MQ-9 Reapers. Beside him, sensor operators manipulated TV cameras, infrared cameras, and other high-tech sensors on board the drones. By squeezing a trigger on a joystick, Tyler and the other earthbound pilots let loose Hellfire missiles on a person or building half a world away. They called the moment of kill that appeared on their "Death TV" monitors the bug splat, but for Tyler, it was death by boredom, especially after all the excitement in North Korea. Going out of his mind with the monotony of it all, he went on R&R leave to Hawaii just to get away for a week. When he returned, he found an order to see his CO as soon as he arrived on base.

"Enter."

The door of the CO's office opened and in stepped Tyler, his hair not cut to regulation length despite repeated admonitions. He had, until recently, two official duties, one of which was piloting the MQ-9 Reapers that were used as sky snipers in the Middle East. The other was trying to make the Olympic taekwondo team. His efforts in that regard, however, came to an abrupt end when he committed *gamjeom*, the serious offense of throwing an opponent out of the ring. He had done so when his opponent refused to engage him in anything more than dainty sparring for points.

But neither of his duties allowed him to sneak half a gallon of beer secreted in a CamelBak hydration unit onto a military transport from Honolulu's Hickam Air Base. It was by no means his first indiscretion in the military. He came to attention in front of the CO's desk and saluted.

"Captain Tyler Kang, sir."

Colonel Bartoe just stared at him as he twirled a pencil around his fingers. Kang stood impassively, giving no indication that he found anything at all uncomfortable about waiting at attention for a full minute. Finally, Bartoe broke the silence.

"Kang, how old are you?"

"Forty-one, sir."

"Forty-one. And don't you think it a bit immature for a man your age to be acting like a frat boy?"

"I missed that part of college life, sir, so maybe I'm unconsciously making up for the gap in my social education. Or maybe I was just thirsty, sir, since there didn't appear to be any flight attendants with a booze cart, and it was a six-hour flight from Hawaii, sir."

"Are you an alcoholic, Kang?"

"No sir, just a nervous flyer."

"A nervous flyer in the Air Force."

"Chair Force, sir."

Colonel Bartoe stared at him, shaking his head slowly back and forth.

"I don't know what to say, Kang, I really don't. Maybe you have a Peter Pan complex or something. I do know this, though: if it were up to me, I'd have you busted down a rank and transferred to Greenland."

"That would be a nice change from all this heat, sir."

"Unfortunately, it's *not* up to me, and the brass above me seem to have a higher estimation of your worth than I do. You've been ordered to go on TDY to Tokyo for the Olympics. You've been given the rest of the week off to prepare and get there."

"But I didn't make the taekwondo team, sir."

"Dismissed, Kang. I hope we don't get too used to peace and quiet when you're gone."

After leaving Colonel Bartoe's office, Tyler drove the thirty-five miles back to his apartment a few miles off of the Strip in Las Vegas. He still kept a landline, and he checked the five messages that had been left, four of them from various women he had romanced and dumped. As he absentmindedly deleted them while sipping a beer, his mind went to his upcoming trip to Tokyo. "The Olympics," he said out loud, and his spirits instantly sank. Here in the privacy of his apartment, his "shame cave" as he sometimes called it when he became depressed with the erratic course his personal life was taking, he thought back to the news he had gotten before the 1988 Seoul Olympics. His aunt and uncle, whom he was staying with in Seoul while his parents were teaching abroad, came to him together one morning, not a good sign. A worse sign was that both had obviously been crying. They then broke the news that his parents had been on board Korean Airlines Flight 858, which had been sabotaged by a North Korean agent. There were no survivors.

Tyler took out the pack of cigarettes he kept for times when he couldn't dispel the memory. Chugging back his beer while inhaling deeply on the cigarette, he let his head drop onto his chest. All the booze and women in the world couldn't put the broken soul of an orphan back together. With all the self-control he could muster, he stood up and forced himself to stub out the cigarette. Then he noticed that there was another message on his voicemail. He hit the button.

"Tyler, it's Patrick. If you haven't heard, you're coming to Tokyo. You can thank me with a lap dance when you get here. Just make sure you bring your Nightforce ATACR scope. The only brands they have over here are made in Japan. Haha, get it? Peace out, my brutha."

Tyler's face broke into a broad smile. He'd be seeing his old friend again. He'd call him later when the beer he'd chugged wore off a bit. In the meantime, he found the ATACR scope in the silverware tray of his kitchen drawer among the other scopes and silencers he had accumulated to the point that there was no more room for silverware. Just as well, since he practically lived on pizza out of the box and beer from the can or bottle. He put the scope in his go bag along with a favored silencer, since Patrick had intimated that there might be some rough stuff involved, otherwise he wouldn't have asked Tyler to bring the ATACR. He debated taking a nap and then calling Patrick, but then decided that since he had been given the rest of the week off, he would first enjoy a night of blackjack at the casinos using the stash of chips he'd earned during his six-month deployment.

Having been "escorted" from a casino for counting cards, Tyler knew he was on thin ice, and that one more offense would leave him banned at every blackjack table in town. Still, there was no game in town with better odds, so he chose a smaller joint off the Strip, far away from the one that had blacklisted him, and took a seat. Smiling at the pretty dealer, he made a neat stack of $20 chips in front of him and took stock of the other player at the table, a balding older guy with whiskey breath dressed in a light blue tux that fit him like a sausage casing. The young woman dealt each of them their cards and the game was on. Within two minutes, the other man had lost all his chips except the one he tipped the dealer with and made an unsteady exit from the table. Tyler gave the dealer a wink. "Just you and me, I guess," he said, and she smiled back. But just then another Asian man, older than Tyler, carried his drink over from another table.

"Mind if I join you?" he asked Tyler and the dealer. Tyler was somewhat disappointed but put on a friendly face. "Not at all," he said, and moved his chair back to make room.

"I just hope my luck changes over here," the man said with what sounded like a Chinese accent. After five games it was clear that his luck was back in full force, and he soon had over a thousand dollars' worth of chips rising like towers in front of him. Tyler had watched to see if he had been counting cards, but the man had barely looked at his or the dealer's cards during his winning streak.

"That's pretty impressive," Tyler said. "Got any tips?"

"Sure. And here's one for the young lady," the man said, pushing a hundred-dollar chip to the dealer. "Larry Suh is the name. I'm going to stretch my legs and have a shot at the bar, if you care to join me," the man said to Tyler. Tyler introduced himself to the man and told the pretty dealer he'd see her later. The dealer lowered her eyes and smiled.

At the bar, the man walked over to the bartender, ordered two shots of Jameson, passed one of them to Tyler, and began a rap about how he was able to "feel" the natural tendency of playing cards to turn a certain way in a certain order. Tyler's next memory was of being back in his apartment.

CHAPTER 12

JIA HEADQUARTERS, TOKYO
July 20

Patrick's smile would have been broader when Tyler entered his office several days later had it not been for the attacks on SDF forces at the Budokan and Yasukuni Shrine. He was midway through his bento lunch of inari sushi.

"Here he is, Lord Commander of the Game of Drones," Patrick said and went over to his old friend standing in the doorway. Patrick and Tyler Kang had developed almost a choreography of camaraderie over the years whereby their sarcastic repartee hid a deep brotherly love. After recent events, he welcomed an opportunity for lighthearted banter.

"What up, bitch?" Tyler said, as he walked in and dropped his duffel bag on the floor. The two old friends embraced. They had not seen each other in the four years since their ad hoc mission to North Korea had brought down the Kim regime.

"I'm really glad you could come," Patrick said. "I needed someone top-notch, smart as a whip, and good with a rifle. He wasn't available, so I called you." Tyler gave him a mock kick to the groin.

"You can only hope to reach my level someday," he said.

"I'll aim low," Patrick said.

After the mutual ribbing, they sat down.

"You're late, bro," Patrick said. "Weren't you supposed to be here two days ago?"

"Yeah, but I caught a bug the night before I was supposed to leave. Totally wiped me out." Tyler shuffled uncomfortably in his seat.

"Bimbonic plague?" Patrick asked with a grin.

Tyler shook his head. "I tried calling, didn't you get my message?" He took out his phone and checked the call history. "Yup, right here."

Patrick took out his. "Nothing showing up here."

"Well, mine's an upgrade, maybe I screwed up somehow. Anyway, here I am."

"Glad to hear you've made a full recovery from your mystery illness," Patrick said. "How are things otherwise?"

"Not too bad after sitting in a dark room ten hours a day seven thousand miles from my target zone for six months." He wiped a drop of sweat from his eyes. "Damn, the heat in this city is fucking heinous. And I just came from Vegas."

"Yeah, it's the humidity," Patrick said and reached over to turn up the AC. "Want a beer? I've got Bud."

"I thought you said you had beer."

Patrick laughed. "Kohai, you've been here five minutes and you're already going native. Alright then, I've also got Kirin."

"Top of my all-time list, Sempai."

Kohai and *Sempai* were Japanese terms that indicated relative ranks of people in an organization based on length of service. Patrick and Tyler were roughly the same age, but Patrick had entered the Joint Special Operations Command first. Thus, he was the *Sempai* and Tyler was the *Kohai*, but like much of their conversation, they used the words with a faux-mocking tone. They sipped their beers as they chatted. Patrick passed the plastic bento tray of sushi to Tyler.

"You guys still using the MQ-9's?" Patrick asked.

"Yup, can't beat the Reaper. Get it?" Tyler said with a mouth full of sushi.

"Yeah, Tyler, it wasn't all that deep. Or original."

"And the Hellfires are still hell on wheels for any *muj* who gets in the way." He referred to the AGM-114 Hellfire air-to-surface missiles that packed one hundred pounds of high explosive. "So what's the deal, Sempai? How come they brought me over for the Olympics?"

"You must have been in transit when the news broke. There's been three attacks on Olympic sites and the Games haven't even begun. The first one was at the stadium. Two guys on either side of me got shot during a briefing by a sniper high up in the stands. Whoever it was got through all sorts of high-tech security but spared me for some reason. Disappeared without a trace. Then just the other day the judo venue and a nearby shrine got stormed by these young assholes with assault rifles."

He handed Tyler photos of the two victims of the sniper shooting in the stadium.

"You were between these guys?" Tyler said, holding the photos from the double assassination at the stadium close to his eyes. "Whoever fired these shots was a pro. Incredible shot placement."

Patrick nodded. "And he used a North Korean Type 58. As did these guys."

Patrick passed him photos from the attacks on the SDF soldiers at the Budokan and at Yasukuni Shrine. Tyler's eyes widened.

After giving Tyler a chance to get squared away and rested at his billet in the SDF's headquarters in Shinjuku, Patrick met him at the range on base. They carried their M4 rifles and one hundred rounds each and checked in with the sergeant in charge. A half hour and only fifty rounds later, their friendly competition had been decided.

"Not to rub it in, Tyler, but you've got some work to do. I brought you over as my main man, bro."

"Jesus, Patrick, I don't know what to say. I've always thought of shooting like riding a bike, but this is piss-poor."

Patrick waited a minute to let Tyler's shame work on his sense of professionalism. "I know you'll have your chops back in time, man."

Tyler shook his head. "How about we end this for today, it's just too embarrassing. I promise I'll be out here every day, though. I won't let you down, my brutha."

"Let's hit the lounge for a quick one. No sense reinforcing any bad habits. And I know you won't let me down, so don't even mention that."

Later that night, Tyler reflected on his sniper career and wondered if he had lost some of his talent to disuse and age. Forty-one years old. He seemed so ancient to himself. He tried to cheer himself out of his crisis of confidence by recalling an assignment he'd been given right after the Rising Tide revolution in North Korea four years earlier. He'd gone back to his old job in the Joint Special Operations Command and been tasked with clandestinely crossing the border into the Balochistan area of Pakistan and taking out the leader of a vicious Haqqani branch of the Taliban. The leader was reputed to be working with a Pakistani general who provided him with direct military and intelligence aid, resulting in the deaths of scores of U.S. soldiers. The hope was that taking out the Taliban leader would also send a message to the Pakistani general, America's "ally," that the U.S. was on to his double-dealing and would come looking for him next.

To anyone who knew him well, Tyler came off as cocky, outspoken, and ready for any bar brawl with his fighting skills and utter lack of fear. For the exigencies of the short-term assignment in Afghanistan, though, he cultivated an inner calm that he had gained through meditation techniques his taekwondo teacher had insisted he learn. Thus, from the day he arrived in Afghanistan, his air of serenity earned him the nickname "the human Quaalude." He kept to himself for the most part, and planned every detail of his illegal one-man mission to take out the Taliban leader. The illegal part never bothered him. His and Patrick's first sniper trainer, SSGT Eric "Pineapple" Shimoda from Hawaii, gave them a training exercise early in their course which they performed by the book but still got greased in the simulated scenario.

"What did you do wrong?" Pineapple asked.

"Nothing," Tyler and Patrick insisted. "We did everything you said."

"You treated the enemy as an equal."

"That's what you told us to do…'Never underestimate.'"

"I didn't say play by the rules."

From that day forward, Tyler never played by anyone's rules but his own.

When intelligence on the Haqqani leader indicated a firm location just across the border, Tyler moved out the next morning at 0200 hours carrying a bolt-action Remington M24 which shot a 7.62-mm 175-grain match bullet and was equipped with a fixed 10-power scope. Once he had found his way by the weak rectangular beam of his taped flashlight to the Zero Line border between Afghanistan and Pakistan, he began a tortoise crawl in the direction of the coordinates he had been given. A sniper has two missions, only one of which is delivering precision fire on selected targets from concealed positions. The second mission is gathering information, and Tyler was also tasked with scoping out the Taliban's immediate area for any civilians they may have embedded themselves among as human shields.

A mile from the Haqqani encampment, the faint light of false dawn began spreading against the eastern sky. Actual sunrise was an hour away. He was right on time. Moving a mere half yard with each shimmy forward, it would take exactly that hour to get into his final firing position and set up his shot.

When he arrived at the FFP, a small rise a mile from the encampment, he stopped and looked in all directions for sentries. Nothing. He had brought his STA sniper blade, but was glad that this job would require only a rifle. Apparently, the terrorists assumed they were protected by the Zero Line border. Bad assumption.

He filled a canvas bag he had brought with sandy soil and set it on a large, flat rock, then placed the M24 on it and estimated his elevation. Once that was dialed into his scope, he checked the wind. A constant five miles per hour from the east. The mountain air was thin, so aerodynamic drag would be less than at sea level, and he needed to adjust the minute of angle—that is, compensate for the bullet's downward deviation due to gravity and air resistance. There was also the cold temperature to factor in, since it made the air denser and would cause the bullet to impact lower.

Once all of his ballistic arc preparations were taken care of, he waited. Soon he saw movement in the encampment through his binoculars and switched to the scope. The Haqqani leader was described as having a long beard and wearing a *salwar kemeez*, or "man-dress" as the GIs called the traditional outfit. Great. That explained everything except anything. Everyone in the encampment fit that description as they began their morning prayers. But there was one man, taller and older than the others, who was immediately brought the morning meal after their prayers. He sat apart from the others and appeared to be leafing through documents of some kind.

Tyler centered the crosshairs just above the man's head. A feral glint born of total self-assurance came into his eye. He would be going for a center-mass shot, and he needed to account for the bullet's drop over the mile it would travel. He sat in coiled stillness and monitored his heartbeat. When it was between beats, he squeezed off a single shot. The bullet flew for two seconds and hit the man squarely in the chest, raising a puff of dust as it pierced the fabric of his clothes. The others didn't react until they saw the man fall backward. Then they began looking in all directions, since the report from the shot was now echoing all around the valley. Tyler pocketed the spent cartridge, the kill brass that had done the job, crawled back to the border, and was met by a patrol of GIs. Radio chatter among the Haqqani encampments confirmed the hit. Not long after, he transferred to the Air Force Command at Creech AFB, lay down his rifle, and gripped a joystick. The money was better, and it was close to one of his favorite places, Las Vegas. He remembered all this in every detail as he lay on his bunk in the SDF officer's quarters he had been assigned, and as he drifted off to sleep, he vowed to spend the days ahead at the SDF range.

The next morning, he was the first one on the range. He set up shot after shot while recalling Pineapple Shimoda's watchwords of "99 percent right is 100 percent wrong." In real life sniping situations there is a great deal of difference between a center-mass hit to the left side of the chest and one to the right. To the right, and the target might live to shoot another day. To the left? Only if the guy was a Vulcan. On this first morning Tyler's ears burned with embarrassment with each botched shot, knowing that the SDF guys on either side of him were keeping peripheral eyes on his every failure. Two of them who were paired up as shooter and spotter dared to snicker to each other. After two hours, and after the SDF sons of bitches had left, thinking him a total amateur, he started getting an occasional bull's eye, but his grouping was still all over the place. He was mortified to think that he used to brag that the JSOC brass had once called him an "apex predator" and joked that he should be kept behind a panel reading "Break Glass in Time of War."

It wasn't until the afternoon of the following day that his talents as a sniper, long left unhoned, began to rise from whatever psychosomatic crypt they had been languishing in. Going back to basics, he recalled the shooter's mantra: BRASS: breathe, relax, aim, slack, squeeze. With each shot getting closer to the bull, time drained from the world, and after his third grouping of six successive bulls, a thrill went up his spine. He looked around triumphantly but in vain for the snickering SDF assholes. No matter. He was back. Then his internal celebration came to a halt: he knew that it was one thing to hit the ten ring on the range, and totally another to do it on the move in the midst of a full-on adrenaline dump.

CHAPTER 13

July 22

After the debacles at the Budokan and Yasukuni Shrine which had resulted in the deaths of all six of the Bonghwajo attackers, three of the remaining six members had been chosen by Mr. Pung to mount an assault on the grounds of Tokyo Tower in hopes of inflicting massive civilian casualties. But despite Pung's riflery and tactics training sessions in Chiba Prefecture, all three were cut down by off-duty SDF members even before they could even aim their Sig Sauer collapsible machine guns. Thus, only three members of the Bonghwajo advance guard remained before the reinforcements arrived.

These last three were childhood friends and took the collective name "Bong Boys" for their clique after one of them brought back a marijuana pipe from a trip to Vienna with his diplomat father. The three had been meeting in secret at the corpse hotel, trying to come up with a way to advance Mr. Lee's battle plan without getting killed in the process, as had now happened to nine of their original number. One of them was elected to approach Pung and ask for an emergency meeting with Mr. Lee. His pitch was that there had to be a better way to effect the desired mayhem without all of them dying in the attempt. After all, he reasoned, who would be left to be the young military regents, as Mr. Lee had called them, gallant lads who would pave the way for the restoration of the regime of the Kim family? Mr. Lee agreed to come over and stay the night, and after listening over dinner to the plan the Bong Boys had devised, gave his consent to the use of cutouts, or surrogates, who would be used as willing dupes until the arrival of the second wave of attackers.

Back in the DPRK, the Bong Boys had been allowed to watch all the South Korean TV they could stomach, and they were particular fans of the boy bands who appeared nightly on shows like *Superstar K*. They knew all the words to the songs, and they would ape the dance moves and exaggerated expressions of romantic ardor as they sang along with the interchangeably androgynous lads onscreen. They furthered their image by dyeing their hair blonde and giving themselves the American-style monikers used by three of their favorite K-pop idols.

The good-looking boy with the rascally twinkle in his eye and a reputation as a charming ladies' man took the name "Casanova." The quiet, brooding one who wrote love poetry dubbed himself "Dreamboy." And the tough guy with the scar in the middle of his eyebrow, who practiced taekwondo by punching and kicking metal utility poles was "Tyson."

The son of the Pyongyang's chief prosecutor, Tyson (born Yun Tae-sen) was raised in a luxurious home on the desirable north bank of the Taedong River. He and his friends all attended Mangyongdae Revolutionary School, and as a boy of thirteen, he was chosen for the honor of executing his middle school teacher. The teacher had been found guilty of treason for collaborating with the Rising Tide movement that eventually toppled the Kim regime.

Tyson hated the teacher both for his disgusting dandruff and for the way he never deferred to the Bonghwajo rich kids the way their other teachers did. The teacher didn't seem to realize the nature of privilege, at times going out of his way to make disparaging comments about their laziness. And so Tyson accepted with relish his patriotic duty to rid the nation of a traitor. On the day of the execution, after the teacher was tied to a gibbet in Kim Il-sung Stadium with all of the school's student body there to witness his end, Tyson took aim and shot the teacher in the gut, which is a famously excruciating way to die. He had been instructed to make it a shot to the chest. An officer in the Korean People's Army, who could tell immediately that the gut shot was intentional, came up to him and commended him for his marksmanship as the teacher writhed in agony on the gibbet in front of them. When the regime fell during the Rising Tide revolution, the boy was spirited out of the country to Japan where his father was an adviser to the Rengo-kai, a Japan-based organization with ties to the Kim regime.

After agreeing to the Bong Boys' proposal of using surrogates for their attacks until the reinforcements arrived on the scene, Mr. Lee listened to Tyson's idea for a cutout based on the latter's research into recent Japanese history. Of all the Bonghwajo, he was the most fluent in Japanese, and Mr. Lee gave his blessing to his idea, especially since it would ideally result in a huge number of casualties. To get his plan rolling, Tyson would first visit a madman.

CHAPTER 14

July 22

With Tyler squared away at the SDF headquarters, Patrick's mind turned to South Korea. He had one more space on his roster to fill. He logged in to a Yahoo email account used by only two people and wrote a short message that he saved to the "drafts" file. The sent-mail and inbox files for this account had never held a single message. His draft message read, "Under the stones?" He then sent a text message on his phone to a South Korean number. It read, "Got my nails done today."

Having lived all his life in the dark labyrinth that was the Kim Jong-un regime, it seemed only natural that after he was granted defector status, forty-eight-year-old Choy Jung-hee should gravitate to a job as a cave guide. And having spent far too many winters in an unheated police car in Pyongyang, the former *Inspector* Choy chose sunny Cheju Island off South Korea's southern coast as his new home. Even now in mid-July, when the temperature and humidity were rising daily, he could instantly cool off while leading tourists down into the Manjanggul system, or relax at the beach with his thirty-one-year-old girlfriend, who was from the area.

He had given the girlfriend firm instructions never to divulge to anyone that he had been part of the *Inmin Boanseong*, North Korea's People's Security, or state police. When he crossed the border after the fall of the Kim regime, he told the immigration officer who processed him that he had been employed in a movie theater that showed films directed by Kim Jong-il. Technically, this was not a lie, since he had worked just such a job while a student at Pyongyang's elite Film Institute, where he studied acting and English. He was then recruited into the People's Security state police, but he wanted to expunge the latter completely from his personal history. He still carried guilt at some of the things he had been forced to do, such as arresting a man on the day of his daughter's wedding after a neighbor who had not been invited to the wedding turned him in for possessing a Bible.

But the main detail of his employment with the *Inmin Boanseong* that he wanted to hide was that he had been chief technical adviser to none other than Comrade Moon himself, founder and head of the infamous Bureau 39. Moon was an idiot when it came to computers, and Choy inveigled his way into Moon's good graces, eventually looting a staggering sum of money from Bureau 39. The source of the theft had never been discovered because Choy had funneled it to Patrick Featherstone, who in turn kept it in five secret accounts in Dubai, Panama, Liechtenstein, Luxemburg, and Switzerland, all of them under a shell investment corporation. Patrick promised Choy that he would only use the money for the people of North Korea. Choy had kept a much smaller portion of the money and had it stashed away at the back of Manjanggul. He still accepted a monthly defector stipend from the South Korean government so as not to draw attention to his independent means.

On this sunny day in late July, he relaxed on the beach with his girl-friend's son while the boy's mother, who was a *haenyeo*, or free diver, surfaced off the beach from time to time with an abalone or octopus which she deposited in her small skiff. A wave to her son and boyfriend and she was under the waves again. As Choy sat reading a history of Go, or *Baduk* as the classic board game is known in Korea, his cell phone vibrated. He let out a long and joyful laugh when he saw the text with the words "Got my nails done today." He excitedly switched over to his email account on a VPN (virtual private network) of his own creation and went to the drafts file. It was the only file with anything in it. He opened the new draft that was in the file. It read, *"Under the stones*?" Only one person in the world would use those words from Go, the "stones" of which referred to the disc-like pebbles that are arranged on the grid of the playing board.

Ten minutes later, Patrick noticed that a new draft had appeared in the mailbox. He opened it.

"Security question: Open with black to 4-4..."

Patrick typed back: *"White to 1-1..."*

He and Choy went back and forth in the same vein several more times. Finally, Choy declared, *"Capture! You're rusty!"*

Patrick laughed out loud. If he was going to be beaten at Go/*Baduk* by anyone, he really didn't mind being crushed by Inspector Choy, his old friend from his mission to North Korea four years before.

Choy switched to his satphone with 256-bitkey encryption and called the number from which the original text had been sent.

"Inspector Choy, how nice of you to call," Patrick said. "By the way, this is a secure line."

"Please, Patrick," Choy said. "Never call me 'Inspector' again. I've left that life behind."

"Oh, sorry. Well, what should I call you, then? *Mister* Choy? Seems a bit formal. Your first name? Wasn't it Jung-hee?"

"I need something more clandestine. Let me think...How about 'Vito'?"

Patrick laughed. "Perfect! Vito Corleone from your favorite film!"

Choy laughed with him. "You remembered! I was just kidding, go ahead and call me Jung-hee."

They caught up with each other's personal lives from the four years since they had seen each other last, and then Patrick's voice turned serious.

"I've been hired as the chief security consultant for the Tokyo Olympics, and I was wondering if you might want to come and give me a hand."

"Actually, I'm quite fine here on Cheju Island, thanks very much. The weather is perfect, my young girlfriend is very pretty, and her young boy thinks the world of me. I feel like I'm twenty-five again. But it's nice to be in touch with you anyway."

"Would it help if I told you that some of your old friends from the DPRK might be up to their usual nonsense?"

There was silence on the other end. Then, "I would have thought that the uprising had at least slowed those bastards down."

Patrick said nothing. He wanted Choy to come to his own decision.

Finally, Choy cleared his throat. "If you have an enemy, that enemy becomes my enemy.

But you have to give me free rein over the cyber stuff. I don't want either the Japanese or American governments telling me what I can and can't do."

"It's fine on my end. And I know you'd be able to detect if they were monitoring you, anyway."

The next day Patrick took a taxi to Haneda Airport to meet Choy, his computer whiz friend formerly of North Korea's Bureau 39. As Choy exited customs and immigration, he looked around for anyone familiar but saw only people holding up cardboard placards with names on them. He did a double-take when he saw one of the placards that was marked "Michael Corleone" and laughed when he realized that the man in the sunglasses and baseball cap holding it was Patrick. They embraced and looked at each other the way friends do after a long absence from each other's lives.

"You let your hair grow out," Patrick said, beaming at his friend who used to sport a buzz cut. "And the glasses make you look even smarter, if that's possible."

"And look at you!" Choy said. "Very distinguished," he said as he brushed his hand against the shock of white hair that now covered mostly just the right side of Patrick's head.

After a cab ride back to Patrick's office at the JIA and Choy having a chance to freshen up, he accepted Patrick's challenge of a game of Go over some Chinese takeout. Patrick had played only a handful of times with Yasuhara Roshi since his adventures in North Korea, and he missed the specific type of discipline the game imposed on his mind. He was convinced that there was an actual center of the brain that was stimulated by the game in a way he had only experienced in combat situations, where the slightest wrong move can lead to death. The stakes were much lower in the game, of course, but the important thing to Patrick was reengaging his brain in Go mode.

He loved the ritual of war that lay beneath the game's apparent simplicity of placing black and white stone discs on a board, with the stones advancing in slow motion across the cross-hatched wooden board as on a battlefield. The object of the game is to control a larger portion of the board than your opponent. Stones are captured and removed if a player is unable to prevent the opponent from surrounding a grouping. Placing the stones close to each other is a cautious defensive strategy that can aid in preventing them from being surrounded. Placing them far apart, on the other hand, is a more aggressive but potentially risky approach. Thus, the skilled player strikes a balance between strategic planning and tactical expedience, much as in combat.

He found the symmetry of the stone disc arrangements appealing to his artistic sense, and he also appreciated the way the game's multiplicity of strategies imposed a discipline on his mind, forcing him to fully consider the placement of each stone.

A mere fifteen minutes later, all of that went out the window as he conceded a quick defeat at Choy's hands.

"Out of practice," Choy said dismissively while lighting a cigarette. Patrick wasn't sure if Choy was referring to Patrick or to himself at needing a full fifteen minutes to kick Patrick's ass. Choy's meaning became clear in his next sentence.

"You gave yourself no *hwallo* [escape route]. You used to try that same strategy when we played in Pyongyang. Every time you attack right away like that, you give away your position. You have to lure your opponent into attacking you first."

Patrick asked for a rematch, but Choy reminded him why he had come all the way from Cheju Island and insisted on getting right to work in a small room off of Patrick's office in the JIA. Patrick had him set up with a computer on a desk, but Choy took one look at the desktop and snorted. He opened his briefcase and took out the thinnest laptop Patrick had ever seen.

"Is that what you're going to use?" Patrick asked in what he hoped wasn't too skeptical a tone.

"I'll have you know I made this myself. I bet you a bottle of the best sake in Tokyo that there's not a computer in this building that can even come close. Now if you don't mind, I'm going to see if I can find any evidence of this North Korean connection you mentioned."

Patrick left him alone. But part of Choy's desire to get right to work was so that he could keep himself occupied and also, hopefully, to finish up early and get home to his girlfriend and her son. At the Cheju Island airport, his girlfriend had squeezed her eyes shut in an effort to stanch a flow of tears, and her young son, who had grown attached to Choy as a father figure, began bawling openly. Before that, Choy hadn't realized how deeply they felt about him and he for them.

After Patrick closed the door behind him, Choy found his spirits darkening further from the desktop wallpaper that appeared on his screen when the computer booted up. He'd seen the image hundreds of times before, but somehow being in an unfamiliar place caused them to cut into his soul. He lit a cigarette and gazed at the image…

Over twenty-five years earlier, Choy had graduated from the prestigious Pyongyang Film School where, along with film history, he also studied acting and became fluent in English, although as a result of his passion for American action films, his English had an unmistakably colloquial cast. After he graduated, he decided that it was high time to settle down and find a wife. Shy around women at that age, he could never quite bring himself to even start up a simple conversation with any of his female coworkers at the film school. So he sought help from a *chungmae*, or go-between, who had an almost infallible instinct for match-ups. After only two mutual rejections on the basis of photos, she found Choy a young woman who proved to be the ideal companion for someone like him. Jae-mi's father had been a war hero as had Choy's, and she loved movies almost as much as he did. Their dates nearly always consisted of watching one of the first two *Godfather* movies in the screening room of the film school. He laughed until he cried when she tried to sound tough while saying, "I'll make him an offer he can't refuse," or "They got Sonny on the causeway."

A year into their marriage, Jae-mi gave birth to a young boy they named Kwang-sun, or "wide goodness," and aside from the chronic food shortages, their lives were a picture of domestic contentment. Choy's expertise with computer technology at the film school had been noticed, and he was offered a job with the Ministry of People's Security, or the national police force, a significant step up in the world. His main duty would be transferring the Ministry's massive number of criminal files to electronic form. If he accepted the appointment, he would have to spend the initial six months of his training down by the DMZ, a requirement of all new recruits. In the interest of state security, family members could not accompany recruits, nor was any communication allowed. Choy would be assigned to track down thieves who had stolen from the State's granaries in the Kaesong area not far from the Demilitarized Zone where theft had been rampant.

This was during the Arduous March, the great famine of the late 1990s, and even otherwise honest people were reduced to food theft. Jae-mi begged Choy not to go so soon after the birth of their child, but Choy gently explained to her that at the end of six months they would be given a modest apartment of their own in Pyongyang as a reward.

They would also have plenty to eat as he rose through the ranks. On the day he left for duty, he rocked his wife and child in his arms. "My body will be a hundred miles from my soul," he whispered to Jae-mi as their tears mingled.

But the famine grew worse over the coming months, with even residents of Pyongyang resorting to stripping bark from trees and boiling weeds for something to put into their stomachs. At the end of his six-month training tour, Choy came back to discover that his infant son had died of malnutrition, since Jae-mi was unable to lactate owing to the food shortage. Jae-mi, the neighbors said, simply gave up after young Kwang-sun died, and she lay on her bed listless and unresponsive when Choy returned. He tried as best as he was able to nurse her back to health, but she blamed herself for the death of her son and was dead within a week of Choy's return.

Choy never forgave himself. But most of all, he never forgave the system that was directly responsible for their deaths, a system aided and abetted above all others by the very man he worked for: Comrade Moon and his Bureau 39. He vowed then and there to do all he could to eradicate the organization from his native country, along with all the Comrade Moons who had made it possible. Now, years later in Tokyo, he could throw himself into his work for Patrick, investigating the probable North Korean connection to the recent attacks. He saved the image of his dead wife and child as a .gif file and got to work with the Olympic rings as his new screen background.

An hour later, he called Patrick back in. He had another cigarette dangling from his lips despite the large *Kin'en* sign above his desk. His usual air of distant serenity while working had been replaced by look of bewilderment that creased his face as he pointed to the screen.

"Before I defected to South Korea, I installed a backdoor virus on the Bureau 39 computer system. A backdoor allows you to get into a system undetected, and Bureau 39 seemed a good place to start looking for a North Korean connection. A little while ago I used it to get into their system, but they must have some new kind of firewall. I can't just roam around in their old files, but I did manage to find an email exchange from the other day between 39 and someone else whom I can't identify. Not yet, anyway. At any rate, I think I may have found a connection between 39 and the attacks."

"Bureau 39, you sure?" Patrick asked excitedly.

Choy rocked his head from side to side equivocally. "*Possibly*. Best not to say anything until I can be sure. For one thing, Bureau 39 was disbanded and outlawed by the new government, so if there really is a 39 connection, it's got to be people who are operating illegally. Which is kind of ironic considering that *illegal* is what 39 was all about."

"Alright, I won't tell anyone till you give the okay. So what was the email? What did it say and who sent it?"

"I can't figure out who it came from—they must have sent it to the 39 computer from a virtual private network that's hiding their Internet Protocol number. IP numbers are unique to every computer, but the private network keeps it hidden. It just said, 'Congratulations on Budokan gold medal.' It looks an awful lot like a reference to the attack. Why would someone be congratulating Bureau 39 about Budokan unless it had something to do with the attack?"

"Well, from what I've seen of Bureau 39, they're evil enough to find something to celebrate," Patrick said. "Can you figure out exactly who in 39 was being congratulated and by whom?"

"That's what I'm going to look for now. I'm going to pose as the person in 39 who got congratulated and send an email back to the original sender thanking them for it. But I'm going to embed another backdoor virus I wrote so that if they open the email I'm sending, I can get into their system and have a look around."

"Are you sure that won't blow your cover? What if the original person at 39 sends a thank you email to them too? Wouldn't that look suspicious?"

"I can just say, 'Thanks, more later' in the subject heading and leave it at that. It's more than likely that they'll still open it to see if there's anything else in the body of the email, but then figure they'll hear back when they don't see anything. That way, if someone else from 39 writes, it could look like they're sending a more elaborate thanks to the one I'm sending. There's no guarantee that this will work, but from the looks of things with the attacks, we've got to try every angle to find out what's going on and what might happen next. Do I have your okay?"

Patrick replied without hesitation. "Absolutely. It sounds like a good plan to me, and like you say, we've got to do something fast about these attacks."

"Alright, let me send that now. If and when they reply, I might be able to get into their system and find out who these people are. And maybe even who their Bureau 39 connection is."

CHAPTER 15

AMERICAN EMBASSY
July 23

In light of the attacks on SDF soldiers at the Budokan and Yasukuni Shrine, as well as the attempted attack on Tokyo Tower that off-duty SDF members had thwarted, Patrick requested an emergency meeting with JIA Director Hayashida and CIA Station Chief Norm Hooper to take up the obvious North Korean connection. He would hold off on any mention of Bureau 39 until Choy had confirmed the association. The last thing anyone needed was another communication screw-up. Hayashida rushed into Hooper's office having just come from a meeting with Prime Minister Adegawa. He was trailed by his assistant, Minoru Kaga.

"I'm very sorry to keep you waiting," he said breathlessly.

"Quite alright, Mister Hayashida," Hooper said. "Can I get you some tea? Water?"

"Nothing, thanks," Hayashida said. Hooper held up a bottle of water to Kaga, who bowed his polite refusal.

Hayashida looked at Hooper and Patrick, and his eyes became guarded.

"If I may begin," Patrick said, "it's very clear that the attacks we've had...so far...have had a connection to North Korea. And every indication points to further attacks. My question is, when will the public be alerted? I ask in my capacity as chief security consultant for the Olympics."

Hayashida sucked air through his teeth while nodding vigorously. "That is actually the same question I put to the Prime Minister this morning, Mister Featherstone." He gave no indication of a follow-up statement.

"And?" Patrick asked, not attempting to hide his impatience.

"Well, it's a little difficult," Hayashida said.

"What's so difficult?" Hooper asked, no less irritated than Patrick at Hayashida's seeming inability to give a straight answer.

"Well, none of the targets so far have been civilians. And we can't really say for a fact that the attacks have been on specifically Olympic sites. Tokyo Tower and Yasukuni Shrine, for example…"

Patrick cut him off. "Tokyo Tower was one of the main viewing areas for the carrying of the Olympic torch that day. And the attack on Yasukuni Shrine was aimed at contestants in the judo competition who…"

Hayashida cut him off in turn. "…who are members of the Self-Defense Force. Similarly, the attempted attack on Tokyo Tower involved a gunfight with members of the SDF. There is no way to know if these attacks were aimed at Olympic sites or at the Self-Defense Force."

"But so what?" Patrick said, his voice rising in frustration.

Hayashida kept his voice level. "At our meeting, the Prime Minister reaffirmed his stance that these Games be an opportunity to lift the spirits of the Japanese people and to show the world what the Prime Minister likes to call 'Japan's Gross National Cool.' We can't allow a situation where people are too frightened to even come to the events."

Patrick and Hooper stared at him agog. Patrick spoke. "Begging your pardon, Mister Hayashida, but how 'cool' would it be to have the Olympic stadium littered with dead bodies if whoever is behind these attacks decides not to confine themselves to military targets? I mean, the Opening Ceremony is tomorrow."

"I'm very sorry, Mister Featherstone, the Prime Minister has made up his mind. There will be no official announcement on the alleged North Korean connection to the alleged attacks on the Olympics. I am telling you that as your immediate superior."

"Alleged?" Hooper thundered. "How much more evidence do you need?"

Hayashida's cell phone rang. He looked at the number and hurriedly mimed excusing himself as he left the room. A pained look crossed Kaga's face as he trailed his boss out the door. He looked at Patrick and opened his mouth as if to say something but checked himself.

Hooper and Patrick watched the door close behind them.

"So you were born in this country, huh?" Hooper said wearily after it became clear that they would not be returning.

Patrick nodded. "Yes. But that's not to say I understand it."

"Tell me about it," Hooper muttered as he went over to the coffee urn.

"Japan is never what it seems," Patrick sighed wistfully. "Then again, it's never anything else either."

Hooper's arm was halfway to pouring a cup of coffee, but he stopped in midair and looked back at Patrick. "You and Japan are made for each other. I have no idea what you just said."

Patrick shrugged. "That's why I couldn't live anywhere else."

Hooper shook his head and poured his coffee in total bafflement.

A moment later, Hooper broke the silence. "Hayashida said 'no official announcement,' correct?"

Patrick turned to him with the barest hint of a smile creasing his lips. "I believe he might have been referring to the NHK Broadcasting Corporation."

Hooper nodded. "The government's mouthpiece."

That afternoon
TOKYO

(AP) "An unconfirmed source has told the Associated Press that the attacks at the Budokan and at Yasukuni Shrine have a possible connection to North Korea. Again, this information is unconfirmed. Stay tuned for updates on this breaking development."

TOKYO
NHK Broadcasting Corporation

"Contrary to a report this morning, the Prime Minister's office has categorically denied any evidence of a North Korean connection to yesterday's attacks on the Budokan and Yasukuni Shrine. Minister of State for the Cool Japan Strategy Takeo Miki dismissed the reports as 'irresponsible.' We'll have more on this story later today."

AMERICAN EMBASSY

"Are they serious?" Kirsten Beck said as members of the combined security command watched the NHK news report in Hooper's office. Director Hayashida had sent Minoru Kaga as his representative to the meeting. "They have an actual Minister of State for 'the Cool Japan Strategy'?"

"I'm afraid so, Ms. Beck," Kaga said. "It's aimed at presenting a more modern image of Japan to the world."

"Well," Kirsten said, raising her eyebrows and choosing her words carefully, "I'm not sure how 'modern' it is to sit on information that might save lives."

"I agree with you," Kaga said. "The same thing happened before Fukushima." Kaga's hometown, ten miles from the Fukushima nuclear power plant, had to be forcibly evacuated after the Japanese government failed to take measures to prevent the 2011 explosion at the plant.

CHAPTER 16

July 23

After giving himself a fresh buzz cut and donning a torn motorcycle jacket, Yun Tae-sen, a.k.a. "Tyson," admired himself in the mirror and drove a mini truck to a neighborhood in the Yotsuya section of Tokyo. Among assorted college dormitories, eating establishments, and condominiums sat a squat, single-story cinderblock building painted bright blue. He parked and locked the truck, went to the front door, and pressed the intercom button. The person on the other end mumbled almost inaudibly, "Hikari no Kami" ("Light of the Gods"). Tyson lowered his voice to a growling bass and said that he had heard about the organization and was interested in finding out more.

A disheveled man in his mid-forties shuffled to the door a moment later and ushered Tyson inside. He introduced himself as "Sekitori," no first name given, and explained that due to a recent ruling by the unjust Japanese judicial system, his organization was under heavy surveillance. Tyson nodded sympathetically and told Sekitori that he and his family had defected from North Korea years earlier because they could no longer stand the microscope the government kept them under. He also told the man that he was searching for meaning in life, and Sekitori launched into a long discourse on Hikari no Kami, including its previous iteration as Aum Shinrikyo, founded by the infamous Shoko Asahara.

They talked long into the afternoon, first about the group's roots in Christian, Buddhist, and Hindu teachings, then about Aum Shinrikyo's 1995 attack on the Tokyo subway system using sarin nerve gas. As he detailed the attack, Sekitori's voice and demeanor became agitated, and spittle went flying from his lips. He told Tyson that Shoko Asahara had been the first savior of mankind, and that he, Sekitori, was the last, now that Asahara had been executed. He then told of an apocalypse that he prophesied would coincide with the upcoming Olympics. Toward the end of his peroration he stood, and with an unblinking gleam in his eye, he again declared himself the savior of the world with supernatural powers. He told Tyson that only his followers would be spared, and he vowed revenge for Asahara's 2018 execution.

Tyson listened with rapt attention throughout the long harangue. Mr. Lee had emphasized the importance of establishing rapport with his contact, and he gave every impression of being Sekitori's newest and most eager acolyte. So when Sekitori stood and declared himself the Messiah, Tyson jumped up and bowed at his feet, blubbering convincingly, something he had practice doing from the 2011 state funeral of Kim Jong-il.

"I've found my home! I've found my home!" he shouted over and over. Then he imparted some important information: perhaps the Messiah would be interested in some materials that might hasten the apocalypse?

July 24
6 p.m.

Many commuters in Japan wear surgical masks to avoid catching or spreading germs, especially since the Covid-19 pandemic, and thus a solitary masked man on this day in late July attracted no undue attention as he entered the Sendagaya station of the Tokyo Metro. Security directly around the Olympic Stadium had been massively beefed up after the double assassination, as well as the attacks on the Budokan, Yasukuni Shrine, and Tokyo Tower, but the station is a twelve-minute walk from the stadium and not as heavily guarded as the stadium area itself.

Unlike most of the other commuters, the man in the mask had purchased a paper ticket at an automatic vending machine as opposed to using a Pasmo or Suica commuter card, which are more convenient but contain detailed information on the date, place, and time of purchase. The man carried in his hand a shopping bag from an upscale *depaato* nearby, but the items inside the bag were unavailable at that or any other department store.

After inserting his ticket into the receiving slot on the ticket gate, he hurried along with the others in the rush-hour crowd to the escalators leading to the trains. Once on the platform he waited three minutes for the local to Shinjuku Station and got on with the others. A few minutes later the train arrived in Shinjuku, and all but the solitary man alighted. He rushed over to a highly prized seat near the door, and as the train filled with a sea of humanity headed in the opposite direction to the Olympic stadium, he reached under his seat to his shopping bag and unscrewed the lids of two jars. When the train pulled back into Sendagaya Station a few minutes later, he poured the contents of the containers into a large metal can, which began bubbling and emitting smoke. When the door of the train opened, he kicked the bubbling can onto the middle of the platform and ran off toward the escalator, where he began pushing others aside and sprinting up the moving stairs, disappearing among the crowds. The Opening Ceremony began in an hour.

CHAPTER 17

Earlier on the same day

Beginning on the day after the double assassination, Patrick had taken to walking the perimeter of the stadium every morning at daybreak, like a pilot inspecting a plane before takeoff. And because he had missed any hint that an assassin had been hiding inside the stadium, he now also included a walkthrough of the inside, up and down the stairs, around the track and playing field, scanning the empty seats with binoculars for anything unusual. He had been assured by a JIA technician that their AI security would pick up any anomalies, but that hadn't been enough to save the two assassination victims.

As a sniper, Patrick had painstakingly practiced for months picking out details that might seem even minutely out of place. He had had an easier time than most because he had studied with the most exacting of teachers for his sumi-e ink-brush painting, where a turn of the brush even a millimeter too soon or a millisecond too late can render an entire painting worthless. *Kan,* his teacher had called it, the intimate connection between sight and mind that receives everything without prejudgment before a stroke is executed. The lesson was easily transferrable to his sniper's "eye." Only after intuiting the sight picture in his sniper's scope would he make a judgment to pull or not pull the trigger.

On this morning of the Opening Ceremony he had awoken at 3 a.m. for his walkaround and was greeted by a cacophony of electrical tools wielded by workers absorbed in the task of making the stadium ready for the world in a few hours. Although Japan had hosted two Winter

Olympics in the past half century, the 1964 Games had been its reentry into the civilized world after its murderous rampage through Asia less than two decades previous. Now, with the 2021 Games, Japan hoped to present to the world its new image of "Cool Japan," a paragon of political tranquility, technological ingenuity, and its enviable *omotenashi*, the hospitality even the most jaded world traveler cannot help but be awed by.

By now a fixture in the stadium, Patrick's foreign appearance elicited no surprise or alarm among the workers, and he freely paced the stadium floor with his eyes roaming from side to side. One of the main lessons he had learned in sniper training was that nothing in nature is regular. Now as he scanned the seats, aisles, and exits, he looked for anything that was even remotely *irregular*, since everything about the Olympics was designed to be a model of attention to detail.

He finished up his security inspection of the lower reaches of the stadium just as day was breaking, and he trained his binoculars up to the roof oculus one last time before heading over to his JIA office. He had a meeting at the American embassy later in the day, but he needed to sign off on paperwork before heading over. Today they would be meeting with Jack "Fitz" Fitzroy, another alleged "cultural attaché" who was actually a CIA spycraft expert, with dirty tricks as a specialty. It was Fitz who had outfitted Patrick with the Griffin 1-A flying suit on its inaugural mission to North Korea four years earlier. Without Fitz, he probably wouldn't have been able to save Yumi.

Several hours later as he was finishing up at his JIA office, his phone pulsed with an incoming text. Patrick smiled, thinking it was from Yumi who often texted him around this time of day. It was not. He squinted at the phone.

"Discern what cannot be seen with the eye."

THE AMERICAN EMBASSY
TOKYO

A small group had assembled in CIA Station Chief Norm Hooper's office, which had been designated the forward operating base of the combined security command for the Olympics. CIA Case Officer Harmon Phibbs and FBI Analyst Kirsten Beck sipped coffee at the round table that dominated the room, while JIA Director Kazuo Hayashida sat off by himself, hoping to avoid a repeat of the scene in Hooper's office where he had been reamed by Hooper and Patrick for not sufficiently alerting the public of danger during the Games. After a while Hooper looked at his watch and spoke.

"Folks, Jack Fitzroy will be giving a briefing down in his basement lair today. Fitz is our resident expert on everything to do with spycraft that might come in handy for the Olympics. Patrick is still at his JIA office, but he'll join us shortly. He's pretty familiar with Fitz's work, so it's okay if he misses the overview."

They all then filed downstairs via the ornate curving staircase leading to the main floor and to a nondescript door that Hooper unlocked. He ushered the group down a narrow spiral staircase that opened onto Fitz's top-secret technical area. The staircase was like something out of a European hotel of the 1920s, but it served the dual purpose of impeding progress up or down in the event of a security breach in either direction.

Once downstairs they were greeted by Fitz, a tall, thin, bearded man in his sixties who greeted them warmly with his usual cup of coffee in hand.

"Here's where the magic happens," he said with a smile as he came over to them. "Come on in and feel free to take a seat anywhere."

After everyone was seated and Fitz was about to begin his briefing, the door to the basement flew open and Patrick entered, out of breath. "We've gotten another message." He held up his phone.

"What's it say?" Hooper asked. Patrick read the text.

"Discern what cannot be seen with the eye."

"Is that another quote from the samurai guy?" asked Phibbs.

"That's right, Miyamoto Musashi. It's from his *Book of Five Rings*."

"Did you trace the phone it came from?" Fitz asked.

Patrick nodded. "It was a burner. Probably a single-use and then straight into the Sumida River."

There was a knock on the door, and a Marine guard burst into the office.

"Very sorry to interrupt, Mister Hooper," the guard said in an urgent voice, "but there's just been a nerve gas attack on the Sendagaya metro station. There's been at least fifty fatalities." The room erupted into confusion.

"Sendagaya? That's the closest station to the Olympic stadium," said Fitz. "What kind of nerve agent was it? Sarin? That's what was used back in 1995 on the subway."

"They think it was Novichok, sir," said the Marine, trying to catch his breath. "It could have been a lot worse. Those four-person elevators in the subways the foreign tourists have been complaining about backed things up a lot, otherwise there would have been twice as many people on the platform." With that, he turned and hurried out of the room.

"Well, I guess we know what that text you got was all about," said Kirsten.

"Novichok. That's ten times more lethal than sarin," Fitz said.

"Where'd they get that?" said Kirsten Beck. "It's banned every-where, even in Russia."

"The component parts aren't," said Fitz, "and they can be carried safely and then mixed at the site of the attack."

"Hopefully, we'll be finding out soon who did this," said Hooper looking at this phone. "I just got word that they have a good description of the guy."

"I think that a good place to start would be to investigate anyone connected to the 1995 sarin attack," said Hayashida. "They hanged the cult leader, Shoko Asahara, a few years back, and this might be an act of revenge. It also undermines the theory that the attacks have a North Korean connection. This is clearly homegrown." He directed his statement to Hooper and Patrick with a hint of triumph in his voice.

Kirsten Beck weighed in: "We can investigate all we want, but the problem is, the clues Patrick is getting are too vague to use in any kind of preventive way, and it's pretty clear the attacks are going to continue. We can't exactly ask whoever's sending them to be more specific. Plus, we don't know how many attacks he, or they, are planning. Is this going to be like 9/11 or a longer timetable?"

"No way of knowing," said Patrick. "As it stands now, we're totally helpless to predict anything. The Olympics are the perfect target of opportunity for terrorists. The whole world's attention is focused on one thing. Plus, Japan has had more than its share of disasters. Whoever's behind this is probably thinking that the country will just fold in the face of their demands. And unless I'm very wrong, we'll be seeing demands before too long."

"There's one thing we can do, though," said Hayashida. "If this attack *was* revenge for the cult leader's execution, we should be able to track down his followers and see if we can get anything that way. And I know exactly where to start. We've had the offshoot groups under our surveillance for some time." Hayashida tapped the screen of his phone and called his JIA field operatives, relieved that the latest attack seemed to vindicate his and the Prime Minister's decision not to draw a connection to North Korea.

When a SWAT team from the JIA arrived at Hikari no Kami headquarters, sure enough, they found stockpiles of chemicals that could be used for producing enough Novichok to kill tens of thousands of people. However, the packages were labeled in Korean *hangul* characters. The puzzling thing to the Korean language speaker on the team was that the order of the characters was different from what he had learned as a child in Seoul. A child in Pyongyang, on the other hand, would have found nothing at all unusual about them.

The team also found a list of members, and they set about tracking them down for questioning.

TOYAMA STORAGE
YOKOHAMA

The air conditioning at the corpse hotel was not functioning properly owing to the power drain in the area from the ongoing heat wave. The windows were wide open, and the cacophonous racket of cicadas in the trees outside echoed in the viewing room where the young Bonghwajo had recently enjoyed their meal of ortolan songbirds. A disheveled Japanese man in his mid-forties, dressed unstylishly in black slacks and a wrinkled short-sleeved white shirt, walked into the room. Mr. Lee and Tyson rose to greet him.

"Mister Sekitori. Your vengeance is complete," said Mr. Lee, shaking the man's hand. Tyson did likewise. Mr. Lee reached into his pocket for his wallet.

"Thank you for the opportunity," said Sekitori without smiling. Tyson had invited the would-be Messiah to the corpse hotel, where he promised a hefty donation and more followers.

One of the sons of the corpse hotel's manager then came up behind Sekitori and shot him twice in the head with a silenced .22 using hollow points.

"Thank you, young man. Unfortunately, Mister Sekitori was attracting too much attention."

The young man hung his head in guilt. The only reason he had shot Sekitori was because Mr. Lee threatened to kill his father if he hadn't. He bowed quickly and left the room before Lee or Tyson could see his tears.

CHAPTER 18

Saturday, July 25

Early the next morning while Olympic preliminary events were commencing, Patrick, Kirsten, and CIA Station Chief Norm Hooper met again in Hooper's office at the American embassy prior to being joined by Hayashida and Kaga. The subject of interagency communication had been raised, and Hooper brought up the failure of American agencies to coordinate their efforts prior to 9/11. He happened to be looking at Kirsten as he delivered his remarks, and she immediately assumed a defensive posture with her arms folded in front of her.

"I don't dispute that the 9/11 attacks were preventable, Norm, but I do take issue when you say it was the FBI that was at fault for not following up on intelligence with your team."

The issue of intelligence communication was a sore point for Kirsten. Six weeks earlier at her home base in Honolulu, she had been called on the carpet for failing to follow up on a credible lead, resulting in the escape of a possible Chinese agent who had been seen taking photographs at Pearl Harbor. Kirsten's posting to the Olympics wasn't meant as a junket. It was a compassionate move by her Honolulu boss to give her time away from a personal loss she had recently suffered, as well as an opportunity to learn from colleagues in other agencies. Her boss had tried to dissuade her from coming back to work so soon, but Kirsten had insisted that she was fine, when actually she wanted to be back on duty to take her mind off her grief. She vowed to her boss that she would never fail to follow up on a lead again, and the boss agreed to keep the incident off her record.

"Believe me, I'm not casting aspersions on you personally, Kirsten. For one thing you were too young to have been part of the Bureau back then." Kirsten breathed an inner sigh of relief. Her boss in the Honolulu office had been true to his word about not divulging her screw-up.

"But as for the larger issue," Hooper continued, "you're making my point for me. The CIA and FBI were never two teams, or at least they shouldn't have been. My point was that we were one team, the United States intelligence team. The main problem in 9/11 and other attacks was that we relied only on our agencies to define what the security risks were, instead of getting out of our silos and collaborating. In situations like that, anything that isn't defined as a risk doesn't go up on the radar screen until it turns into a full-blown disaster. And then everyone says we screwed up, which we did. But the reason for it was that we defined the problem too narrowly, since we didn't rely on each other's intelligence. The Company was just as guilty as the Bureau, so again, I'm not trying to give you guys a black eye."

There was a knock on the door, and Hayashida let himself in. Kaga followed him.

"Good morning everyone. I hope I'm not late."

"Not at all, Mister Hayashida. We were just having a chat about what happens when there's a communication breakdown in the intelligence community," he said with a barb in his voice. "Come on in, have a seat. Anybody seen Phibbs?" Everyone shook their heads. "Well, let's begin, anyway."

The five of them sat down around the round table in the middle of Hooper's office. Hooper cleared his throat.

"Okay, folks, it's now quite clear who's responsible for the attacks," he began with a look at Hayashida to gauge his reaction through his body language. Hayashida sat still as a stone, his face betraying nothing. Hooper continued.

"This is North Korean all the way, from the Type 58 rifle to the origin of the Novichok components. Plus, one of the three young guys who attacked the SDF headquarters had a map of the area that was marked up with Korean writing."

Hooper paused and waited for Hayashida to say something, anything. His mouth tightened when the JIA director still said nothing. He looked at Kaga, whose eyes were downcast, his lips pressed into half a scowl. Kaga looked over at Hayashida as if willing him to say something, but Hayashida sat unmoving. With an almost inaudible sigh Hooper got to the point of the meeting. "Mister Hayashida, it seems obvious that the public should be alerted of possible danger. The attacks have clearly been coordinated."

Hayashida sucked air through his teeth. "Saaa," he said tilting his head to one side, the universal Japanese expression for not knowing something and/or not wanting to commit one's self by saying something. "I have to wonder who in North Korea would be in a position to do this kind of thing," he said. Kaga let out a breath in seeming exasperation. Hayashida shot him a look.

"Well, it's clear that *someone* connected to North Korea is," Patrick said, his voice rising. He was not going to hide his annoyance. "What difference does it make if it looks like someone's *in a position* to do something?"

Hayashida sucked more air. "But what if the attacks aren't coordinated? What if these are lone wolf attacks?" Patrick winced at the cowardly term. It had been overused in Europe in recent years after attacks that were clearly the evildoing of ISIS or other death cults to avoid the label of Islamophobia.

Hooper shifted in his seat. "Mister Director, please. It makes absolutely no difference if it's one person or ten. You still have a lot of dead bodies in that subway station, and it's looking more and more like the Olympics are the target."

"Yes, of course," said Hayashida, "and that is why the Prime Minister wants us to increase security to a level commensurate with the threat. He's given me authority to detain anyone suspected of being connected to these attacks for the legal limit of twenty-three days, but the JIA will go about this quietly. As I stated in our last meeting, we do not want a situation where people are too afraid to come to the events. This is too important a moment in our history. And as your President Bush said after the September 11 attacks, if people stop going about their ordinary lives, then the terrorists have won."

"Oh, come on," Hooper said. "We have no way of knowing how big this threat is. Are all these incidents related? Are they indicators of more to come? I feel strongly that we should act proactively and at least warn people."

"As I stated, Mister Hooper, the Prime Minister feels it best not to alarm the public. And as I also said, we will be arresting anyone we suspect is part of this."

Patrick stood. He'd heard enough. "It's the Prime Minister's decision to make, Mister Hayashida. But I want to make it clear that I completely disagree with not issuing any warnings to the public, and I won't accept responsibility if anything happens. My job is chief security consultant, but if the PM is going to call the shots on this, I'm not going to be hung out to dry if things go south. Are we clear on that?"

Hayashida nodded with his eyes closed. "Yes, Mister Featherstone, very clear." As Patrick was leaving the room, he could have sworn that Kaga was nodding his encouragement to him in as unobvious a way as possible.

Later that afternoon, NHK interrupted its coverage with an important announcement. They had received a video and Twitter feed from a North Korea-based group called Chosun Restoration, whose members in Japan claimed responsibility for the Novichok attack on the Sendagaya subway station as well as the attacks on the Budokan indoor arena, Yasukuni Shrine, and Tokyo Tower. Further, the group claimed responsibility for the assassination of two officials inside the Olympic stadium two weeks before the Opening Ceremony. It also said that the attacks were in retaliation for the Rising Tide uprising that toppled the Kim regime four years earlier on the day of their Glorious Triumvirate Celebration, North Korea's equivalent of the Olympics in terms of spectacle.

Chosun Restoration announced that more attacks could be expected if the Japanese, South Korean, and American governments did not withdraw their support of President Nahm Myung-dae's Rising Tide government in North Korea and expedite the return of the Kim family to power.

CHAPTER 19

THE WHITE HOUSE
July 26

Director of National Intelligence Jay Garvida was ushered into the Oval Office for his meeting with President Evan Dillard while Dillard was going over the presidential daily brief.

Garvida took a seat at the table in the middle of the office across from the president.

"I was just reading about these attacks in Tokyo," Dillard said, looking up from the PDB. "What do we know about this group behind them?"

"Apparently, they're part of a group in North Korea called Chosun Restoration, sir," Garvida replied. "They're loyal to the Kim family and want to bring them back to power by toppling the current Rising Tide regime. They're growing by leaps and bounds because Rising Tide's been unable to deliver on its promises of economic prosperity once Kim Jong-un was ousted. Instead, now there's widespread hunger throughout North Korea. This terror cell of theirs in Japan seems to be trying to use the Olympics as center stage to air their demands and also to take revenge for the overthrow of Kim Jong-un. The word 'Chosun' is an old name for Korea before the Japanese colonized it in 1910."

"Any of them been captured?"

"No, sir."

Dillard shook his head as he read from the PDB. "'We demand the immediate withdrawal of American, Japanese, and South Korean support of the puppet Nahm Myung-dae.' I'll be damned. Any Americans killed in these attacks?"

"No sir, but here's something odd: the guy who pretty much instigated the overthrow of Kim is an American citizen who was born and raised in Japan and…"

Dillard held up his hand. "Wait a minute. Is this the guy the Agency sent over a few years back to look for the mock defector?"

"Correct, sir. His name is Patrick Featherstone. He's now been hired as the chief security consultant for the Olympics. Anyway, the first attack in Tokyo was a couple of weeks ago, a double assassination of two Japanese security officials inside the Olympic stadium. The strange thing is, this guy Featherstone was standing right between the two guys, but whoever was shooting intentionally left him alone. The question, of course, is why wasn't Featherstone shot along with the other two if these attacks are revenge for the overthrow of Kim? You'd think he'd be the primary target."

"Huh," Dillard huffed. His eyes went up in thought. "What about North Korea itself? Does President Nahm know anything about these guys?"

"Negative, sir, at least not in any detail. Chosun Restoration appears to have started in response to food shortages in the past year or so. The rice crop partially failed after massive flooding a few months back, and Chosun Restoration tapped into popular anger at the government's inability to do anything about it, especially since China cut off all aid when Kim Jong-un was overthrown."

"But we're still sending them aid, right?"

"Correct, sir, but most of it is being looted and sold on the black market, just like under the Kim regime. The big fear this time around, though, is a civil war followed by a refugee crisis. Under Kim, ordinary people had no freedom of movement, but now they can come and go pretty much as they please. The food situation is getting worse all the time, and if there's a popular uprising against Rising Tide, I think it's safe to say there'd be a mad rush for the exits. It would overwhelm the borders with China and South Korea, but especially China."

"Okay, thanks Jay. Let me know if there's anything new from this group that's blowing up Tokyo."

An hour after meeting with Garvida, Dillard personally opened the door of the Diplomatic Reception Room for his next appointment. He smiled and extended his hand to Chinese Ambassador Wu Shin-tao, who had come on urgent business. After an exchange of pleasantries, they took seats on either side of the fireplace.

"Thank you very much for seeing me today, President Dillard. I am sure that you understand the gravity of the situation in Japan and North Korea."

"Of course, Mister Ambassador, I've been briefed about the recent attacks in Tokyo and the crisis on the peninsula."

Wu nodded. "From what I can gather, a number of North Koreans from the Chosun Restoration insurgency somehow gained possession of weapons of mass destruction and are aiming to…well, I was going to say 'disrupt the Olympics,' but perhaps 'destroy the Olympics' would be more accurate. Which leads me to my next point."

He paused to let the gravity of the situation sink in. "The situation in the former DPRK is becoming more and more untenable, Mister President, which is without a doubt providing fuel for these attacks. More and more people are calling for the return of the Kim family, and I know that is not something that your country would accept. People are openly saying that at least under Kim there was political stability, but now there are widespread fears of civil war. On top of that, our reports indicate that large sections of the country are on the brink of famine. And now these attacks by Chosun Restoration on Tokyo. Something simply must be done before there is civil war and a refugee crisis. May I remind you, Mister President, of the 'caravans' at your border in recent years? We don't like that kind of thing any more than you do. Thus, my government would like to make a proposal." Wu searched Dillard's eyes for any indication of openness or hostility. He would then tailor his remarks accordingly. But Dillard was playing his cards close to his vest and kept his face blank. Wu's jaw tightened as he continued.

"Since North Korea has, since its inception, been especially close to my country both ideologically and culturally—what we call 'lips and teeth close'—I've been authorized to offer what my premier is calling 'the China Solution.'" Wu again waited for any sign from Dillard, but Dillard had been coached to keep his famously uninhibited mouth shut. Wu plunged ahead.

"The China Solution would be the establishment of a temporary one-year protectorate over North Korea under the wing of China until the unrest there subsides. Now, as you know, President Nahm of North Korea has been nothing but hostile toward China since he assumed power four years ago. But if you can persuade him to work with us, we would be willing to fully restore aid in the form of food and fuel, which would help alleviate the suffering that is behind the threat of civil war and the success of this Chosun Restoration group. As you also know, a civil war would mean millions of refugees flooding across the border into my country. The world has seen what happened in Iraq after Saddam Hussein was deposed."

Ambassador Wu lifted one eyebrow and paused to let that sink in. He had just reminded Dillard of one of the worst American-made political disasters in history. But as Dillard listened to Wu's pitch, he recalled China's 2012 incorporation of 80 percent of the South China Sea as internal Chinese water simply by redrawing the map. And now they were being ever so generous and offering to create a 'temporary' one-year protectorate in North Korea while working with President Nahm? *What's the catch?* he thought.

Wu continued to outline the details of the China Solution for several more minutes. After he had finished, Dillard stood.

"Thank you so much for your kind offer, Mister Ambassador," he said smiling. He was going to continue to hold his cards close to the vest.

His shoot-from-the-lip style had gotten him into too much trouble in past years, and with the 2021 election coming up, he needed to weigh all options carefully. "I will certainly discuss it with my cabinet." He then ushered Ambassador Wu out of the Reception Room.

As was their practice every week, President Dillard met with his long-time friend and vice president, Paul Coppinger, for lunch in the Oval Office. Dillard had chosen Coppinger to replace Jared Lymon as veep after Lymon collapsed and died of a heart attack a year into their first term. *Just as well*, thought Dillard at the time. Lymon had been foisted on him by the party establishment who insisted that it was Lymon's turn to position himself for 2024. But Dillard never liked him and shed only crocodile tears at his funeral.

Dillard and Coppinger's meal today consisted of baked pork chops and fried Friel. Speaker of the House Jon Friel was Dillard's just-nominated opponent in the upcoming election, and the president and Coppinger relished the chance to take on this middle-aged flower child. For one thing, Friel was an all-but-avowed socialist who promised an end to everyone's financial woes thanks to the largesse of the federal government, thus assuring himself of the college snowflake vote. For another, he had ascended into the speakership as a compromise between the less liberal and more liberal factions of his party as opposed to anything close to a distinguished record.

Friel was also an unabashed opponent of Dillard's actions in the Middle East, and one of his main campaign slogans was "A Time for Peace," a line from Pete Seeger's "Turn! Turn! Turn!" Dillard's party promptly redubbed it "Peace in Our Time," Neville Chamberlain's infamous words of capitulation to Hitler. Dillard and Coppinger both dismissed reports that Friel's message was resonating beyond college campuses, especially since Dillard's last campaign had been about job creation, not handouts. His faithful base couldn't get enough of him, now that the economy was motoring along again like a Ferrari after the Covid-19 crisis. Still, that morning's *Washington Post* poll had the two presidential candidates only five points apart in Dillard's favor.

"Not to worry, Evan," said Coppinger as he picked up his silverware.

"I *am* worried, Paul, especially with these Olympic attacks and North Korea going all to shit. I met with Ambassador Wu this morning," he said.

"And?"

"And he sounded like the tooth fairy. He says that Zhongnanhai is offering what they're calling the 'China Solution' to this business with North Korea. They're afraid, rightly so, I guess, that if there's civil war in North Korea, China will have twenty million starving refugees on their doorstep. So they want me to talk President Nahm of North Korea into playing nice with China in return for restoring aid. The Chinese want to establish a temporary one-year protectorate to help Nahm manage the country, which Wu says would take the gas out of the Chosun Restoration movement in North Korea. Voila, no more threat of civil war. They also think it'll stop the Chosun Restoration terror attacks in Japan, since the North Koreans back home will stop supporting the group if their bellies are full."

"Temporary, huh?"

"That was my reaction too. But when you think about it, the only thing North Korea really has is a starving population, and Nahm doesn't appear to know jack about doing anything about it. If China can prevent a civil war by helping him out, it'll stave off a refugee crisis, and we're talking millions of refugees, Paul. Still, with China you always have to wonder if there's a catch."

"Amen to that. For starters, what if they just want to bring back the Kims and turn the country back into a client state?"

"You're right. I'd never even considered that. At any rate, there's no way we can look like we're knuckling under to the demands of the terrorists in Tokyo. I'm going to call Prime Minister Adegawa after lunch."

CHAPTER 20

July 27

As chief consultant for security at the Olympics, Patrick didn't enjoy the luxury of a regular workday, since security issues of all degrees of magnitude can arise at a moment's notice. Still, no human can work around the clock, and at eight o'clock every evening, he felt his energy flagging, having been up since 4 a.m. inspecting the venues in the Tokyo area, fielding calls from the media wanting updates on the terror attacks, and wondering when, not if, the next attack would occur. He returned to his room in the JIA, called Yumi to make sure she and Dae-ho were okay, took a shower, and sat down on his bed to enjoy a bento meal while watching the news. Days of nonstop thinking about the attacks had left Patrick's head spinning. After his light dinner, he lay his head back on his pillow to rest his eyes, deep sleep being out of the question just yet due to mental overstimulation. He reached over to turn off the reading light on the night table and touched his hand to the photo of Yumi he kept there. But when he closed his eyes with the light out, the first thing that came into his mind was Kirsten Beck. He turned the light back on again and took Yumi's photo in his hands. Then he got out of bed and took down his framed reproduction of Miyamoto Musashi's *Shrike on a Dead Tree*, one of the artist/warrior's most famous ink-brush paintings. He sat back down on the bed as he examined it. He had given it to himself as a present when he graduated from Tokyo University of Fine Arts, and some of the quotes he had used in his thesis came tumbling down through the years:

When you cannot be deceived by men, you will have realized the wisdom of strategy...

Distinguish between good and evil...

The carpenter uses a master plan of the building, and the Way of strategy is similar in that there is a plan of campaign...

He bolted upright in the narrow bed. A *plan* of campaign—of course. Something about the nature of the attacks had been gnawing at him, but he hadn't had the time to contemplate exactly what it was. Now, with Miyamoto Musashi's words echoing in his ears, he realized that there had to be some underlying pattern to the attacks, and if he could fathom what that pattern was, he would be a lot closer to figuring out what might be coming next.

He got out of bed and sat down on his *zafu* meditation cushion and began the zazen practice of counting his breaths until his mind emptied out. Then he waited for what he called "the flash," the burst of inspiration that comes when logical striving for answers ceases and intuition takes over. But before any intuition had a chance to burst forth, the next thing he knew, his alarm clock was ringing at 4 a.m. Somehow, he had lain down on the rug and fallen into a dreamless sleep. Although he hadn't gotten any insights into the pattern the attacks were following, he consoled himself with the fact that he had just had one of the best sleeps of the past two weeks. He was ready for the day, this time with his senses attuned to any flashes of insight that might suddenly take center stage of his mind. Instead of insight into the attacks, though, the first thing that came into his head was Kirsten Beck's eyes.

———————

The next morning, Patrick was on his way to the American embassy for a meeting with the combined security command when he noticed Kirsten walking quickly ahead of him with a cup of Starbuck's coffee. She was wearing a tan suit with a yellow blouse that matched her coloring perfectly. She hadn't seen him. He called out to her, and she turned.

"Oh, hello," she said, smiling.

"Walk with you?" he said.

"Sure. I just needed to get some real coffee. The stuff Hooper keeps in that urn of his is like sheep dip."

"Don't I know it. Maybe that's why my sleep patterns have been so off lately."

"Uh-huh, and it has nothing to do with the attacks," she said, lifting her eyebrows with a grin.

"Oh yeah, that too, I'd almost forgotten," Patrick said, smiling back. "By the way, this is supposed to be a quick meeting at the embassy, and I'm going to have some lunch afterwards. Since we'll be working together on this Chosun Restoration thing, I was thinking it might be a good idea to share our thoughts on how to approach it. Any plans for lunch?"

"Actually, no. That would be a great idea. Know any good places?"

After the embassy meeting, Kirsten excused herself briefly to check her messages with the secretary she'd been assigned. She came back to the vestibule of the building five minutes later.

"Thanks, sorry for the quick detour."

"No problem at all."

"That girl they assigned me is superefficient and easy to work with, but she drives me nuts with that 'uptalk' business. Every declarative sentence is suddenly a question. It's like she's auditioning for *Jeopardy!* all the time."

Patrick laughed out loud. "Oh, I know, it's just so irritating. 'So I went to the store? And bought a new sweater? But it was too small? So I guess I have to return it?' Maddening."

They laughed as they exited the embassy and talked as they walked, making better progress than Tokyo's earnest little eco-cars that were stuck in the noontime rush. A short way from the embassy, they saw a young boy of at most thirteen sporting a T-shirt that read "I Love Every Bone in Your Body, Especially Mine." The wholesome-looking, well-bred kid had no idea what the shirt said, only that it was in English and therefore somehow cool.

Patrick stifled a chuckle when he saw it. "You gotta love these T-shirts," he said in a soft voice, lamely attempting to defuse any embarrassment that Kirsten might be feeling.

"Do I really?" Kirsten said in a sarcastic tone, but Patrick snuck a glance at her and saw that she was grinning. *What a relief. A sense of humor*, he thought.

As they walked, her head kept pivoting off in different directions as she took in the unfamiliar sights and sounds of central Tokyo. Once he had to slow her down when no fewer than four senior citizen security guards held their hands up for them to be careful as they went around a narrow ditch being dug on the side of the road, even though they had plenty of room.

"That's how they keep their unemployment rate so low," Patrick commented with an arch smile.

Kirsten shrugged. "Whatever works. I guess it beats having homeless people all over the place like downtown Honolulu. Sometimes you can hardly walk down the street."

"Really? I had no idea it had gotten so bad."

Kirsten nodded. "Homeless and urban hipsters with man buns. I don't know which is worse."

"I suddenly like downtown Tokyo a lot better," Patrick said as they continued walking.

"So what exactly does an FBI analyst do in this day and age? And how did you decide on that career path?"

"Well, they were looking for people with a strong math background, and I majored in math in college. Mainly because numbers don't lie."

"Unless they're statistics," Patrick said with an impish smile.

"Touché on that," Kirsten said with a smile of her own. "Anyway, we piece together information from different sources and assess threats. Kind of like what we're doing now with these attacks. Pretty boring stuff usually, that's why I'm in training to be a psych profiler." She tilted her head to the left and side-eyed him appraisingly as they walked. "Italian, I'm guessing."

"Pretty good profiling, but no, although a lot of people think that. Actually, I'm Black Irish on both sides, plus an eighth Japanese from my mother's side."

"Interesting. I'm blonde Viking Irish on my father's side, but a quarter Lebanese from my mother's side. Thanks to her, I learned Arabic, which is my official second language in the Bureau. No one can ever guess that I'm part Arab, although that side of the family is Maronite Christian, not Islamic."

Patrick noted a hint of defensiveness in her last remark. She went on.

"I've never gotten any grief for my ethnicity, which I've never hidden, by the way, but when I hear my darker relatives on my father's side talk about some of the names they've been called…

"On the other hand, some of them go around saying things like 'Three thousand people died on 9/11. That's how many are killed in the Middle East in a typical week,' which is true, of course, but the people who died on 9/11 had no part in what happens in the Middle East, except to the wackadoodle fringe Left. Anyway, that was one of my main motivations for joining the FBI, to counter the stereotype. What drives me crazy is that part of me understands the animosity, although I hate the racism on the part of the wackadoodle fringe Right. Stereotypes have a kernel of truth. There's a reason why car rental companies charge more if you're under twenty-five. Kids get into more accidents. Is that ageism? I think it's just actuarial common sense. So I live in two psychological worlds when it comes to the subject. Sorry, I've really gotten the conversation into an unpleasant area."

"No, you haven't," said Patrick. He found something endearing in her use of the word "wackadoodle." "I think you make a lot of sense."

A few minutes later, Patrick led Kirsten to a tiny *izakaya*, a traditional Japanese pub, down a side street off the main drag. They took their seats at the far end of the bar. It didn't offer them much privacy since there were only eight seats total, but Patrick explained to her that in Japan you make your own space where little exists. He smiled at the owner and held up two fingers. The owner, who seemed to know him, nodded and smiled back. In short order he brought over a tray with a small porcelain jug of sake and two tiny cups.

Patrick poured for both of them. "I like a bit of sake with lunch. This stuff is mild—don't worry about getting lit."

"I usually have a little wine with lunch myself," she said, and they toasted each other. Kirsten took a sip. "Oh, this is good." She said with surprise and took another sip. "I'd always heard that sake was a step above lighter fluid."

"Some of it is," said Patrick, "but this is top of the line. It's called *junmai*, which is pure sake without any additives. It's brewed naturally, and they don't add any alcohol like they do with the cheap stuff."

"So delicious," Kirsten said, holding her cup out. Patrick refilled it, then held out his own.

"The custom is never to pour your own," he said with a smile.

"I like that," she said, filling his cup. She looked around the bar.

"All the signs in this area are in English except for this place," she said.

"That's why I like it. I come here to get away from the Foreign Service types from all over the world. Foreigners attached to the embassies around here can spend their entire assignments learning just a few words of very basic Japanese."

"I find that really arrogant. Plus, you deprive yourself of learning about the culture when you don't even make a stab at the language."

"Exactly," Patrick said. "What's the point of being in a different country if you're not going to expose yourself to some different ways of looking at things. I knew a guy in Kamakura who refused to learn the language at all. He said that it sounded like they have fifty words in the whole language, and when they run out, they just start over from the beginning."

Kirsten groaned and shook her head in amused disbelief. "That sounds like something that Phibbs guy at the embassy would say. What's his story, anyway?"

Patrick rolled his eyes. "Believe it or not, Senior Case Officer Harmon Phibbs is supposedly great at recruiting talent. Or 'supposably' as he would say. Somehow, he's got as great a knack for turning spies as he does for insulting people. According to Hooper, he can be a real charmer when he's in the field. He latches on to these lonely sad sacks from Russia or wherever who are far from home and befriends them, hard as that is to believe."

"That's definitely hard to believe. How about you? You said something about being an artist."

"That's right. Traditional Japanese calligraphy and ink painting was my major in college. Tokyo University of Fine Arts and Music, just outside of Ueno Park—not far from the zoo."

"And yet you were a sniper, right? I don't get it." They poured each other more sake and Patrick signaled the owner for a reload which he delivered right away.

"These little jugs are tiny. I'm not even feeling a buzz. Anyway, the art of calligraphy and the art of the sniper have a lot in common," he said taking another sip. "There's the relaxation of the fingers so as not to get in the way of yourself, and you have to see things in a particular way in both. You empty your mind, and you become one with the target or the sheet of paper. I call it 'the flash'—the moment when rational thought ends and pure intuition takes over. I think one of the reasons I gravitated to both arts was for that sense of seeing things. It has a certain pleasure to it, like immersing yourself to the point that everything else disappears. Plus, in both arts you have to keep emotion out of it, otherwise the stroke or the shot will suffer."

"I don't know much at all about the whole sniper thing, but I've always been fascinated by calligraphy. There's something starkly beautiful about it."

"You have a good sense of its underlying aesthetic if you can say that. A lot of people think it's boring compared to, say, oil paintings."

"I like them too, but I hate modern art. So much of it seems to depend on novelty, like that guy who used to get wasted and splatter paint all over canvases that are now worth millions."

Patrick smiled. "Jackson Pollock. Yeah, I can't say I'm much of a fan myself. It's like they'll do anything to not make sense impressively. But I can respect some of it. Like the way Picasso's cubist works show how the eye takes in reality before the brain creates the illusion of seeing it whole. I would imagine that's something like the reverse of what you do as an FBI analyst."

"Right, we break it down to see how it works. By the way, are we getting drunk? Any more of this sake, which is great by the way, and we should start splattering paint."

Patrick laughed. "Not drunk drunk, just a bit relaxed. We can make this little flask our last before we head back to the embassy." They both sipped the remainder of their sake in companionable silence for a few minutes.

"And your wife? Is she also an artist?" Kirsten asked, bringing the cup to her lips.

"Actually, we're not married. Yet. But I'm sure that will happen eventually. You?"

"I'm a widow," Kirsten said without emotion, but Patrick noticed that as she spoke, she instinctively touched the ring finger of her left hand with her left thumb for a brief moment, what interrogators would term displacement activity.

Patrick's eyebrows shot up.

"Yeah, I know. How does someone as young as me become a widow? Well, he was also an agent. Undercover, if that helps clear things up a little. Sorry to be so evasive. It's just not something I'm ready to talk about yet. It's too recent." Patrick nodded. An awkward silence ensued.

"Anyway, we were talking about you. Kids?" she asked him.

"One adopted. Well, we're in the process of making it official," Patrick answered without elaborating any further. His deep-set eyes turned into caves in the downlight of the bar. Like Kirsten, he also wasn't one to open up too quickly, and had developed an allergy to the American custom of grilling near strangers with personal questions. He changed the topic to the items on the blackboard menu above them and gave her a quick lesson in Japanese culinary vocabulary. As they left the *izakaya* a while later, Patrick invited her to stop off at his office at the Japan Intelligence Agency to meet Choy. Patrick had told him he'd be back at 2 p.m.

CHAPTER 21

July 28

Choy came out of his little room off Patrick's office with a cigarette between his fingers when he heard Patrick and Kirsten coming in the main entrance after their lunch. Patrick began the introductions.

"Kirsten, this is my old friend from North Korea, Jung-hee Choy. He's my cyber consultant for Olympic security. He'll deny it, but he's a genius. He once counted to infinity and then turned right around and did it backwards." They all laughed. Choy smiled at Kirsten and turned to Patrick expectantly.

"Jung-hee, this is Kirsten Beck from the FBI. She's liaising with the JIA for the Olympics."

"Jung-hee," Choy said, walking over to her with his hand extended.

"A pleasure," said Kirsten, but then her smile weakened. Choy was looking at her as if he'd seen her before.

"By any chance, are you a fan of the *Godfather* movies?" Choy asked. Patrick rolled his eyes and groaned.

"I've heard of them, but they were a little before my time," Kirsten replied.

"They're *timeless*!" Choy said with mock indignation. "The reason I ask is that you look a lot like Sofia Coppola when she starred in *Lost in Translation*. She's Francis Ford Coppola's daughter and played Michael Corleone's daughter in *Godfather Part III*. Lousy movie, but she's got a great face. Like you."

"Well, thanks," Kirsten said with an embarrassed smile. "I'll try not to make any lousy movies of my own."

They all laughed and went into Choy's little back office. Choy lit another cigarette from the one he'd been smoking as if passing a baton in a relay race and sat down in front of his computer. Kirsten batted the smoke from her face. Seeing her consternation, Patrick said to Choy, "Those things are slow-motion suicide, you know. They're going to take ten years off your life."

"Maybe so, but they're the worst ten years," Choy said absently. As he clicked on the documents he'd been looking at, he mumbled offhandedly, "I quit smoking once. It was the most horrible four hours of my life."

While Choy was cueing up the documents on screen, Patrick turned to Kirsten, who had taken a step away from the cigarette smoke. "Junghee thinks the attacks might have something to do with Bureau 39."

"Remind me what Bureau 39 is," Kirsten said.

"It's the criminal wing of the former North Korean regime. Not that the whole country wasn't one big organized crime syndicate. Bureau 39, though, went above and beyond. 'Diabolical' doesn't come close."

Choy spoke. "I posed as the person in 39 who got congratulated for the Budokan attack and sent a return email to the original sender, thanking them for it. It had the backdoor virus I wrote embedded in it."

"So who is it?" Patrick asked.

"I can't tell."

"But I thought you said that once they opened the email, the backdoor virus would infect their system and you'd be able to get in."

"It looks like they didn't actually open the one I sent. They just sent a new email to the person at Bureau 39 with a fragment of code in it."

"You opened it? How do you know they're not trying to infect *you*?"

"What alternative did I have?"

"I suppose you're right. So what about this fragment of code? I assume you mean computer code."

"Right. There's no way of knowing what it means. Unless…" Choy looked at Kirsten. "Patrick said you're in the FBI?"

"Right."

"You might be able to help me figure this out."

"Me? How?"

"The FBI has a system called Naris 3.0, does it not?" said Choy.

Kirsten's face fell. "How on earth would you know about that?" she said in a tone that was almost aggressive.

"It's what I do, Kirsten. May I call you 'Kirsten'?"

Kirsten nodded. "Please answer my question. How did you know about Naris 3.0?"

"'Don't ask me about my business, Kay,'" Choy said with a chuckle, using the *Godfather* quote to try to defuse the sudden tension. It didn't work. She glared at him with her arms folded.

"Alright, how about letting me into the loop, you two? What's Naris 3.0?" said Patrick.

Kirsten took a long inhalation through her nose and let it out slowly. "Basically, Naris 3.0 is a data management system," she said.

"To say the least!" laughed Choy while Kirsten shot him daggers.

Choy took over the explanation as Kirsten's face hardened into stone and she tightened her arms in front of her. "The original Naris 1.0 allowed the FBI to get every email that everyone in the world has written for the past ten years. It can process zettabytes of emails, and a zettabyte is a trillion gigs. Naris is how the FBI got that guy Petraeus out at the CIA. You have to wonder what that was all about. Anyway, they store all this data, and when they're curious about someone, they've got all sorts of info on them.

"This new 3.0 version also gives them the ability to analyze fragments of code associated with email, like the strings of cookie code you sometimes see in the address bar of your computer. Not that the FBI routinely looks at all this data, but they *have* it. When they're looking at someone of interest, they just have to process the info through Naris

3.0 and pull out their metadata. What's really interesting is the program they use, which…"

Kirsten Beck smoldered. "Please stop. That's highly classified information. And you still haven't answered my question. How did you even know about it, let alone how it works?"

Choy smiled. "Actually, I *did* answer your question. It's what I do. And finding out about what the FBI is up to is what Lazarus does."

"This is like getting into some kind of alternate reality," said Patrick, flustered that he was so far out of the cyber loop. "Alright, I give up. Who or what is Lazarus?"

"Lazarus is the computer system developed by North Korea's Reconnaissance General Bureau. When I worked in Bureau 39, we used Lazarus for that 2014 attack on the Sony Hollywood studio," Choy said.

Kirsten Beck shook her head. "You are good," she said. "Okay, you have all this inside information, so why do you need me?"

"I need you to access Naris 3.0 for me," Choy replied as if the answer was obvious. He pointed to the line of code on his computer screen.

qd7wr-6669re34+57sto+49rat737+ion082638##sg

"Hey look, there's the word 'restoration' in there," said Patrick.

"That's right," said Choy. "It looks pretty encrypted except for that word, right? But the problem is, it doesn't have any of the fingerprints of the encryption systems we used at Bureau 39. I think it's just the digital remains of something bigger. I need to see if I can take it to the next level, and that's where Naris 3.0 comes in."

Kirsten still had her arms folded in front of her and a look of resistance on her face. She didn't move.

Patrick spoke in a voice that was low and stern. "Kirsten, I'm hoping to adopt a North Korean orphan who may or may not make it. That's how malnourished he was. And it was all because of Bureau 39 and people like them. That's who we're dealing with here."

Kirsten looked him in the eye as he spoke, then broke eye contact, sighed, and waved Choy off of his seat in front of the computer. "Both of you turn away from the screen, please," she said, and Patrick and Choy turned their backs to her.

A minute of typing and clicking later, Kirsten had them turn around.

"This fragment of code leads to a Tokyo craigslist ad for a used wedding gown," she said.

"What? Who the hell is going to want a used wedding gown, especially in Japan?" Patrick said. "No one here would even think of buying something like that secondhand."

Choy had an impish smile on his face. "And no one goes on craigslist anymore, not since they got rid of the personals. It's a great place to send the code. But you're right," he said, "the only person who would go to an ad like this is someone who was looking for it and knows about pixel embedding. Kirsten, may I sit down again, please?"

Kirsten stood and Choy took her place in front of the computer. He opened a program on his desktop and copied and pasted the image of the wedding gown onto a template. Immediately, two Korean *hangul* characters appeared on the screen. One read "sky" and the other read "heart."

"'Sky Heart.' Isn't that a toy?" asked Kirsten. Her manner had softened slightly but her arms were still crossed in front of her. "My little niece was playing with something called Sky Heart back in Honolulu."

"I doubt anyone's going to be emailing Bureau 39 about toys," Choy said. He looked out the window absently and thought for a minute. Patrick and Kirsten said nothing. After a minute, with his eyes shifting back and forth at some unseen object, Choy spoke again.

"I'm thinking the best thing might be for me to pose as the person who sent the Sky Heart email. I can cover my tracks using a virtual private network I created. Then I could send the recipient at Bureau 39 another embedded message along with a new backdoor virus I wrote and see if they'll reply directly to me. It's kind of a desperation move that might blow my cover if they get suspicious, but we don't know when the next attack will be. If we get lucky, they'll inadvertently give me some clues as to who sent the 'Sky Heart' thing."

"I agree," said Patrick. "At this point we've got to try all the angles. Who knows, maybe like you say, whoever this is at 39 will give up some useful information without realizing it."

Choy opened the program he had used to decode the original pixel-embedded message. He then typed an email and embedded something in the pixels of the same craigslist image of the used wedding gown, along with the new backdoor virus he had written. He pressed Send. "Now we wait to see if they take the bait," he said.

"What did you tell them?" Patrick asked.

"I embedded the Korean characters for 'heart' and 'sky.' Just a reversal of the original they got from the person on the other end, but I'm guessing they'll be puzzled enough to open it to find out why it's reversed."

The three of them sat staring silently at the computer with their arms folded. After half an hour, Choy said, "No sense the two of you waiting around here. I'll let you know if anything comes in."

Patrick and Kirsten agreed and left Choy alone in his office. After they left, Choy opened the .gif file of his dead wife and child and put his hand on the screen. "*Igeon neol-wihangeoya*," he said to them. "This is for you."

CHAPTER 22

That same day

Kirsten returned to her office at the American embassy and decided to lay down for a nap on a small couch that looked designed for a child. Her head ached from the lunchtime sake as well as from culture shock that seemed to be getting worse by the day. Even the miniature couch seemed as if from a dreamlike parallel universe where things were just a touch too bizarre for reality. The miniaturization of so many things in Japan, Patrick had told her, was part of a phenomenon called *kawaii*, or cuteness for its own sake. On their walk back from the *izakaya*, they had seen gaggles of high school girls dressed all alike in short, pink skirts and carrying plush backpacks out of which poked the heads of oversized teddy bears. At one point, she found herself face-to-face with Minnie Mouse as another girl pulled a small piece of rolling luggage from which a plastic applique of the cartoon character grinned vapidly. Further on, two prepubescent girls sported white frilly dresses and carried parasols, which Patrick told her was the latest in what was known as Lolita fashion. *How do their parents even let them out of the house dressed like that?* Kirsten thought, especially when she noticed a pair of obviously tipsy middle-aged "salarymen" ogling the girls. There was much about Japan that she had taken an instant liking to, but this cuteness thing was not one of them.

When she woke from her nap an hour later, she went over to her desk and decided to have a look at some of the documents that had been coming in regarding the situation in North Korea. One of them in particular piqued her interest: a graph of the economic health of the country before and after the Rising Tide revolution. It illustrated the reason for the fears of a massive refugee crisis. The economy had actually been performing slightly better during the Kim regime, although an inordinate amount of the food supply had been making its way to the army and the black market rather than to the starving masses. Still, it pointed to a Rising Tide regime in crisis, one that had promised far-reaching improvements before the overthrow but that was simply not delivering once it assumed power. A huge factor was that China had cut off all aid to the country the day after the overthrow, and this had included oil subsidies that had powered the factories. But the fact remained that in terms of agricultural productivity and bringing food to the table, the Rising Tide Party was woefully inefficient to say the least. As Kirsten was taking notes, she heard a knock on the half-open door.

"Come in," she said.

In walked Harmon Phibbs. The hot, humid weather added a sheen to his pulpy complexion that looked like plastic that had exploded in a microwave.

"Just checking to see how you're doing here in sashimi-land," he said with a probing smile. He was already closing the door behind him when Kirsten held out her hand and said, "I like to keep it open."

"Oh, sure, no problem," he said. He came into the room and helped himself to a seat in front of her desk. "So. How do you like this country so far? Kind of like 'Goodbye America, Hello Kitty,' right?"

Kirsten started to answer, but Phibbs was just getting warmed up. "I been here like five years and can't seem to get a rotation out of it. I guess Langley really wants me here. I'd love to have my last assignment before I retire be someplace like Costa Rica where they appreciate the U.S. of A. and don't go around stabbing us in the back like this country does. Or maybe Scotland, but that's probably because I've spent so much time drinking the place. Hey, you ever wonder why you never see any American cars in the streets here? It's 'cause they have these humongous tariffs on anything from our country. American beef? Forget it, they got this thing where they say that Japanese intestines can't digest it, therefore it can't be imported. Then they've got the whole guilt trip they try and lay on us for Hiroshima and Nagasaki, which was the only thing that would have ended WWII. Plus, it's not like they were sitting around singing 'Kumbaya' in Esperanto during the war. Ever hear of the Rape of Nanking? There were these two lieutenants in the Imperial Army who competed with swords for the number of beheadings they committed, and the newspapers reported it every day like they were McGwire and Sosa. Don't suppose you remember those two, do you? Baseball sluggers?" Kirsten shook her head, too aghast to say anything. Phibbs shrugged. "On the plus side, they don't have all the nonsense we have with the diversity thing, mainly because they only have one race."

"I'm part Arab," Kirsten said with a weak smile.

"Whoops." To change the subject, Phibbs reached over and picked up one of the files Kirsten had been reading. Kirsten looked at him with her mouth half open in astonishment, too shocked at his serial boorishness to say anything.

"I see you've gotten the latest data on the situation in Norkland," he said. "Hard to believe, isn't it?"

"Yes, it is," she said guardedly.

"Actually, I think I may have an inside track on where this is all going," Phibbs said with a look of I-know-something-you-don't-know. "I know you're an analyst and psych profiler for the Feeb, so you might find this of interest. I met a guy from the Chinese embassy the other night at a bar I go to in Roppongi. Nice guy, down to earth. Likes his booze. Maybe too much. Anyway, he was being coy about it, but the gist of what he was inferring was that there might be more to China's interest in North Korea than meets the eye."

"You mean more than fortune cookies and Hu Flung Dung?" Kirsten said. Phibbs chuckled and looked down in amused embarrassment.

"Yeah, I know, I sometimes let loose with some stupid stuff," Kirsten was nodding, "but I've got a pretty good track record when it comes to getting juicy inside dope. You know how in movies there's the big boss, and then there's the guy who actually gets things done in the background but doesn't get credit? I'm that guy. My second language training was in Chinese, by the way, I'm nowhere close to fluent, I'm the first to admit it. To my ears, it's always sounded like sound effects for a kung fu movie, but I can read it pretty good. Anyway, I was talking to this guy, Chen was his name, and we got to discussing communism and capitalism. He kept saying that capitalism is done for because the work ethic in the West is gone and that's the only thing that keeps capitalism going. He said once we run out of people willing to haul butt and make a lot of money at the top end of the salary scale, there's not going to be any wealth to trickle down. I had to agree with him. Everyone in the U.S. is looking for instant gratification, especially these snowflakes in college who go off to Europe on their junior year abroad and see places like Germany where the government pays for their education and gives them a stipend, but that's only because we're paying for their defense. At the end of four years, the kids are commies and the parents are bankrupt.

"You seem pretty smart and savvy, so you probably understand something that a lot of people don't realize, and that's that there's no one more practical on the face of the earth than the Chinese. I told that to Chen, and he was all flattered that I understood that fact, but I was, pardon my French, bullshitting him to get him to open up, so I went on to say that the Chinese are so practical that none of them could possibly believe in communism, which is as impractical a system as is possible. You follow where I'm going with this?"

Kirsten shrugged. "Not really, but what else did he say?"

"He kind of agreed with me without coming out and saying it, but he did say that everyone in the Zhongnanhai—that's their Politburo…"

"I know."

"Everyone in their Zhongnanhai believes in the whole China as Middle Kingdom thing, but not in the sense of 'between two other kingdoms' or something. They see it as China as the center of the universe. Chen said that his country needs communism in order to keep 1.2 billion people in order. That's the whole reason for it, not any kind of belief in the ideology. To my mind, communism and fascism are two suits in the same closet."

"So what did he say about North Korea?"

"He said…man, he was getting wasted…he said that there's a lot more to this China Solution than anyone thinks. I bought him another drink and asked what he meant, but the guy got this distant look and then fell asleep right there on the bar. Anyway, I thought I'd pass that on to you for your analysis. It looks like China has something up its sleeve. I'll see if the guy shows at the bar tonight, and maybe I can pin him down. I'll let you know if I find out anything else."

"I appreciate it, Mister Phibbs."

"Harmon. Call me Harmon. Maybe we could have a drink sometime? Kirsten?"

Kirsten smiled queasily. *How about when hell freezes over? Harmon?* she thought.

She saw him to the door and thanked him for dropping by. She closed the door behind him.

CHAPTER 23

TOYAMA STORAGE
July 27

A grim-faced Mr. Lee returned to the corpse hotel. His heart had sunk when he learned earlier in the day that the second wave of attackers had been caught up in the dragnet that the JIA had established throughout the country. Hundreds of people of Korean ancestry who were even remotely suspected of having ties to Chosun Restoration had been quietly arrested, among them Mr. Lee's reinforcements. Further, Prime Minister Adegawa had just issued a statement that Japan would stand firm in the face of terrorism and that the Games would continue. As Mr. Lee entered the building, Pung immediately summoned the Bong Boys, who hurried downstairs to the viewing room. Once they had come to attention, Lee began.

"I have the unfortunate duty to inform you that your reinforcements have been arrested. It is now all up to you."

The Bong Boys stared at him with shock in their eyes. *That means there's only three of us left!* they thought in unison. Lee continued.

"But as I said after we suffered our first casualties at the Self-Defense Force headquarters, we are united in our desire to restore our glorious Kim family to the seat of power, and thus, although our numbers are small, if we think as one, we shall prevail. Make no mistake: there is nothing easy about reclaiming one's rights, especially when the whole world sees our country as backward and insignificant. But, believe me, when we are finished, the whole world will know that the DPRK is a great nation thanks to courageous young men like you who are willing to sacrifice everything for the cause of justice."

At the words "sacrifice everything," the three young men shifted on their feet. The great battle for which they had been recruited was now not so much one of glory but rather one that could well end their lives. It was too late to back out now, that much was certain, so the only option left was to continue to follow Mr. Lee and trust that his leadership would see their efforts to a triumphant conclusion.

"It seems that our message has not yet penetrated," Lee continued in an acid tone, referring to the Prime Minister's official statement that the Olympics would continue. "Therefore, we will be moving to the next phase of our mission." Lee turned to Mr. Pung, who spread out a map of Tokyo on the large dining table where they had enjoyed their ortolan feast. Lee proceeded to outline in minute detail the next attack which would usher in Phase Three of their mission: attacks on infrastructure. After his presentation, he looked up at the young men. "Hahn Doo-won, step forward."

The lad's eyebrows shot up like circumflexes. He had not expected to be charged with a mission of the magnitude that Mr. Lee had just described. Mr. Lee looked deeply into his doe-like eyes.

Like all of Mr. Lee's squad of North Korean rich kids, Hahn Doo-won took his nickname from a member of a South Korean boy band—in his case, "Dreamboy." The name was fitting, since he was of a wistful, introspective nature who enjoyed reading and art and wrote original poetry, most of it love poems to one of his many crushes. What he could never let on to anyone, though, was that all of his crushes were fellow students. Male students. Although homosexuality is not addressed in the North Korean criminal code, it is regarded as decadent and "against the socialist lifestyle," with a number of gay couples having been executed during the Kim years.

Dreamboy had actually been looking forward to his ten years of mandatory military service starting at age twenty, since he saw it as a chance to rub shoulders (at the very least) with fellow conscripts, some of whom, by the intransigent laws of human nature, had to have sexual urges like his own. With the downfall of Kim Jong-un, though, those dreams perished along with his privileged Pyonghattan lifestyle.

Now, living with Casanova and Tyson, he struggled mightily to tamp down his feelings, especially for Tyson, the tough guy of the trio. Dreamboy sometimes caught himself staring with his mouth open at the older boy, admiring his studly physique and aura of danger, especially after Tyson's role in the Novichok attack. One time, when Tyson turned quickly and caught him gawking, Dreamboy saved himself by pointing to Tyson's nose and telling him he had a large snot hanging precariously, and when Tyson rubbed his nose, Dreamboy said, "Got it," with an air of having saved Tyson from a grave social faux pas.

Now he was face-to-face with Mr. Lee, who was obviously fully aware of his secret.

"You know why I have chosen you, yes?" Lee said with his head tilted down and his eyes looking up at the lad. He handed Dreamboy a glossy color photo of a smolderingly handsome man in his mid-thirties with chestnut hair and cobalt-blue eyes.

Dreamboy gulped and nodded. "I reaffirm my commitment to Chosun Restoration!" he fairly shouted, his heart beating wildly against his ribcage.

Mr. Lee made an about-face and exited Toyama Storage, and Pung dismissed Tyson and Casanova. He then met with Dreamboy, outlining the logistics of his mission. Dreamboy took the photo of the handsome man with him to his room. He would study it, he told Pung, who sneered in disgust and walked quickly away.

CHAPTER 24

July 28

After Chosun Restoration had issued its demands several days earlier, nothing more was heard from the group, and everyone involved in Olympic security was cautiously hopeful that the group's demands would not be backed up by further attacks, especially after the JIA had been given extraordinary and sweeping powers in an effort to root out the group. Anyone suspected of having ties to Chosun Restoration was being held without charge for the legal limit of twenty-three days, which would go well beyond the duration of the Games. So far hundreds of people of Korean descent, including Mr. Lee's contingent of ninety-four reinforcements, would be spending the Olympics being interrogated under harsh conditions. The draconian measures appeared to be working.

With the pressure somewhat off halfway through the track-and-field events, Patrick and Kirsten made plans to meet again for lunch after their respective morning meetings. Patrick's daily calendar was free for an hour or so before he was scheduled to meet Kirsten, and as he sat at his desk thumbing through paperwork with the outline of the Olympic stadium in the distance, he suddenly bolted upright in his chair. He had completely forgotten to call Yumi. He immediately picked up his office phone and was relieved when she answered on the first ring. They spoke for five minutes, mostly about Dae-ho's condition, and he signed off by telling her how much he loved her and how much he missed her and the boy.

He sighed in reassurance when he hung up. But then he felt butter-flies in his stomach and realized why: he was a bit too eager to meet Kirsten for lunch.

Idiot, what are you thinking? You and Yumi are making such good progress together, don't jeopardize it, for God's sake!

Lighten up, it's just lunch! I'm not going to do anything stupid, okay?

For her part, Kirsten's mind wandered during her morning meeting with the JIA bigwigs. They were conducting the meeting in Japanese with only an occasional translation for her from young Minoru Kaga. As she sat nodding at them without comprehension, her mind went back as it always did when she wasn't occupied to the man she had married and divorced, the man she still found herself calling her husband. She and Landon had been in the same FBI Academy graduating class, and while she went into intelligence analysis with an assignment in Hawaii, Landon's risk-taking nature and dislike of a regular schedule had led him to surveillance and a posting in Southern California, although they alternated visiting each other every month. His half-Puerto Rican lin-eage had given him a smoldering sex appeal and fluency in Spanish, and his first undercover assignments were as a midlevel coke dealer to low-er-level gangs in the Boyle Heights section of Los Angeles. He thrived on the thrill that filled his days, to the point that Kirsten had to wonder if she had made a mistake in at least not waiting a while longer before accepting his marriage proposal.

After her misgivings grew into suspicions, and she hired a Honolulu private investigator to keep an eye on him during one of his monthly visits. Sure enough, his risk-taking personality type had taken him into the beds of at least four other women that he admitted to when she con-fronted him with the evidence. Less than half a year after they had com-mitted to each other for life, they stood in awkward silence outside the office of a lawyer she had hired to take care of the formalities. Even as he was about to sign the papers ending their marriage, he told her tear-fully that he had made "a" mistake that would never happen again. The lawyer cleared her throat, urging them to get it over with, and although Kirsten might have forgiven him had it really been "a" mistake, four mistakes constituted a deal breaker. Still, aside from his incorrigible weakness for women, she knew he was a decent sort at heart, and she grieved for what might have been between them. He would have made a wonderful father, although a terrible role model had they had sons.

Anyone observing her face during the JIA meeting would have noticed a gradual look of muted agony creeping into her eyes. She was recalling the day when her immediate supervisor, Ronan Coyle, had broken the news that Landon had been outed by unknown people while undercover as a member of a San Bernardino motorcycle gang that had entered into a business arrangement with a Mexican drug cartel. She remembered knowing as soon as Ronan had come on the line that Landon was dead. She didn't ask for details of his murder, and Coyle was not forthcoming with any. They both knew what had happened to Kiki Camarena of the DEA when he was outed back in 1985, and the cartels had become even more sadistically violent in the intervening years.

After a morning of morbid thoughts during a meeting she could not understand, Kirsten found that her step was nothing short of springy as she left the meeting room and began walking to her upcoming lunch with Patrick. She told herself that her eagerness was a function of wanting to pass on to him the information that Phibbs had given her. Now that she was sufficiently oriented to the area around the embassy, she had told Patrick that she felt comfortable finding her own way to the soba restaurant where they would meet. Five minutes later, she saw him waiting outside, smiling and waving.

"This place has AC," he said.

"Oh good, I wasn't looking forward to a muggy lunch. Shall we go in?"

They walked to a table that the owner's wife led them to. She apologized to Patrick that they were extra busy today but gave them cups of water. Patrick told her there was no rush. After she had left, he turned to Kirsten. She was grinning.

"You'll never guess who I was talking to," she said. Patrick shook his head.

"Harmon Phibbs," she said with a chuckle.

"Harmon, is it? On a first name basis already?" Patrick teased.

"In his dreams."

Patrick laughed.

"He's a classic. The whole time he was in my office, he was bad-mouthing everything about this country. I'll definitely be keeping him at arm's length. How did he ever make senior case officer? He must have a rabbi in the Agency."

"Oh, I'm sure he's got the goods on someone high up in the Agency, an affair or something, otherwise he'd have been posted to Djibouti ten years ago. Definitely a strange bird. Divorced, no surprise. But like I said last time, he's got a real knack for turning people. Apparently, he has some kind of raw genuineness that makes turncoats trust him a lot more than our usual spooks, especially when he's drinking, which is every night. According to Hooper, he was a disaster at the CIA Farm when it came to tradecraft like shaking surveillance and making brush contacts. But he was top of his class in MICE, which I'm sure you know all about."

Kirsten nodded. "'Money, ideology, compromise, ego.' The main motivators for someone to turn."

"Right. But in Phibbs's case, believe it or not, there was also something that spooks found charming, for lack of a better term. I know, sounds ridiculous, right? But he once turned someone who was actually surveilling him just by going up to the guy and offering to buy him a drink. The guy was so taken aback that he accepted, and from there he became one of Phibbs's Agency conquests."

"And here I pictured him trawling the dark underbelly of the spy world."

"Oh, he does that too. There was another guy he found out had a weakness for junior high school girls, and he was prepared to turn him in to the cops for the images he had stored on his phone. Phibbs had gotten a friend of his in the No Such Agency to hack the phone. The perv was more than willing to accept a drink from Phibbs to find out what else he knew. I guess we have to give the devil his due. I wouldn't take him up on that offer of lunch, though."

"Believe me, there's no danger of that."

"Actually, I think he still holds the Rising Tide thing against me," Patrick said. "'Spooky kabuki,' he calls it. But it's not as if I actually set out to bring down Kim Jong-un, it's just that things have a way of spiraling out of control. Most of what I did was out of self-preservation." He felt a pang of guilt as he said the words. He had just conveniently omitted the fact that his main motivation had been saving Yumi from Senghori Prison. Kirsten nodded sympathetically. He noticed for the first time the tiny flecks of gold buried in her hazel eyes.

Kirsten said, "Oh, I almost forgot. He said something interesting about China when he came to my office." The owner's wife came up and gave them their menus. The woman bowed and rushed off to another table. Patrick turned back to Kirsten and found himself studying her eyes more intently, finding an allure in their faint spiderwork of tiny wrinkles at the corners.

"China, huh? He didn't call it 'Commie-land' I hope," Patrick asked, hoping to draw attention away from his obvious attraction. "He's used that one before."

"He came close. Plus, he didn't seem to think that I knew that the Zhongnanhai is the Chinese Politburo. He said he met a guy at some bar he goes to who works at the Chinese embassy. The guy got drunk and told him that there's more to this China Solution than just a desire to keep out North Korean refugees."

Patrick squinted. "Hm. He didn't say what?"

"Apparently his new drinking buddy passed out before he gave up anything else. Phibbs said he's going to see if the guy shows at the bar again tonight."

"Well, let's see what he finds out, if anything. I wouldn't be surprised if he made the whole thing up as an excuse to come see you. I know I would." He cursed himself at first for taking such a major step forward with that last comment, but then he felt a sense bordering on triumph when her cheeks pooled with color as she smiled and lowered her eyes to one side, classic body language for sexual attraction. She quickly recovered her sense of feminine restraint and looked more intently than was necessary at the menu.

"So what does this restaurant have?"

"Something called 'Japanese food.'"

"Very funny. Hey, by the way, I got a phrase book. What do you want for lunch?"

He studied the menu. "I think I'll have the tempura soba. How about you?"

She pointed to a picture of one of the dishes and asked him how to pronounce the Japanese words beneath it. He told her, and she lifted up her hand to get the busy woman's attention.

"Watch this," she said to Patrick. "*Sumimasen,*" she called out, and the woman rushed over. "*Tempura soba kudasai,*" Kirsten said, pointing to Patrick, "*Zaru soba kudasai,*" she said, pointing to herself.

The woman smiled indulgently and said, "*Kashikomarimashita!*" (Certainly!)

"Very impressive," Patrick said. "And your pronunciation was perfect."

She thanked him. When the woman set their bowls in front of them a few minutes later, they started right in. Noting her initially dainty approach, Patrick told her that slurping was considered a sign of appreciation.

"This is fabulous!" Kirsten said between slurps. To the owner she called out, "*Oishii desu!*" ("It's delicious!")

"*Arigato gozaimasu,*" the owner bowed and thanked her with a smile. Patrick watched the look of schoolgirlish delight on Kirsten's face and felt a warmth in his belly that had nothing to do with the hot noodles. After the meal as they made their way back to their respective offices, they made plans to meet the next day at the same place for dinner, ostensibly to talk over any information that Phibbs may have gleaned from his new Chinese booze buddy.

Patrick rationalized that since they both were required to be on call near the embassy, it made sense to have some company for at least some of their meals. And he *was* calling Yumi every day, after all. After a few days, though, still without any more sign of Chosun Restoration, he and Kirsten were having all of their meals together. Except breakfast.

After getting off the phone to Yumi one afternoon, he was wracked with guilt over the thought of her being alone at home with the boy while he was savoring his little seduction fandango with a much younger woman. The time had come to dial things back with Kirsten. That night after dinner at a new place, as he and Kirsten settled into their seats with tea, Patrick immediately steered the conversation in the direction of their need to stay vigilant. The Games were only halfway finished, he said, and there was no guarantee that all the members of Chosun Restoration had been arrested in the huge JIA dragnet. Kirsten looked at him strangely, as if he were breaking some unspoken rule of etiquette, and as Patrick was going on about how the terror group might just be keeping its powder dry for something big, Kirsten held up her hand and smiled.

"No shop talk, okay? Besides, I have a surprise for you," she said and reached into a bag on the rack behind their seats. She took out a small package.

"It's for you," she said. He opened the package and saw that it was a professionally mounted print of a selfie he had nonchalantly taken of the two of them a few days earlier. The frame was a stylized heart.

He felt his face flush. "Kirsten, I really appreciate this," he said in a serious tone, sighing. The smile on her face faded. "But I really want to emphasize that this can only be a friendship. Nothing more."

Kirsten's lips and eyes slowly tightened. "Of course. I completely understand," she said. The silence became intolerably awkward.

"Uhh, hmm," Patrick began. He sighed again. "I'm sorry if I led you to think it was anything more than…"

"Actually, you did," Kirsten said, hard fibers of grievance in her voice. "I'm not letting myself completely off the hook here, but when I saw how much you were enjoying our time together, I guess I jumped the gun. You really did put out some pretty strong signals."

"I know, and I'm sorry, Kirsten, I really am. If I were unattached, I would be…"

"Please. Don't. Let's just leave it at that." She gathered her things and stood.

"I'll see you at the embassy," she said with an unconvincingly cheery tone. Patrick stood but accepted the rebuke in penitent silence. Then he raised his hand to the bartender for a round of sake. Just as quickly, he canceled it. If what he had just told Kirsten was true, there was no telling when another attack would happen and how big it would be. The situation was too unpredictable to risk anything more than the light buzz he had going from the predinner sake mixed with a stiff shot of self-loathing. *When a man decides to make an ass of himself,* he thought, *there's very little that can stop him.* He paid the bill and left. The heart remained on the table.

CHAPTER 25

July 31

With Patrick in Tokyo for several weeks, Yumi tried to keep busy in order to quell the memories of her time as a captive in North Korea's notorious Senghori Prison. The house she shared with Patrick was simple but spacious, with several extra rooms that inevitably had filled with boxes of their possessions. One afternoon after feeding Dae-ho his lunch, getting him to take his supplements, and putting him to bed for his nap, she decided to make use of the Marie Kondo book she'd ordered online by bringing order to at least one of the extra rooms. She began arranging items into three stacks: definitely keep, maybe keep, and definitely toss. Two hours later, she felt herself fading, and she lay down on the tatami to rest her eyes. Before long she was sound asleep with fragmented images flitting through her mind.

The first image was of Pung kidnapping her off a beach in northwest Japan, and the next was of being driven to Senghori Prison. She was sent to Senghori by order of Comrade Moon after her father stole a backpack nuke from Moon, who planned to use it to instigate a coup and proclaim himself the new Great Leader of North Korea.

As she languished in the prison camp, despondently waiting in vain for Patrick, Yumi's heart plummeted to the depths of despair. In her dream she was seized by memories of the torture chamber the size of a basketball court where prisoners were trussed up like hogs, hung upside down, and lashed with a steel-tipped bullwhip, with Bastard Cho, the head guard, presiding. Once, she watched as the lifeless body of one young man was dragged from the torture room by his fellow prisoners. She asked someone she had befriended what had happened to him.

"Suffocation," one of them whispered.

"Strangled?" Yumi whispered back, knowing that suffocation was a euphemism for garroting.

"No," came the reply. "He screamed to death."

Her dream was haunted by an image of herself lying night after night on a thin, rotting mattress, consumed by the scraped-out pain of abandonment and thinking, *Patrick, where are you? I feel so alone. So alone, so alone, so alone...*

Even now, almost four years after her imprisonment, the nightmarish images and sensations woke her several times a week. One of the most frequent of them, and the one that consumed her now, was of being repeatedly gang raped by the guards. After she returned to Japan, she was told that she would probably never be able to bear children as a result. As she descended deeper into the hell of that memory, she awoke with a muffled scream in her throat, the fragments of her disjointed dream falling apart like pieces of a broken kaleidoscope. But then she sensed that something was wrong in the house, and she jumped up from the tatami floor and ran to Dae-ho's room. His breathing was labored and wheezing, and he had a look of panic on his face as he turned to her. She gathered him up, raced to Patrick's truck, and drove as fast as she could to Kamakura General Hospital.

Patrick's phone rang. Yumi was calling, and she hated talking on the phone.

"I'm at the hospital. It's Dae-ho," she said in a frantic voice as soon as Patrick answered. "His breathing suddenly got all wheezy."

"I'm on my way," Patrick said.

On the way down to Kamakura from Tokyo, Patrick pulled his motorcycle over and called Yumi. The doctor had released Dae-ho, and they were now at home. Half an hour later, he pulled his Harley up to his house. When he went inside, Yumi was holding a sleeping Dae-ho.

She looked emotionally and physically exhausted, and Patrick was overwhelmed anew with guilt from his close call with Kirsten Beck. On the ride down from Tokyo, he recalled something he had read in a college philosophy class where Plato claimed that human shame arises solely from the threat of being discovered. He didn't believe it. He knew he would feel shame about his behavior even if no one ever found out.

"The doctor gave him an antihistamine for his breathing, and it made him drowsy," Yumi said. "He did a thorough exam and said that Dae-ho's breathing would be okay. It was probably from the awful humidity along with malnutrition."

She smiled, and her eyes began to tear. "I'm so, so glad that you're here," she said, barely controlling the sob she felt forming behind her eyes. Dae-ho woke up in her arms and as always, held out his hand for Patrick. Patrick smiled, placed his fingers into his hand, and stayed with him until he fell back asleep. He carried him to his room and lay him down on his futon.

"You need to go back to Tokyo for your job, Patrick, you'll get in trouble if you're not there."

"It's alright, I told them I needed to check up on the sailing preliminaries this evening at Enoshima Yacht Harbor down the road. God, I missed you so much."

Then it was his and Yumi's private time together. Their intimacy was that of two hearts, souls, and bodies that became absolutely one, neither of them knowing where one began and the other left off. They then lay in each other's arms for a late afternoon of indescribable bliss that went beyond mere happiness. It was like being in the midst of the place where all phenomena issue out of the universe, and he knew he would never feel this way with anyone else. But after an hour, he awoke with a start and found himself immersed in dread, as if waiting for the proverbial other shoe to drop. He rose and kissed them both. Then he was back on the road.

But instead of returning immediately to Tokyo, Patrick made a snap decision and turned his motorcycle down a familiar road. Another secret he had buried deep inside had become intolerable to carry anymore. There was only one person he could ever talk to in this kind of situation.

"You're back so soon," Yasuhara Roshi said when Patrick knocked on the door of Eiwa-ji Temple. The roshi's voice became wary when he saw the look in Patrick's eyes.

"I want to kill them all," Patrick said in a scary voice, as he stood in the doorway of the temple with unblinking eyes.

"Come in," Yasuhara Roshi said. He had seen Patrick like this before. Once they were seated in the teacher's study, he asked Patrick who exactly he wanted to kill.

"Everyone who made that system in North Korea possible. Everyone who had a hand in kids like Dae-ho dying from malnutrition. And not just them. Everyone who's ever hurt a kid. The people who abused the orphans at Yukinoshita Orphanage. I want them dead."

"And the one who accidentally shot a young boy in Serbia?"

Patrick's chin went to his chest. His teacher had seen right through him. "Yes. Him too."

"But he deserves to live, I think. I also think he needs to stop carrying around the children who are dead and do something about the children who are living. Which he is doing."

Patrick didn't look up. The roshi continued.

"You asked about killing before. I told you it was sometimes justified in self-defense or to prevent a worse evil than the killing itself."

"But what about killing out of vengeance?" Patrick asked. "And what if someone commits an even worse evil than he's avenging?" His shouted words echoed through the temple. For the first time to anyone, Patrick then unburdened himself of a deed he had committed in North Korea after the fall of Kim Jong-un, when he and Yumi were working at the children's shelter near the DMZ....

In their first days at the shelter Yumi mentioned a rumor that the commandant of Senghori Prison, a sadistic thug known to the prisoners as the Rat Catcher after his practice of depriving them of their only source of protein, was still living alone in the prison. He had executed scores of prisoners on the flimsiest of pretexts, including an eleven-year-old girl whom he shot in the head for attempting to escape. As Yumi told him of the girl, Patrick felt a familiar rumbling in a dark part of his heart. After lunch that day he picked up an axe and told her he was going into the forest for firewood. But as soon as he rounded the corner leading away from the shelter, he made a beeline for the prison four miles away.

Senghori is an enormous compound and appeared to be deserted when he got there, but he wanted to make sure there were no guards still holed up inside after the overthrow. He moved stealthily among the shabbily maintained wooden barracks where the prisoners had been held and saw the one where Yumi had been imprisoned for months. He went up to it and laid a hand on it, as if conjuring the evil that had been perpetrated upon those held there for so long. If he ever encountered any of those guards, he would direct that evil back upon them.

He moved on to what he remembered as the "interrogation" building and stood transfixed. He was smelling once again the appalling stench that had hovered like a toxic cloud over this building back when he was captured. His gut contracted involuntarily, bringing up a throat-searing surge of bile and acid. He remembered being dragged into the building from the barbed wire fence he had cut in order to gain access to where Yumi was being held.

One of the guards, nicknamed Bastard Cho by the prisoners, wielded a wooden club, and Patrick felt again the repeated jabs to his ribs as they dragged him to the building he now stood in front of, where the stench of death and disinfectant competed for dominance, with death the hands-down winner. They then bound him hand and foot with barbed wire to a thick wooden pillar the size of a small tree. And he heard as if today the metal cleats on the Rat Catcher's heels tap-tapping a slow tattoo on the rough-hewn porch planks before he landed an uppercut on Patrick's chin where a guard's rifle butt had opened up a gaping wound.

As he stood outside the torture building all these weeks later, Patrick was secretly hoping that the rumors were true: that the Rat Catcher who ordered these and other atrocities had indeed survived. Because if he had, Patrick had the perfect sendoff for him from the evil karma he had created in this life. That what he was contemplating doing was evil in its own right never crossed his mind, so unslakeable was his thirst for revenge. Revenge for Yumi, revenge for himself, and maybe most of all, revenge for the children who had been murdered at the Rat Catcher's hands.

He drifted slowly through the camp with the axe on his shoulder, not attempting to muffle his footfalls, and hoping that they might flush a certain someone out of wherever he was, if indeed he was still in the camp. As he walked, Patrick heard a churring sound coming from the direction of several large glass jars of honey next to an active hive. The flowers in the area were in full bloom, and the bees looked as though they had been well looked after. He picked up one of the jars and continued walking, sipping the cloying nectar as he rounded the main administration building. The honey was a pleasant change from the steady diet of rice, kimchee, and bits of pork everyone had been living on at the shelter. Then he stopped in his tracks. On the side of one of the buildings was a large portable wire pen holding at least fifty rats. They looked ravenous and screeched in fear as he approached. He dripped some of the honey into the pen and the rats were all over each other trying to lap up every precious drop that hung from the wires.

A moment later Patrick heard what sounded like a shower running in a barracks-like structure fifty feet away. As he got closer to the barracks, he began to make out the sound of humming. Whoever it was seemed to be enjoying his shower. Patrick racked his brains to remember the sound of the Rat Catcher's voice, but no doubt owing to the shock of his last encounter with him, couldn't even recall if the commandant's voice had been high or low in pitch. He slowly and deliberately ascended the wooden steps of the barracks, allowing the heels of his boots to scrape along the planks of the porch. He tried the door. It was locked. The humming stopped. After another moment the shower was turned off.

"Who's there?" a voice called out authoritatively in Korean. The voice of someone in charge. Then it came to Patrick: the Rat Catcher's voice had been a high baritone that he jammed down into his larynx for an extra layer of resonance, like an adolescent trying to impress a date. *But there is only one date awaiting this son of a bitch*, thought Patrick: *a long overdue date with destiny.* After the Rat Catcher called out again, louder this time, Patrick swung his axe several times into the door and kicked it open. A rifle was propped against the opposite wall.

"Who's there, dammit?" the now-terrified voice called out. Patrick answered back with a voice uninflected with emotion. "*Jiog*," he said. "Hell." He could hear the Rat Catcher moving quickly, so he kicked in the partially open bathroom door and saw the bag-of-bones sadist who had inspired so much fear in the prisoners cowering in the corner of the shower stall, trying frantically to get his pants on and no doubt regretting the fact that he had left his rifle so far from the shower. Patrick aimed it at him.

"No!" the Rat Catcher called out.

"That's right," Patrick said with an otherworldly smile. A bullet would be too easy. He was a firm believer in karma, and the Rat Catcher's payback should and would be hellish. Patrick welcomed the prospect of being the Angel of Death, not realizing, in the heat of vengeance, that he himself was about to go over to the dark side. He set down the rifle and picked up the axe again.

He ordered the former superintendent out of the barracks and told him to take off the trousers that were half on, half off. The man quickly complied, apparently thinking that he would be shown mercy if he did as he was ordered. Wrong. Gesturing with the axe, Patrick ordered him over to the nearby interrogation room, where Patrick and thousands of others had been tortured.

Once inside, Patrick tied the Rat Catcher to the same pole where he himself had almost been murdered. His heart beating wildly at the imminent prospect of retribution, Patrick felt as though he had been taken over by an unnatural force that impelled him to his next act. He went outside to the wire pen where the rats were kept and carried it back inside. The rats screeched even louder when they saw their nemesis. Patrick flung down the axe and poured the contents of the honey jar all over the Rat Catcher, whose eyes went wide with terror as he realized what was about to happen. Patrick then recited the words that Yumi had told him the Rat Catcher delivered before the many executions he had ordered: "Traitors who betray their nation and its people will meet the same fate." Then he opened the wire pen and left the building, walking back to the makeshift orphanage and humming the "Dies irae" from Mozart's "Requiem." It wasn't until he was about a half mile down the road that the screams came to a halt.

When he got back to the orphanage, Patrick said not a word about what had happened, but slowly a rumor began to circulate about how the Rat Catcher had been eaten alive by rats and that a foreign-looking man with graying hair on one side of his head had been seen walking from the prison, ignoring the screams of the person inside.

As Patrick was relating his story, Yasuhara Roshi had been leaning closer and closer in. When Patrick finished, he blew out his cheeks, sat back in his chair, and looked out the window at the night sky for a long moment. Then he looked back at Patrick.

"I don't think I've ever heard anything like that."

Patrick hung his head in shame. His teacher continued.

"I'm not going to sit in judgement of you. I don't know what it was like for you and Yumi at that prison. But people have two natures, Patrick. One inclines to do good things and the other inclines to do bad things. Sometimes *very* bad things. But no matter how bad a person appears to be, that other side almost never dies. It just lies dormant, waiting to wake up."

"Are you talking about him or me?"

"Both. Everyone. I'll tell you this: If we take a person's life, we take his future, his potential, away from him. And also from the world. We never know when someone will change and realize their mistakes and do wonderful things for others, but if we take their lives away, we take away that possibility." He paused and held Patrick's eyes.

"Now. There are also people whose karma is such that nothing will change them for the better in this life. And sometimes it becomes necessary to send such people into their next life before they can destroy others." He cocked his head to one side. "But maybe not so dramatically," he said in a low voice as he poured them tea from the pump thermos on the low table.

"You once wanted to become a monk, and I told you no. You were very upset. Do you remember?"

"Yes. Of course I remember."

Yasuhara Roshi nodded his head. "The life of a monk is not for you. But you have found your true calling with Yumi, correct?"

Patrick nodded and again felt a wash of guilt come over him. "Yes, even though I don't deserve her."

"Everyone feels that way at some time. But your duty now is to protect Yumi, the boy, and all of those people who are in danger at the Olympics." The old man began to smile. "You should be glad you're not a monk like me. All I do is meditate and lead sutra services. If I were your age, I would welcome the chance to be in your shoes." His face turned serious again.

"Now you need to go and do your duty."

He rose from the table, and Patrick rose to join him. The old Zen teacher and his favorite student embraced for several long moments. Then Patrick was on his way.

CHAPTER 26

August 1

In a typically Japanese blending of tradition and continuity, the planners of the 2021 Olympics went to great lengths to establish a tie-in to the 1964 Games by creating the Heritage Zone, where most of the events of the earlier Olympics had taken place. One reason for this was to show off the lasting beauty of the architecture from the earlier Games, as opposed to venues in other countries that often fell into decrepitude after a few years. One of the signature venues from the 1964 Games was the Yoyogi National Gymnasium, a Tokyo landmark famous for the striking design of its suspension roof. It was a natural for the image shown between programs on the NHK national broadcasting system located directly next door. The thirteen-thousand-seat gymnasium was scheduled to be used for the 2021 handball competition. But only if it stayed standing long enough.

With a twinkle in his cobalt-blue eyes and a ready smile for all he came in contact with, Lionel Moreau was what some in the town of Shibata in Niigata Prefecture called "a good *gaijin*" to distinguish him from the shady Middle Eastern characters on the edge of town who were said to traffic in stolen cars and drugs. How the Middle Easterners had even made it past Japan's draconian immigration checkpoints at every port of entry was beyond anyone, and the citizenry all had what came to be known as "the talk" with their children. It had nothing to do with the birds and bees. Rather, it was a firm admonishment that every kid heard from kindergarten age on up that they were never to walk alone and to always run to the nearest *koban* (neighborhood police box) if any of the "dark people," as the Middle Easterners were called, spoke even a single word to them.

Although Moreau had chestnut-brown hair, he was not a "dark person" in skin color. The former Catholic schoolboy had grown up in the upper-middle-class Paris suburb of Montreuil. As a journalism student at the Sorbonne, he quickly earned the nickname "Moreau le montant" or "Moreau the stud," for the number of women, young and old, he had seduced with his smooth manner and tender charms. What he kept under wraps, even in permissive France, was that he also played for the other team, and his string of male conquests was as long as that of his female ones. He was particularly attracted to the passive late-teen catamite type.

Moreau was drafted into the French army with a specialty in high explosives owing to the fact that he had earned a blasting license at age sixteen and worked for a construction company in high school, demolishing old buildings in the fourteenth arrondissement to make way for underground garages. Stationed in Kosovo as part of a UN peacekeeping force, he witnessed firsthand the carnage that had befallen the Muslims of the populace at the hands of a Serbian paramilitary group known as the Scorpions. His stomach turned at the sight of a Scorpion killing field his unit came across in the forest outside the town of Podujevo, and he wondered far into the night how the ostensibly Christian Serbs could have perpetrated such atrocities on a group of fellow human beings solely on the basis of their religious beliefs.

Upon his return to France after a year in the Balkans, Moreau became depressed by what he saw every night on the television, especially a documentary on the 1982 Sabra and Shatila massacres in Lebanon told from a viewpoint that was sympathetic to the Arabs. For the most part, though, attack after attack on Arab countries was rationalized by the talking heads, with the Islamist retaliatory attacks condemned as terrorism. In the small room he rented in Paris, Moreau cheered the underdog in these TV battles while drinking Bordeaux from the bottle and exercising his old habits of seducing any and all willing women and young men.

But after a while he grew disgusted with his life and began to read the Koran as part of a search for meaning that included quitting drinking and completely abstaining from non-*halal* food items. Sometime later he decided to formally convert to Islam, so he took the Metro to a mosque located in one of Paris's *banlieus* where the imam regularly urged the faithful to wage holy war on the infidel. Moreau's point of radicalization took place on 9/11, when he cheered in front of a TV with his fellow believers as the Twin Towers of the World Trade Center collapsed. They took particular mirth in the sight of people jumping from windows on the upper floors.

"It's your turn now!" they screamed at the TV screen over and over as they high-fived each other.

Soon thereafter Moreau joined an al-Qaeda cell that was active in the *banlieu* near the mosque and cut off all contact with his infidel family. His leader in the cell was Mohammed al-Tikriti, one of the original followers of Abu Musab al-Zarqawi, the founder of al-Qaeda in Iraq. After a rigorous vetting process to make sure he wasn't a plant of the *jahili* nonbelievers, al-Tikriti gave Moreau the fighting name of "Dergham."

"It means a tough and fearless lion with magnificent sharp teeth," explained Tikriti at Moreau's initiation. Moreau beamed with pride in front of his fellow initiates. "But you mustn't bare your teeth until you are ready to strike," al-Tikriti added. He told Moreau that he would eventually be sent undercover to various locations around the world as one of the terrorist group's "striking lions."

Caucasian converts are prized by radical Islamic groups for the ability their skin color gives them to operate freely in Europe, North America, and Asia without arousing the suspicion that Middle Easterners draw. But converts are not just tools to get past security. They are a way for the terror groups to become a global movement. For their part, many of these same converts are eager to prove their devotion to jihad by volunteering for the most dangerous assignments around the world, as Moreau did soon after his initiation.

"That will come in time," al-Tikriti assured his young convert. He could see great potential in this "Dergham," possibly even rising to be a leader who would command a cell of his own, plot strategy, and launch attacks. First, though, he would cut those magnificent sharp teeth by raising money and organizing cells in Asia, which is how he ended up in the town of Shibata, Niigata Prefecture. Despite lacking any kind of background in restaurant work, Moreau somehow wangled his way into a job at a sushi restaurant, where he bused tables and washed dishes.

What al-Tikriti couldn't see from Paris was the change taking place in Moreau's brain during his initial time in Asia as the result of a head injury he had sustained in Kosovo. A newly inducted squad mate had instinctively swung the rifle he was cleaning at a mosquito, of all things, and had caught Moreau in the side of the head, causing what seemed at first a slight concussion. But over time the injury got worse and was now manifesting itself as psychotic symptoms that began with sudden episodes of agitation and hostility.

After moving to Tokyo, Dergham Moreau took up residence at one of the local mosques without letting anyone know of his al-Qaeda affiliation. After he began talking to himself and lashing out at the other worshippers, they began to wonder if this brother was possessed by some *jinn*, or evil spirit, and they purposely began going out of their way to avoid him. Officials at the mosque were required by custom and religious tradition to continue to offer him hospitality, but everyone desperately hoped that the man would become tired of living in a country whose language he didn't understand and which was riddled with *haram*, or unclean things prohibited by Islam.

Moreau was a daily avid reader of *Milestones*, an inflammatory screed by Sayyid Qutb, an Egyptian Islamic radical who was executed in 1966 for conspiracy to assassinate the Egyptian president, Gamal Nasser. Qutb was also one of Osama bin Laden's main guiding lights, and his call for "true" Muslims to destroy anything or anyone deemed *haram* spurred Dergham to action. But he could not completely shake his own *haram* instincts, and in order to make these forbidden urges less conspicuous, he moved out of the mosque and took up informal residence at one of Tokyo's many internet cafes, not an uncommon way for people of straitened circumstances to find lodging. He then created a website from which he exhorted fellow believers to wreak apocalyptic retribution on this ungodly culture, where alcohol and pig's meat were freely consumed, and where, beneath a veneer of quiet respectability, so many vile reprobates freely indulged in shockingly repugnant vices. Meanwhile, he trawled the back streets of Shinjuku's 2- chome area for the young male pickups he favored above all others.

Meanwhile, back at the Yokohama corpse hotel, Dreamboy stared for hours at the photo he was given of the man with the cobalt-blue eyes and began to write daily poems to him. "*My heart burns with sublime incandescence,*" one poem began, and he counted the hours until they would meet. Pung had given him detailed instructions on how to establish contact.

CHAPTER 27

August 1

Choy worked best alone. It was a habit he developed as a member of the *Inmin Boanseong*, North Korean State Police. Back in 2012, he had worked with two high-ranking inspectors who were now languishing in a *kwaliso,* or concentration camp, because an underling turned them in for sharing a single beer during the official mourning period for Kim Jong-il. The two inspectors' relatively low rank kept them from the fate of Kim Jong-un's defense minister, who was strapped to the barrel of an antiaircraft gun. What was left of his body was then fed to pigs. So if nothing elsc, self-preservation dictated that Choy spend as much time alone as possible during the Kim regime. During his long hours of solitude he had elevated his cyber expertise to the equivalent of a Level 10 Google senior fellow, a prowess he put to use in siphoning off $4 billion from Bureau 39 into Patrick's offshore bank accounts before he defected.

Now, four years later, he sat in a small room adjoining Patrick's office with his hands behind his head, wondering what on earth the pixel-embedded *Sky Heart* characters could mean. And who had sent the email containing the characters? He set out to find an answer by disguising himself behind a virtual private network as the original sender and simply reversing the characters in a follow-up email. His email also included a backdoor virus embedded in the image of the characters. One click on the attachment by someone on the other end and Choy would be in the Bureau 39 recipient's system. He would then be one step closer to finding out who was communicating with the Bureau he once worked for.

He had now been waiting over a day for the person at the Bureau to be curious enough about the reversal of the two characters to open the attachment and respond. As he sat looking out the window at Hibiya Park, he let his mind wander through other strategies he might consider next. This one was looking like a bust.

Patrick called out from his front office asking if Choy wanted some of the coffee he was brewing. Choy instinctively made a face. He had tasted Patrick's coffee.

"I'm good with my tea, thanks," he called back breezily. Just then, his computer emitted a blip sound. He sat up in his chair. "Patrick…" he called out.

Patrick came into Choy's workspace and looked at his computer screen. An email had just come in from the person at Bureau 39. He had opened Choy's email with the backdoor virus. The message in the body of the email was a single word in Korean: "*Ye.*" ("Yes.")

"'Yes'?" Patrick said. "'Yes' what? You didn't ask him a yes/no question, did you?"

"I don't know what it means either, and I don't want to risk asking him. But the main thing is that I can now look around in his system. What's really interesting, though, is that his Internet Protocol number hasn't been disguised."

He typed some more, then looked at the screen. "Huh. So that's what's going on," he said under his breath.

"What? What's going on?" Patrick asked, his voice rising in excitement.

Choy pushed back from the desk and interlocked his fingers on his belly. "We've been looking in the wrong place, according to this IP number. I assumed the guy was in 39, but it looks like someone hijacked 39's system to make it look like it was coming from them. It's the reverse of what we used to do in 39, which was to invade computer systems and put the blame on China. This isn't the real Bureau 39 at all."

"Well, who the hell is it?" Patrick said, urgency in his voice.

"I'm not sure exactly. But it's pretty clear it's coming from somewhere in China."

Patrick looked at him. "So what now?"

"Now? Now I have to narrow it down to *who* in China. Only 1.3 billion possibilities. But I think I know where to start." Choy hunched closer to the screen, cutting off Patrick's view.

Patrick knew that body language. Without a word he turned and exited. Choy worked best alone.

CHAPTER 28

August 1

With the unshakeable confidence of the deranged, Dergham began arguing arcane points of the Koran on the website he created and viciously attacking anyone who voiced a contrary opinion. He also praised ISIS leader Abu Bakr al-Baqara for training the "striking lions" who had been committing attacks around the world.

Days after he created his website, Dergham was approached online by someone who described himself as a seeker from Korea. He wrote, *"I am a great admirer of your courage and depth of knowledge. I am wondering if you would consider perhaps instructing me in the ways of true Islam?"* The two made plans to meet at the internet café where Dergham was living.

At their meeting the young Korean seeker treated Dergham to tea and a bowl of instant ramen, what looked to be the man's first meal in several days. He sat in rapt attention when Dergham went on a long harangue against the United States and the developed world in general. As the afternoon progressed, Dergham's "lessons" became more and more self-righteous and hate-filled, with the Korean taking notes all the while. But what he found much more interesting was the passion in his teacher's cobalt-blue eyes.

He parroted Dergham's rantings and told him of his disgust at the licentiousness of places such as the Kabukicho red-light district, and also the Shinjuku 2-chome area, which has the world's highest concentration of gay bars. But as he spoke of this latter place, he held Dergham's eye and noticed a change come over the zealot's face. Those cobalt-blue eyes went inward, and his breathing quickened. Neither of them spoke for a long moment. With the air in their little cubicle fairly pulsating with sexuality, Dreamboy brushed his hand up against Dergham's bearded cheek. Dergham shuddered and pulled Dreamboy into an embrace that turned into a passionate kiss. Wordlessly, they left the internet café and took a taxi to Shinjuku 2-chome.

After an afternoon of impassioned lovemaking, Dreamboy and Dergham lay back in the bed of the gay-friendly love hotel they had checked into. The mirror on the ceiling had powered their libidos for the past several hours, and they now lay sprawled across the bed in blissful repose. Dreamboy lowered his voice and thanked Dergham for the most passionate time he had ever experienced, but Dergham's face was knotted with profound remorse. This was exactly as Pung had predicted. Dergham would now be fully primed to expiate his evildoing. Dreamboy thanked him for accepting him as a pupil and then whispered that he wanted to kill as many corrupt infidels as possible. "Is this allowed in true Islam," he asked.

Dergham, in full self-hating penitence, said that not only was it possible, but it was incumbent upon the true believer in Islam to wipe out idolaters and purveyors of all that is *haram* wherever he may find them. Dreamboy then whispered that he knew where to find a supply of high explosives, but that he himself didn't know the first thing about them. Pung's research into the Frenchman's past then paid off. Moreau/Dergham said that he himself had been a member of the French Army, and that he just happened to have trained as an HE specialist. "Where do you have this store of high explosives?" he asked Dreamboy.

"In a place called Yoyogi. Have you heard of it?"

AMERICAN EMBASSY

August 1

Combined security command for the Olympics

"Another text just came in from our friend," Patrick said in a call to Hooper the next day.

"I'll get everyone together. Come right over."

Ten minutes later the de facto task force met again in Hooper's office.

Patrick read off his phone. "Listen to this: *'If necessary when attacking, you must pull the stakes out of a wall and use them as spears and halberds.'"*

"Fuck is a halberd?" muttered Phibbs.

"Some sort of weapon, obviously," said Hooper in a caustic tone. "The question is, is this something symbolic, or does he mean it literally?"

Kirsten had only spoken to Patrick with arctic aloofness, if at all, since the incident at the *izakaya*, but now she directed her comments to him as chief security consultant.

"Actually, I think the real question is when this is going to happen. It doesn't matter so much what the weapons will be as it does what the next target is. My own feeling from my profiling training is that whoever this is is going to escalate the attacks. It's been so long since the last one that the next one is going to make the others pale in comparison."

"Thanks for that input, Kirsten, I totally agree," Patrick said. If he had hoped that her comments indicated a thaw in the dynamic between them, he was mistaken. The closest she came to a smile was a slight crimping in the lips.

CHAPTER 29

August 2

As Dreamboy had promised, Dergham found a Canter Class R-F truck parked in an alleyway near Yoyogi Park. He had shaved his beard and was wearing coveralls with a small French flag emblazoned above the pocket. An observant eye would have noticed that the top portion of his face was sunburned, while the recently shaved lower part was milky white. The side of the truck sported the Olympic rings with the words "Jeux Olympiques de Tokyo" painted on the side.

He took the keys Dreamboy had given him and unlocked the driver's side door. Then he went around the back of the truck and opened it after making sure no one was in the immediate area. The pungent scent of ammonia and diesel fuel brought back memories of the time he had trained in the French countryside with his al-Qaeda brothers. Today he would show them what a true striking lion looked like.

The truck was loaded with twelve five-hundred-pound barrels of ammonium nitrate fertilizer, nitromethane, diesel fuel, and a mix of ball bearings and jagged pieces of metal, with the barrels arranged in the shape of a backwards J to direct the blast laterally toward the Yoyogi Gymnasium. Dreamboy had told Dergham he could expect to find in the truck's cab a ten-minute time-delayed fuse that branched off and led to two sets of nonelectric blasting caps which would ignite 350 pounds of high-grade explosives. The time delay would allow Dergham to activate the bomb and escape before detonation. If all went as planned, the exploding blasting caps would send a shock wave radiating outward at three miles per second through the ammonium nitrate and fuel, which would then vaporize, forming a huge volume of oxygen gas. The hot oxygen gas along with the energy of the detonation wave would then ignite the fuel.

As he approached the gymnasium's Harajuku Gate, Dergham slowed the truck to a stop and began vehemently gesticulating and shouting in a nonstop stream of French to the elderly security guard who had flagged him down. The Japanese are notoriously reticent in speaking even a single phrase of English to a foreigner, despite having to take the language all through middle and high school. The thought of engaging a foreigner speaking French, no less, was enough to freeze the security guard's blood. Despite the guard's strict orders to inspect all vehicles entering the gate, Dergham could see the man wavering as he considered his next move.

As he had been trained back in his al-Qaeda cell in the French countryside, Dergham had also slotted into the guard's expectations. The human mind doesn't like uncertainty, he'd been told, and takes measures to explain or eliminate it. "Imagine if you see a dog running behind a fence," his trainer had said. "The dog disappears every time the fence covers him over, but one hundred percent of people will tell you the dog is still there. If you give the right signals, the other person will fill in the blanks." Dergham filled in the blanks now with the security guard who was face-to-face with a foreigner speaking a language he didn't understand driving a truck that had the Olympic rings on its side. He waved the foreigner through with his orange wand.

Once the truck was in place in the entranceway to the concrete gymnasium, Dergham lit the fuse in the cab, and with the serenity of the faithful, began walking briskly away from the truck while praying in a low voice, "In the name of Allah, most gracious and most merciful..." He was no more than five feet away when the bomb ignited, creating a pressure wave traveling at eleven hundred feet per second and instantly vaporizing him. There was no way Pung was going to allow Dergham to be captured. The fuse was ten seconds, not ten minutes. When Pung leeringly told Dreamboy of the betrayal back at the corpse hotel, Dreamboy screamed and wept bitter tears as he clutched Dergham's photo close to his heart. He would not come out of his room for two days.

The explosion measured 3.0 on the Richter scale and demolished forever the notion among Japanese that their country was too isolated for outside terrorism. Patrick was out on a run on the footpath surrounding the Imperial Palace when he heard the blast and then the doppler wail of the emergency vehicles. Word-of-mouth news of the attack spread from runner to runner. He took out his cell and called Yumi to make sure she and Dae-ho were okay. The likelihood of anything happening forty miles away in Kamakura was remote, unless it had been a simultaneous attack across the Kanto region, but the magnitude of the explosion ignited his protective instincts. Assured that they were safe, he began running back to the embassy.

Along the way he suddenly stopped in front of a three-hundred-year-old sweet gum tree in the Ninomaru Gardens, whose spreading canopy had made it one of his favorites in the entire Imperial Palace compound. He forced the explosion from his mind and plucked a star-shaped leaf from a low-hanging branch of the seventy-five-foot tall tree and twirled it in his fingers. Then he picked up one of its spiky seed balls off the ground, rolled it in his hand, and dropped it again. In the face of the insanity of what had just happened, he needed to reaffirm life by literally regrounding himself in the infinite intelligence of the natural world. He then took a deep breath and ran as fast as he could back to the embassy.

In the hours immediately after the blast, the leaders of several Olympic delegations from the Middle East marched over to the television cameras in whatever sport venue they happened to be and declared firmly that their countries categorically condemned the violence. Word had spread quickly that the blast had destroyed the Yoyogi Gymnasium and killed upwards of a thousand spectators. Luckily, the blast had occurred during a two-hour break before many of the expected thirteen thousand spectators had arrived for the afternoon match between France and Israel.

The NHK main studio next door was still standing but heavily damaged, with many killed and injured from the debris that flew from the exploding gymnasium like, well, like "spears and halberds" traveling at over the speed of sound. Later in the day, NHK reported that it had received a video from Chosun Restoration claiming responsibility for the attack.

CHAPTER 30

August 3

Hooper, Phibbs, JIA Director Hayashida, and Kirsten Beck sat around the table avoiding Patrick's eye. None of them had ever seen him this angry. He paced the floor back and forth in Hooper's office and held something in his hand.

"So, Director Hayashida, tell me again why the Prime Minister was reluctant to release information about the attacks. It was so the people wouldn't be alarmed, right?"

Hayashida sat in his chair with his eyes down and said nothing in the face of Patrick's tirade.

"And now over a thousand of those people are dead, and the death toll keeps going up!" Patrick continued, becoming even more livid. His free hand shot out in the direction of the flat-screen TV that hung on the wall opposite Hooper's desk.

"And it's my face that's on that television screen! Is this why I got hired, so the Prime Minister could conveniently blame the foreign security consultant when the shit hit the fan?"

Hayashida exhaled and bowed in his seat in Patrick's direction. "I'm very sorry, Mister Featherstone. I had no idea that your face would be shown on the television, or…"

"It's not about my face on TV!" Patrick shouted, cutting him off. "It's about all those people who were murdered! An announcement advising extra caution might have saved even one of those lives!"

He paced even faster and then came to a halt in the middle of the room which crackled with tension. Not even Phibbs dared offer one of his inane comments.

"Alright, here's how this is going to work," Patrick said finally. "You're going to contact the Prime Minister and tell him that unless he takes full responsibility for not releasing all available information on the earlier attacks, then I will call a press conference and tell the Japanese public exactly what happened as I submit this on national TV." Patrick held up an envelope with the characters 辞表, "*jihyou*" or "letter of resignation," written in his own calligraphy.

"Your call," he said to Hayashida and then exited the room, slamming the door behind him. His anger remained in the air like something physical, and the most awkward silence any of the others had ever endured hung over the room. Finally, Hooper broke it.

"Well, it's pretty clear that not alerting the public of the full danger was a mistake," he said. Hayashida remained silent. Phibbs spoke next.

"Cat's out of the bag, folks. All the major newspapers are asking what the government knew and when."

"That's right, and I heard that some Diet members are calling for the Games to be canceled or for the government to just give in to Chosun Restoration," Kirsten said.

Hayashida looked up. "I assure you, everyone, the Games will not be canceled. I will do as Mister Featherstone asks and have the Prime Minister take responsibility for not releasing the information."

"And what if he refuses?" Phibbs asked.

Hayashida looked at everyone in the room in turn directly in the eye.

"Then my letter of resignation will join Mister Featherstone's as I stand next to him on national television." He stood and left the room.

An hour later, Prime Minister Adegawa appeared on national television. He bowed deeply and apologized profusely, telling the citizens of Japan that there was not enough information to go on after the earlier attacks, but that he would personally let the country know if there was any further danger.

"Fucking weasel," said Phibbs, shaking his head in anger as he, Hooper, and Kirsten Beck watched the announcement. "There was plenty of information to go on."

"Yeah, but this is Japan," Hooper said. "He's gotta save face."

"Unless it's Patrick's."

Hooper and Kirsten both looked at Phibbs in surprise. It was the first either of them had ever heard him say anything in Patrick's defense, let alone call him by his first name.

Patrick watched the broadcast from a nearby *izakaya*, not wanting to go back to his JIA office unless it was absolutely necessary. When he saw the Prime Minister's disingenuous attempt at washing his hands of blame, he came close to throwing his bottle of Kirin draft at the TV screen. He took out his letter of resignation and was about to go deliver it to Hayashida when he stopped and thought it through. "That's probably what they want," he said out loud to himself. The owner looked over at him. Patrick waved him away.

But I'm not going to give them the satisfaction, he thought.

CHAPTER 31

JAPAN INTELLIGENCE AGENCY HEADQUARTERS
TOKYO

Director Hayashida set down that morning's *Asahi* newspaper and picked up his phone. A minute later his assistant Minoru Kaga, recruited from Cabinet Intelligence and Research, walked into his office and bowed. Hayashida indicated a chair next to the desk with his hand. His secretary followed Kaga in and set a teapot and cups onto a trolley to one side of her boss's desk.

"Kaga, what I have to say stays between you and me," Hayashida said after his secretary had left. Kaga nodded. "Yes, sir."

Hayashida opened a drawer of his desk and pulled out a color photo of a twisted piece of metal, which he set in front of Kaga.

"This is a fragment of a license plate from the attack on Yoyogi Gymnasium." Kaga picked it up and held it close.

"Were they able to get any information from it, sir?"

"I'm expecting a report any minute."

"Shall I alert Mister Featherstone? He might be able to have the young FBI lady analyze it at their labs…." Hayashida was already shaking his head emphatically as Kaga spoke.

"No, I don't think so. I want the JIA to be solely in charge of this angle. We don't have to take a backseat to America all the time." Kaga looked at him with his lips parted.

"As for Mister Featherstone," Hayashida continued, "I was the one who recruited him as the chief security consultant for the Olympics. But that was before I or anyone else had any idea that there would be these attacks. I hired him for several reasons: One, of course, is that he was one of the top operatives in the American JSOC. He also happens to be bilingual. I thought it would be a good idea to have someone of his reputation in that very visible position with strong ties to Japan but who isn't actually a Japanese citizen. The international angle of the Olympics. I think the Americans call it 'optics.' My other reason, which is between you and me, is that I wanted to demonstrate the transparency of our Agency after what happened with the previous director."

"The office building, sir?"

Hayashida's predecessor had purchased a North Korean-owned building in Tokyo for far less than it was worth, leading to questions about his loyalty to Japan.

"Yes. But now Featherstone is acting much too independently and actually second-guessing me and the Prime Minister. I guess he really is an American at heart, despite having been born here." He probed Kaga's face for a reaction, but Kaga's expression didn't change, and he gave no indication of either agreeing or disagreeing with Hayashida. Hayashida had hoped for a bit more toadying from his underling, but he pressed on.

"The latest indication of trouble was when he threatened to resign over the Prime Minister's refusal to knuckle under to the terrorists. I find it somewhat unfortunate that he's not following through with his threat."

"Actually, sir, I'm fairly sure he was against the Prime Minister's decision not to issue a warning after the earlier attacks. He thought it might have saved lives."

Hayashida wasn't prepared to be contradicted and it showed in his tone. "Actually, the Prime Minister and I were against releasing it for fear that it would cause undue panic and keep people away from the Games. There was no way of predicting the attack on Yoyogi Gymnasium. And the Prime Minister's and my main concern has always been showing Japan to the world in the best light possible."

Kaga said nothing. Hayashida leaned in.

"I'd like you to work closely with Featherstone. Offer your services, that kind of thing. Just don't let on that I put you up to it. It doesn't look as though he's all that close to the CIA people at the American embassy, but that might work in our favor. He'll probably want someone to confide in."

"It sounds like you want me to spy on him, sir."

Hayashida shrugged and affected a weary look on his face. "Whatever you want to call it. I just need to have a closer sense of what he and the other Americans are up to. I have a feeling he'll want to pick your brain to find out more about what we're doing at the JIA, so you'll be in a good position. When people ask questions, they reveal what they don't know."

Hayashida went over to the trolley on the side of his desk and poured them both a cup of tea. He set one in front of Kaga, who bowed in his seat.

"I realize now that I dug myself into a deep hole by hiring him. Featherstone is not a team player—that much is clear. Don't you think?"

Kaga looked away while nodding his head half-heartedly. His body language was not lost on Hayashida.

"But I know *you* are a team player, right, Kaga?"

"Yes, sir," Kaga said with no discernible uptick in enthusiasm. Hayashida turned his head and side-eyed his underling.

"Kaga, what was your job at Cabinet Intelligence and Research?"

"I reported to the director of the International Division, sir. Since I lived for a while in the U.S., I was recruited to analyze any intelligence that the American CIA shared with us."

"And would you say they shared a lot?"

Kaga lowered his eyes and smiled weakly. "Almost all of what I learned from them I had already read in the newspaper. They were very nice, but I'm afraid any modest talent I might possess was not really being fully utilized."

Hayashida nodded vigorously. "That's what I mean when I say we need an inside eye on what's going on there, and that's where you'll come in. It must have been frustrating for a man of your talents." He picked up Kaga's dossier and scanned through it. "Your English is perfect, you were second in your class in marksmanship at the Academy, and it says here that you are a 'dogged investigator.' Plus, you're very good-looking. Do you agree with that assessment?""Well, sir, based on the scores I was able to achieve in all those areas, I humbly accept the compliment. As for the latter…"

Hayashida was placing the dossier carefully back on his desk, aligning its corners with the edges of his desk as Kaga spoke. "Too bad you're a bachelor," he said, cutting him off. "Actually, I'm glad. You'll be working long and irregular hours for a while, so no time for hostess bars and the like." Kaga's face blanched.

"Another thing: between you and me, the real reason the Prime Minister and I proposed using the American embassy as security headquarters for the Olympics was so that we could keep an eye on them. We knew they'd be meddling in Japan's affairs as they always do, and this was a way of keeping tabs on them. With you keeping Featherstone in your sights, we'll have an even closer look." He held Kaga's eye before continuing.

"By the way, you were involved in a little incident at Yale when you were doing graduate work, is that correct? Something to do with a party and cocaine…and compromising positions with a faculty member's wife?"

Kaga's face darkened. "Sir, my apology was accepted, and…"

"No need for the details, Kaga. It's between you and me." Hayashida moved his head closer to Kaga. "Agreed?"

"Agreed," Kaga said dourly. He did not say "sir."

"Good." Hayashida stood and went to his office window overlooking Hibiya Park.

"On one side I have the Prime Minister who thinks I'm his little errand boy, on the other I have all these second-level bureaucrats who hate me because the PM put me in charge of this agency. But it's not my fault that my predecessor sold out to the North Koreans and these bureaucrats were part of his inner circle. After the Olympics, assuming any of us survive the stress, I will be looking into just how dirty their hands are. For now, though, you're the only one I trust. And I know I can trust you, Kaga," he said, looking back at Kaga steadily. He turned back to the window. "The Americans think I'm completely useless. Did you find them to be arrogant when you lived there?"

"Only some of the people in charge, sir. Not the ordinary people."

"Hm. Just like here, then. One thing in our favor in Japan, though, is that the ordinary people and the people in charge are all Japanese. We don't have all that racial nonsense going on." He sat back down at his desk and began neatly arranging a stack of files.

"That might be because there's really only one race in Japan, sir," Kaga said.

"Exactly. How long can it continue like that, though? Our birth rate is too low, and twenty percent of the population is over seventy, but we can't bring in immigrants without losing our uniqueness. I know that flies in the face of the whole 'internationalism' theme of the Olympics, but I can't help it, I'm from a different generation. Maybe your generation will find a way to keep Japan going without turning it into the chaos they have in America."

"Sir, to tell you the truth, I didn't find a lot of chaos over there, at least not where I was. In my opinion our news media likes to focus on the worst things that happen there in order to make Japan look good by comparison."

Hayashida looked up at Kaga. "Really? I'm glad to hear that." His gaze turned inward. "Maybe."

He stood again and went back to the window.

"I was born during the Great Pacific War with the Americans. I don't know what they're teaching in our schools these days about the war, but I have a feeling it's more leftwing propaganda to rub our noses in defeat. Why is it that only Western countries got to establish colonies, anyway? Didn't the Americans do that in the Philippines? The French in Morocco and Vietnam? But when we did it in Korea and China, we were suddenly 'aggressors,' when actually we were bringing the enlightenment of Japanese culture to backward places. Don't you agree, Kaga? Don't worry, you can speak freely."

"Well, I'm not sure how enlightened it was to chop off people's heads when they disagreed, sir."

Hayashida snorted. "Gross exaggerations from socialist TV commentators. Oh well, as I say, I'm from a different generation. I suppose it's natural that we disagree. Don't worry, I won't chop your head off, though," he said with a smile, which Kaga didn't return. Then his phone rang. He picked it up, listened, grunted, and hung up.

Hayashida regarded Kaga unblinkingly. "That was our forensics lab. They couldn't find anything of value on that license plate fragment." Kaga checked himself from suggesting that perhaps agencies other than the JIA might have better luck.

"I know that deep down inside you're a loyal Japanese," Hayashida said. "Please keep me apprised of what's going on with the Americans. You may go."

Kaga bowed and left without a word.

CHAPTER 32

THE WHITE HOUSE
August 4

Director of National Intelligence Jay Garvida entered the Oval Office. He did not look forward to the next twenty minutes. The president was pacing behind his desk. Garvida waited to be acknowledged. Finally, Dillard looked up from the ground. His face was ashen.

"Seventy-three Americans? Is that number correct, Jay?"

"Actually, Mister President, I'm sorry to report that it's gone up to seventy-nine overnight."

Dillard took a long, slow inhalation and released it in a loud sigh. "Jesus. What the hell's going on with security over there? Didn't those earlier attacks light a fire under their asses?"

"According to our Agency station chief in Tokyo, the Japanese thought they had all the members of Chosun Restoration rounded up."

"Well, obviously they missed a few," Dillard said heatedly. He turned his back to Garvida. "What do you suggest?" he said to the fireplace in a somber tone.

"Well, sir, it's Japan's Olympics, and…"

Dillard spun around. "And those were American lives, Jay! What's the situation over there, isn't there some kind of joint task force between us and the Japanese for the Olympics?"

"That's correct, sir, they're calling it the combined security command. The problem as I see it, though, is that no one person is really in charge. That guy Featherstone was hired by the Japanese government to be the chief security consultant, but from what I gather, he's being shafted by the bureaucracy."

Dillard sniffed. "Imagine that," he muttered. He turned back to the fireplace and thought for a long minute. Then he turned back to Garvida.

"I'm sending Garrett Proctor over. We need results fast. 'A new broom sweeps clean,' and all that." Dillard sat down at his desk, took out a legal tablet, and swiveled his chair away from Garvida.

"Yes, sir," Garvida said to his back. He didn't move. Dillard swiveled back around.

"Anything else?" he asked.

"Sir, I'm just wondering about this 'China Solution' thing. It seems to me that if anyone can rein in the North Koreans, it's China. If they could establish a protectorate in North Korea, I'd bet they could get to the bottom of this Chosun Restoration group and shut them down. They're pretty efficient that way."

"I don't doubt that they are, Jay, but I'm worried that it might just be a ruse to bring back the Kim family. Still, maybe they're sincere, I don't know. I haven't taken it totally off the table, but I want to see if Proctor can do something about these North Korean attacks in Japan before committing to something as drastic as letting China to run North Korea."

"Understood, sir," Garvida said. He turned and left.

CHAPTER 33

Hooper hung up the phone. He was wincing. "That was Langley Seventh Floor. After the Yoyogi explosion, the president figured we weren't doing an effective job with this terrorist group, especially after all those Americans were killed. He's sending over someone from the National Counterterrorism Center. The guy's been given full authority and is reporting to the president directly. Turf war alert."

"Why do you say that?" asked Kirsten Beck. "He's one of your guys."

"Actually, he isn't. Ours is the *CIA* Counterterrorism Center. Two different entities."

Kirsten shook her head from side to side. "No wonder things get siloed and screwed up. Couldn't they even have made them *sound* like two different agencies?"

Dillard rubbed his face. "I've given up trying to fathom why Washington does anything anymore," he said in a weary voice. "It's not worth the effort, and it won't change a thing. At any rate, they're sending over this guy named Garrett Proctor. He was one of the main people behind TIDE."

"Acronym translation, please," Patrick said in an irritated voice without looking up from the messages he was checking on his phone.

Jack "Fitz" Fitzroy answered for Hooper. "TIDE is the Terrorist Identities Datamart Environment. It's a database of a million or so probable terrorists. This guy Proctor's a piece of work. Norm, have you met him?"

Hooper shook his head. "I've only heard of him. That was enough."

Fitz continued. "I had the pleasure two years ago. Prepare to have your toes stepped on at the very least. He carries a chip on one shoulder and a china shop on the other."

————————

Garrett Proctor, fifty-two years old, won the Navy's "Chris Dobleman Most Improved Boxer Award" in his senior year at Annapolis following a humiliating defeat to a much lower ranked pugilist in his junior year. His defeat, he was convinced, came as a result of a prank. One of his teammates had told him before the match that his opponent that day was an undefeated boxer from Naval Base San Diego who had knocked out his last four opponents. Proctor charged the opponent at the opening bell of the first round, but quickly found himself on the ropes as his teammate's words about his opponent ran through his head. The opponent scored point after point in the first round, but when Proctor returned to his corner, the offending teammate frantically told him he had been joking and that the opponent was actually a no-account palooka, the goat of his brigade. Emboldened by his success in the first round, the palooka managed to stay fairly even with Proctor in the final two rounds and took the bout on points. Although Proctor had to settle for the Most Improved Boxer award the following year, when he had been aiming for the Grand Championship, he took from the whole experience the importance of skepticism of received wisdom coupled with unflinching aggression. The Marine first lieutenant who recruited him out of Annapolis assured him that his worldview was wholly consistent with the philosophy of the Corps.

After he earned a master's degree in Russian studies from the University of Pennsylvania with a thesis on Ivan the Terrible, Proctor's military career eventually took him to Afghanistan for two year-long tours of duty. But with three weeks to go before the end of the second tour, the helicopter in which he was riding was struck by a shoulder-launched missile that nicked the tail rotor and sent a hot shard of steel into his right eye. The missile was later determined to have come from the CIA's Operation Cyclone, which armed the mujahedin against the Soviet Union. Proctor's opinion of the Company plummeted and never recovered, especially after his eye had to be removed and fit with a prosthesis.

As the plane carrying Proctor and four others made its final descent into Tokyo's Haneda Airport just outside the city, Proctor gazed out the window and tried to pick out Olympic landmarks he had memorized from looking at Google Maps on the flight over. Directly below was the Olympic Village and further to the west were the remains of Yoyogi Gymnasium not far from the Olympic Stadium. He braced for the "Navy landing" he had requested of the pilot, one that came down hard on the runway and left some rubber as a calling card, as if coming down hot on an aircraft carrier. Not for him the wimpy Air Force landing that all-too-gently featherbedded the plane back on earth with barely an impact. When the wheels hit even harder than he was expecting, Proctor let loose with an unbridled and wholly uncharacteristic "Hooyah!" and enthusiastically punched the unoccupied seat in front of him with the heel of his hand. Then his face reverted to kick-ass mode, his emotional dial set on "grim determination."

Rather than a simple ride to the American embassy, Proctor had ordered a three-Humvee motorcade that bulled its way through downtown Tokyo and came to a stop behind the main gate of the embassy. A Marine guard rushed over to open the door of his Humvee just as Proctor was exiting it of his own accord. The fifty-two-year-old, 230 pounds and built like a clenched fist, still sported a high and tight haircut ten years after his retirement from the military. He strode assuredly to the main door of the building, where CIA Station Chief Norm Hooper was waiting. Seeing the set in Proctor's jaw, Hooper changed his game plan and walked down the stairs to meet him. Like most people, he was disoriented by the steady gaze of Proctor's glass eye contrasted with the slatelike glare of his good one. His enemies dubbed him "Cyclops," but only in private.

Once inside the embassy with a minimum of chitchat with Hooper on the way in, Proctor called for an immediate situation report from everyone involved in the effort to ferret out those behind the attacks. Hooper hastily assembled Phibbs, Patrick, Jack "Fitz" Fitzroy, Kirsten Beck, and Minoru Kaga, whom Hayashida had assigned to work with— and spy on—the Americans. Proctor began without waiting for Hooper to introduce anyone.

"As you may have already heard, I'm not a patient man, especially where American lives are concerned," Proctor began, pacing back and forth with his head down on the carpet in front of the fireplace in Hooper's office. "Let's get to work. I'll entertain all credible ideas on how to identify and eliminate this Chosun Restoration group."

Hooper raised his hand, and Proctor acknowledged him with a curt nod. "Garrett, I just want to clarify something: this is Japan's Olympics, and in terms of a chain of command, they have final say over everything. Their Prime Minister did request that we take an active role in the counterterrorism effort, but ultimately they call the shots."

"And what shots have the Japanese taken?" Proctor said. "Because from what I've seen and heard, they've been pretty hands-off, and that just doesn't work when American lives are at stake. We need to first find out who the enemy is, which is an effort I'm frankly not seeing a lot of evidence of, and then we need to bring the fight to that enemy. Now, these attacks are obviously of North Korean origin, correct?"

Everyone in the room nodded. "Then why aren't stones being turned over in that area? I understand that the JIA has detained a number of Koreans, but they obviously haven't detained the right ones. Is anyone else being questioned? If not, why not? Another angle is this: I know that Chosun Restoration has claimed responsibility for the Yoyogi attack, but from what I saw of the remains of the building, it looked a lot to me like Islamic terrorism. So what about this scenario: Chosun

Restoration has banded together with Islamic terrorists as part of the global terror network. Have these questions even been asked? Right now, President Dillard is being pressured to accept this so-called 'China Solution,' and he isn't happy about being backed into a corner by a country he doesn't trust."

Patrick raised his hand. Proctor turned to him. "Go ahead."

"I'm Patrick Featherstone, chief security consultant hired by the Japanese government to oversee the entire security effort, and…"

"I was just reading about you on the plane," Proctor interrupted, picking up his phone. He held it up a moment later. "Pyongyang. The coup that brought down Kim Jong-un. So on one hand, we have the Japanese who don't want to fight, and on the other, their security consultant who engineered a regime change. On his own."

"Actually, an overthrow had been developing for years by the Rising Tide democracy insurgency. I played only a small part in what happened."

"You're too modest, Featherstone. The after-action report here says you, quote, 'lit the fuse.'"

"Does the file also say anything about the satchel nuke that I prevented from blowing up on the Kumgang Dam? Do you know how many people would have been killed if that succeeded? And as far as 'lighting the fuse' is concerned, the people were ready to get rid of the Kims for years. The fuse had been in place for a very long time in North Korea. I just helped them light it."

"Be that as it may," Proctor quickly retorted, "no one will be helped if the Japanese continue to sit on their asses and you do anything that smacks of what you did in Pyongyang. And besides, why on earth is an American in charge of security at the Tokyo Olympics?"

"Because for one thing, I was born here, Mister Proctor, and they feel I have the military background along with the language skills. The leadership of the security consortium they were going to use was deemed, shall we say, 'unready,' and so they asked me. Plus, they wanted to project an international image on the Games. They're sensitive to charges that Japan holds the rest of the world at arm's length and only pays lip service to being part of the 'outside' world."

"That sounds like an accurate self-assessment," Proctor said. "They've always skated around the margins of the war on terrorism and never really committed to fighting it."

A hand was raised and recognized by Proctor. "I'm Minoru Kaga of the Japan Intelligence Agency. Part of the reason for that, Mister Proctor, is our constitution, which prohibits us from taking more than a role of self-defense."

"Well, from the looks of your former National Gymnasium, I'd say the war on terror is now firmly on your soil. The giant moat called the Pacific Ocean has been breached, and Tokyo has become one big HVT, would you not agree, Kaga?"

Kaga's face scrunched in incomprehension.

"*High value target*," Proctor said, as if it should have been obvious. Kaga shrugged in resignation and nodded.

"Starting now, I will be in charge of the counterterrorism effort, and…"

Patrick's hand shot up. "Let me remind you, Mister Proctor, that I'm not part of the American military or any American agency. My contract gives me full autonomy."

Proctor turned sharply to Hooper. "Is that true?" he demanded.

"Yes. He's his own man."

"What about the thing in North Korea?" Proctor scrolled through the file on his phone.

"He was NOC. Nonofficial cover."

"I don't need any help with the acronyms," Proctor said as he confirmed what Hooper had just said from the file on his phone. "Well, that's one too many chiefs, especially since I have at my command all the technology of the United States. I also have the military intelligence necessary to track down these clowns."

Fitz raised his hand. "Mister Proctor, Jack Fitzroy, CIA tradecraft specialist for Asia. Not to boast, but we're in pretty good shape when it comes to technology and military intelligence for this area of the world."

"Really? Do you have Predator and Sentinel drones on hot standby?"

"No, but we're…"

"Look, I'm not trying to take anything away from the CIA, the JIA, or you, Featherstone, but my office has the experience and resources to make sure we have enough spank to get the job done, especially if push comes to shove it up their asses. It's too important to be anything but a coordinated effort, and I'm the one positioned to coordinate it. That's just the reality of the situation, not the free rein of my ego."

No one in the room spoke until Patrick raised his hand again. Growing up in Japan, he had been raised to acquiesce to authority, to go along to get along, but the hard-knock experience of being a *gaijin* had cured him of the habit early on.

"I can only reiterate what I said before, Proctor," he said, purposely calling the Big Man from Washington by his last name. "My contract gives me complete autonomy in everything connected with Olympic security. I've agreed to join forces with all other aspects of the security effort with the embassy here as our de facto forward operating base, but please be clear that I'm not your underling and I'm not accepting orders from you."

Proctor looked stunned and was silent, but not for long. "Alright, have it your way. But don't come crying to me when you're in over your head."

"I won't if you won't," Patrick said in the same tone and got up to leave. *Let the power games begin, asshole*, he thought. The now-silent room seemed to pulsate with an electric charge as he closed the door behind him.

CHAPTER 34

OLYMPIC STADIUM
August 5

The more he thought about it, the less likely Patrick felt it would be for him to develop a workable relationship with Proctor, if only because of the latter's overweening arrogance. But how to bring about that split without it being too obvious? The entire security command, including Director Kazuo Hayashida of the JIA and Patrick himself, had already agreed to designate the American embassy as its CSC, its combined security command. But that was before Proctor and his ego had landed. Now, he was in danger of losing his leverage and autonomy. He decided to chance it and called Hooper to tell him that he wanted to move his operation to his office here at the stadium. Hooper seemed amenable at first but asked Patrick to hold on. Patrick could hear him talking to Proctor with the phone muffled against his clothes. When he came back on the line, he relayed Proctor's response.

"Garrett's not all that keen on it, Patrick. I reminded him that you're an independent contractor for the Japanese government, but you your-self *did* agree that we would all coordinate our efforts with the embassy here being the forward operating base." Hooper muffled the phone again, but Patrick could hear Proctor talking to Hooper in the back-ground. "Tell Featherstone we can't lose unity of command. The worst sin you can make in the field. I have a feeling he might be a bit deficient in that area."

Thinking back to a sergeant with a similar personality in his military days, Patrick hit upon an idea. He told Hooper to tell Proctor, who apparently was too important to speak to Patrick directly, that he, Patrick, was merely establishing a TOC, a tactical operations center, at the stadium. He would meet with Hooper, Proctor, and the others of the combined security command on an unspecified 'regular basis' at the embassy. He had told the sergeant way back when much the same thing, only the TOC was the quartermaster's warehouse where the beer supply was stored.

Hooper seemed completely taken by Patrick's proposal, partially because it made perfect sense, and partially because Patrick's tone was one of uncharacteristic cooperativeness. He relayed Patrick's idea to Proctor, who seemed to reluctantly agree. Hooper came back on the line. "Garrett says, how about we meet over here tomorrow at 0800? Just to compare notes and make sure we're all on the same page, that kind of thing…"

"Let me get back to you on that, Norm. There's a possible confidential informant I've got a bead on, and I need to have some flexibility in my schedule." Hooper again relayed Patrick's response, and Proctor finally came on the line personally.

"Featherstone, Proctor. Tell you what: I'll send Case Officer Phibbs over, and he can liaise with the CSC and your new TOC. Sound good?" There was a note of triumph in Proctor's voice. Patrick's stomach fell. Out of the frying pan, into the fire. "Sure, sounds good," he said, kicking his desk as he hung up. Proctor couldn't stand Phibbs either, so he fobbed him off to Patrick. Patrick had been bested.

He phoned Choy and told him where they would now be based, and Choy brought his laptop over half an hour later from JIA headquarters. As he and Patrick were settling into their new digs, the sound of footsteps echoed through the hall. Whoever it was was muttering something in English. It got clearer as the person neared the corner that led to Patrick's office. "Fucking morons, everywhere I turn," the voice said. A moment later, Harmon Phibbs appeared around the corner.

"Oh. Hi. Didn't know you were in."

"What's up, Phibbs?" Patrick said. "I hear Proctor designated you as liaison between here and the embassy."

"Yeah, lucky me. It was Fitz's idea, by the way. Proctor kept giving me grief and I told him I couldn't work with him and he said I had to and I told him no I don't because he's not Company and da-da-da. Guy thinks he's hot shit, but he's only half right. I've known corpses with more personal warmth. It all went downhill from there, acronyms as verbs, the whole bit. So just when you called Hooper a while ago, Fitz suggested that I be a liaison between you and the 'team' at the embassy. It's basically to keep me away from Proctor. So here I am."

"Fitz's idea, huh?" Patrick said. "Remind me to put salt in his coffee."

"Hey, I'm not that bad once you get to know me. I've got all sorts of experience and contacts in this town. We'd make a good team."

"No, we would not. Because I'm not looking for a team, at least not one of equals." Patrick turned his head to one side and thought. Phibbs was right on one count, at least: he did have a lot of experience and contacts in Japan and he might well be useful.

"I tell you what: You won't work *with* me. But you can work *for* me."

Phibbs's head went back with a look of disbelief on his face. "You mean take orders and shit? I've been in the Agency my whole career. I'm the ranking case officer here."

Patrick folded his arms. Phibbs thought a moment and sighed. "Oh alright, if it makes you feel better, I'll take orders and shit."

"And please watch your mouth. No nasty comments."

"Aye aye, snowflake. Just kidding." Phibbs looked at his watch. "It's almost five. Buy you a drink, sailor? I know a good place nearby."

Patrick opened his mouth to refuse, but checked himself. He didn't know Phibbs at all except for his annoying manner, and he might indeed be a good addition to the "team" if he had as many contacts and inside information as he constantly reminded everyone. And at the very least, Phibbs was buying.

"Sure, a quick one, though. I've got a meeting at 6:30 with one of the JIA squads that are running the stadium surveillance."

"Nice that they let you drink on the job," Phibbs smirked as they walked to the door.

"I'll be having Calpis," Patrick said.

Phibbs's face contorted in pain. "Friends don't let friends drink that shit."

Ten minutes later they arrived at a bar that catered mostly to foreigners. Phibbs was familiar enough with the proprietor that he was welcomed by name. He ordered for both of them, and the waitress carried their drinks back to their booth.

"Thanks," Patrick said, taking a sip of his Calpis. Phibbs watched him drink, shook his head in disgust, and took a long gulp of his bourbon and soda before setting it down. "Ahhh, I do love that first drink," he said, smacking his lips. "It's like breakfast: the most important one of the day."

Patrick chuckled. The guy wasn't totally bad.

Over the next fifteen minutes he listened as Phibbs launched into the type of nonstop riff that most people found insufferable, but Patrick found himself actually enjoying it. Noting Phibbs's usual attire of an old dark green sport jacket, short-sleeved shirt, and clip-on tie, he learned that this was a legacy of Phibbs's early days in the field as part of the CIA's political action wing of the Special Activities Division when he needed to "go gray" and not stand out on a crowded train platform in Krakow.

"I can understand Eastern Europe, but how do you get away with never wearing a suit in this posting?" Patrick asked. "Isn't that standard work attire for 'cultural attaches' in this town?"

Phibbs smirked and took a sip of bourbon. "The last suit I owned was so long ago the thing had a codpiece." Patrick found out that Phibbs was divorced from a much younger wife from his home state of Kentucky, and that he now spent his free time gambling at the race track in the Fuchu area, near Tokyo's main prison.

"Horses, bikes, powerboats, and motorbikes, you name it, and I've bet on it," Phibbs said. "Correction, I've lost on it. Like they say, luck never gives, she only lends, and I never know when to walk away. There's a saying where I come from: pigs get fat, hogs get slaughtered. I bought into Bitcoin early on but held on too long till it turned into Shitcoin. Now I gotta keep working to pay alimony. Hard to even stay afloat in this town, though. They really bend you over for everything, especially booze."

He shrugged, drained his glass, and called out for another. Patrick signaled that he was good. The waitress brought Phibbs a fresh bourbon soda. As he took a sip, he slapped his belly.

"It might not look it now, but I was a pretty good tight end at Murray State. Football's something that teaches you about how fast life goes by. You see your childhood hero as the rookie of the year, and then twelve, fifteen years later they go on waivers even after a fabulous career. Life." He stared wistfully at the table and then continued.

"I remember when I first came into the Agency. You were in Serbia, right? I was probably over there the same time as you, but I was recruited directly into Special Activities from college. Fitz was my first supervisor. Kind of regret I hadn't gotten some military experience under my belt first, but what the hell. Saw all sorts of shit over there. What a mess."

"I didn't know Fitz was over there."

Phibbs nodded and squinted into the middle distance. He then turned to a foreign patron who was smoking and drinking with his friends in the adjoining booth.

"Gimme one of those things, will you?" he demanded of the man, a Frenchman judging from his Gauloises. The man looked as though Phibbs had asked him to donate a kidney, but he held out his pack. Phibbs thanked him, lit the cigarette like a pro, and inhaled it like it was pure oxygen. Then he stubbed it out into the ashtray. "Damn, now that's a fuckin' head rush. Four years next month off of those things. That's one thing I like about Japan. I go into those little smoking cubicles they have and just breathe."

He turned serious again. "You heard about Srebrenica, right? I was one of the first ones in there after the massacre. Young kids, old guys, five thousand of them. Didn't matter to Milosevic and his crew." His eyes went inward. "Man, I've seen some heavy shit," he whispered raspily to himself as he took another slug of bourbon and soda.

"You gotta wonder if it's human nature for people to do that kind of evil. We did it to the Indians, oh excuse me, 'Native Americans,' and the Japanese did it all through Asia. Same shit, different toilet."

Phibbs showed no sign of slowing down from his monologue, and after he let drop that he had also been in Serbia, Patrick was inclined to let him just keep talking to see what came up next.

"I'm from a dirt-poor family in Kentucky. We practically had to draw straws to see who ate at night, so I've never understood this whole 'white privilege' thing. *Or* the ethnic sensitivity thing, for that matter, not that I give a rip what color anyone is. I wouldn't know sensitivity if it bit me in the ass. And, you know, Japan gets along fine without diversity. They don't have the chaos you have in other places, and they don't need to build a wall. They've got a giant moat around the whole damn country. Well, not anymore. That's one thing Proctor got right."

Patrick checked the time and remembered something he wanted to ask.

"Kirsten mentioned something about a conversation you had with a Chinese diplomat. That there's more to the China Solution than meets the eye?"

"Oh yeah, that guy. He hasn't been around to the bar for a few days. Hope nobody heard him blabbing away to me. That's a one-way ticket back to Beijing and probably a firing squad. He didn't elaborate on it, so it might have just been talk, trying to impress me kind of thing. Oh, by the way, I don't know if I mentioned it, but I'll be going on vacation right after the Games officially end. It's my usual time off, and I can't stand those after-action circle jerks. I put in for leave before all this shit happened with these Nork knuckleheads. Gonna go lose some money at my favorite Macau casino."

Patrick nodded. He had one more question but hesitated before coming out and asking it. Finally, he blurted it out. "I've got to ask you. How do you get away with everything? Saying whatever you like, pissing people off left and right. I mean, what's the saying? 'You can catch more flies with sugar than vinegar'?"

Phibbs relit the cigarette he had stubbed out. He took a single drag and stubbed it out again. Then he gulped the rest of his drink.

"I don't catch flies, Featherstone. I kill them," he said, unexpectedly serious as he set his glass down. His tone threw Patrick off guard. "Actually, I know all sorts of shit. That Srebrenica thing I mentioned? Milosevic had help, and not just from other Serbs. That's all I'll say. And no matter what anyone tells you, he didn't die of natural causes. I'll also tell you this: if I turn up facedown in a ditch..." He left the thought unfinished and called for the waitress to bring his check, which he signed with the speed and legibility of a seismograph.

"Well, I guess it's time for some people to get back to work. Me? I'm going to head over to Kabukicho," he said, referring to a notorious red-light area of Shinjuku. He bid Patrick a good night, and Patrick stared at his back, wondering exactly what Phibbs knew about whom.

CHAPTER 35

THE WHITE HOUSE
August 5

President Dillard sat at his desk rubbing his eyes with one hand and sipping dark roast with the other. He had hardly slept the night before, thanks to the latest poll numbers in the upcoming presidential election which had dramatically shifted after seventy-nine Americans, among victims from many other countries, were killed in the attack on the Yoyogi Gymnasium. One poll from the previous day had Dillard's opponent, Jon Friel, pulling within one point as a result of his seizing on the acceptance of the China Solution as a platform plank. He had even hinted that Dillard was a racist for not accepting it. The presidential race was now a statistical tie.

Dillard was startled out of his grim daydream by the trilling of his phone. His appointments secretary was on the line.

"Mister President, Ambassador Wu to see you."

"Give me a minute." He carried his coffee cup over to a tea trolley at the other end of the room, straightened his tie, and checked his face in the wall mirror. "Jesus," he said out loud to the old man who stared back at him.

"Send him in," he said over the intercom. A moment later, in walked the Chinese ambassador. Dillard walked over to greet him.

"Welcome, Mister Ambassador. Please have a seat."

"Thank you, Mister President."

Wu sat down at the coffee table across from Dillard. From the president's demeanor, Wu sensed that polite chitchat was not on the agenda, so he opened his briefcase and took out a file folder.

"Mister President, if I may get right to the point. We have new estimates on both the economic situation in North Korea as well as the number of refugees who might be expected to pour over the border into China in the event of a civil war."

He handed the file to Dillard.

"As you can see, the rice crop is expected to be half of what was predicted. Here are some photos we've gotten of malnourished citizens." Dillard looked first at the economic charts, then at the photos, which were shocking in their depiction of barely breathing human cadavers, the likes of which were commonplace in North Korea during the three Kim regimes. Nahm's government had been predicated on reversing Kim Jong-un's agricultural failures and turning the once-fertile Hamgyong and Kangwon provinces into the breadbasket of the country. Instead, Nahm had chosen a friend from his insurgency days as agricultural minister rather than someone who actually knew something about farming, with the result that the country was now approaching famine.

Wu continued. "Chosun Restoration has increased in popularity the hungrier the population has gotten. Nahm may have succeeded in deposing Kim Jong-un, but he's been a disaster as a leader. He needs help. He needs the China Solution, as does the entire region."

Dillard set down the document and photos. "Ambassador Wu, what assurance does the rest of the world have that China won't bring back the Kim family? Or that the China Solution will be in effect for a maximum of one year?"

Wu angled his head to one side and chuckled. "Mister President, I assure you, Kim Jong-un was never a friend of China's. He was like an untrained dog, and we were always having to clean up after the mess he made. In terms of the duration of the China Solution, North Korea is the last place on Earth that China wants any long-term responsibility for. It is of no strategic importance, and our only interest, as I've said, is to prevent twenty million refugees from coming over the border. That's the sum and substance of our interest in North Korea. It was a millstone around our necks during the Kim years, and now it threatens to be far worse. And as I indicated last time, we would be willing to fully restore aid and work with the Rising Tide government of President Nahm to put the country back on its feet. Believe me, we just want to protect our borders from being overrun. I'm sure you understand it from that perspective alone." Wu tilted his head again and gave a knowing smile. Protecting borders had been one of Dillard's main platform planks four years earlier.

"I just can't get the South China Sea out of my head for some reason," Dillard said pointedly.

Wu closed his eyes and let out a nose laugh. "Mister President, let me be completely frank: The South China Sea has value. North Korea is less than worthless."

After Wu made his exit ten minutes later, Dillard noticed that he had left the file folder of documents and photos on the coffee table, no doubt intentionally. Dillard picked up one of the photos and winced at the starving child it showed. Then he caught himself. That's exactly the reaction Wu would have wanted.

But what's the catch? he found himself thinking yet again.

At the next morning's news conference, several reporters grilled Dillard on the China Solution, and the president said that although he appreciated China's offer, he preferred to exercise restraint, given China's track record in recent years. The same reporters were all over him with the point that every minute he waited might result in more deaths at the hands of the terrorists in Tokyo. Dillard repeated his point about exercising restraint, then fed his press secretary to the lions for the rest of the conference, claiming an urgent cabinet meeting.

Vice President Paul Coppinger came over that afternoon for the postmortem.

"Listen to this," he said, reading from the evening edition of the *Washington Post* as he sat down in front of Dillard's desk. "'It is clear that voters are tired enough of terrorism in the Middle East. The prospect of it now spilling over from North Korea, as it appears to be doing in Japan, is the final straw. *If China wants to help North Korea put an end to the terror, we should get out of their way*, seems to be an increasingly common sentiment among voters. President Dillard's implication that China might possibly be trying to expand its hegemony over Asia is falling on deaf ears.'"

"Yeah, I saw that," Dillard said dejectedly. "Idiot voters know jack shit about China, and I'm the only one standing in the way of them controlling the whole continent. They're also looking to dip their chopsticks into Africa, did you know that? And I don't care what Wu says, this bullshit move about a 'temporary one-year protectorate' over North Korea is just the next step in completely taking over Asia. I bet you anything the first thing they'd do is bring back the Kim family. Wu kept saying Kim Jong-un was no friend of China's, but he was a lot more valuable to them than this President Nahm has been."

Coppinger nodded sympathetically, but he knew that his boss's frustration was the result of his cratering in the polls, which was at least partially the president's own fault. The televised debate two nights before had been a disaster. An overconfident Dillard had dismissed the advice of his handlers, Coppinger included, to prepare with several mock debates, and as a result Friel mopped the floor with him, citing statistic after statistic to support his claims, while Dillard tried to smirk him off as a lightweight flower child.

"You're right about you being the only bulwark against Chinese hegemony, Evan, but we need to get reelected first."

Dillard narrowed his eyes. "Oh shit, don't tell me, Paul. You're thinking I should accept this China Solution too."

Coppinger lowered his head to one side. "We definitely need a finger in the dike of these poll numbers. If you're still leery about the China Solution, how about we come out with some kind of major policy announcement to counter all the negative shit? The Space Force, for example? We've been quiet on that lately. It might show strength of the kind voters would favor. We definitely need something after yesterday's poll. Otherwise, we may be looking disaster in the face in November."

"Tell me something I don't know," Dillard said, stubbing out his cigarette. "The good news is that the next debate isn't for another few weeks, so maybe Friel's numbers yesterday were soft." Dillard poured them both some coffee while he thought.

"I've got it," he said, setting down the pot, a look of triumph on his face. "We're both going to the Olympics."

"The Olympics? I thought your daughter was going as the U.S. rep."

"That won't cut it. The public has to see you and me in a high-profile setting, something Friel can only wet dream about, and there's nothing more high-profile this year than the Olympics. Reagan and Clinton both did it and got reelected in landslides."

"But what about the rules of succession? There must be something in there that says the president and vice president can't be out of the country at the same time. And what about the terrorism going on over there? What if we're targets?"

"Obama and Biden were both abroad at the same time once. And we just have to be sure to duck if there's any trouble in Tokyo. Otherwise, next in line is Jon Fucking Friel."

"That's taking a helluva chance. With us *and* the country."

"We'll be fine. We'll be our brave and fearless selves," he said with an ironic smile. "That's one of our main strengths in the polls. The voters, in their infinite wisdom, see Friel's inexperience as a weakness. We can hammer that distinction home just by showing up in Tokyo."

"Well, alright, but let's make it a brief appearance and then come right home. I can't get Friel taking the presidential oath of office out of my head if the voters in their infinite wisdom choose him instead of us."

CHAPTER 36

August 5

Almost as a way of distracting himself from his sense of helplessness over the carnage at the Yoyogi Gymnasium, not to mention his frustration with Hayashida and Proctor, Patrick looked over his notes from the past few weeks. He had gotten into the habit of jotting down stray ideas whenever they occurred to him so that he might pursue them when he had more time. He paged through his little pocket notebook and was baffled by most of what he had scribbled. "Cadenza on smartphones" one seemed to read, but he couldn't recall what it was supposed to mean. On the opposite page, though, there was a scrawl he was able to decipher: "Bozu stress out chain smoke patriotism." He looked out his window and recalled the look on his young Korean friend's face the last time they had met. He took out his phone and thumbed in a text.

"Lunch?"

An hour later Patrick met Bozu at the Shinagawa Aquarium south of the Tokyo city center. They parked their motorcycles and climbed the steep stairs to the upper deck of the restaurant which was almost empty, since the oppressive heat had worsened and all the other customers were in the air-conditioned downstairs section. The haggard waitress who seated them managed to be polite despite being swamped in her downstairs section, and she took their orders of coffee for Bozu, Calpis for Patrick, and burgers for both. As she went off to fetch their drinks, Patrick noted the same preoccupied look on Bozu's face as last time as he took out his cigarettes and a book of matches and fired up a Melvius. Patrick leaned in over the table.

"What's going on?"

"What do you mean?" Bozu said, clearly startled by the question.

"Something's happening that you're not letting me in on. The last time we met, I got a definite sense that you wanted to tell me something."

They stopped their conversation as the waitress brought their drinks. When she had left, Patrick continued.

"Did something happen?"

Bozu sighed. "I can't say."

Patrick stared at him and said nothing. They waited in silence until the waitress brought their hamburgers, and Bozu hurriedly began wolfing his down, even though he had texted that he'd eaten not long before. Patrick began eating too and kept watching his friend. Halfway through the meal, he tried a different tack.

"What did you mean last time we met when you said, 'If someone was trying to harm your country, would you kill them?' Was it about these attacks in Tokyo?"

Bozu put down his half-eaten burger and lit a cigarette. "I can't tell you," he said, his voice piped up several keys higher than usual.

"Are you in danger?" Patrick asked. Bozu shifted uncomfortably in his seat and used a paper napkin to wipe the sweat on his forehead, sweat that had nothing to do with the heat and humidity. Suddenly, he got up from the table. "I'm sorry, Patrick, I have to go," he said, grabbing his cigarettes and walking quickly out of the restaurant. Patrick's eyes followed him. He didn't want to add to his stress, but Bozu obviously knew something about the attacks. He briefly contemplated following him at a distance but dismissed the idea. Bozu was no idiot, and he would realize immediately he was being followed. Then a book of matches on the ground where Bozu had been sitting caught his eye. Patrick held it up: "Toyama Storage."

Patrick eased his Harley down a narrow road near where the warehouses fronting the Yokohama docks meet a run-down residential area. A quick Google search had given him the location of Toyama Storage. It was now around 7 p.m., and with the normal workday over, all the warehouses except one were shuttered for the night. A light on the second floor gave Patrick all the bearings he needed. He locked his bike a block from the makeshift morgue and picked up an empty plastic soda bottle that lay on the ground. He took out his knife and cut off the top and bottom, leaving just the middle section, which he cut into a long strip, folded in half, and pocketed. He then began walking unsteadily, as if he'd had one too many in the nearby red-light district. When he was directly in front of Toyama Storage, he staggered down the alley on the side of the building and waited silently for his eyes to adjust and to see if he could pick up any bits of conversation from the second floor.

All he could make out were muffled snippets of sentences spoken by one person, punctuated by low laughter, as if that person was making a presentation of some sort and the others were his audience. One of the skills he had learned years before in JSOC was parkour climbing, in which one made use of whatever details of a building or terrain that could be used for accessing another part of it. He and Tyler had often stumbled their way back to their barracks only to find that they had missed curfew and that everything was locked up. However, resourcefulness was the main overall lesson they were learning in their training, and it didn't take long for them to apply parkour skills in vaulting the fence around their compound and climbing the side of the barracks building to their quarters on the third floor.

A storm gutter ran down the side of Toyama Storage from the roof, and Patrick tugged gently on it, testing its sturdiness. It was a bit shaky, but the only other way to climb the building from the outside was by planting his feet into the almost foot-width corrugations of the aluminum siding and somehow shimmying up back and forth, hoping that he didn't hit a wet patch and slide, or more likely, fall to the ground.

After establishing that the storm gutter would support his full weight, he looked around one last time and began his ascent. Halfway up the building, he heard the muffled conversation inside stop suddenly, and he held onto the gutter without moving. His arms began to burn; he wasn't in reach of any of the support braces of the gutter to use as a foothold. His muscles became more and more rubbery. Sweat poured down his face onto his hands. Just when he thought he'd have to risk a controlled fall down the side of the building, a burst of laughter came from inside. Apparently, someone had been telling an involved joke with a particularly good punch line.

Using the laughter as a cover for any noise he might make, Patrick pulled himself hand over hand to the top before there were any more lulls in the conversation. Once on top of the building, he walked carefully over to the fire door which was locked from the inside but luckily not with a deadbolt. He removed his boots and took out the length of plastic he had cut from the soda bottle and inserted it into the space just above the doorknob. When it was all the way through to the other side, he eased it down between the faceplate and strike plate of the latch and slowly cracked the door open until it began to squeak, at which point he took out a tube of lip balm from a utility pocket, dug out a thick chunk, and worked it thoroughly into each of the rusty-looking hinges. A minute later; he ever so gently opened the door, the hinges still squeaking slightly but not as much as before. He continued easing the door open a millimeter at a time until he could squeeze through.

Once on the other side, he switched on a tiny penlight whose cone of illumination was narrow but all he needed to make his way down the stairs at the same snail's pace. He paused when he reached the landing and listened. The conversation had continued as before, but he couldn't take a chance that his unfamiliarity with the upper floors of the building might suddenly give him away when, say, one of the hardwood boards began to creak.

He pointed the penlight at the first room he came to. Its door was slightly ajar, and he slowly pushed it open. Shining the light around the room, he could see it was the bedroom of a generic young male, with clothes hanging off of chairs and several items of dishware sitting unwashed on the desk that fronted the room's only window. Something on the desk caught his attention: a group photo, indistinct in the low light, showing four men, one of them older, and three of them in their late teens or early twenties. He took his phone from his pocket and snapped a flash photo of the photo. Then he noticed that the conversation downstairs had died down.

He pocketed his phone and moved more quickly out of the room and over to the stairway leading up to the roof. Sure enough, just as he was creeping up the stairs, he heard the voices of two men, one older and one younger, coming up a lower flight. They appeared to be making small talk before heading off to bed, but he decided to wait on the landing outside the door leading to the roof until he was sure he wouldn't be detected. The two men were moving up the stairs more slowly than might be expected, with the older man lagging behind with what appeared to be an injured leg judging from the way he took the stairs one at a time. They said goodnight to each other, and Patrick had a fleeting glimpse of the older man as he limped into his room. About fifty years of age, Asian, no unusual facial features. He didn't appear to be one of the men in the photo, but then again, Patrick couldn't really make out any details in the low light of the room. He would enlarge the image later.

After waiting almost an hour on the landing, he heard the sound of snoring coming from the room in which he had taken the photo, so he slowly began climbing the stairs leading to the roof. Once there, he grabbed his boots and walked toe to heel in his socks to the other side of the roof. Since space is at such a premium in Japan, the buildings are often constructed directly next to each other, and the one adjoining

Toyama Storage was two feet away at most. Desperately hoping that the roof of the adjoining building was sturdy, he crouched on the ledge of Toyama Storage, threw his boots across the divide, and launched himself across to the other building. He lay on the roof for several minutes until he was sure his jump had gone undetected. Then he reverse-shimmied down the drainpipe to street level, where he walked to his Harley, rolled it down a slight hill, and started it up. A minute later, he was on the Shuto Expressway leading to Tokyo.

After parking his bike in his usual spot at the stadium, Patrick was walking to his office suite when he felt a jolt of apprehension. Kirsten was standing outside his door.

"Kirsten. Everything okay?" he said, tension tightening his voice.

"Yes. Well, no." She took a breath before continuing. "Please please please don't take this the wrong way, but I need to get out of that embassy. Proctor is driving me and everyone else nuts. Is there any possibility at all I can join you and Mister Choy over here? Again, please don't read anything else into it."

Patrick relaxed and smiled. "Of course. I completely understand. Come on in, but I should tell you, Phibbs is also here."

Kirsten grunted and rolled her eyes, but followed Patrick into his suite. Once inside Patrick waved his hand around. "It's not much, but I call it hell."

Kirsten smiled, the first time he'd seen her anything but morose since he'd broken off whatever had been developing between them.

"Charming," she said facetiously, indicating the takeout boxes littering the floor. Patrick pointed to a small desk off to one side.

"It's all yours, if you're still interested in relocating to this dump."

"I've seen worse, believe me," Kirsten said, and she set her briefcase down on the desk and took a seat. "Where's Phibbs?" she asked guardedly.

"Probably skulking around dark alleys looking for lost spies. Don't worry, his workspace is in one of these back rooms. He won't bother you." Patrick went directly to his desk and sent the photos he had taken on his phone at Toyama Storage to his computer and proceeded to enlarge them. As the images appeared on his computer screen, he felt a jolt of adrenaline. The older man in the photo with the three young men he recognized right away. All doubt about who was behind the attacks evaporated. He called Choy in from his small lair off of Patrick's office. Choy came out, greeted Kirsten, and took one look at the unsmiling face on the screen. He let out a long "Hmmmm" that started high and ended low and put his hands backwards on his hips as he rocked from back and forth. Hearing the emotion in Choy's voice, Kirsten came over and lowered her head close to Patrick's computer screen.

"His name is Pung Min-ho," Patrick said to her. "I had the pleasure of meeting him in North Korea. I bet you anything he's the one sending the texts."

Choy added, "Comrade Moon's right-hand man. I was sure he was dead."

"And I'm sure he hates my guts for killing Moon," Patrick added. "But I don't see him being the leader of these attacks. If he's the best Chosun Restoration can do, they've got problems."

Choy said "Mmmm" again, but this time in an appraising way. "I agree. The real leader has to be someone smarter."

Kirsten said, "I still don't get why he didn't just kill you at the stadium if he hates you so much?"

"I have to believe it's so he can have the last laugh. When I was in North Korea, I made him lose face in front of Comrade Moon. This is his way of turning the tables. That's my theory, anyway."

He was about to continue when he heard a sound outside his office. Choy and Kirsten had heard it too and were looking at Patrick expectantly. Patrick tiptoed to the door and opened it quickly. Minoru Kaga stood outside with his hand raised to knock on the door, but the look on his face telegraphed the debate going on in his head. He took a step back.

"I'm sorry to bother you, Mister Featherstone," he said sheepishly.

"Patrick. Call me Patrick. Come in. What can I do for you?"

Kaga entered the room and took a deep breath which he then expelled quickly. "I would like to work for your team."

Patrick laughed. "My 'team' is getting bigger and bigger all the time. Aren't you with Hayashida's 'team'?"

"Yes, but..." He looked to one side and paused.

"But what?"

"Actually, he was the one who sent me over here to spy on you. He also told me not to tell you about debris they found at the Yoyogi Gymnasium. There was a fragment of a license plate from the truck that blew up. He said he wanted the JIA forensics lab to analyze it."

"Did he say why he kept that information from me?"

"He wanted the JIA to get the credit."

Patrick shook his head and spat air. "Yet again with these stupid power games. Hayashida on one side, Proctor on the other. And with this license plate thing you'd think he'd want as many hands on board as possible to try and find leads."

Kaga looked down again. "As it turned out, there wasn't enough information on the license plate to follow up on, but that's the way he operates. I don't like it. Or Mister Proctor, to tell you the truth."

Kirsten laughed at the last comment. "You're not going to find a lot of people who would find any fault in that."

"Mister Hayashida also wants it so that if anything else happens, he can blame the Americans. He was the one who gave NHK News your photo that appeared on the television after the Yoyogi attack. He was hoping you would resign."

"Surprise, surprise. That's one reason I moved my office over here. Come on in and close the door. And welcome to the 'team.' You can be the resident double agent and let me know what Hayashida is up to."

Patrick went on to tell the group about Toyama Storage in Yokohama.

"Shouldn't we tell the others?" Kirsten asked.

Patrick stood with his head tilted sharply down to the left, his eyes looking up and to the right, his forefinger pressed against his lips as if telling himself, "Shh." But to the observant eye, the finger was twitching as if pulling a trigger as he thought the situation through. Hayashida would no doubt lead a raid on Toyama Storage for the greater glory of Japan, and any hope of getting to the bottom of Chosun Restoration would be lost. For his part, Mr. Subtlety Garrett Proctor would probably call in a Hellfire strike.

"Tell them what?" Patrick asked Kirsten, all wide-eyed innocence.

CHAPTER 37

The next morning

"*Meet now!*"

Bozu's gut clenched when he read the text from Patrick.

"*Where?*" he texted. It took his fingers several tries to find the right letters.

"*Yokohama Landmark Tower twenty minutes.*"

Patrick arrived at the Tower and was about to go up to the observation deck on the seventieth floor when he saw Bozu sitting off by himself on a bench by the vending machines. From twenty feet away, Patrick could see Bozu's leg jiggling up and down like a piston as he chewed on a plastic straw while squinting at nothing. As Patrick approached, Bozu jumped up. Patrick pointed with his hand to the elevator, which they entered together and rode up in silence. When the door opened to the deck, Patrick led the way to the side of the building facing the dockland area. He pointed to a building that Bozu knew well.

"I went there," Patrick said.

"But how…?" Bozu exhaled instead of finishing his sentence. "Then you know where they are."

"But I don't know *who* they are, and you're about to tell me." Patrick took out his phone and tapped on the photo he had taken of the group photo in the room he had entered.

Bozu could hardly string together a coherent sentence as he told Patrick about Toyama Storage's repurposed function as a corpse hotel and the residence for a dwindling group of young North Korean men, three of whom were in the photo Patrick was showing him. He went on to describe the recent luncheon and ceremony that he had partially witnessed while waiting on those in attendance. The detail of his account that captured Patrick's attention like no other was that of a coffin being wheeled in for the luncheon.

"Comrade Moon? You're sure that's what they said?"

"I know they'll kill me, me and my brother and father," Bozu said.

"What else did they say? Come on, you have to hold it together here, a lot of lives are at stake, not just yours and your family's. What else did they say?"

Bozu forced himself to inhale deeply. As he exhaled, his eyes filled, and his head rocked from side to side. "The leader is a man they called Mister Lee. He had the young North Korean guys do some kind of ritual where they pricked their fingers with pins and set the blood on fire on wads of cotton. Lee said something like 'This ritual was created by Comrade Moon who was the founder of Bureau 39.' I know they're behind these attacks, Patrick. Mister Lee made my brother kill someone after the nerve gas attack on the subway. I'm so sorry I couldn't say anything before, I was just too afraid that they'd..." Despite the heat and humidity, Bozu had his arms wrapped tightly around himself.

"Have you ever fired a gun before?" Patrick asked.

Bozu nodded his head. "Yes. With the motorcycle gang."

"Get on your bike and follow me."

During his friendly shooting competition with Tyler at the SDF headquarters in Tokyo, Patrick realized that although Tyler's skills had been rusty beyond recognition, his own left much to be desired as well thanks to the endless hours he was spending on job-related meetings and paperwork. Since that competition, he had earmarked an hour a day for shooting practice at the same range, sometimes with Tyler, sometimes not. Within a few days, his accuracy had improved somewhat, but he was nowhere near where he wanted to be. Thus, Bozu's need for some serious armament gave him the perfect opportunity both to refresh whatever meager skills Bozu had learned in his motorcycle gang and for Patrick to hone his own prowess.

After they left the Yokohama Landmark Tower, Patrick had Bozu follow him to the SDF's Asaka Shooting Range in the northwest part of Tokyo. It would be the venue for Olympic shooting competitions, and after Patrick flashed his security creds, he introduced Bozu to the sergeant in charge as a member of the South Korean shooting team. The sergeant waved them through.

Once on the range, Patrick placed his tactical backpack on the ground and took out his 9mm SIG Sauer P226. He thumbed the safety on and off a few times, just to get the feel of it, and handed it to Bozu while looking around to make sure no one was nearby.

"Two things: One, if you don't know what you're doing, don't do it faster. Two, don't shoot anybody. Life's short enough without you making it shorter."

Bozu took the gun without hesitation, released its empty magazine, and pinch-pulled the slide to fully clear it. A suppressed smile formed at the corners of Patrick's mouth, and he handed Bozu a box of bullets.

"Nice," Bozu said, holding the box up to inspect. "Nothing says goodbye like a jacketed hollow point."

Patrick shook his head. "You've been holding back."

Bozu smiled. "You have no idea," he said and began pressing the bullets into the magazine.

An hour later both of them had gone through two hundred rounds each. Although it soon became clear that Bozu's skills as an actual shooter paled in comparison to his pose as a would-be gunslinger who read gun magazines, by the end of the hour he was finding the bull about 30 percent of the time and hitting the outer rings the rest of the time with very few total misses. Patrick had been away from any sustained pistol work for months, but by the end of the hour he was shooting bulls 80 percent of the time. Both his own abilities and Bozu's were a source of relief. Plus, he now had an extra shooter.

Later that same evening, after they had gone their separate ways, Patrick got a text from Bozu asking to meet him again as soon as possible at the Shinagawa Aquarium.

"We need to go outside," Bozu said when Patrick arrived. His tone and manner were agitated. Patrick followed him out to the veranda. Bozu went to the extreme far end of the deck and sat at one of the metal tables.

"Water," he said excitedly.

"What are you talking about?" Patrick asked.

"Their next targets have something to do with water."

"You said targets. More than one?"

"I think so. I got back and overheard them saying something about taking a train on the Ome Line for one of the 'picnics,' that's what they call the attacks, and that the other picnic is near Iwabuchi. Both are planned for the day after tomorrow."

"The Ome line leads west, and Iwabuchi is north. Hang on." Patrick began a Google search of the two areas on his phone. He didn't have far to look.

"If it's really about water, then one of the targets has to be the Ogouchi Reservoir and the other one has to be the Aosuimon, the Blue Sluice Gate. Did they say what they're planning on doing?"

"I couldn't hear. I was listening through the wall."

"Well, the reservoir supplies most of Tokyo with its drinking water, so it's huge."

"What about the other one?"

Patrick scrolled down on his phone. "The Blue Sluice Gate is the only thing keeping the Arakawa River from flooding northern Tokyo after this past rainy season." He looked up from his phone. "Who's going to do it, all of them?"

"I'm pretty sure one of them said he was going to try and recruit a woman to do something to that second target you mentioned." Bozu asked Patrick for his cellphone, went to the camera app, and tapped on the photo Patrick had taken at the corpse hotel. He enlarged it with his fingers and pointed to one of the people in the photo.

"This is the guy. He's going to meet the woman tomorrow. He thinks he's a real ladies' man, and he calls himself 'Casanova' like the K-pop singer."

Patrick looked at the photo and memorized the young man's features the way he would memorize faces of the targets he had been assigned as a sniper. Bozu told him where Casanova would be meeting the woman the next day, and Patrick ran to his bike.

"Let me help," Bozu called out, his jaw set in determination.

"You're more help where you are," Patrick shouted back. "I can't risk going back there, and you already have a cover." Seeing Bozu's face, he jogged back to him. "Believe me, if you can get more information like this, then you're going to be saving more lives than I ever could."

Bozu reluctantly accepted Patrick's explanation and walked dejectedly back to his bike.

CHAPTER 38

All through his years at Mangyongdae Revolutionary School, Casanova had lived up to his nickname, with at least two scandals involving freshman girls. His father, a Central Court justice, had to bribe one of the girls' parents, and he forced his priapic son to apologize with a backhand to his face that broke his nose. After it healed imperfectly at the hands of a state doctor, the girls in Casanova's circle of friends found something ruggedly handsome and slightly dangerous about his new face. He was a natural for the next murderous assignment on the docket.

From all appearances, Megumi Noguchi, born on the island of Shikoku, would be regarded as Japanese, but she carried within her a stain that no amount of purification at a Shinto shrine could cleanse. Her forebears of centuries past on her father's side had been butchers and gravediggers, people associated with death, and for this alleged crime against the tenets of Buddhism, they would be called "people of the hamlet" or *burakumin*. A less euphemistic term was *ningai* or "outside of humanity." The Japanese government at one point declared that burakumin were worth one-seventh of an ordinary person, or less than a slave in America at the time of the Dred Scott Decision.

Megumi Noguchi's father didn't help matters any when he married a Palestinian woman, Megumi's mother, although their daughter's features were far more Japanese than Middle Eastern. After high school Megumi moved to Tokyo where she hid her ancestry and place of birth from college officials and matriculated at a junior college in the down-at-heel Taito Ward in the northern part of the city. Soon she gravitated to a political action club sponsored by the radical Japanese Red Army, which had as its mission the liberation of the world from the type of oppression she herself had been the victim of. Her college career came to an abrupt end when, in an attempt at ingratiating herself with the handsome leader of the Brigade, she foolhardily self-published a bomb-making manual that she distributed on campus.

Now Megumi Nonaka was forty-four years old and feeling every second of it. Although blessed with a lovely face, she was single, loveless, and barely scraping by at Fleur, her beauty shop, and despairing of ever finding someone to share her life, especially since her background was so tarnished by her *burakumin* background and the bomb-making manual she had published in junior college. What customers she had these days were mostly fellow middle-aged women with little future. As she sat in the back of her salon in existential dejection, smoking a cigarette and thumbing through gossip magazines, the glasslike bell of her shop door tinkled.

"*Irasshaimase,*" ("Welcome") she called out half-heartedly, stubbing her cigarette into the ashtray and coming out to greet her customer. How she hated this life and the unfairness of Japanese society, which oppressed so many like her in the name of racial purity. But as she parted the beaded curtain and entered the salon, she saw that this was not one of her regulars. She had no male customers except the transvestites who cruised the nearby red-light district at night. And the one entering her shop looked like something out of a rock band, although there was something vaguely foreign about him.

"In town for a concert?" she asked him as she readied her chair for him. He stared at her with parted lips for a moment, smiled, and then nodded.

"My Japanese not good," he said, revealing dimples she hadn't noticed when he was just standing there mutely. "I want make style and blonde hair please."

Megumi smiled back and indicated the seat. Such a cute accent and good manners. "Of course." She snapped a nylon cape around his neck and began styling his hair, snipping just a little here and there. He sat in silence watching her in the mirror. She then went to a closet to get the chemicals she would use.

"What group are you in?" she asked as she brought them back.

"Doki Doki Dokei," he said, still looking at her intently in the mirror. She stopped. "Doki Doki Dokei" meant "timebomb" and was the name of the manual she had written in junior college.

He unsnapped and removed the nylon cape around his neck and took her hand.

"I hear about you from friend. So beautiful," he whispered. Megumi's eyes widened. He held her gaze, and she felt her breathing becoming quick and shallow.

"You're so young," she said shakily, her legs going weak as he continued to hold her gaze. He reached out and ran the back of his hand down each cheek in turn. Her breath turned into short, panicky gasps as he lowered one hand to her breast and drew her face to his with the other. She took his hand off her breast, and for a moment he questioned his charm until she went to the front door, locked it, and led him to the back room where she kept a foldout couch.

Afterwards, they shared one of her Sobranie Black Russian cigarettes and drifted a finger's breadth above the earth in luxurious afterglow. She traced his slightly misshapen nose with her finger.

"You're a fighter," she said with a smile. He turned to face her and smiled back.

"I fight for good things," he said.

"Have you always liked older women?" she asked. He nodded with a bashful smile. In truth he preferred his high school freshman conquests, but he'd make an exception if it furthered his agenda.

"And I fall in love with you from your book," he said in a confessional tone, as if he needed to apologize for coming to her shop on the false pretense of being a K-pop singer in need of a touchup for his locks.

"You are so intelligent. And also so…I don't know Japanese word. It mean 'fight for poor people.'"

"Maybe 'struggle'?"

"Yes, that word. I hear it before but could not remember."

They talked the rest of the afternoon of the ruling classes' oppression of the workers of the world, and they agreed that they both wanted to do something about it. Something big that would make the world sit up and pay attention to them for a change. Then they made love four more times over the course of the afternoon. Afterwards, Casanova kissed her gently on the lips and told her he would be back the following day with the next step of the plan they had devised between lovemaking sessions.

Megumi rejoiced in the fact that she had finally discovered someone in Japan who could fill the empty parts of her soul and body.

And Casanova rejoiced in the fact that he had finally discovered someone in Japan who was not only a damn good lay for an old bitch, but also a willing dupe in the plan that would restore him and his fellow princelings to their former glory in Pyonghattan.

As he made his way back to the corpse hotel, he was so absorbed in his conquest that he didn't realize that he had been followed to the beauty parlor by a man with Italian features who had been waiting outside the whole time. The man cocked his finger like a pistol and aimed it at the murderous boy as he receded into the dwindling twilight.

CHAPTER 39

Patrick sat in his office with Kirsten, Phibbs, and Kaga, with Choy in the back room working on his computer. Patrick addressed the group.

"We don't know how many of them are going to be involved. It could be one, it could be more. Bozu doesn't know how many of them are left. One of them recruited a hairdresser who wrote a bomb-making manual in junior college." Patrick told them. Choy came out to join them when Patrick mentioned this last detail.

"You gotta be kidding, junior college?" Phibbs said.

Patrick nodded. "She's a hardcore radical. Definitely not your typical Japanese office lady."

"Do we know when and where they're planning to do it?" Kirsten asked.

"Two days from now, probably at the Blue Sluice Gate in Iwabuchi, but that's really just a guess."

"I'll go."

All eyes turned to Kirsten. "Go where?" Patrick asked.

"I'll go to the hairdresser and see if I can find out more details."

Phibbs looked at her without speaking, but his doubt came through loud and clear.

"I know some of you are probably skeptical," Kirsten said. "'What can a desk officer do in the field?' you're thinking. But screw you, we all had to do undercover training at Quantico."

"Which was not all that long ago," Phibbs said under his breath.

"You're good at that, Phibbs, muttering stuff and being all wiseass about it. Why not just come out and say you think I'm too green?"

Phibbs looked the other way.

"I think it might be a good idea," Choy said. "It's not as if we have a lot of options." They all looked at Patrick, who was wondering if Kirsten was at all motivated by the murder of her undercover husband. Bravery or bravado? Maybe the psychological profiler had a profile of her own. After a minute of deliberation, he spoke.

"I'm willing to give it a shot. The worst that can happen is that you get a bad haircut."

"Or a pair of scissors in the throat if she's made," said Phibbs.

"I'm not going to be made, okay? I'm not a total fucking idiot."

"I didn't say you were, it's just that you haven't done this before."

"Which means I'll have my eyes open and not think I know everything, unlike some people." Phibbs opened his mouth but closed it again.

"Alright," Patrick said. "You need to come up with a good cover story. Think of all the possible questions she might sound you out on."

"Hey, maybe she's looking for a girlfriend," Phibbs muttered under his breath.

"Fuck off, Phibbs, not everyone's as horny as you." Kirsten went back to her worktable. Phibbs's laugh rang loud and tinny, like the peal of a dented bell.

CHAPTER 40

"*Irasshaimase,*" Megumi called out to an incoming customer more ener-getically than usual. Ever since she had met the Korean boy who called himself Casanova, her step had become lighter and her outlook infinitely brighter than before. He would be coming over again later that night. The customer now walking in was a foreign woman in her thirties with softly alluring features and dark blonde hair. She nodded to Megumi uncertainly, and it was clear that she didn't speak any Japanese. But she saw that Megumi had been watching Al-Jazeera on the television, and she tentatively asked Megumi if she spoke Arabic after introducing herself as Amira.

"*Na'am!*" said Megumi enthusiastically, and the two of them began to converse in Arabic, first in polite generalities, and then about what the woman wanted hairstyle-wise.

"Just a little trim to get rid of the split ends, nothing drastic. And what do you think about a little color? Can you bring out some highlights?"

Megumi started in. "So are you in town for the Games, Amira?" she asked as she cut.

"Yes, I'm here to cover the Olympics for a magazine."

"Oh, an Arabic one?"

"Yes," the woman said in a softer voice, as if trying to decide whether to say more. She looked at Megumi in the mirror, and said, "It's called *al-Iirjae.*"

Megumi stopped cutting. "I've heard of it. It means 'return,' yes?"

The woman nodded. "My father is from Palestine. I was always raised to do what I can for the return of Palestine."

Sensing no negative reaction from Megumi, the customer got more specific about exactly what she had done for the cause of wresting Palestinian territory back from Israel, including being a member of an underground group that provided safe houses for fugitives suspected of being terrorists. Suddenly Kirsten/Amira stopped in midsentence. Her head moved forward, and her eyes went to a thin volume on the magazine table. Megumi followed her eyes and became flustered. She hurried to the magazine table and placed the day's newspaper over what Amira was looking at.

"Wait," Amira said. "Can I see that?"

Megumi hesitated but then removed the newspaper and brought the pamphlet over to Amira. It was an English translation of the bomb-making manual she had written in junior college. She had brought it out for Casanova to look at when he came by later.

As Kirsten/Amira read, she nodded her head and smiled. "I didn't realize how committed you are to the cause of justice," she said to Megumi.

Megumi looked intently at Kirsten for several moments before continuing. "I'm also a member of an underground group. We're called the Pan Asia Anti-Japan Armed Front." Kirsten/Amira listened attentively as Megumi spoke and thumbed through the beautician's bomb-making handbook. She stopped at one of the illustrations, and Megumi said, "Anyone with an intermediate knowledge of chemistry can do that one." She explained that it made use of sodium chlorite-based herbicides which can be gotten without suspicion in large quantities out in the more rural areas.

After Megumi had finished explaining, the customer opened her handbag and took out her wallet. She gave Megumi a healthy tip as well as a business card.

"We should meet again soon, I think," she said to Megumi pointedly.

"How about tomorrow?" Megumi said.

The two women, strangers just a few short hours earlier, embraced like sisters. Sisters in the cause. They would meet again the following day.

CHAPTER 41

Unlike the Miyamoto Musashi texts that came in before the earlier attacks, the next one to appear on Patrick's phone was less cryptic, thanks to Bozu's tip: *"Water is sometimes a trickle and sometimes a wild sea."*

Patrick knew that one of the targets was most likely the Ogouchi Reservoir in the far western part of the metropolis that holds the water supply for most of Tokyo. The immense reservoir holds about 190 million tons, and there was no way Patrick and his little team could be effective there. He had no desire to meet or even talk with Hayashida, so he told Kaga to let his boss know about the possible plot at the reservoir, saying nothing about the Blue Sluice Gate.

Set on a floodplain of reclaimed swampland on an active earthquake fault line, the harbor city of Tokyo seems as unlikely a location for a world capital as any in the world. Much of the metropolis lies below sea level, and its eight rivers contribute even further to the city's vulnerability to flooding, as in the Great Kanto Flood of 1910 when the Sumida River broke through its embankments and turned the city into a vast inland sea. One of the government's responses was to build the Aosuimon, or Blue Sluice Gate, which prevents the Arakawa (literally "wild river") from overflowing during a hard rain by shunting the excess water into a drainage canal that flows to the sea. In the weeks leading up to the Olympics, the gate had come down so often due to torrential rains that the government had decided to leave it down until at least the end of typhoon season in September.

Kirsten had gone back to Megumi's salon the day after her first visit, at which time Megumi had enlisted her for what she called "direct action" against the Islam-hating world. They would set out the following day. She cited the 1972 Munich Olympics and promised her new recruit that what she had planned would make those attacks seem puny and amateurish in comparison.

The next day, as the train slowed its approach into the Tokyo Metro station a few blocks from the American embassy, Kirsten thumbed back the hair over her right ear and turned her head from side to side to examine her reflection in the windows of the decelerating train. Dressed in a lightweight tracksuit, she wondered for an instant if anyone might be thinking she was an athlete in town for the Olympics but then immediately dismissed the thought. Ten years ago, maybe. Her eyes gave her away, and not because of the crow's feet that she tried unsuccessfully to hide under a layer of foundation. It wasn't as if she were stuck in the past, she thought to herself. Landon was dead and wasn't coming back and that was that. It was more like being stuck in an unchanging present that held no promise of anything more satisfying on a level she desperately missed. In a word, she felt unloved. But as she boarded the train and sat down, she remembered where she was going and why. She touched her ankle to make sure that the 11.5 ounces of metal she was carrying had no chance of falling off.

A half hour later, as the train approached Akabane-iwabuchi Station, the end of the line, she began to feel a sense of deepening apprehension, and she ran through a mental checklist of things she needed to be fully aware of: surveil the area to be sure that only the one young Korean was there with Megumi; allow their mission to proceed up to a point where no one would get hurt but would allow enough time for Patrick to neutralize the hostile actors; always have access to the Colt Mustang that was irritating her ankle.

Exiting the station, she could see the coffee-colored Arakawa River in the distance, and she checked the time on her phone. Megumi would meet her at the riverbank in twenty minutes, and they would maintain their pose as two youthful fitness enthusiasts out for a noontime jog. She'd been told that the temperature would be slightly cooler near the river, but when she considered what she had gotten herself into, it suddenly felt like the sun had traveled a few million miles closer to the earth.

Waiting at the New Arakawa Bridge, Megumi waved to Kirsten in a hurry-up gesture, and Kirsten began jogging toward her. Unlike her look of excited anticipation at her beauty shop, Megumi's face was tense.

"We're late. I heard from him that he wanted to start early," she said in Arabic.

Kirsten's brow knit, but she didn't protest. "Alright. Does he have the…"

"Yes," Megumi said, holding her hand up and cutting her off. The only people around were a group of visibly drunk men staggering to a recycling truck carrying plastic bags full of empty cans, but Megumi was acting as if they were surrounded by undercover Arabic-speaking JIA agents.

"Don't worry, I'm not new to this," Kirsten said as they began jogging along the Arakawa Greenspace on the bank of the Arakawa River.

"Sorry, I don't want to take any chances," Megumi said. She looked at the digital watch/pedometer on her wrist and squinted into the near distance at the Blue Sluice Gate a quarter mile away. "There it is," she said, and Kirsten looked to where she was pointing. Three metal barriers, each twenty feet across and sixty feet high, were suspended between four huge concrete stanchions. The barriers had been lowered into the river against a tide that was raging as a result of the torrential rainy season.

"It's a pretty simple arrangement," Megumi said as they jogged. For a woman who smoked as much as she did, Megumi was in more than decent shape. She panted slightly but was fully able to carry on a conversation. "We'll each take one of the gates."

"Got it," Kirsten said. As they approached the Blue Sluice Gate, they saw a young man in a track suit stretching on the grass next to a gym bag. He didn't acknowledge them as they got closer until they were directly in front of him. They all surreptitiously looked around at the few runners and homeless people on the footpath. It was nearing noon, and it became clear why the young man wanted to start early. The nearby office buildings would be clearing out in a short while for lunch, and he wanted a high body count.

Megumi made a show of being surprised at the young man's presence. "Oh, I didn't know you jogged here too!"

Casanova smiled dyspeptically as he looked at Kirsten. Megumi spoke again. "This is my very good friend Amira I told you about," she said. Kirsten/Amira smiled nervously and said, "Nice to meet you," in English. Casanova continued to stare at Kirsten suspiciously before finally inviting them to sit down on the grass. He brought the gym bag in front of him. Opening it, he took out a box of cookies that he offered to them. After they had nibbled on the cookies, he took out three bricklike objects wrapped like presents.

"I have *omiyage* presents, so please..." he said in English, handing them each one of the bricks. Then he continued in a low voice. "Climb to top of gates. Megumi, you take number one, and Amira, take two. I will take three," and he pointed to the closest of the three gates. "I am here today one hour, and also yesterday. Nobody watching." He then explained that once up on the platform of the Sluice, it was a simple matter of climbing as quickly as they could up the ladder grips that ran along the sides of the three gates, packing the C4 bricks into the hinges that ran along the tops of the gates, and coming back down again. The bombs were remote-controlled, he said, indicating his cell phone.

A quarter mile on the other side of the Sluice from where Kirsten and Megumi had jogged in, Patrick sat in the grass next to a bicycle with a pair of binoculars. He had been intently observing the avian life of the riverbank, a not uncommon pastime, and occasionally he had followed a "bird" as it flew in the direction of the Blue Sluice. As he saw Kirsten, Megumi, and Casanova get up with the bombs in their hands, he looked around the area one more time. From what Bozu had told him, there might be more of the young Bonghwajo involved in the attack on the Sluice, but Kirsten, Megumi, and Casanova looked to be the entire crew. He set down the binoculars, turned his back on the Sluice, and removed his Glock from the saddlebag of the bike and racked the slide to feed a round into the chamber. As he turned back to face the Sluice with the gun in his waistband with the safety on, he saw Kirsten reaching down to "scratch" her ankle, making sure that her Colt Mustang was good to go. It was also Patrick's signal. He looked around one more time to be sure there were no other Bonghwajo in the area and began pedaling toward the Sluice.

On Casanova's go, Megumi and Kirsten followed him up the stairs of the concrete landing below the water barriers, and they all walked quickly to the rungs protruding from the concrete stanchions. Once on top of their respective gates, the three went directly to the large metal hinges that controlled the up and down motion of the gates, all of which were firmly closed against the enormous volume of water that had accumulated in the river as a result of the rainy season's twenty-three days of steady precipitation. Kirsten looked around nervously for Patrick. The plan was to go along with Casanova and Megumi until it was clear that reinforcements would not be coming and then for her and/or Patrick to shoot them both. Now with a brick of C4 in her hand, her breathing went into panic mode as she searched the area for Patrick, who had not yet arrived on the scene. Suddenly, Megumi called out.

"Wait!" she shouted to Casanova. "There's a playground right over there." She pointed from her perch atop her gate at Meisho Kindergarten, where children were playing less than a few hundred yards away. The school had not been visible from the ground.

"Keep going," Casanova shouted.

"But you said it would only be government buildings," Megumi called back. With both of them arguing back and forth, Kirsten surreptitiously dropped her brick into the river and climbed back down.

"It's too late," Casanova yelled, and he took out his cellphone/detonator. "Get off now," he screamed to Megumi and jumped the remaining eight feet off his gate onto the concrete landing. He began running toward the riverbank next to the Sluice.

"You can't just kill those children!" Megumi shouted. She climbed back to the hinge where she had left her C4, ripped it out of the hinge casing, and threw it into the river. Casanova swore and looked down at his phone. Before he could trigger a detonation, Kirsten grabbed her Colt from her ankle holster. Casanova looked over at her just as she was bringing the gun up. He jumped to avoid being hit and fell off the concrete, landing onto the ground ten feet below, where he lay unmoving. Megumi looked down at Kirsten in shock but then began climbing the rungs to the top of Casanova's gate to retrieve the block of C4 he had left on top. "Come down, Megumi!" Kirsten shouted, but Megumi continued climbing. Patrick arrived just as Megumi reached the top of the gate. "Where's Casanova?" he shouted to Kirsten, but she was too involved in what Megumi was doing to even hear him.

As Megumi was about to throw the other block of plastic explosive into the river, Casanova lifted his head up off the ground, saw what she was trying to do, and pressed the screen of his phone. Immediately the block of C4 exploded in Megumi's hand, leaving only a flash of light where she had been standing. The gate became dislodged from its tracks, allowing the swollen Arakawa River to pour through the gap, but the other two gates held firmly against the torrent. Water rose twenty feet up the bank and then leveled off, sparing Meisho Kindergarten and most of the other buildings above the riverbank. Kirsten and Patrick swam ashore and turned to look at where Casanova had been lying, but the area was now completely inundated.

CHAPTER 42

AMERICAN EMBASSY

The after-action review by the combined security command quickly went from bad to worse. Hayashida had sent hundreds of JIA agents to the Ogouchi Dam, but they found nothing. It was obvious that he and Proctor had discussed the situation before Patrick had arrived.

"Featherstone, I have to ask," Proctor began. "For some reason, I can't get out of my head the possibility that there never was a threat to the Ogouchi Dam. Meanwhile, your heroics at the Blue Sluice Gate get front-page coverage. It was as if someone wanted the JIA out of the way. After all, no terrorists were anywhere to be found except at the Sluice."

Patrick's mouth dropped. "You think I made up the threat to the Dam in order to hog the glory at the Sluice?"

"Nothing like that, Mister Featherstone," said Hayashida, "but what Mister Proctor and I were wondering was if you have some kind of inside source. I mean, how did you know there would be an attack on the Blue Sluice Gate?"

Patrick was ready with an answer. "I found a fragment of a license plate, Mister Hayashida. You know, like the one from the Yoyogi Gymnasium you kept from me?" Hayashida's face fell, and he glared at Kaga. Kaga glared back.

Patrick continued. "And Proctor, you don't know enough about anything here to even be opening your mouth, so how about keeping it shut for a change?"

Predictably, Proctor didn't. "Hayashida and I want you to step down. There's just too many cooks in all this, and we want you to resign."

Intense indignation blazed in Patrick's gut, and he turned from side to side in disbelief at what Hayashida and Proctor had just suggested. Then he saw Kaga. His jaw was set, and he was ever so slightly shaking his head, telling Patrick not to even think of quitting. It was all Patrick needed. He stilled his breathing to regain his composure and turned to Proctor and Hayashida.

"My contract is ironclad, and there's no way I'm going to step down, especially if you two are proposing it. But from now on you can count on one thing: I'm on my own. And so are you."

He turned on his heel and made for the door. He hesitated briefly when he heard footsteps right behind him. He turned and saw it was Kaga. Together, they began to exit the room.

Hayashida called after Kaga. "I knew you weren't a loyal Japanese."

Kaga turned back. "It's because I'm a loyal Japanese that I'm no longer working for you. I resign."

Patrick laughed as they continued out the door. "And I hereby hire him."

CHAPTER 43

President Dillard demanded from his chief of staff a rare fifteen minutes alone prior to his meeting with two senators and a congressman from his own party several hours before his departure for the Olympics. A naturally gregarious man who derived energy from crowds, especially crowds of adoring supporters, he had been feeling uncharacteristically spent and weary lately, and a gnawing part of his psyche had been whispering in his ear that he really wouldn't mind all that much if he weren't reelected in November. But then the loathsome face of his opponent, Jon Friel, crowded out all else, especially Friel's condescending smirk during the first of their televised debates.

Unlike his opponent in the last election, who was a genuinely good man, if politically misguided, Friel had a Machiavellian dark side that he tried to mask under a persona of "man of the people," which the media ate up. It killed Dillard to think that Friel had fooled so many people, when actually he was the most duplicitous, underhanded son of a bitch in politics with the exception of Evan Dillard himself. Friel had been on the attack in recent weeks, and Dillard feared he was being beaten at his own game of nonstop blitzkrieg. The media had used Friel's embrace of the China Solution to marginalize Dillard as a "racist isolationist" out of touch with reality in Asia. And Dillard feared that this morning's meeting with party members was all about caving. He stubbed out his cigarette with an envious look at the antlike tourists on Pennsylvania Avenue and wished he could be as blissfully carefree as they were. He pushed the button on the intercom on the desk.

"Send them in, Maddie."

In walked the Senate majority leader and the whips from the House and the Senate. The grave look on Senator Carl Davis's face told Dillard all he needed to know about the next excruciating twenty minutes. After they had all sat down in wing chairs in front of the Resolute Desk, Davis took it upon himself to begin the proceedings.

"Mister President, all of us here in this room today are up for reelection in November. And as you've no doubt seen in this morning's *Post*, Friel has pulled one point ahead in the presidential race." Actually, Dillard had been too afraid to look at the *Post* that morning, so Davis's news came as a gut punch. Davis continued.

"The three of us have been discussing party strategy for November, along with analysis of why Friel's numbers have been going up so dramatically, and it seems clear to us that his improvement is largely due to his embrace of the China Solution. People are just sick and tired of terrorism, plain and simple."

Dillard began nodding halfway through Davis's last sentence, and he held up his hand as Davis finished it. "I know where you're going with this, Carl, and part of me agrees with what must be your conclusion as to the way forward. I can't say I totally agree with the analysis that Friel's numbers are the result of his embrace of the China Solution. There are several factors going into this home stretch that are working against us, including the downturn on Wall Street. But I'll grant you that at least some of his uptick is due to the China and North Korea thing. What I told the vice president last night is what I'll tell you all now. He and I are going to the Olympics tonight, and we're hoping that our appearance there will strengthen all of our positions in the polls for November...."

As he got to the last point, the three members of Congress shifted in their seats almost in choreographed fashion. "Mister President, I'll be candid," Davis said before Dillard could start again. "We're all tanking. That's the only word that comes to mind that fully captures the situation. We lost the House in the midterms, and if things go as the polls are indicating, we'll not only lose the Senate but the White House too. We need a total reversal in the polls, and fast. I don't think an appearance by you and Paul at the Olympics is going to cut it. Now, forgive my presumptuousness, but I commissioned a national poll by Pew Research last night, with the main question being, 'Would accepting the China Solution affect your vote?' According to their results, which I just got before coming over, ten percent of likely voters would change their votes in our favor. Ten percent, Mister President."

"I understand the dilemma we all face, Carl," Dillard said with weary impatience. "And as I was about to say, when Coppinger and I appear at the Olympics, if there's no immediate uptick in our polls, I'm not going to hang any of us out to dry. But I do want to wait till then."

"And at that time if there's no improvement, you'll accept the China Solution?" Davis pressed.

Dillard nodded. "You have my promise. I'll do everything in my power to prevent Jon Friel from inflicting himself on this country."

CHAPTER 44

Very few people actually choose to travel to North Korea even once, let alone twice, but when the love of your life is languishing in a gulag just north of the DMZ, one sets aside common sense and goes searching. That is the position Patrick found himself in before the Rising Tide revolution of 2017, when Yumi Takara was abducted from a beach on Sado Island and spirited away to Pyongyang on the orders of Comrade Moon.

Patrick's first trip across the border was as a non-official-cover CIA operative, disguised as a Canadian art dealer, with an ostensible mission of finding and, if necessary, killing Tyler Kang, who had mock-defected to North Korea but forgot to tell his people back home about the "mock" part. But Patrick's old comrade in arms had a whole deck of wild cards up his sleeve, one of which was to assassinate Kim Jong-un, which came to naught with the Rising Tide revolution.

Patrick's second, more personal trip to the North was to find and rescue Yumi, and to that end, he wound up flying over the DMZ in a Griffin 1-A flying suit straight out of Tesla Labs. Once on the other side, he established contact with Nahm Myung-dae, leader of the Rising Tide insurgent movement that toppled the regime, and now the president of North Korea. But Nahm's ability to lead an insurgency did not translate into leading a nation, and his disastrous agricultural policies had led to widespread food shortages rivaling those of the Kim years. The ineptness of his leadership had also spawned several opposition groups who yearned for the stability of the Kim dynasty, much like Russians who to this day hearken back to the days of Stalin. The most visible of the opposition groups was also the newest: Chosun Restoration.

Into the breach had stepped China, but Nahm vehemently rejected the China Solution, fearing that the PRC would promptly bring back the Kim family. Once back in power, the Kims would wipe Rising Tide from the face of the earth. On the other hand, Nahm faced a rebellion much like the one he had led four years earlier if he couldn't find a way to improve the economy and soon. Then came news of an unexpected development, one that involved an old friend from the Rising Tide revolution, a foreigner who spoke fluent Korean. His secretary placed the call. A minute later, the foreigner answered.

"Nahm Myung-dae, is it really you?"

"Yes, Patrick, it's so good to hear your voice."

"It's good to hear from you too." He waited for Nahm to get to the point of his call. It certainly wasn't to exchange pleasantries.

"Patrick, I have a very important favor to ask."

"Of course. You know I'd help you in any way I can."

There was a time gap on the other end of the line as Nahm searched for the right words.

"I'm sorry to keep you from your duties, Patrick, but I'm wondering about the young boy that you and Yumi took for adoption."

Patrick's heart froze. What on earth could be coming next? He waited for Nahm to continue.

"Patrick, can you please let me know if the boy has a birthmark on his neck?"

Patrick wrestled momentarily with the urge to say no, politely end the call, and hang up. Instead, he replied. "Yes. On the left side."

Nahm sighed before continuing. "As I'm sure you know, things have been tough ever since the Chinese cut off aid." Patrick didn't bring up the added factor that Nahm's policies were also a major factor in the situation in North Korea, and he let his old comrade in arms continue.

"What we need for the long term is something I've only heard rumors about, but which could not only feed the people, but put them to work for decades. Do you know what 'rare earth' is?"

"I've heard of it."

"I just recently learned exactly what it is myself, and why it's so valuable. It could be the start of a whole new economy over here, independent of foreign aid. I was reading an online report this morning, and it said that rare earth elements are typically not found in one place in high concentrations." Nahm paused before continuing.

"Patrick, someone in this country has discovered the world's biggest deposit of it in one place. It's worth trillions of dollars. Trillions."

"So have you started mining it?" Patrick asked.

"We will as soon as we find it."

"I thought you said someone found it already."

"He did. But he won't say where it is. Until he's reunited with his son."

Patrick numbly disengaged from the conversation as Nahm continued with his account of the miner.

OUTSIDE OF KAESONG, NORTH KOREA
Four years earlier
May 1, 2017

A man in his early thirties walked with his wife and very young son into the forest just outside of Kaesong near the DMZ. It was the day of the Glorious Triumvirate Celebration in Pyongyang, a day commemorating the ineffable magnificence of Kim Il-sung, his son Kim Jong-il, and the current Brilliant Commander, Kim Jong-un. A national holiday had been declared, and citizens all across the country were exhorted to watch the celebration on large screen televisions set up in public places. Chief Engineer Ahn Mun-yin had lied his way out of attending the broadcast in Kaesong by telling his work unit supervisor that his young son was feared to have contracted tuberculosis and needed to be kept quarantined. He knew someone else who had successfully used the same lie to escape that year's dreaded February 16 commemoration of Kim Jong-il's birthday.

So with a spring in their steps, the young Ahn family made their way to the father's workplace, which was only accessible across a high and steep ravine. He carried the boy on his back and led his wife by the hand. She hated heights and kept her eyes closed when they reached a short but particularly treacherous part of the trail where he guided her steps. When they arrived at their destination, they were rewarded by a glorious spring day shining over one of the loveliest parts of the country.

The plan was to enjoy a picnic at the waterfall that ran above the cave where Ahn had been exploring for new seams of coal. He had recently found several tiny diamonds in the cave in the course of his prospecting, and he hoped to find one large enough today to have fashioned into a ring for his wife. The little boy carried a plastic pail and shovel, the mother a lunch basket, and the father a headlamp. His tools were already in the cave. A half-hour's walk later, they reached their destination, and the wife spread out blankets. The boy began digging in the dirt with his plastic shovel, and his mother asked him what he hoped to find.

"Gold, Omma, for you and Appa!" Ahn smiled as his wife wrapped the boy in her arms. "We don't need gold or anything else, as long as we have you, Dae-ho!"

Ahn then told his wife he would be gone just a short while, keeping secret that he would be searching for a diamond suitable for this woman he loved so much.

As he entered the cave, he savored the cool mustiness and the silence that echoed his footfalls. Half an hour later, he dug his hammer into the cave wall a quarter mile below the surface, and his headlamp picked up a yellow glint. At first, he thought it was his eyes conjuring up kaleidoscopic shapes as they became accustomed to the dark. He rubbed his eyes, but the glint remained, so he began chipping away steadily at the rockface until he was finally able to use his hands to pull out a large section of rubble. As he did so, the yellow glint expanded. He opened the tool bag he had carried in, took out his X-ray fluorescence analyzer, and aimed it at the seam, just to be sure it was really gold. But the list of elements in addition to gold that appeared on the readout screen of the XRF analyzer sent a shiver up his spine. He then pointed the device all around the rocky matrix containing the gold and confirmed his suspicion. He had stumbled upon a huge concentration of all seventeen rare earth elements in one place. But how extensive was the deposit?

Half an hour later of aiming the XRF at the rockface all through the mineshaft, it was clear that the deposit extended far into the cave, possibly for miles. He would need to return to the surface and call this in right away, but so absorbed had he been in his task that his brain hadn't even registered the distant thunder of a flood pulse.

Meanwhile, his wife sat topside with her son drinking the cold barley tea she had prepared and waiting for her husband to reappear at the cave entrance. She began to worry. Down below, the sound of rushing water got louder, and Ahn finally realized the danger he was in. He hurriedly made for the cave entrance a quarter mile above as the rumble of floodwaters grew in intensity, like a freight train hurtling through a tunnel. Carefully threading his way through a mineshaft partially blocked by a rockslide set off by the flooding, it took him a full hour to reach the surface, the entire cave shaking as if by an earthquake. He was only fifteen yards from the cave entrance when an enormous torrent of white water spewed from the cave ceiling, and he barely dodged tons of falling rock and debris. Within seconds, his exit from the cave was almost completely blocked. He could see daylight, but there was no way he could get out without help, so he checked for a signal on his cellphone. He was picking up one bar, but it flickered in and out of reception.

He repeatedly tried calling his wife, but there was no answer, so he yelled toward the cave entrance over and over but again heard nothing. Sensing that something had gone wrong with her husband in the cave, the wife had hurried back forty minutes earlier in the direction of Kaesong to try to get help. As the late afternoon light outside faded,

Ahn decided to see if his phone signal would carry to Pyongyang, and he dialed a number.

PYONGYANG

"Rising Tide! Rising Tide! Rising Tide!"

The ecstatic chant resounded throughout Pyongyang on the day of the overthrow of the Kim Jong-un regime. Shopkeepers, barbers, factory workers—people from every walk of life shouted themselves hoarse long into the night as they realized that a yoke had finally been removed from their necks. Thousands had dutifully arrived in the capital that morning, expecting the usual depressing celebration of socialism, but by the end of the day, the people had risen up and thrown off their shackles.

By the time Chief Mining Engineer Ahn phoned from the cave in which he was trapped, the Rising Tide revolution was in full swing, and government activity had quickly come to a halt in the capital as the state security apparatus collapsed. Pihl Do-yun, the mining engineer's supervisor in the People's General Industry Group, breathlessly picked up the phone when a call came in.

"Yes, what is it?" Pihl shouted excitedly into the phone.

"Comrade Pihl, can you hear me? This is Chief Engineer Ahn Mun-yin at a mine down south. I'm trapped in the cave and need help. Can you call someone from your end to come help?"

"I can't, Comrade Ahn, Pyongyang is…" Pihl's next words were garbled, and Ahn could not make them out. He shouted into his phone. Maybe Comrade Pihl just needed some more motivation to send help.

"But I think I've just made an important discovery. Tons and tons of rare earth, the kind we've been looking for…"

"There's been trouble here, Comrade Ahn, the Brilliant Commander has gone into hiding, and the streets are filled with people. Someone said the government has collapsed. I can't do anything right now, I'm very sorry. Where did you say you made this discovery? I'll make a note of it, but then I have to get the hell out of here. Are you there, Ahn? Comrade Ahn, are you there?"

But Comrade Ahn had ended the call. It had finally happened. The rumors had been true about the Rising Tide group going to Pyongyang for a mass demonstration, and now it looked as though the demonstration had turned into a full-scale overthrow. Ahn was jubilant and depressed at the same time. It would take him hours to tunnel out of the cave, and he still couldn't reach his wife by phone. He shouted for her over and over. Still nothing. Finally, after sitting on the ground frantically going over his options, he turned on his headlamp and began digging his way out of the cave. The next morning when he finally emerged, he went straight home. There was no sign of his wife or son.

CHAPTER 45

Patrick and Yumi, along with a sleepy-eyed Dae-ho, took the early morning Japan Air flight to Seoul and were met by an official who drove them from Kimpo Airport to the Seoul Government Complex in the capital's Jongno District. There they were photographed and fingerprinted for their extraordinary travel visas that would enable them to freely cross the DMZ. Once in North Korea proper, they would meet President Nahm Myung-dae, who would be personally escorting them to the village of Darang-ri, where Chief Mining Engineer Ahn lived alone. His wife had gone missing on the day that Ahn was trapped in the cave. She was presumed dead, probably from a fall down the ravine that led to the cave. Dae-ho was found wandering in the forest alone and starving, and was sent to the children's shelter that Patrick and Yumi worked at. Patrick had already sent Nahm a photo of the boy, and Ahn had confirmed he was his son.

When Patrick came home on the day he had spoken by phone to Nahm, Yumi could tell that something was gravely amiss, not only because he was supposed to be staying in Tokyo, but from the morose look on his face. Her anxiety turned to devastation when Patrick broke the news that the boy's father had been found. A welter of conflicting emotions ran like an electric charge through them both. On the one hand, they were of course happy for Dae-ho that he would be reunited with his father. On the other, they had grown so attached to the boy that they were heartsick.

As they drove up to the DMZ, the boy hummed to himself, the first time they had ever heard him do that. He seemed to sense that he was going home. Patrick and Yumi sat looking out the window in dispirited silence. As promised, Nahm met them on the north side of the DMZ. His beaming smile at seeing his old friend from the revolution vanished as he noted Patrick's and Yumi's misery. After perfunctory small talk, they got into his government car, and Nahm's driver took them along the Reunification Highway past the city of Kaesong. Patrick was able to pick out landmarks from his several motorcycle trips back and forth to Pyongyang when he was rescuing Yumi from Senghori Prison.

When they came to a maple tree by the side of the highway that had been struck by lightning, the driver slowed down and began negotiating an unimproved road up into the surrounding mountains. Soon they came upon a village: Darang-ri. Along the way Dae-ho had become increasingly animated, and when he saw the first building of the village, he let out a loud "Haaa" sound and began pointing at every new building that came into sight. Finally, the moment Patrick and Yumi had dreaded the most was upon them. A man in his mid-thirties was walking toward them with a searching look on his face.

"Appa! Appa!" Dae-ho called out. Patrick held a sobbing Yumi in his arms. The boy jumped out of the car and into his father's arms. He began babbling nonstop to his father, the first time Patrick and Yumi had heard him speak. Now they finally understood the boy's upward inflection when he said "Appa?" and "Omma?" He was not asking them if they were his parents. He was asking where his real parents were.

After they had had a small lunch that the villagers brought out for them, Dae-ho's father formally thanked Patrick and Yumi for looking after his boy for the past four years, then huddled to one side with Nahm, Dae-ho watching his father the whole time, as if afraid he might lose him again. After a short discussion with Nahm, the father reached out two fingers, and Dae-ho jumped up, ran over, and took them in his hand. He looked back at Patrick and Yumi and waved with a beaming smile on his face as his father led him out of the building and down the street. Patrick and Yumi watched silently as they disappeared from view. Yumi squeezed the amulet she had lain on Dae-ho's pillow in Kamakura. It was all she had left to remember him by.

After allowing them some time together to process what had just happened, Nahm came up to Patrick and Yumi and thanked them again for seeing the boy through the worst of his malnutrition. Then he excused himself. He needed to meet with the boy's father again about the location of the discovery he had made in the cave.

Patrick needed to return to the Olympics right away, and Yumi wanted to distance herself as soon as possible from what she had just experienced. They left on the return flight to Tokyo late that afternoon.

After just a few hours' sleep at home, Patrick rode his motorcycle to the Olympic Stadium at 3 a.m., the Shuto Expressway dimly lit by a perfectly sliced half-moon that hid timidly behind a scrim of cloud. The lights of the metropolis on the horizon had the soft glow of a thousand Tibetan butter lamps. The whole ride up to Tokyo, he was consumed by the look of hollowing grief on Yumi's face when they returned from North Korea and saw Dae-ho's empty bed, as though the fabric of her universe had been rent from top to bottom. When Patrick had to leave, she insisted that she had cried most of the pain away, but he knew it was a brave front for the loss that had devastated her. He forced her image from his mind, and opened the bike up to over a hundred miles per hour, making use for the first time of the red gumball flashing light he had been issued for the duration of the Games.

Pulling into the stadium, he parked his bike in his underground spot and went into his office for a quick cup of coffee. On the way out again, he checked his face in the mirror, and the eyes that looked back at him were stitched with raggedy crimson threads of fatigue. When he rubbed them, he saw a paisley design. Then it was time for his usual walkaround, both to check for anyone or anything that looked out of place and to keep his mind occupied so that he didn't start wondering what Dae-ho was doing at that very moment. The last event the previous evening had finished at 10 p.m., and now preparations were being made for the start of the marathon and the Closing Ceremony that would follow it. As he swiveled his head up and down and side to side, searching for anything amiss in the stadium, he was struck anew at the refined elegance of the structure and the ingenuity of its architect, who had seamlessly blended form and function on such a magnificent scale. And its stated goal of oneness with nature was accentuated by the mother hawk that flew up to the rafters every dawn with fresh fish from the nearby lake for its hatchlings.

All around him as he walked, the stadium buzzed with the muted activity of people who knew exactly what they needed to do. No one waved or called out as they usually did during his walkarounds. Time was tight with the 7 a.m. start of the marathon only a few hours away. He stopped briefly to look at a dozen or so gracile runners from around the world warming up already, and he knew that he would never in a million years have been anywhere close to their level. Even the runners coming in a half hour after the winner today would be sprinting at the end of twenty-six miles. He chuckled as he thought of Indiana Jones's adage, "It's not the years, honey—it's the mileage," and knew that Indy was wrong. After the age of forty, it was the years *and* the mileage. He sighed and turned toward his office.

At 6 a.m., he sat drinking coffee with Kirsten, Tyler, and Kaga, while Phibbs napped off a hangover in a chair and Choy sat at his computer in the adjoining room, sipping ginseng tea. Tyler was on his third cup, and his leg jumped up and down like the needle of a sewing machine. Kirsten made no attempt to hide her irritation. Everyone's sensibilities were sharpened to a razor's edge.

"Can you please stop?" she said. Tyler looked at her uncomprehendingly.

"Your leg is bouncing. It's driving me nuts."

"Whoa, sorry," Tyler said in a wounded voice.

Patrick said, "I think we're all a bit on edge from lack of sleep."

"Especially at zero stupid thirty in the morning," Phibbs grunted with his eyes closed and his chin on his chest. For Patrick, the maddening unpredictability of the attacks along with the hurried trip to North Korea had stolen from him any restful sleep for several nights running. The others were no less physically exhausted, but Patrick had the added emotional drain of seeing the look on Yumi's face when he brought her home to a house that was missing one of its key members.

While they waited to go outside into the stadium proper, they talked about the attacks and how they should prepare for this, the final day of the Olympics.

"I don't think we *can* prepare," said Phibbs, his head still on his chest. "We can't expect anything predictable from whoever's been doing this. All the previous attacks have been random."

"I'm not so sure," Kaga said. "You know the old story about the elephant and the blind men? One thinks the tail is the elephant, another the trunk, and so on. The point is, it's all about perspective. We need to stand back, open our eyes, and see the whole elephant."

Kirsten said, "You're right, Minoru." Her foot had fallen asleep, and she got up and started pacing to restore circulation to her legs. "Patrick, can you see any pattern in the Miyamoto texts you've gotten, the whole elephant, as it were?"

"No, I've been trying to do that for weeks," Patrick said glumly. "The only pattern I can see is that each attack has been an escalation of the previous ones. First the shooting here at the stadium, then the Yasukuni, Budokan and Tokyo Tower attacks, then the Novichok attack on the subway, then the Yoyogi Gym attack, then the Blue Sluice Gate attack. Each one was potentially more lethal than the last, but that doesn't really give any indication as to what the next target will be."

Kirsten stopped in her tracks, her brow furrowed and her eyes focused down on something inward.

Patrick waved his hand in front of her eyes. "Hello? Calling Kirsten? You still with us?"

Kirsten said nothing but opened the web browser on her phone. She typed in a search word: Warden.

CHAPTER 46

OLYMPIC STADIUM
Office of Security

"Five rings!" Kirsten said excitedly as she held up her phone.

"But I told you already, the whole Miyamoto Musashi thing is a nonstarter," Patrick said, irritation in his voice. "Pung or whoever else is just jerking my chain."

"No, I'm talking about *Warden's* Five Rings!"

"What the hell is that?" Tyler asked.

"John Warden was a U.S. Air Force colonel, and he came up with this system of five graduated attacks designed to completely incapacitate an enemy." She began reading off her phone: "Here, listen to this, 'Each level of a system, or "ring," is considered one of the enemy's centers of gravity. There are five such rings.' The first of Warden's Five Rings is 'fielded military,' and we can think of that as the two security chiefs who were assassinated on the Olympic field and then the attacks on the SDF and Yasukuni Shrine."

"How is that shrine part of 'fielded military'?" Tyler asked skeptically.

"The shrine is dedicated to Japanese soldiers and sailors who were killed in battle. Then there was the failed attack on Tokyo Tower and the subway nerve gas attack, which could be the second ring: 'terrorizing the population.' The third ring is 'infrastructure,' and that could have been Yoyogi Gymnasium, if you think of it as Olympic infrastructure."

She read off her phone. "The fourth ring is 'system essentials.' What's more essential than water?"

"So you mean the attempt to blow up the Blue Sluice Gate," Patrick said. "It's not exactly a clear line, but for the sake of argument, let's suppose you're right. That's four rings so far. What's the fifth one?" Patrick asked.

Kirsten scrolled down her phone and stopped. Then she held it up for him to see.

Patrick read off her phone: "Warden's Fifth Ring is 'Destroying the Leadership.'"

He jumped up out of his chair.

"Who's scheduled to be here today?" he shouted as he ran over to his desk. Then he read off his list of dignitaries who would be seated in the VIP box for the Closing Ceremony.

———————

In the interest of solidarity on the day of the greatest potential threat to the Olympics, Hooper called Patrick at 6:15 a.m., suggesting a truce between Patrick, Hayashida, and Proctor. Everyone needed to put their differences aside for this final day of the Games, Hooper argued. Patrick reluctantly agreed. The peace that Hooper was brokering made perfect sense in terms of unity, but it didn't lessen the intense dislike the three men had for each other. They agreed to meet a short while later at the embassy. As Patrick and his team were going over the VIP list, Choy called them into his little room off of Patrick's office. Phibbs remained in Patrick's office, dozing.

"Whoever has been communicating with the bogus Bureau 39 just sent a new message," Choy said when they gathered around his computer.

"Was it encrypted?" Patrick asked.

"No. I posed as the person they communicated with and sent an infected reply email. They opened it and emailed me back right away, so I now have a backdoor into their system." Choy peered closer to his computer and read the Chinese characters on screen. "It says 'People's Central Bank.'"

"Who specifically sent it and who at the bogus Bureau 39 is it directed to?" Kirsten asked.

"The sender is identified only as 'Z,' and the recipient is 'LJT.' Probably people's names. The subject heading is 'Sky Heart.'"

"That 'Sky Heart' thing again. But what the hell is it?" Patrick asked.

Phibbs came alive when he heard the word and entered Choy's small office. He looked fully refreshed from his nap. "Did you say Sky Heart? That's one of the things the Chinese diplomat I was grooming kept saying. I thought it was broken English." He typed the word into his phone. "Got it!" he called out a moment later. "This is off a classified Agency intel report: 'Sky Heart is an office of the Chinese People's Liberation Army based in the Western Hills of Beijing.' Well, there's your connection. The PLA works hand-in-hand with the People's Central Bank in surveillance and intelligence gathering."

Patrick turned to Choy. "Can you get anything more from the files in their system?"

Choy shot him a look. "You mean the 4,862 files in this compressed file folder? Oh, I'm sure I can find all sorts of things. Just give me a year or two."

"Sorry," Patrick said. He looked at the wall clock. "We've got to get over to the embassy for the meeting with the others, especially if Kirsten's right and there's going to be an attack on leadership. The emperor of Japan is going to be there today, people."

"As is the president of the United States." Everyone turned. In the doorway stood Garrett Proctor, flanked by Hooper, Fitz, and Hayashida. "You people were late coming to the embassy, so we came over here," Proctor said. The four men walked into the room. Kirsten filled them in on her working theory about Warden's Five Rings and the possible attack on the world leaders at the Closing Ceremony.

"Sounds pretty thin to me," Proctor said.

"What else do we have to go on?" Kirsten insisted.

Hayashida spoke up. "I would like to remind everyone that the Prime Minister is adamant that the Games not be disrupted in any way, especially today when the whole world is watching. We have a state-of-the-art AI system, and we will use it to screen everyone who comes into the stadium. Our Japanese technology can distinguish identical twins apart as well as people who have had plastic surgery. It can also pick up the tiniest traces of explosives and sharp weapons."

"But that only works if they enter through the gates," Patrick said. "What about the sniper three weeks ago? He got in undetected, and the AI was fully functional at the time. I hope you're right about how wonderful your system is, but if it isn't, we'll be the backup."

He then signaled for everyone to gather around his computer. "Take a look at this photo. These are at least some of the Chosun Restoration people behind the attacks." He proceeded to tell them about Toyama Storage, the Yokohama corpse hotel.

"When was this taken," Hayashida asked.

"A week or so ago," Patrick said.

"A week? Why wasn't I informed of this?" Hayashida demanded.

"Why wasn't I informed of the license plate you found after Yoyogi?" Patrick countered.

"I already told you it was untraceable."

"But you didn't know that at the time. You held back from me, Mister Hayashida, so you're in no position to complain."

Fitz looked up from the photo. "I bet you these young guys are just the cannon fodder. It's gotta be the older guy here who's behind it." He pointed to Pung.

"I disagree, Fitz," Patrick said. "That guy tried to kill me in North Korea, but he's just the tail of the kite."

"Patrick's right, that's Pung Min-ho," Choy added. "He was Comrade Moon's main enforcer. Nasty guy, but he's no leader, at least not of these attacks. It's got to be someone else in charge."

Patrick said, "There's one other person involved in this, probably the top guy, who's not in this photo. I saw him at the corpse hotel, but only briefly. I think I can still ID him, though."

Proctor had been keeping uncharacteristically quiet through this exchange, but now he spoke.

"It would be nice and neat if we could predict what they're going to do next, but the fact is, we have no idea. No offense, Agent Beck, but that theory of yours is pure speculation, and we need a lot more than that." Kirsten said nothing, but her jaw tightened. Proctor looked at his watch. "It's now 0643. The marathon begins in seventeen minutes. Before we go, there's one thing I want to make clear. As you know, I have Predator and Sentinel drones on hot standby. If it becomes necessary, I intend to use them."

Everyone instinctively turned to Hayashida who, predictably, had turned ashen.

"Mister Proctor, I have already told you that the Prime Minister has the final say in the use of this type of weapon. These are the Japanese Olympics, not the American Olympics, and certainly not your Olympics. Any use of that sort of weapon will go through the Prime Minister first, and I demand your acceptance of those terms."

All movement stopped in the room. Proctor turned to Hayashida. "Mister Hayashida, I'll make this as brief as I can. We don't have much time, obviously." He took a deep breath and began. "Back in early summer of 2001, a Predator flight that one of my predecessors ordered over Afghanistan produced probable sightings of Osama bin Laden. My predecessor lobbied for a targeted killing with Hellfire missiles. But he received so much pushback from people who were offended by the fact that he had gone over their heads that the president didn't give authorization until September 4 of that year. By that time bin Laden was gone. I think we all know what happened a week later."

"Be that as it may, Mister Proctor, I am not authorizing you to use those weapons on Japanese soil or in Japanese airspace. I'll say it again: these are not your Olympics."

Hayashida and Proctor stared each other down. Finally, Proctor spoke.

"Let's saddle up and get outside. The crowds were pouring through the gates when we were coming in here. Check weapons."

Everyone hurriedly complied before the confrontation could begin anew. For good measure, Patrick slipped an M9 knife into his boot.

Before leaving, Patrick spoke to Choy. "Jung-hee, I know there's a lot of files in that compressed folder, but can you stay here and see if you can find anything else on them that might narrow down who's behind this?"

Choy sighed. "Sure. Never mind that I didn't sleep at all last night and haven't eaten since yesterday. Can you please reach into the refrigerator and grab me the sandwich in there?"

Patrick turned to the refrigerator and brought a giant sandwich to Choy. "Smells good," he said as he handed it to Choy.

"Best bulgogi in town," Choy said as he went into the back room and resumed his search while devouring half of the sandwich in two bites.

When everyone else was armed and ready, they assembled and made their way to the door, walking wordlessly down the corridor until Phibbs broke the silence.

"Showdown at the hoedown, folks," he said, but his voice lacked its characteristic bluster.

CHAPTER 47

OLYMPIC STADIUM
7 a.m. start of marathon

Several members of the Olympic security team, including hardened agents of the Japan Intelligence Agency, practically jumped out of their skins when the starting gun went off to begin the marathon. They were still skittish from when the two security officials were cut down by a North Korean assassin's bullets three weeks earlier.

The marathon was the final event of the Games, and immediately at the sound of the starting gun, over a hundred runners glided around the track effortlessly despite a blistering pace that they would maintain and even surpass during the race. After some ungentle jockeying for position near the front of the pack, the runners settled into a single organism that bobbed up and down in unison with little if any wasted effort as they made their way out of the stadium to the main part of the course.

Spectators lining the streets marveled at how easily these human gazelles made a sub-five-minute-mile pace look. At a little after 9 a.m., the runners who had survived the heat and humidity would face a steady 1 percent incline over the final mile-and-a-half return to the stadium, having completed the twenty-six-mile route that would take them past the Imperial Palace, around Sensoji Temple with its imposing Thunder Gate, past Tokyo Tower, and finally back to the stadium for a final quarter-mile lap around the track. The awarding of medals to the top finishers in the male and female divisions would double as the first event of the Closing Ceremony, while the expected capacity crowd of sixty-seven thousand would snack on sushi, dried squid, rice crackers, and "hotto doggu" purchased from the concession stands as they watched the runners' progress on the Sony jumbotrons on opposite sides of the stadium. It was safe to say there was not a single citizen of Japan who wasn't desperately praying at that moment that there would be no more attacks on this, Japan's showpiece Games of the twenty-first century. The new emperor, Naruhito, had made an unprecedented fifteen-minute appearance in a hastily put-together TV special on the heightened security measures that had been taken which, he assured his subjects, had rendered the rest of the Games "impregnable."

After Patrick and the rest of the combined security command left for the stadium, Choy began to sift through the thousands of files he had accessed through the back door virus he had sent to the mysterious sender of the Sky Heart file. He shook his head in frustration at the sheer volume he had to choose from, most of which were spreadsheet or ordinary word processing files. But one caught his eye, a .gif image file which he clicked open. It looked a bit like the universal "six-pack" that police agencies around the world show to witnesses for them to identify suspects. Looking at the date and time it was last saved, he noticed that it seemed to be paired chronologically with a large compressed text file which he began to extract. The .gif file was of six grim-faced older Asian men in military uniforms which he printed out in color while waiting for the compressed file to open. When he saw the military men, he decided to bring it immediately to Patrick along with the first twenty pages he had been able to print of the text file. As he was exiting the office, he stopped. The other half of the giant bulgogi sandwich called out to him, and he grabbed it on his way out the door.

As the combined security command fanned out around the stadium field, Patrick felt his phone vibrate. He looked at the screen: *"The spirit of fire is relentless."* He called over the others and showed it to them. "Here's the latest Miyamoto Musashi text." After some discussion, Proctor hit on an idea and pointed to the center of the field.

"Take a look at the fireworks display they're setting up. I've heard of those things being repurposed as WMDs." Everyone's eyes went to the six men on the field from a private company who were preparing a portion of the pyrotechnics for the Closing Ceremony. Hayashida spoke into his sleeve and ordered JIA agents disguised as course marshals to go over and interrogate them. Sure enough, a short time later one of the JIA agents radioed back that two of the fireworks operators did not have proper credentials to be on the field. Hayashida ordered that portion of the fireworks to be shut down and for all other launch points to be thoroughly checked out.

There was a qualified sense of relief on the part of the combined security command, but Tyler was having none of it.

"Let's not spike the ball on the five-yard line, folks. The text about fire and then it being the fireworks is just too obvious. I'm betting it's a misdirect, if anything."

Choy trotted out of breath onto the field, holding the copy he had printed of the six-pack photo along with the twenty pages of the text file he'd been able to extract so far. The CSC members gathered around him. A prickle of sweat broke out on Patrick's back as Choy held up the photos. He pointed to one of the headshots. "This one here is the guy with the limp from the corpse hotel.'"

Tyler peered intently at the photo of the man Patrick had just identified. The face looked vaguely familiar. Then it hit him.

"Sempai, I know this guy. You remember I told you I was sick before coming out here?"

"Yeah, what about it?"

"To tell you the truth, I'm not sure what happened. I went to the casino for some blackjack and sat down at the table. This guy in the photo bought me a drink at the bar, and next thing I remember, I was back in my apartment."

"Were you missing anything? Sounds like you got rolled."

"Just any memory of what happened. But I'm sure it was this guy. He must have spiked my drink."

Choy translated the caption under the photo. "This is General Liu Jintao of the People's Liberation Army of China."

"Well, whatever his name is," Kirsten said, "I'm not taking the chance that the next attack isn't on leadership, just like it says in Warden's Five Rings." And with that she began running toward the VIP box halfway up the stands.

Proctor called after her. "Hang on, Agent Beck, we need to maintain unity of command."

Patrick interrupted him. "Let her go, Proctor, if anyone's going to be issuing orders in this stadium, it's me."

Proctor turned to him. Like most people, Patrick found it disorienting to look at one eye that was motionless and devoid of expression while the other was animated with emotion—in this case, self-righteous indignation. Proctor pointed to the VIP box. "The President of the United States is going to be in that box, Featherstone, and that's my operation, not yours. If anything you do or don't do leads to any harm to that man, I will personally come after you with everything I've got."

Tyler listened to the confrontation and decided not to get involved. He could do no good by taking sides, as if he would take any side but Patrick's. He began a fast-walk off the infield and up to where Patrick had assigned him his position for the day: a recessed gap between the nosebleed seats at the top of the stadium and the rafters of the oculus. The gap was originally scheduled to be used for TV cameras during the Games, but Patrick had commandeered it as a sniper's hide. It was the same hide where the Type 58 rifle had been found, the rifle that Pung had used to gun down the security officials on either side of Patrick three weeks earlier.

But before Tyler got far, his phone rang. He looked at the incoming number. It was a familiar area code. Las Vegas. He answered it. The person on the other end was not big on social niceties.

"Kang."

"Colonel Bartoe. What an unexpected surprise." It was Tyler's CO at Creech AFB outside of Vegas.

"The surprise was all mine, Kang, when I got a call from Yokota Air Base a short while ago. They said that the remote-control capability on one of their MQ Predators was taken over using your security credentials. It was hijacked to an unknown location."

Tyler went numb. "Hijacked? With my security credentials? How is that possible, sir?"

"I was hoping that *you* would clear up that mystery."

"Well, I'm as mystified as you are, Colonel. Did they say how the drone was accessed?"

"We've checked on our side here, and the breach didn't come from any of our modules. The guy I spoke to at Yokota seemed to think it was accessed by phone GPS with the access codes fed into a classified app. They're checking on that now. You were working on creating a phone app like that, were you not?"

"Sir, this is totally impossible. I'm *talking* on my phone to you now. I haven't used it for anything else, I swear it. And I just bought it a few weeks ago."

"I have to take another call on this. Be sure you answer when I call back." Bartoe rang off. Tyler's mind raced. How could his phone have been breached? And by whom? He remembered Patrick saying that he never got the text message Tyler had sent saying he would be getting to Tokyo late. He ran over to Choy, the computer expert, and filled him in on what Bartoe had just said.

"Dial *#06#," Choy said. "That will display your IMEI."

"What's an IMEI?" Tyler asked as he dialed the code into his cell.

"International Mobile Equipment Identity. It's a unique numerical identifier for every mobile device."

A sixteen-digit number appeared on the screen, and Tyler showed it to Choy, who looked for the number on the phone itself. That number was different.

"You've been cloned," said Choy.

"But that's impossible, I just got it from an official Apple dealer a few weeks ago and it's never out of my sight!"

As he spoke, though, Tyler's mind went back to the man who spiked his drink at the Vegas casino.

"Holy shit," he said softly. *Larry Suh*. He turned to Choy. "The guy in that photo you printed out. Who did you say he was?"

Choy looked down at the photo. "General Liu Jintao of the Chinese Air Force."

"I just remembered him being in my apartment when I was doped up. He was looking at my phone and my computer. He must have left me a clone of my phone, kept the real one, and uploaded my security credentials from my home computer."

Just then, a roar went up in the crowd as Emperor Naruhito waved to the crowd while walking to the VIP box. His image, and a split screen of President Dillard applauding him, was projected on the jumbotron on opposite sides of the stadium. Focusing on what he could control at the moment, Tyler started off again to his hide.

At the same moment, Patrick's attention went to Proctor who was shouting into his phone. "What the hell do you mean, a hijacked MQ Predator?" He paused and listened to the person on the other end of the line. "How far away is it?" he shouted into the phone. "Jesus," he whispered upon hearing the reply. "Arm two MIM-104 Patriots. Await further instructions."

Patrick was about to speak when Hayashida ran over after hearing Proctor ordering antiaircraft missiles to be armed.

"You can't even think about using missiles anywhere near the stadium, especially not with the Emperor here!"

"If we don't take it down, not only the Emperor but every person in this stadium could be vaporized. That text about 'fire' could mean it has some kind of nuke on it." His phone rang again. Listening to the person on the other end, he relayed the progress report to Patrick and Hayashida.

"It's still pretty far, but those things can go three hundred miles per hour."

"Can't they divert it to the ocean?" Hayashida asked frantically.

"Someone else is controlling it remotely. Plus, it's purposely being flown over high population areas. If we shoot it down and there's radioactive material on it, the fallout area could be worse than Fukushima." Proctor turned to his aide. "We need to get close enough to it to lase it for radiation." He referred to a technique whereby a low-powered laser is aimed at a suspected source of radioactive material, thus freeing electrons from oxygen ions, at which point a second laser energizes the electrons and starts a cascading breakdown of the air. The rate of the breakdown of air molecules indicates the presence or absence of radioactivity. He ran off to his mobile command center outside the stadium.

Patrick decided it was a good time to call in to his team, who were situated in various parts of the stadium. He hailed Kirsten first. "I'm about five rows back from the VIP box. No sign of any trouble."

"Roger that, keep me posted." Patrick was about to check on Phibbs when his stomach dropped. He called Kirsten back. "Kirsten, is the Chinese head of state in the VIP box?"

"Wait one…"

He heard her asking the Secret Service agents who surrounded the box the same question and came back on the line.

"Negative. The Chinese Premier begged off. He sent a representative from the military."

Patrick's heartbeat raced. "What branch?"

"No idea. His back is to me. I'll have to go down below the box and get a visual of his uniform."

"I'll wait...."

But as he looked in the direction of the VIP box, a call came over the radio from Proctor.

"Featherstone, my Sentinel hovering overhead just picked up movement on top of the oculus roof." He ended the call as abruptly as he began it, and Patrick lifted his binoculars and focused on the underside of the oculus. Two men in leotards appeared to be preparing to rappel down, and Patrick thought they might be a part of the Closing Ceremony festivities he hadn't heard about. He was about to ask Kaga to make sure, but just then Kirsten came back on the line.

"Patrick, you still there? He has three stars on his shoulder boards and a whole fruit salad of medals on his chest. He's sitting off by himself on his phone."

"Kirsten, this is important. Is he *talking* on the phone?"

"No, it's more like he's texting."

"Wait there, I'm coming up. Alert the Secret Service people. He might be the one behind the attacks." There was the sound of an argument on Kirsten's end.

"Patrick, the Secret Service just kicked me out of the area. They said President Dillard is about to do a live press conference."

"At the Olympics?" Patrick shook his head in exasperation. He cut off Kirsten and hailed Proctor on the radio.

"Proctor, did you know that the President is planning to do a live TV presentation from the VIP box?"

The silence on the other end gave Patrick his answer. "He's the POTUS, Featherstone, he can do as he damn well pleases. I've got to keep this line open for info on that Predator." He broke the connection.

Patrick swore and called Kaga.

"Minoru, take a look at the roof at the far end of the stadium from where you are and tell me what you see."

Kaga brought his binoculars up and scanned the area. "Looks like maybe they're getting ready for the Closing Ceremony. A couple of acrobats or something."

"That's what I was thinking, but I want to be sure. You need to go up where Tyler is and get a closer look."

Kaga got a sinking feeling in his gut but climbed the stairs to the upper level of the stands above which Tyler was situated.

Patrick ran across the field to the entrance to the stands leading up to the VIP box. Halfway there, he looked up at the box and saw the Chinese general Kirsten had mentioned. He was intently fiddling with this phone, but the brim of his military hat covered his eyes, preventing a clear view of his face. Patrick called Kaga again. "Break off from Tyler's position and meet me on the field directly below the VIP Box." Kaga heaved a sigh of relief and ran to Patrick's position.

———————

Outside the stadium, Proctor sat in his mobile command center waiting for word on the Predator drone. His phone rang, and he answered it immediately. He quickly rang off and spoke to his aides in the vehicle.

"That Predator is headed this way. Elevation: fifty thousand feet."

———————

Patrick's assignment for Tyler was to surveil the stadium the way the two of them had surveilled Kim Il Sung Square four years earlier looking for a would-be assassin of Kim Jong-un. Because the dimensions of the Olympic stadium were so immense, he had brought with him a bolt-action M24 that had been rechambered from its original 7.62x51mm NATO round to one that could accommodate a carrot-sized .458 Winchester Magnum round, giving it an effective range of one thousand meters. He scanned the stadium with his scope, becoming more and more frustrated by the utter improbability of spotting something suspicious, but he systematically divided the stadium into grids that he scrutinized one after the other.

Up in the area of the VIP box, the portable TV cameras from the international news outlets and their operators were examined carefully by Secret Service agents in preparation for President Dillard's imminent news conference. Based on that morning's polls back in the States showing no improvement against his opponent despite his Olympic appearance, he had decided to announce to the world, but most of all to the voters of the United States, that he would accept the China Solution to bring the rule of law back to North Korea and hopefully bring to justice the perpetrators of the crimes committed in the name of the group calling itself Chosun Restoration.

Five rows back from the VIP box, Kirsten called Patrick over the mic network. "Patrick, I hope I'm wrong, but one of the ushers in the VIP area looks a lot like the guy from the Blue Sluice Gate, the one called Casanova."

"What? Are you sure? I thought he drowned."

"Let me go take a closer look. Out."

Kirsten exited the VIP area, took the stairs two at a time to the top row, and looked down in the direction of the man she thought might be Casanova. He was turning every few moments to look at Emperor Naruhito, Prime Minister Adegawa, and President Dillard. Not suspicious behavior in itself, but coupled with his unmistakable pretty-boy face marred only by a slightly misshapen nose and minus the blond hair that he had dyed back to black, the guy looked to be a highly probable match. She patted the gun in the shoulder holster under her suit jacket and began walking back down the stairs at a normal rate.

Patrick ran to the section of the grandstands where the VIP box was located and squinted up. Television cameras had been brought over, and President Dillard was examining himself in a mirror an aide had brought over. TV lights were on in anticipation of his announcement. Off to the right of the VIP box, Patrick saw the older man he had seen limping up the stairs of the corpse hotel. Now dressed as a Chinese Air Force general, he was busy on his phone and didn't look up despite the activity in preparation for Dillard's press conference. Patrick began mounting the stairs with his head down and spoke into his sleeve mic. He got the Secret Service on the line. After identifying himself, he spoke to the head agent.

"You need to end that press conference right now."

"Are you out of your mind? The POTUS is planning a major policy announcement."

"Look, moron, it might be a posthumous policy announcement if you don't shut it down right now. Get him out of the box and into safety immediately. We have at least two probable active shooters in that area."

The line went dead and Patrick looked up to the box. Secret Service agents were swarming over Dillard and VP Coppinger, and Japanese JIA agents were hustling the Emperor and Prime Minister out as well. Patrick could hear Dillard's muffled protests that he wanted face time as he was being led to safety, but the Secret Service ignored his pleas.

From her vantage point, Kirsten watched as the VIPs were escorted to safety, and panicked spectators nearby began running toward the exits. Despite the confusion, she was able to keep an eye on the young man she was now sure was Casanova, but when she was ten feet away from him, he suddenly turned to face her. She reached for her gun, but he had the jump on her, and he sprang cat-quick with a pistol he produced from under his suit jacket. The chaos in the area around the VIP box was doubled as Casanova held up his counterfeit security credential to the spectators in the area and began dragging Kirsten down the stairs in a choke hold. Patrick was ascending the stairs from the opposite direction, and when he saw what was happening to Kirsten, he turned away to avoid a confrontation from that distance. As he did so, his eye was momentarily caught by the man in a military uniform who was limping while looking at the phone in his hand.

Patrick called Kaga on his sleeve mic and told him where he was, then turned back to Casanova and Kirsten, who were now halfway down the stairs. Patrick drew his gun, but Casanova had seen him all along.

"She will die!" he called out to him. Patrick lowered his gun and let them pass. He signaled the other security personnel in the area to stand down, fearing that any sort of gunplay in the stands would quite likely result not only in Kirsten's death, but in the deaths of more than a few spectators as well. Kaga ran over with his gun drawn, but Patrick held up his hand and shouted at him to put it away while pointing in the direction of the Chinese general who was still on his phone, seemingly oblivious to the commotion around him.

"That phone might be what's controlling the incoming drone," Patrick said.

"I'm on it," Kaga said, and he began running toward the general. Patrick headed back in the direction Casanova had taken Kirsten. He waited until they were out of sight before he cautiously began following them from a safe distance.

Kirsten struggled against Casanova, but the youth was all wiry muscle, and every time Kirsten tried to break free, he applied more pressure to the choke hold he had her in until she ceased to resist. Her only other choice was losing consciousness. They got to the bottom of the stadium stairs, and Casanova dragged her to the tunnel leading to the bowels of the stadium. Now that his assassination attempt had been thwarted, he had nowhere else to go, and it was his best option for establishing any kind of defensive position. Once they were out of sight, Patrick ran to the tunnel entrance.

When Kaga got within five feet of General Liu Jintao, the man suddenly looked up from the phone he was engrossed in and tried to limp away, but Kaga easily caught up with him and grabbed him by the arm. The general threw the phone down, and Kaga watched it clatter down the stairs. Knowing it was in all likelihood controlling the Predator hovering overhead, Kaga gave up the chase and ran down the stairs toward the phone. One of the cameramen from the aborted news conference picked it up and handed it to Kaga, who looked up to where he had last seen the general, but there was a stampede of humanity trying to escape the chaos of that section of the grandstands. Surprisingly, the spectators in the other sections didn't move from their seats, largely because the uproar of applause for the marathon runners who were now entering the stadium was drowning out everything else. Kaga raised his head to the oculus and called Tyler on his sleeve mic. He had something for him.

CHAPTER 48

Up in his sniper's hide, Tyler was seized by a horrifyingly unfamiliar sensation: a panic attack, his first experience of disabling fear in a combat situation. The fear was not for his own safety, but rather that his actions had quite possibly led to a situation where mass murder was a real possibility. He forced himself to take deep breaths, hold them, and release them gradually, a sniper technique known as tactical breathing. The technique worked to a certain degree, but he couldn't keep from his mind his atrocious performance at the firing range with Patrick. Although his target scores had improved over the week following that embarrassing display, he knew that in a fighting situation, he would not only have to deal with the enemy outside, but the enemy within that might well succumb to an overwhelming adrenaline dump with its attendant tunnel vision and loss of motor control. He continued with his breathing technique as his head alternately swiveled between the floor of the stadium and the mouth of the oculus, where the hijacked drone might come diving in at any moment at over two hundred miles per hour.

Tyler's breathing exercises were interrupted when he saw Kaga inching toward him. Kaga held something in his hand, and his arm was outstretched. Tyler's head shot forward to see what it was.

"I believe this is yours?" Kaga said with a nervous smile as he forced himself not to look down from the dizzying height. He handed Tyler his original phone. "We found the guy who's been using this to control the UAV [unmanned aerial vehicle]."

"Where is the son of a bitch?" Tyler growled as he took the phone and began scrolling down its screen.

"He got away, but Patrick thinks he's the brains behind this whole thing."

"Yeah, well, if I find the bastard, those brains will be spread out all over this fucking stadium," Tyler mumbled as he fiddled with his phone.

"I've got to get back down," Kaga shouted in a voice just short of panicky, slowly descending the girders by feel, rather than looking down. Tyler was too absorbed by the phone in his hands to even hear him.

On his way down the girders, Kaga's fears lessened with each step closer to the bottom. He looked up at the preparations underway for the Closing Ceremony and wondered how on earth the two acrobats who were scaling down the oculus on the other side of the stadium were able not only to stand the vertiginous heights but to actually gambol from girder to girder as if skipping along an earthbound sidewalk. The acrobats were carrying props on their shoulders that no doubt they would be wielding in some dazzling display of what the Closing Ceremony director had called "Japan's traditional wit."

But as Kaga jumped down the final rung of the metal ladder leading up to the girders, something about the acrobats looked amiss as they got closer. Their props suddenly didn't look like anything Kaga had ever seen in a circus or carnival. He *had* seen something similar in his JIA training, though, and when one of the "acrobats" took the "prop" off his back and unfolded it, doubling its length, Kaga recognized it as a Sig Sauer collapsible machine gun of the type he had trained on. His senses went on high alert when one of the two men began aiming in the direction of the now all-but-deserted VIP box. Kaga estimated that the closer of the two men was maybe a hundred yards away, well within the effective range of his Glock, but he would be firing upward. He steadied the gun on a support rail and took aim. The round found its mark, and one of the shooters hung suspended from the cords that were supporting him.

When Patrick reached the entrance to the tunnel, he called out to Kirsten but got no response. The glare of the brilliant sun had rendered him temporarily blind in the darkness, but with his gun drawn, he began moving down the tunnel as cautiously as possible so as not to waste precious time while Kirsten was in mortal danger.

In a meeting room at the far end of the tunnel, Casanova kept one arm around Kirsten's neck while removing her handcuffs off her belt and securing her right wrist to a water pipe. He told her he'd kill her if she made a sound. As Patrick inched his way closer to the double door leading to the meeting room, Casanova followed his every move in a convex mirror used by support staff to round corners safely. When Patrick finally sprang around the corner in what he thought was a surprise move, Casanova was waiting for him with a knifehand strike to the inside of his elbow, knocking his gun away. Since the young North Korean hadn't just shot him outright and Kirsten was obviously being held as a bargaining chip, Patrick sensed an opening.

"You're all being used!" Patrick yelled in Korean. Casanova squinted, taken aback by an obvious foreigner speaking his language. Patrick continued.

"That's right! The man you think is 'Mister Lee' is really Liu Jintao, a general in the Chinese Air Force. He doesn't care about you or any of your friends. You're just pawns. The reason for these attacks he's had you carry out isn't about restoring the Kim family to power in your country. It's about taking over North Korea for its trillions of dollars' worth of minerals that belong to the people. Here, look at this," he said, and reached for the printout he had in the back of his waistband. Casanova raised his gun and was about to shoot when Patrick yelled again.

"This is evidence of everything I've just told you. Read it, and if you don't believe me, then you can shoot me." He slowly reached behind him and took out the printout that Choy had made, the most prominent feature of which was the image of "Mister Lee" in the uniform of a Chinese general. "Look, here he is. Your glorious leader."

Casanova's head moved forward to get a better look at the document Patrick held. His grip on Kirsten had lessened with each word Patrick spoke, and he reached his hand out to accept the printout.

"I tell you what," Patrick said, "I'll guarantee you safe passage back to North Korea if you let her go." Casanova looked up from the document.

"This is real?" he asked. Patrick nodded emphatically. Casanova's eyes went side to side, and Patrick knew he was weakening.

"I'm going to pick up my gun, and I want you to put yours down. And I want you to open the handcuffs. It's the only way you're getting out of here alive."

"You promise safe passage?"

"I swear it," Patrick said even more emphatically. Casanova set his gun down and released Kirsten from her handcuffs.

"Run," Patrick said. Kirsten was about to exit through the same door Casanova had used, but Patrick called after her. "Use that door on the far side of the room." He didn't know if other members of his team would be looking for them with guns drawn. Kirsten took off across the wide hall and exited through a door leading to safety down a different part of the tunnel. Patrick watched her leave and then turned back to Casanova. At the sound of footsteps running toward the meeting room from the original door, Casanova immediately picked up his gun again. Patrick desperately hoped that whoever was there would not come in with guns ablaze. He knew he could still make the deal with Casanova, but since the youth had his gun aimed at him, he didn't dare turn around. He called out.

"Minoru? Tyler? No weapons!"

But the surprise in Casanova's eyes when he saw who was coming in made Patrick turn just in time. Pung was attempting to clap his hands over Patrick's ears in the *happa-ken* "rupturing fist" attack of martial arts, one aimed at breaking the eardrums and causing instant violent pain and disorientation. Patrick saw him just in time before Pung could make full contact, but when he defensively reached for his ears, his Glock dropped from his hand.

"I've been waiting so long for this moment," Pung said in Korean.

"Why didn't you just shoot me when you shot the others?" Patrick asked in the same language.

"What, and deprive myself of seeing your face when you realize you're going to die? That would have been too fast. I want to take my time and enjoy this."

He took a hunting knife from his pocket and began moving toward Patrick.

"Here, hang on to this," he said to Casanova, passing him his hand-gun. Casanova took it but looked imploringly at Patrick.

"Don't forget what I told you," Patrick said to the youth.

Pung looked at Patrick and then at Casanova. "What did he tell you?" he demanded.

"He said that Mister Lee is a Chinese general."

"And you believed him? Idiot!"

Casanova's eyes cut side to side. Suddenly, he threw the gun down and ran from the room through the same door Kirsten had used.

"Come back here!" Pung shouted after him. But Casanova was gone.

"Alright, never mind. Now it's just you and me," he said to Patrick with a malicious grin. He came toward Patrick with his knife at the ready, but Patrick threw himself at the much larger man and began slapping him back and forth across his face, a martial arts move designed to short-circuit the brain and throw the opponent off balance. The knife fell from Pung's hand, and he stutter-stepped, recovered, then countered by stamping on Patrick's foot while grabbing him by the hair. Patrick could tell a headbutt was on the way, so he pulled back at the last second, softening the impact, but throwing himself off balance and dropping to his knees. Despite the relatively mild contact Pung had made, a cut opened up above Patrick's eye, and blood began pouring into his eyes. Pung picked his knife up off the floor. Thinking he had done more damage to Patrick than he actually had, he called to him in a loud voice.

"I hope you can still hear me, because I'm sure everyone in the stadium is about to hear you," he shouted as he extended his arm out for a stab to Patrick's kidney. But Patrick's instincts from his JSOC training resurrected themselves before Pung was able to plunge the knife. Despite the blood in his eyes from the headbutt, Patrick began thrusting a finger of each hand in rapid-fire jabs at Pung's throat, hoping to land at least one directly above the super costal notch, a martial arts move known as *atemi* which is designed to crush the bundle of nerves that control the movement of the neck, instantly incapacitating the opponent.

He finally landed one squarely into that exact nexus, but Pung's neck was half again as wide as the average man's, and he merely was thrown back a foot or two. When Pung came back for another attack, he attempted a slanting blow with the side of his hand just below Patrick's nose, but Patrick fended it off with an arm bar, giving himself enough time to take the knife out of his boot. In JSOC Patrick had learned that in a knife fight, one should always kick and punch first rather than try to stab someone outright. Stabbing is a sucker move, since it exposes the body for too little potential gain. So he kept the knife close in and tried to slash Pung's knuckles, or better yet, the insides of his arms and legs with their major blood vessels. If he got Pung in an artery, he would likely bleed to death, but Pung's powerful leg-thrust kicked the knife out of Patrick's hand and sent it skittering across the floor.

Patrick hobbled as fast as he was able with his injured foot to the opposite side of the room, and Pung smiled. He was now toying with his prey, allowing Patrick to do as he liked. But a surprised look came over his face when Patrick tore off a foot-long section of sharp metal from the bottom of a storage rack and again began jabbing at Pung, who flinched in surprise. Now was the time to stab, Patrick knew, and he saw his opening: when Pung flinched, he lifted both arms, exposing his visceral cavity, and Patrick lunged forward in an attempt at driving the razor-sharp piece of metal deep into Pung's gut.

But Pung knew immediately what Patrick was up to, and he pivoted on his heels in a roundhouse kick to Patrick's head, knocking him backwards and dazing him further. The right-hand man of Comrade Moon had toyed with his prey long enough. He was now going in for the kill.

As he raised the knife over a disoriented Patrick, he called out, "Revenge for Comrade Moon!" But before he could complete the arc of the knife's trajectory, he turned to the sound of someone running into the room.

"Patrick!" a voice cried out. Patrick's head immediately swiveled in the direction of Choy's voice. The instant he had entered the room, Choy had assessed the situation and kicked Patrick's knife back to him. Patrick grabbed it, and while Pung still had his arm lifted, he plunged the blade deep into Pung's left side just below the ribcage and tore it straight up to his sternum with an awful ripping sound. Blood immediately began gushing out of the wound and a moment later out of Pung's mouth. His legs went out from under him, and as he lay bleeding out on the floor, he turned his head to face Choy.

"Traitor," he rasped through blood-soaked lips, his face contorted in agony. He was seconds away from death, but Choy thought of his wife and child who had perished in the Arduous March as a result of people like Pung. He picked Patrick's gun up off the floor and spoke the official words of the executioner in North Korea.

"This is how miserable fools end up. Traitors who betray their nation will meet the same fate.'" He took aim at Pung's head. Pung just stared at him with unrepentant hatred until the top of his head flew off.

Choy hurried over to attend to Patrick.

"Shall I get a doctor?"

"No. Let me just rest for a few minutes and get my balance back." The two of them sat together in silence while the stragglers in the marathon entered the stadium to enthusiastic support from the gracious audience. After ten minutes of slow, deep breathing to replenish the oxygen in his bloodstream, Patrick took hold of the storage rack and slowly pulled himself up into a standing position. Choy purposely didn't come to his aid; he wanted to make sure Patrick had a good sense of what he could and couldn't do next. When Patrick was fully upright, he turned his head from side to side, testing his balance as he took a few steps forward.

"Not too bad, actually," he said. "I was expecting worse."

Choy chuckled. "You and your powers of recovery. You sure you don't want to run a victory lap around the track?"

Patrick smiled wearily and walked back to Choy. "Too old for that shit," he muttered.

Choy set Patrick's gun down on a laundry storage rack, took a sheaf of paper from his back waistband, and handed it to Patrick. It was a hard copy of another file he had printed off the Sky Heart folder.

"Before you go run any marathons, read this first. It lays out pretty clearly the whole plan they had for North Korea. All the attacks were an attempt to get the world to accept the China Solution. When that didn't happen, they were going to kill the U.S. president and vice president so that the next person in line would approve it."

Patrick took the document and began reading. "Dillard was going to accept the China Solution when they attacked. If they had waited ten minutes, they could have gotten what they were after." Patrick scanned through the rest of the printout of the Sky Heart file, shaking his head from side to side. "Just incredible." He looked up at Choy.

"When you say 'they,' do you mean General Liu and the People's Liberation Army? I mean, how high up does this thing go?"

"Hard to say just from these files. I haven't seen anything that implicates Zhongnanhai directly. There's a lot more files I'll need to look at first to find that out. I had to go through over a hundred just to find this and the other one."

"Thanks for sticking with it."

Choy shrugged. "It's what I'm here for." He went over to the door and retrieved the sandwich he had dropped when he first came into the room.

"Lunch? After all this?" Patrick asked.

Choy nodded. "Plenty for both of us," he said, dangling the paper bag.

"I think my appetite's going to need a little more time," Patrick said with a laugh.

Choy picked up Patrick's gun off the storage rack and passed it to him.

Patrick reached for it. "Leave the gun. Take the bulgogi."

Choy laughed. "Bastard. I've been waiting forever to use that line."

Outside in the hallway came the sound of footsteps. Patrick pointed his gun at the door, but then immediately lowered it when Kaga's face appeared. He had one of the two Bong Boy "acrobats" handcuffed and walking in front of him and two other JIA agents. The youth hung his head to his chest.

"This guy and another one were the backup execution team. They were going to machinegun the VIP box from the oculus if Casanova wasn't successful. I shot the one called 'Tyson.' This guy wisely surrendered and came down on his own. Allow me to introduce 'Dreamboy.'"

Patrick walked over to the youth. "Do you know who you were working for?" Dreamboy continued to stare at the floor, saying nothing.

"You were being used," Patrick continued. He held the photo of General Liu Jintao under Dreamboy's face. "You recognize this man, I'm sure." Dreamboy looked at the photo and lifted his head. His eyes widened slightly.

"Mister Lee," he said in soft surprise.

"'Mister Lee' is actually General Liu Jintao of the Chinese People's Liberation Army. He doesn't care anything about your country, and he was willing to sacrifice you and all your friends."

Dreamboy looked up. His eyes narrowed as though assessing the truth of Patrick's words. "What will happen to me?"

"That's up to the judicial system," Kaga said, and signaled for the other two JIA agents to take Dreamboy away. Just as Patrick and Kaga were about to exchange high fives, Kaga got a call on his cell which he took and quickly hung up after answering. "That was Proctor. The drone is seventeen minutes away from the stadium." They both ran out of the room and up to the stadium floor.

CHAPTER 49

Drawing on his years of experience as a drone operator, Tyler opened an app on his smartphone and began scanning. Whether from a command module at Creech AFB or from a smartphone, control of a drone makes use of electrons in motion, and Tyler was easily able to locate the Predator hovering at fifty thousand feet, seemingly in a holding pattern and waiting for its next command. But it was also possible that it had been preprogrammed to attack at a specific time. With adrenalin-heightened senses, he ran through a dozen possible scenarios in his head.

Meanwhile, down in his mobile command center outside the stadium, Proctor got word that a laser radiation analysis of the drone taken from a fighter jet that got to within a thousand feet established that the UAV had no radioactive materials aboard. However, nothing could detect if an airborne vehicle carried chemical or germ agents such as anthrax spores which could be dispersed throughout the stadium via an aerosol cloud. After kicking himself a thousand times for going to the Vegas casino and having his phone hijacked, Tyler forced the guilt from his mind and went back on high alert. When Patrick spread the word on the mic network that the drone was not equipped with a nuclear weapon, Tyler ran through one possible outcome after another, all of them lethal in varying degrees. One such scenario had the Predator running out of fuel and crashing down somewhere in the Tokyo area with who-knows-what as its payload. Or it could very well have been programmed to go into a death-dive directly into the stadium. In any case, Tyler desperately needed to somehow deconflict the UAV and bring it down safely. But where?

He decided to try and redirect the drone by jamming any satellite and land-originated control signals it might be receiving, followed by a GPS spoofing attack that fed the UAV false geopositional coordinates to force it down in an area of Tyler's choosing instead of crashing into the stadium. His phone was equipped with an Avtobaza radar-jamming and deception system, a sophisticated form of signals intelligence. After establishing access to the drone's avionics, he began feeding it spoofing signals that might possibly allow him to override its avionics programming—unless the system had been programmed not to accept any overrides. When the UAV didn't respond after repeated attempts, he had his answer. The drone would not accept overrides. Unless…He opened a hidden app on his phone, one he had created that didn't show up on the phone's settings.

One of Proctor's team had calculated that if the drone were suddenly to be sent into a dive from its current height of just under fifty thousand feet, it would hit the ground within four minutes, leaving not nearly enough time to evacuate the Olympic stadium. A thoroughly unfamiliar sense of helplessness came over Proctor as he sat watching the radar monitor of the UAV as it went through its seemingly endless lazy circles nine miles above Tokyo. Sooner or later, it would run out of fuel and fall from the sky. The solution that ran through his mind was to destroy it at a high enough altitude that the debris would at least be dispersed over a wide area. He switched to a closed frequency and spoke to the base commander at Yokota AFB.

"Prepare MIM-104 Patriot for immediate launch. Await my command."

Proctor kept that information from Hayashida. He just told the JIA director and everyone else that the drone was in a harmless hover at fifty thousand feet and to hope for the best.

Tyler opened the hidden app on his phone, one he had created but never used before. Making use of the knowledge he had learned for his master's in aerospace engineering, he had designed it after a disastrous mission in Afghanistan where a Sentinel drone was hard programmed to monitor Kandahar, when, without warning, a mayday came in from a squad stranded near the Helmand River about fifty miles away. The Sentinel was the closest UAV to the area, but since its course had been hard programmed, another Sentinel eighty miles away was called in to assist, but was too late on the scene to save the eleven men of the squad. A dark silence had filled the operation room at Creech after the squad was lost, and Tyler took it upon himself to try and prevent the same thing from happening again. The app was untested, but he could think of no alternatives if the Predator hovering above had been programmed to attack. He took a deep breath and closed his eyes, fighting the instinct to panic and willing himself into what others had called his "human Quaalude mode." After a minute of stilling his mind, he went back to his phone. Just then, a call went out on the mic network. The Predator was going into a full-engine dive. Ordinarily, Tyler would have been too late to control its descent. But not this time.

Proctor had just given the standby launch alert to Yokota for the surface-to-air missile (SAM) when he got word that the Predator had gone into its full-engine dive. The UAV apparently had been programmed to hover until a certain point had been reached and then to come straight down at the stadium. Proctor spoke to the commander at Yokota. "Launch SAM on my three. One, two…"

"Sir, wait," the Yokota commandant called over the mic. "The drone's engine just shut off. There's no heat sig for a SAM to track."

"What? Well, what about a visual, for god's sake?"

"It's free-falling at three hundred miles per hour. There's no way we can guarantee a hit at that speed. If we miss, the SAM could come down in a populated area."

"Let me worry about that, dammit. I want a SAM launched at best visual. Do you understand? We have to mitigate the destruction!"

"I'm very sorry, Mister Proctor, our defense pact with Japan prohibits any launch over a populated area that's not one hundred percent certain of success."

"Screw the defense pact, that Predator needs to be destroyed now, do you hear me? Hello? Hello?"

––––––––––––

As soon as the drone had gone into its full-power descent, Tyler used the app he had created to send a general override command to shut off the propeller and also signal the left elevator to go full up simultaneous with the right rudder going full down. This sent the UAV into a tailspin at terminal gravitational velocity, as opposed to with full power. At least now Tyler had more of a cushion of time as it got closer to the ground. Then he peered around the environs of the stadium. Spying the large lake on the grounds of the Akasaka Palace lying slightly to the east, he did a mental calculation of its distance from the stadium.

He picked up his M24 rifle which had been rechambered from its original NATO round to one that could accommodate .458 Winchester Magnum rounds, giving it a range of one thousand meters. His breathing became faster as he considered the task in front of him. His longest shot had been just over a mile. But that had been more or less on a level plane. For what he contemplated now, he would be firing almost straight up, probably no more than one thousand meters, but with the wind taking the rounds in completely unpredictable directions. And he would need the drone to come to a near standstill for him to have anything close to a shot at it.

He peered through the scope at the coordinates his app had calculated. Then he saw it. A small white object getting larger by the second. He wiped his palms, and taking the phone in his hands, sent a signal engaging the left rudder full up while simultaneously restarting the propeller engine, but in reverse rotation to produce thrust to the rear rather than pushing the drone to the front. Immediately the UAV began turning in midflight until it flipped topsy-turvy and was pointing straight up. At that point, its downward momentum was approaching the point where it was exactly canceled by its upward thrust. He sent one last signal nudging the aircraft a single degree east toward the lake, dropped his phone, and picked up his M24.

He caught the drone in his sights at around eight hundred feet and took one last deep breath. When the drone reached a zero G standstill at the top of its parabola, he fired four shots at the propeller, destroying it so that no autorotation could affect its final vector. The drone hung suspended in the air for a moment and then began a tight corkscrew. Nine seconds later, it reached its terminal velocity of two hundred miles per hour and plunged tail-first into the lake.

CHAPTER 50

After all the threats had been neutralized, Patrick made a phone call and sent a text. No response to either. He ran to his motorcycle. Twenty minutes after leaving the stadium, he pulled into the parking area next to Toyama Storage, making no attempt to hide his arrival. He had his Glock out with the safety off, and he half hoped that there would still be someone from Chosun Restoration at the corpse hotel to give him what would surely be a one-sided fight. He ran around to the front door ready to kick it in when he saw that it was half open. To the side of the door lay a Suzuki Bandit motorcycle on its side. His heart sank. The owner would never have willingly left it like that. He dreaded going inside but forced himself up the steps.

Bozu lay bleeding on the floor with a sucking chest wound. The SIG Sauer P226 Patrick had given him lay on the floor. When Bozu saw Patrick, his eyes opened as much as his waning strength allowed, but Patrick put his hand on his head.

"Shhh." He keyed in 110 for emergency and told the operator to send an ambulance as quickly as possible. Then he grabbed the table-cloth off the long banquet table and applied direct pressure to Bozu's wound. Bozu tried to speak, but Patrick shushed him.

"Just wait, help is coming."

Bozu's eyes went to the opposite side of the room where two bodies lay on the ground.

"I ran away...but then I came back...I couldn't leave my father and brother...when I got here...Pung had just shot them...I tried to shoot him...but he got me first. I made believe I was dead. It was easy." He managed a wan smile. "I think I might have slowed him down a little bit."

Patrick nodded his head as he held Bozu's hand. It was true. Pung had arrived late on the scene at the stadium. Had Bozu not put up a fight, Pung might have been able to cover for any of the other would-be assassins, and Dillard might now be dead. Patrick too.

The dopplering of sirens in the distance got closer, and less than a minute later an ambulance and a police car came to a screeching halt in front of Toyama Storage. Even if they had arrived right after Bozu had been shot, it would have been too late. After the bodies of Bozu and his father and brother were taken away, police strung crime-scene tape across all the entrances. The CSI with the tape looked at Patrick expectantly but didn't hurry him along. Just as Patrick was about to leave, he noticed the casket in the middle of the viewing room. He walked over and lifted the lid. Just as he thought. Empty.

CHAPTER 51

Three days after the close of the most tumultuous Olympics in history, the combined security command met one last time, this time at JIA headquarters in central Tokyo. Following an outcry of wounded patriotism when word got out in the media that the American embassy had been the forward operating base for security during the Games, Director Hayashida moved all remaining meetings to his home turf, especially since the Paralympic Games would begin in less than three weeks, and his office was again charged with security but without Patrick, whose contract was officially over after this meeting. As Patrick looked around the room filled with faceless bureaucrats, he envied Kirsten, Tyler, and Choy, who had hightailed it home two days earlier.

Patrick had finally persuaded Yumi to see a doctor, and she was now waiting for her appointment at Kamakura General Hospital. She texted him that she was just exhausted, and there was no reason for Patrick to hurry home. The doctor had been called away on an emergency, but she was being well looked after. Patrick promised to come directly to Kamakura as soon as this final meeting was over.

When the last member of the combined security command entered the large meeting room at JIA headquarters, Hayashida called the summary-and-review session to order.

"What can I say?" he began, and the silence in the room became even more pronounced. It was a rare day that Hayashida was at a loss for words. The next hour was largely filled with the ritual blowing of smoke up any convenient posterior with the exception of the announcement that Hayashida was retiring and Minoru Kaga would be in charge of security for the Paralympics that began in a matter of weeks. Everyone silently wondered if Hayashida's retirement was voluntary.

When the meeting was finally coming to a merciful close, Hooper signaled Patrick that he'd like to meet briefly afterwards. He held up the fingers of both hands and mouthed, "Just ten minutes." Patrick nodded and looked at his phone for a text from Yumi. Nothing. He limped behind Hooper into a nearby empty room with two pains, one in his head from the glancing headbutt he'd taken from Pung, and the other in the foot that Pung had stomped on. The two pains throbbed in time with his pulse but a split second apart since it took the blood longer to reach his foot than his head.

When they were inside the room, Hooper closed the door. "Well, I suppose I have to eat the proverbial crow and thank you," he said without meeting Patrick's eye. Patrick said nothing. He wanted Hooper to twist in the wind a bit. "I guess I should also apologize for suggesting that you might turn Tokyo into a replay of Pyongyang four years ago."

"Apology accepted," Patrick said. He briefly looked out the window and turned back again. "So what's the upshot on everything? I take it that Liu Jintao wanted Dillard and Coppinger dead so that the next person in line would accept the China Solution."

"That's not the half of it. The documents your man Choy got hold of were the tip of the iceberg. Our analysts found a ton of other stuff that laid out the rest of the plan: Liu Jintao and his gang were planning on assassinating President Nahm of North Korea once the China Solution was in force and then installing Liu Jintao as the new leader. We don't know how far up the chain of command that went, though, they hid their tracks pretty good. It's within the realm of possibility that Liu Jintao and his people in the Chinese military were going rogue. We'll have a clearer idea soon, though. Our guys are analyzing the rest of the files as we speak."

"Holy shit. And what about North Korea? Any prospect for things settling down a bit? They were looking at civil war before all this…."

"Oh, hell yeah. Now that they've got all those minerals—and it's not just rare earth, by the way, there's also literally tons of gold and platinum in that mother lode—countries are lining up right and left to offer aid until they're able to mine the stuff. Out of the goodness of their hypocritical hearts, of course. Nobody ever heard from them until the mineral deposits came to light. The biggest loser in all this is China. Between you and me, Dillard got Nahm Myung-dae to agree not to give them even a speck of the stuff. That wasn't a hard sell, Nahm hates China for propping up the Kims for so long."

"And Liu Jintao?"

"Escaped. Nobody knows how, but he and one of the young kids…"

"Casanova."

"Is that what he called himself? Jesus. Yeah, Liu and 'Casanova' are nowhere to be found. Hey, by the way, let me show you something."

Hooper opened his briefcase and took out a multi-paged file. He wetted his thumb and riffled through it until he found what he was looking for.

"Here, take a look at this. I know everyone thinks Phibbs is a total fuckup, but the man's got damn good research skills. Here's his analysis of what's been going on in China."

Patrick took the file and began reading. Under the heading "Dual Use Technology," the file was a detailed breakdown of the alliance in China between the People's Central Bank, the People's Liberation Army, and various allegedly civilian corporations, foremost being Wuahei and Daibu, which worked behind the scenes on military applications for their artificial intelligence projects.

Patrick looked up when he finished reading. "And all they needed to take everything to the next level was another source of rare earth."

Hooper nodded. "They've had their hands in the fortune cookie jar all along, although again, we don't know yet if Zhongnanhai was involved."

Patrick closed his eyes and snorted. "Oh, by the way, since we're on the subject of Phibbs, I had a drink with him last week."

"Lucky you," Hooper said, rolling his eyes.

Patrick ignored the comment. "Did you know him in Serbia? He told me we were all there at the same time, you, me, Tyler, Fitz…."

Hooper scratched his face and looked away. "Sure, I knew him. He was new back then. Hadn't gotten that layer of personality that we've all come to know and love." He smiled with everything but his eyes.

"He said he knows where all the bodies are buried…."

Hooper spat air. "That's so typical of our Harmon. He still thinks he's in deep cover. I think he misses the intrigue."

"He said that if anything happens to him, he'll spill the beans. He's got information somewhere, and if he turns up facedown in a ditch, it'll be released somehow." Phibbs hadn't actually said that last part, but Patrick wanted to see Hooper's reaction.

Hooper's face darkened, and he turned to one side. Then he turned back. "Alright. Here's my take on Phibbs. I'm only telling you this because I can see that you've got all sorts of suspicions, no doubt about me too. I've also heard that he's got damaging information on people, some of whom are still in the Agency. My guess is that being a douche bag is his way of throwing people off the scent. He's never come out and said it point blank, but my feeling is that he's working for someone very high up. In what capacity, I don't know. To what end, I don't know. But it's an ongoing kind of thing."

"Meaning what?"

"Meaning ongoing," Hooper said with a note of impatience. "Again, I don't know all the details, but you hear bits and pieces here and there. That's really all I know, promise."

Hooper's eyes were steady, as was his body language. No apparent deception. On the other hand, Agency guys were good at that. But Patrick decided to take him at his word.

"Well, when he gets back, tell him I said thanks."

"I'll do that."

There was an awkward silence. Neither of them knew how to end this impromptu meeting. Finally, Hooper put his hand out. Patrick shook it with half a grip and left the room.

Once outside the room, his phone vibrated. It was Yumi texting from her doctor's appointment. "*All done!*" the text read, exclamation point and all. Patrick took a deep breath and slowly released it.

An hour later, he arrived at Kamakura General Hospital. Yumi was waiting in front.

"You look so much better," he said as he took her in his arms.

She beamed up at him.

"I was worried about you, you know," Patrick said, pulling her head into his chest. "I love you so much," he whispered, rocking her gently from side to side.

"I love you too," Yumi said.

Patrick pulled back to look at her. It was the first time she had used those words since before he had broken off their engagement years before. Then she lifted her head, looked deeply in his eyes, and took hold of his hand. She placed it on her belly.

"Appa," she said, with a warmth he'd never heard from her before.

EPILOGUE

THE WHITE HOUSE
One week later

"Your 11 a.m. is here, Mister President."

"Send him in."

President Evan Dillard remained seated as Ambassador Wu entered. Wu's usually upbeat demeanor was nowhere in evidence.

Dillard indicated a seat across from him at a worktable.

"Did you do what I asked?"

"Yes," Wu replied sullenly. "Zhongnanhai is willing to comply with your request in the interest of regional stability and also as a gesture of thanks for helping us uncover the rogue element."

"'Rogue element.' You mean General Liu Jintao?"

Wu nodded and looked long and hard at Dillard. "The traitor. You do understand, I'm sure, that he was acting completely on his own without the knowledge of the Chinese government."

Dillard held his eye for a moment. Then he smirked and held out a pen.

Wu signed the document in front of him, rose, and exited the Oval Office.

An hour later, regular programming on BBC International was interrupted for breaking news.

> This just in from our Asia Bureau. We have received unconfirmed reports that the People's Republic of China agreed this morning to reset its territorial borders in the

South China Sea back to those of 2011. The same source tells us that General Liu Jintao, alleged mastermind of the recent attacks on the Olympics, along with a number of co-conspirators, were arrested last night and put on trial where a military tribunal found them all guilty of treason. They were summarily executed without making final statements. Stay tuned for confirmation of these reports.

THE END

ACKNOWLEDGMENTS

The author gratefully acknowledges a number of people who helped bring this book to fruition, especially my literary agent, Susan Gleason, for her expertise in identifying areas where the dramatic thrust of the story could be enhanced and the characters brought into sharper focus.

Many friends and colleagues were of immeasurable help in reading through the manuscript and offering critical insights and corrections, and to them I extend my deepest thanks. Among these were Michael Breen, Monica Chung, Thomas Grollman, David Hagberg, Dale Hall, Deborah Hayden, Gary Hughey, Richard Lessa, Bradley K. Martin, Barbara Phillips, Naomi Shepherd, Todd Shimoda, Robert Vieira, and John Wehrheim.

Many thanks also to my brother and former NASA aerospace engineer Dr. William Shepherd for his technical insights on the operation of UAVs (drones).

ABOUT THE AUTHOR

Photo by Janet Ohuchi

Gregory Shepherd spent his early years in New Jersey, London, England, New York City's Lower East Side, and Honolulu. He lived in Japan for four years studying Zen Buddhism at a temple in Kamakura and traveled regularly to Seoul, where he smuggled democracy literature into the country.